CITY OF FEAR

ALSO AVAILABLE BY LARRY ENMON

The Burial Place

CITY OF FEAR

A ROB SOLIZ AND
FRANK PIERCE MYSTERY

Larry Enmon

CROOKED
LANE

NEW YORK

Copyright © by Larry Enmon

Published in the United States by Crooked Lane Books, an imprint of The Quick Brown Fox & Company LLC.

Crooked Lane Books and its logo are trademarks of The Quick Brown Fox & Company LLC.

Library of Congress Catalog-in-Publication data available upon request.

ISBN (hardcover): 978-1-64385-031-3
ISBN (ePub): 978-1-64385-032-0
ISBN (ePDF): 978-1-64385-033-7

Cover design by Andy Ruggirello
Book design by Jennifer Canzone

Printed in the United States.

www.crookedlanebooks.com

Crooked Lane Books
34 West 27th St., 10th Floor
New York, NY 10001

First Edition: June 2019

10 9 8 7 6 5 4 3 2 1

For Betty, Natalie, and Eric

1

Antoine Levern opened the top middle drawer of his desk and felt for the bag taped to the underside. He tore it loose and sprinkled a little coke on a sheet of paper. After dividing it into two lines, he took a short straw and pulled a line into each nostril. He squeezed his nose and shook his head a couple of times. His eyes watered.

Damn, that's some good yeyo.

What he had to do next could only be done if you were a little high. After he tucked the straw back into the plastic bag and re-taped it under the drawer, he sniffed, wiped his nose, and picked up the phone.

"Okay, let's get this over with."

A moment later Benny strolled in, followed by Tabor. One look at Benny and Levern had second thoughts about what he planned to do. Little Benny, the guy he'd known all his life. Arms and neck tatted up and that stupid, self-confident smirk he always wore. A hustler second to none. Still dressed like a New Orleans gang-banger.

As he approached, Benny showed his customary grin and extended his hand. Levern didn't smile or offer to shake. Tabor placed a straight-back chair in front of the desk and directed Benny to sit. As Levern pulled his thoughts together, Benny's confident smirk faded and he squirmed. Instead of speaking to Benny, Levern spoke to Tabor, behind Benny's chair.

"You know how long me and Benny have been friends?" Levern asked.

1

Tabor didn't talk much, preferring instead to roll the toothpick between his lips.

"Twenty-two years," Levern said, staring at Benny. "Ain't that right? About twenty-two years?"

Benny had an expression that screamed, "What's wrong?"

Levern chuckled. "Yeah, since we played in the lower Ninth Ward as kids. And when Katrina broke the Industrial Canal Dam, I even helped his family get out. Didn't I?" Levern's gaze bore down on the little man in the chair. The sound of the toothpick in Tabor's mouth snapping caused Benny to jump. Beads of sweat formed on his brow.

Benny fidgeted and stared at the floor. "Yeah, sure."

Levern massaged his bad knee, and his eyes narrowed. "And after I got established in Dallas, who was the first guy I sent for?"

Benny looked like he might bolt at any time. "Me . . . you sent for me, Antoine," Benny said in a quiet, apologetic voice.

"That's right." Levern jumped up and limped toward the aquarium in the corner, which was draped with black cloth. Benny had gone a shade paler.

"And I gave you a job with my new organization, didn't I?"

Benny couldn't answer, although he croaked some kind of response. Levern didn't blame him. Most people lost their voices about this time. Some pissed themselves.

Levern slid the cloth off. Inside the aquarium, a cottonmouth water moccasin coiled around the tree branch.

"Check out this bad boy," Levern said, gazing through the glass.

Benny kept his eyes glued to the floor, sweat drops the size of dimes skating down his cheeks and forehead.

"He looks skinny," Levern said. "You been feeding him?"

Tabor smirked and spit the two pieces of toothpick on the back of Benny's neck. Benny jumped, and a whimper escaped his lips.

"No, wait," Levern said, slapping his forehead with his palm. "I'm supposed to feed him."

The reptile slithered against the glass, watching the group through its malevolent dark eyes, its black tongue sliding in and out as it tasted the air.

"Well, hell," Levern muttered, "this is awkward." He slowly opened the aquarium lid. The snake raised its head. "Easy, boy," Levern whispered. The snake froze and opened its mouth, showing its creamy white throat. A hiss floated from the aquarium.

"Easy, boy," Levern whispered again. He turned to Benny, who wasn't the blackest guy he'd ever known, but who had just turned another shade whiter. Levern calmed himself. Reptiles know when you're afraid. "Steady boy," Levern slowly reached into the aquarium behind the snake. He moved his fingers to within a couple of inches of the thing. Levern kept his breathing even and eyes fixed on the reptile. Some folks said snakes could smell your expended carbon dioxide. Didn't want to spook him.

Levern stroked the snake on the back a couple of times and it relaxed. Letting out a shallow breath, he gently lifted the thing from its lair. After a few more strokes on its scaled back, the moccasin relaxed a little more, wrapping all fifty inches around Levern's arm, resting its head in his palm.

Grandma would be proud.

"I guess since he hasn't been fed in a while, he's just in an ugly mood," Levern said, staring at Benny. "You know, since he hasn't bit anything lately, his venom is probably fully charged."

Benny turned his head slightly, watching Levern. "Please don't."

Levern smiled as the reptile's tongue flicked in and out. "You ever heard any of those stories, Benny?"

Benny stared at the floor and seemed to find his voice. "What . . . stories?"

Levern limped toward him. "You know, the ones about my grandma being a Voodoo priestess?"

Benny shrugged and attempted to stand. Tabor pushed him back into the chair and held him down. "Sure," Benny said, his breath coming out in pants. "Everyone's heard those, but I never believed them, honest."

3

Levern lowered the snake to waist level. "That's too bad, because they're all true," he whispered.

The snake cast its gaze on Benny. It opened its mouth and an evil hiss filled the air.

Levern approached the chair and pushed the snake to within a foot of Benny's hand. He froze with a wide-eyed stare.

"Speaking of stories," Levern said, "I heard a bad story about you, Benny." Levern shook his head and glared. "Real bad. You know the one, right? The one about you stealing from me?"

Benny leaned back, his lips forming a terrified frown.

"After all I've done for you and knowing you so long. Figured I could trust you." Levern reached and grabbed Benny's shaking and sweaty hand. The snake flinched and slithered to the edge of Levern's palm, inches above Benny's arm.

"Don't move. He hates sudden movements," Levern whispered.

The moccasin wiggled a couple of inches closer to Benny, opened its cotton mouth, and hissed again.

"Now, I'm giving you a warning and a chance to pay me back for skimming off the cargo hijacking." Levern turned to Tabor. "How much?"

Tabor produced a slip of paper from his shirt and showed it to Levern, who examined it for a couple of seconds. "Eighteen thousand should just about cover it. Do you agree with my audit?"

Benny kept his eyes on the snake. Sweat dripped off his nose and chin. He nodded.

"Good. I'll expect the money by next week. Try this again and it won't go so smoothly, understand?"

Every muscle in Benny's body relaxed. "Thank you."

Levern returned the snake to the aquarium and slid the lid closed. He looked at Tabor. "Get him out of my sight."

Tabor grabbed Benny by the collar and dragged him to the stairs—giving him a good shove. The sound of Benny tumbling down the stairwell floated through the room as Levern wiped his hands on his jeans and reclaimed his chair. Every so often he liked to make an example. Keep the rest on their toes. They'd all tell the story among themselves until it became another legend.

Tabor returned to Levern's desk. "What do we do afterward?"

Levern massaged his knee again. "What, after he pays the money back?"

Tabor nodded, rolling a new toothpick between his lips.

"The usual. Benny knows the rules," Levern said. "Take him frog gigging."

Tabor grinned. "My pleasure."

2

Detective Roberto Soliz stared out the car window at the rough neighborhood and sighed. No way to spend a Sunday night.

Midnight surveillances suck.

The streets were deserted. Only a siren in the distance and a howling dog in a backyard broke the silence. Working the Criminal Intelligence Unit meant keeping an eye on the known crooks in hopes they might lead you to the unknown ones. The fact that he and his partner sat down the street surveilling a notorious gang leader's home was bad enough. But working the night shift really pissed him off—they had seniority.

Rob checked his watch—two o'clock. He looked through the binoculars again at the house—quiet as a cemetery.

A garbled snore sounded from the passenger seat. His partner, Franklin Pierce, slept peacefully in the full slouch position. Knees on the dash with his head resting against the passenger window.

May as well have a little fun.

Rob opened his notebook and removed a feather. He leaned over and lightly touched Frank's ear with the tip. Frank swatted away the imaginary fly. Rob clasped his hand across his mouth to muffle the laugh, waited a few seconds, and did it again. Frank twisted his head and groaned. Rob eased closer and directed the tip of the feather toward Frank's nose.

"If you tickle me with that again, I'll shoot you," Frank mumbled, never opening his eyes. He shifted to a different position. "I didn't think Mexican cowboys even had a sense of humor."

Rob laughed. "Rise and shine, cracker. Two o'clock—your shift."

Frank opened one eye. "That's impossible. I just went to sleep."

"Yeah, three hours ago."

Frank moaned, stretched, and pulled himself to an upright position. He ran his hand through his long hair and looked around. "Anything going on?"

Rob spit the dip of Copenhagen into the Styrofoam cup and sat it back on the dash. "Not a damn thing. Place is dead. Wake me at five."

Rob slumped in the driver's seat, crossed his arms, and closed his eyes.

* * *

Frank yawned and opened the thermos of coffee. One sniff and he made a face. Nothing worse than old coffee, just enough time for all the bad flavors to assemble in one place, ready to assault the unsuspecting drinker. He poured a cup and tasted it. Yup, nasty.

He rubbed the dull ache on his right side. Sometimes sleeping in a car caused the old knife wound to act up. Frank scanned the gang leader's house with his binoculars. Just like Rob said—all quiet.

Movement in the front yard caught his eye. He zoomed in on a woman walking across the lawn in the shadows, approaching the porch. Tall. Bright red hair. Fair complexion. She moved with cat-like ease across the damp grass. The black, almost formal, flowing gown whipped in the light wind.

What tha . . . ?

She strolled to the door. After gazing down the street in both directions, a trace of a grin swept across the full red lips. A large bush partially blocked Frank's view, and he couldn't tell if she opened the door or if someone opened it for her. She disappeared completely behind the bush and the front porch light went out.

Frank snatched up the night vision scope and punched Rob. "Someone's on the porch."

Rob sat up. "What?"

Frank trained the night scope on the gang leader's house a couple of hundred feet away. He scanned the area, but the woman had disappeared.

"She's not there anymore," Frank said.

"She?" Rob chuckled and settled back into his sleeping position, crossing his arms again. "Probably some call girl Ricardo ordered. He likes hookers."

Frank searched the yard and sides of the house with the infrared scope. Working vice, he'd seen enough hookers to know she wasn't one. Rob might be right, but Frank still had doubts. "I don't think she turns tricks."

"Did she go inside?" Rob mumbled, keeping his eyes closed.

"Must have, the light went out. By the time I grabbed the scope, she wasn't on the porch anymore."

Rob turned his head toward the window. "Wake me if she shows up again."

Frank spied with the scope for another five minutes, but the woman never reappeared. A lone car cruised down the street toward them. Its bright headlights blinded Frank, but he recognized the silhouette. The Dallas Police patrol car's spotlight came on, searching the curb and adjacent residences, probably looking for house numbers. When the car stopped at Ricardo's house, Frank had a bad feeling. He shook Rob.

"Hey, uniforms just pulled up."

"Huh?" Rob sat up and eyed the patrol unit. "Why are they here?"

"Great question," Frank said. "Let's see."

Rob cranked their car and rolled up to Ricardo's. Frank and Rob held up their badges as they exited. Approaching uniforms when driving a "cool car" and in plain clothes had to be done with care—especially at night.

"Police," Rob said.

The closest uniform, the younger of the two, swung his flashlight toward them. His hand rested on his pistol.

"Dallas Police—Criminal Intelligence," Frank announced. "What's going on?"

Before the officer could answer, a scream came from inside the residence. A dozen gunshots followed. Muzzle flashes lit up a second-story window, and a chorus of barks and howls from neighborhood dogs broke out.

"They're shooting at us!" the younger uniform bellowed as he dove behind the patrol cruiser.

They all took cover and Frank steadied his nerves while checking to see if Rob was all right. Fighting the adrenaline wasn't easy for Frank—not why he became a policeman.

Rob gave the okay sign from the other end of the patrol car. He'd bunkered in behind the car's engine block. Safest place when bullets were flying around.

The senior officer yelled into his handheld radio. "2416, shots fired at our location—need backup."

The dispatch answered. "2416, copy, shots fired at your location. Any unit clear and close for back up?"

She gave the address. A supervisor came on the air. "Five-nineteen, I'll also be checking by with 2416."

Frank peeked over the trunk of the car, the breeze from the cool October night ruffling his hair. All was quiet again. No lights from inside the place. He ducked back down. "I don't think they were shooting at us." He pointed at the second floor. "All the shots were directed inside."

Rob popped his head above the hood for a look.

Frank shifted the pistol to his left hand and ran his sweaty right palm down his pants leg. He didn't like this part of police work—the shooting part—but just sitting there wasn't an option. Bad things happened when you waited too long after shots were fired. Victims bled out, suspects fled, and witnesses drifted away.

"We have to check it out," Frank said.

"We'll take the front." Rob stood and motioned for the senior guy to follow him.

Frank sprinted to the side yard with the younger uniform in tow. It was dark, but a light shined from the back, illuminating the side yard. A wooden gate with vines growing over the top looked like the best way in.

The rookie shined his light over the gate into the yard. His voice had an uneasy edge. "Shouldn't we wait for backup?"

Frank reached over the top of the waist-high gate, searching for the metal release clasp. "No time." As he lifted it, a sharp edge sliced into his wrist. He jerked his hand back. *Damn.* Frank shook off the pain and charged around the house to the backyard. The area was well lit thanks to a light atop a thirty-foot pole in the corner of the yard. No dog in sight. Frank stayed low and eased to the back door. He tried it—not locked.

Frank turned to the young officer behind him. "Get ready. When we go in, you break to the left, and I'll take the right."

The kid had an excited or frightened look, Frank couldn't tell which. *How long has he been on the streets?*

The rookie keyed his radio. "We're going in."

The voice of the other officer with Rob replied, "We're already in."

Frank rushed through the door and fumbled for a light switch on the dark kitchen wall. He flicked it a couple of times. Nothing. The kitchen smelled of grease and old food. The floors were slippery.

"Frank, you in?" Rob shouted through the darkness from the opposite end of the house.

"Yeah, coming to you," Frank said.

The younger officer's flashlight guided the way through the gloom. As he and Frank moved toward Rob's voice, they kept their guns in the tactical shooter position. When they rounded a corner, Rob and the senior officer stood beside the sofa, shining their light on two Hispanic gangsters slumped back in the cushions. Both were in their twenties.

"They shot?" Frank asked.

Rob had his fingers against the neck of the closest one. Rob shook his head and gazed at Frank with a perplexed expression. "Not a scratch on 'em, but they're out cold."

Something bumped upstairs, like an object falling. Everyone crouched and swung their pistols toward the dark staircase. The senior officer toggled the light switch on the wall—nothing.

"Did we have a complete power failure?" Rob whispered.

Frank pulled back a curtain. Lights from other houses were on, and people milled in their yards. "If we did, it only affected this house." He pointed to the senior uniform and motioned up the staircase. "Lead the way."

The man frowned and stepped to the front. Frank didn't blame him. Any staircase can be a kill zone—especially in the dark. But the uniforms wore ballistics vest. Frank didn't.

"Back up your buddy," Rob said, positioning the younger guy behind his partner. Rob pointed at a specific dark corner of the staircase. "Keep your gun and flashlight to the right."

All four eased up the stairs, guns at the ready.

Frank gnawed his lip. This felt like one of those no-win academy training scenarios in which a cop always got shot. Frank's skin prickled.

He touched the back of the senior officer. "Hey, there may be a woman up here. Don't know if she's armed."

With each step Frank's stomach churned. He took long even breaths. The uniforms reached the top of the stairs and peeked around the corner of the second-floor landing.

"Clear," the senior officer whispered.

Frank and Rob scooted up closer behind them as the uniforms shined their beams down the dark, empty hall. Everyone stopped and stayed low and flat against a wall. Frank took a knee and his hair bristled. The bedroom door at the end of the hall was shrouded in shadow. An ominous looking thing. The absolute stillness of the place scared him. Something felt very wrong.

Too quiet.

Was this a set up? The sound of someone in their group trying a hall light switch only increased Frank's anxiety. A bead of sweat trickled down his cheek.

They began their steady advance down the creepy corridor. Before passing each room, the uniforms cleared it while Frank and Rob kept them covered from the hall. The moon shining through the skylight cast eerie cloud shadows that danced over the carpet. They looked like tiny ghosts skimming across the floor. Only the master bedroom remained unchecked. Frank released a breath as sirens died away and the sound of other patrol vehicles skidded to a stop.

The senior uniform pointed at the younger cop. "Get out there and let them know where we are," he whispered.

Moments later the sound of feet stomping up the stairs caused them turn their heads. A uniform sergeant and two other officers join them in the hall.

"What do we have?" the sergeant asked, catching his breath.

Rob flashed his badge. "The guy who lives here is Ricardo Salazar—a gang leader. May be a woman in there with him. Heard shots earlier. All quiet since then."

The sergeant nodded and gazed around the hall. "What happened to the damn electricity?"

"No idea," Rob said.

Frank moved back as the sergeant motioned for the uniform officers with shotguns to come forward. The sergeant banged on the bedroom door. "Police! Come out with your hands up." Only silence answered his demands. He scanned the faces of the others.

Rob wiped his hand across his mouth. "Okay, let's do it then." He crouched, balancing on the balls of his feet.

The sergeant pushed the door open, and stepped back.

As Frank rushed into the dark room, the smell, the feel, and his own anxiety caused him to shiver. The place reminded Frank of a tomb. Something brushed his pants cuff. In the dim light, a terrified tabby bolted out and raced down the hall. It hit the stairs at a dead run. Something about the way the moon shined through the skylight made it look as if a cloud hovered over the animal as it made its getaway.

Frank sucked in a lungful of air and again steadied his nerves. They spread out, guns at the ready. No one was in the pitch black room, but a sliver of light shined from under the closet door. The sergeant, using hand signals, posted the officers in a quarter circle around the door. He motioned at Frank to open it. Frank knelt, braced himself against a wall, and eased his hand to the handle. If he didn't move quick enough, he could get shot from the crook or the cops. It was a bad position.

He pulled in a breath, jerked the door open, and flattened himself against the bedroom wall, waiting for the shots.

No one fired. The group stared into the closet, slack jawed. After a few seconds they lowered their guns and advanced. Frank edged his head around and peeked through the open door.

Ricardo Salazar, dressed only in a pair of plaid boxers, sat slumped against the back wall. He held a flashlight in his left hand. A cloud of smoke still lingered inside. The stench of gunpowder hung thick in the air. At least a dozen spent shell cases littered the carpet around him. Ricardo held a .45 in his grip, slide locked back—empty. His eyes were fixed and staring straight ahead, his mouth twisted, as if in a scream.

Rob walked in and did a pulse check. "He's dead."

On the floor, beside the body, lay a small crudely sewn black cloth doll. Uneven stitches formed the mouth, and tiny red buttons served as eyes. A long silver pin extended through the head.

Rob reached for it, but stopped. He withdrew his hand, glanced at Frank, and then back at the doll. Like a good Mexican Catholic, he crossed himself and mumbled something in Spanish. No one else spoke. There was nothing to say.

An old scene from *The X Files* resurfaced in Frank's memory.

Yeah, this was going to make for a screwed-up report.

3

Rob suppressed another yawn. He glanced over the low cubicle wall at Frank typing away. Working with Frank the last few years had been especially good for Rob. Frank's sharp mind and work ethic had lifted them both to recognition by the highest levels of the command staff. If Rob had not been partnered with him, his career wouldn't be on the rise. But working with Frank had its challenges. Rob's wife, Carmen, thought Frank was a little crazy. Rob never considered him exactly crazy. Weird, but not crazy.

Last night the scene supervisor at Ricardo's house told them to go home, get some rest, and be back at Criminal Intelligence Unit by two in the afternoon to write a supplement to the report. Rob had his one-page supplement done; Frank continued typing. Guy was a stickler for details. He would pause every so often and readjust the Band-Aid on his arm. Frank getting his wrist sliced open on a gate last night was par for the course. He was an injury magnet. That was one of the challenges. Hanging around Frank too long could get you hurt. Carmen couldn't handle Rob getting hurt now. Not in her condition.

As of late, Rob had started calling Frank, Dark Cloud. This seemed appropriate since he wasn't the luckiest cop in the world. The name originated in Rob's old Marine unit while deployed in Iraq. There always seemed to be one guy who just couldn't get a break. If a grenade was thrown, or a mortar shell exploded, that poor schmuck always caught shrapnel. If a bullet was fired or an IED detonated, that guy got hit. Some guys got patched up and returned to duty, only to get hit again a few weeks later. Other Marines tended to shy away from him—bad luck. They gave the unlucky guy a goofy name, Dark Cloud.

Rob was glad he didn't have to do any additional investigation on the case from last night. The whole thing creeped him out. All he wanted was to get back to traditional CIU investigations and let someone else handle the dead guy in the closet.

"How's it hanging, buddy?"

Rob looked up and met eyes with Paul Sims. He and Paul had worked together in Homicide a few years back. Rob transferred to CIU, but Sims liked working murders and stayed with Homicide. He was happy-go-lucky and jolly—fat guys usually are. Rob was stocky and short, Frank was tall and thin. When all three stood side by side, they looked like a carnival sideshow.

Frank looked up from typing. "Hi, Sims."

Sims downed the last few nuts in the packet. He always seemed to be eating. He held up a wad of papers. "Looks like I've got this new homicide case on Ricardo Salazar." He flipped a few pages and eyed Frank and Rob. "According to the preliminary, you guys are the star witnesses." Sims tugged at his tie. He never kept his top button buttoned. His neck grew faster than his ability to buy new shirts.

Frank slid into his slouch position, one leg hanging over the arm of the chair. "Star witnesses. Hear that, Rob? At least we're stars at something." Frank handed Sims a four-page supplement to the report. "Figured you'd want a copy."

Rob handed over his one page. Sims lifted an eyebrow while comparing the two.

"Frank's showing off again," Rob said.

Sims opened a Baby Ruth candy bar and took a bite. He held a clear evidence bag with something black inside. The doll found at Ricardo's was visible through the plastic.

"Hey, every report I've read mentions this thing." Sims took another bite and stared at it. "Any particular reason?"

"The doll was right beside Ricardo in the closet," Rob said. "Spookiest thing in the house, other than the dead body."

Sims finished the Baby Ruth and dropped the wrapper over the top of Rob's cubicle, missing the garbage can on the other side. "Any other toys around?"

"Nope, Ricardo lived alone," Rob said. "As far as we know, no kid ever visited." Rob looked to his partner for confirmation, but Frank was typing again.

Sims picked something from his tooth with his finger as he turned to leave. "Okay, I'll look these over and talk to you later."

Rob gazed at the CIU area, which was one large room with numerous short-sided cubicles. About eighteen desks dominated the middle, and private offices with glass walls circled the open area. These were occupied by the supervisors. Rob and Frank's sergeant, Terry Andrews, and their lieutenant, Edna Crawford, had been talking in her office for the last half hour with the door closed. Every so often Edna looked out her glass wall toward them. She had this look when she wasn't happy, something between a frown and grimace. Edna appeared to be doing most of the talking. She reclined in her executive chair, playing with a Rubik's cube.

"Think they're rehashing last night?" Rob mumbled.

Frank glanced at the pair as Terry nodded at something Edna said. "Yup. Get ready for the call." Frank sat back and laced his fingers across his chest.

As if on cue, Rob's phone rang.

"You and Frank step in here," Edna said.

Rob turned his head toward her glass office. "Yes, ma'am." Rob stood and slipped on his jacket. "They want to see us."

Frank didn't move. "Big surprise." He continued lounging while examining the cut he got from the gate last night. The ambulance attendants had sprayed something on it, slapped a couple of butterfly Band-Aids across the top, and advised him to see his doctor about a tetanus shot. *Might need a stitch.* Of course, Frank ignored them, but then again, Frank ignored most people.

Finally, at the speed of a human sloth, Frank rose and raked his surfer-cut hair back. As usual, he didn't bother putting on his jacket. Rob led the way to Edna's office.

When they entered, she dropped the Rubik's Cube on the edge of the desk. "Have a seat, guys."

She wore her hair twisted into a tight bun. Her office always smelled of gardenias, one of those plug-in things. Almost every time Rob visited her office there was something bad to discuss, so he'd begun associating the smell of the place with controversy. This led to him hating sitting on his own back porch. Gardenias were planted along the back wall of the house.

Terry sat in the only chair, so they headed toward the sofa, "the lecture couch," as Frank called it. He picked up the unsolved cube as he passed Edna's desk.

In Rob's career he'd had good sergeants and good lieutenants, but never both at the same time—until he got to CIU. Terry was senior in time to everyone and had twice as much experience as Edna. Solid and stoic, he gave her good advice she counted on.

Edna would never be satisfied being the first black female lieutenant to lead CIU. She had her eye on being the second black female chief of police.

Frank slid into his usual place on the right side of the sofa, closest to Edna. Rob flopped down on the other end. Edna got right to the point. She held her favorite pen and slowly clicked it, then pursed her lips for a moment before speaking.

"Had a meeting on the sixth floor this morning," she said.

Rob tensed. *Oh, Christ.*

When neither answered, she continued. "Major Higgins wanted to know how four DPD officers allowed Ricardo to get hit while they stood in front of his house bullshitting."

"We weren't bullshitting," Rob answered. "We'd just walked up and identified ourselves to the uniforms when the shooting started."

Edna turned to Frank, but he didn't react or agree. He tilted his head side to side as he attempted to solve the cube.

Edna lifted a page of handwritten notes from her desk and reviewed it. Her brow rose. "What happened to the red-haired woman?"

Rob's stomach tightened and he clasped his hands together. Again he wanted Frank involved in the conversation, but he sat mute.

"She wasn't in the house when we made entry," Rob said, "must have split out the back."

"Did you see her?"

"Not exactly," Rob said.

Edna turned to Frank and showed a cocky smile. "You appear to be the only person who saw this mysterious lady. Any explanations as to what became of her?"

Rob figured Edna would hone in on that. Just another reason to drop this case and let Homicide figure it out.

Frank leaned forward with a deadpan expression, placed the cube on her desk with all the same colors matching, and said, "No."

Terry cleared his throat. "Guys, they had an engineer go through the place this morning. Someone tripped the main breaker out back." He interlaced his fingers over his slim midsection. "See any sign someone had been in the backyard last night?"

Rob shrugged and shook his head.

"Nothing," Frank mumbled.

Edna picked up the cube and checked each side. Her brow furrowed as she dropped it in her tray. Frank melted a little deeper into the sofa. His long legs stretched out, shoes almost touching her desk. She cut her eyes in his direction and had that expression she probably reserved for her two young daughters.

Edna and lots of other supervisors always gave Frank a pass. That's the way it was with Medal of Valor holders. Every cop likes to think of themselves as tough and a little dangerous. Frank never thought of himself that way. He was an analytical thinker who enjoyed the problem-solving aspects of law enforcement—never cared for the macho end of it. But Frank *was* tough and more than just a little dangerous. Killed five people, been shot, stabbed—yeah, he was dangerous. Thing about Frank, he never looked for trouble, but shit-storms always seemed to find him. *Dark Cloud*.

Edna exhaled. "Nine-one-one got a call to the house a little after two this morning. A voice that sounded like Ricardo's was screaming about some intruder. That's why the patrol unit was dispatched." She glared at Frank. "We need to find the woman. When a drug gang leader gets killed for no apparent reason, it makes people jumpy. Gang wars have started over less."

Edna looked at Terry, Terry looked at Rob, Rob looked at Frank, and Frank looked at Edna. No one spoke for a few awkward seconds before she said, "That's it, get to work."

"Let's go." Terry stood.

Rob and Frank followed him into his office. While Edna's work area reflected a cool professional environment with certificates lining the walls in tight formations, Terry's felt like a home. Oil-on-canvas vistas of the Texas Hill Country gave the place warmth and a relaxed feel. Terry poured coffee from his private pot and stood beside his desk. His cool blue eyes were hard to read.

"How's the wrist?" Terry motioned to Frank's hand.

"Just a scratch," Frank said.

"He needs a stitch," Rob chimed in.

"Any ideas about last night?" Terry asked. He leaned back against his desk and blew into the cup before taking a sip.

"Can't explain it," Frank said. "She was there one second and gone the next."

Terry dropped into his chair. "Major Higgins and the Drug Task Force supervisor are meeting later this afternoon. They want a plan to present to the chief. I'm really hoping it doesn't involve us. This thing sounds like a mess. The less we have to do with it the better."

Rob hated messes. Nothing good ever seemed to happen when a case started off as shitty as this one did. After a few years' experience, you could always spot the good cases from the shitty ones. This thing stunk up the whole room.

Terry gave them his fatherly smile. "You guys grab some down time, see you tomorrow. We'll figure out something by then."

They strolled back to their cubicles, and Rob slipped on his jacket and adjusted the collar. Frank eased into his chair and typed something into Google. Images of dolls similar to the one at Ricardo's popped up on the monitor.

"You coming?" Rob asked.

Frank must have found one he liked. He clicked on it and waited for it to load. He looked up. "Yeah, I'll be along in a minute."

Rob knew better than to wait on him. Frank's "minute" usually took an hour or more. Rob took one last look at the monitor before leaving. The doll image had a caption below it.

Voodoo.

*   *   *

Just before five o'clock Edna strolled to Terry's office. He sat behind his desk, leaning on his forearms as he studied the computer monitor. He had a pinched expression.

She needed his advice again. He'd never let her down. "Busy?" she asked.

He jumped. "Just looking at the gang stats this year."

She walked through the door and closed it behind her. "Actually, that's what I wanted to talk about."

Terry poured her a cup of coffee as she took a seat. "I think I know what you're going to say."

Edna took the cup and nodded, settling back into the chair. "You were here during the gang wars of '91 and '92, right?"

"I'd just come on the job. Hadn't been on the street a month when all hell broke loose."

"How did it start?"

"Stupid kids just started killing each other and innocent civilians for no apparent reason. The old Family Violence Division that oversaw the Gang Unit had a top-to-bottom shake out. Several demotions and transfers."

Edna gazed in her coffee cup and didn't speak for a moment. When she looked up, she said, "Higgins told me this morning he was holding CIU responsible if this thing escalates. Said we were the eyes and ears of the department in the intelligence unit, and should have had our fingers on the pulse of the city."

Terry's brow crinkled. "He can't be serious. That's the Gang Unit's job more than ours."

Edna kept her voice under control. She didn't want Terry knowing how furious she was with Major Higgins. Good leaders support their superiors. "Higgins isn't over the Gang Unit. He's over CIU. Said we shared equal responsibility with them."

"We have a little time to work it out. This might be a one off," Terry said, "besides we really don't have to worry until civilians get into the crossfire. That's when the shit gets real."

Edna didn't answer. Terry had just said a mouthful. *Until civilians get into the crossfire.* Just sitting and waiting for something to happen wasn't in her nature. It felt like being in a stew pot waiting for someone to turn up the heat. Her whole police career hung in the balance. Once transferred or demoted, it was almost impossible to make a comeback.

She'd not touched her coffee. Acid gnawed at her gut, and she just wanted it to stop before she became sick. She stood and sat the cup on the desk.

"Thanks, Terry. I guess we'll just have to wait and see what happens."

Terry also stood. "Try not to let it upset you. The guy getting hit last night was probably just an anomaly."

4

Tuesday morning after his workout, when Rob strolled into CIU about nine o'clock, Frank was already there, still sitting in the same position Rob left him yesterday. One might assume he'd spent the night there, except he had on different color Dockers and Polo shirt. He stared at the computer monitor, biting the inside of his cheek.

Nothing about this case gave Rob any comfort. He'd told his wife, Carmen, about it last night, but she didn't show much interest. She didn't show much interest in anything anymore as her depression worsened. Rob felt as if his twenty-years-plus marriage was fading like an old photograph, an image that got hazier every year. Now Frank even had a zombie look.

"Morning," Rob said.

"Hey," Frank mumbled, without taking his eyes off his monitor.

Terry meandered from his office sipping coffee, his brow wrinkled, his expression pained. He paused at Frank's desk. "The sixth floor decided what they wanted to do. It's going to be a joint investigation. Narcotics, Homicide, and Criminal Intelligence will work the thing. There were enough drugs in the house to hold the two gangsters you found on the sofa. Narcotics is sweating them. Since they're investigating it as a homicide, Paul Sims is handling that part. They want you guys to concentrate on identifying and locating the missing red-haired woman. Higgins is hoping for quick action on this," Terry said. "If another gang leader gets killed before we figure it out, well. . . ."

No one needed to tell Rob about Major Higgins. Guy always rolled as much shit downhill as possible. Staying on his good side was a full-time job for Edna and Terry.

Terry opened his mouth to say something else, but instead strolled in the direction of Edna's office.

Rob removed his jacket and hung it on the back of his chair. He eyed Frank. Guy always had the kind of laid-back expression that caused you to wonder if he was about to go to sleep or just waking up. Since they were pulled back into the investigation, Rob figured Frank must be calculating on how to find the mysterious woman. But then again knowing Frank, he might be wondering if fried peanut butter and banana sandwiches were really the preferred meal of Elvis during his later years.

*   *   *

The thing Frank loved about working CIU was also the thing he hated the most. Unlike other units like Homicide, Missing Persons, and Burglary and Theft, CIU could work any case the department investigated. But not being in the specific unit investigating the case always left CIU detectives unable to control it. Frank hated not being in control. The case officer always had more leeway into how the investigation was run. Most of the time CIU had to wait for them to share information before they could do much.

He doodled and scratched out questions that needed answers. Why did they trip the power circuits at Ricardo's? How did they kill the guy without touching him? A poison? What rendered the two guards unconscious? And the last, and possibly most important, what happened to the red-haired woman? Frank examined the doodle beside the list of questions. He'd subconsciously drawn the likeness of a Voodoo doll. The M.E. had the body, and DPD forensics had the trace material from the scene. Might have a preliminary report in the next couple of days.

Whoever left that moronic Voodoo doll at Ricardo's was singing to the wrong person if they thought it would intimidate Frank. No one in the police department was more grounded in reality than he was. His religious doubts were well known, and no amount of hocus pocus could distract him. As far as ghosts, he believed in Casper and that was it.

Frank handed Rob a sheet of paper over the cubicle wall. It was a printer copy of the doll he'd been studying the day before.

Rob looked it over a moment before asking, "What about it?"

"The answer to the red-haired woman," Frank said.

Rob glance at the paper again. "I don't get it. How does this help us find the woman?"

"Connect the dots."

"Huh?"

"I pulled that doll photo off of a Voodoo website. And Ricardo was a drug gang leader, right?"

"Right."

"Ricardo was found dead with—" Frank pointed at the image of the Voodoo doll Rob held, "—that thing beside him, right?"

"Yeah."

"So if you think of a criminal in the drug business and Voodoo, who comes to mind?"

"Antoine Levern," Rob answered.

Frank clasped his hands behind his head, rocked back in his chair, and said, "Brilliant."

Frank and Rob strolled into Terry's office, and Frank explained his theory. Terry studied the photo of the doll as they waited. The hum of the cubicle jungle drifted into the office. Frank liked the hum—it relaxed him. Made him feel at home. Terry lounged back in his chair. "So you believe Levern is somehow involved?"

"Won't know till we interview him," Frank answered. "Know who in Narcotics might be working him?"

"No one that I'm aware of," Terry said. "Since Ferris retired, Narcotics has moved on to easier fish. Popular opinion is Levern has an industry contact that keeps him informed what drugs are going to be on what trucks. Makes it a lot easier to hijack the right shipment. Ferris knew everything about him. Worked him for years."

Rob took a sip of coffee. "He still around?"

"Yeah. Fell on hard times after he retired. Wife booked out. I've heard he's hitting the bottle pretty bad."

Frank stood. "Think we'll swing his place by for a chat before we see Levern. You know the guy?"

Terry pointed to a photo on the opposite wall. "We went through the academy together over twenty-five years ago." Terry strolled to the picture and Frank followed. "That's him." Terry pointed to the third row up. The tall officer in the photograph wore his police cap low, almost touching the bridge of his nose, the sides of his hair buzzed close to the scalp. His intense eyes stared directly into the camera with a determined resolve.

Terry had that sentimental look he always showed when a fellow officer went down hard. "Give him my regards."

As they walked out of Terry's office Frank said, "I'm going to check my hair and make-up before we go. Be right back."

Frank meandered to the men's room down the hall. Terry's expression and last words were burned into Frank's memory. The thought of having his mind and wits erode bothered Frank almost as much as the thought of being killed. As he aged, he had no one to look after him. Going to a home was out. What kind of life could he have there? If only Carly were still alive. But life's twists and turns never ask you what you want before doing their thing. *Just go with the flow.* Perhaps someday another might come along that he'd want to love—perhaps not.

When he walked back into CIU, a round of laughter erupted from a group of detectives gathered around Rob's cubicle. Once or twice a week Rob would go on a joke-telling binge. Rob had a lot of funny jokes.

Frank caught his eye. "Ready to go, Seinfeld?"

5

Most of the apartment complexes off Harry Hines Boulevard and Northwest Highway in Dallas would not fall into the plush or luxurious category. Some would not fall into the safe, comfortable, or well-kept category either. But that's where retired officer Ben Ferris lived. Rob craned his neck, searching for the building number. Frank slept in the passenger seat. *How does he contort his long legs and back into that weird position?* Rob poked him.

"Hey, we're here."

Frank gazed around and ran a hand down his face. "Already?"

"Get a load of this place. Ben lives in a dump," Rob said. The car bounced from one pothole to the other in the parking lot. Few vehicles were around. A stray dog sniffed a paper bag beside the nasty swimming pool that looked like a biology experiment that had gone terribly wrong. The building's walls were tagged with gang graffiti. The complex had that "we've spent all we're going to on this joint and now we just want our money back" look.

Rob swung into a parking place beside a rusted '92 Toyota Corolla with a busted passenger window covered with plastic and duct tape.

"This isn't where I'd like to end up in another ten years," Rob mumbled.

They walked through a grimy breezeway. The smell of Mexican food floated through the air. Apartment forty-one was on the right.

An overflowing bag of trash drooped against the wall. About a hundred flies were searching for a way in. Taped to the door—a note.

Jim,
Had to step out for a while. Door's unlocked and cold beer in
the refrigerator.
Be back in a bit.
Ben

Rob frowned and turned to Frank. "Has he lost his mind? He'll be cleaned out."

Frank tried the doorknob—unlocked. He cracked it open. The interior was a dark cave. "Ben, hey, Ben . . . you home?"

Rob got that kind of feeling he used to get in Iraq. Just before he knew it was time to run for cover.

Frank pushed the door open a little more before Rob touched his shoulder. When Frank turned around, Rob shook his head and put his index finger to his lips.

"Hold on a second," he whispered. "Hey, Ben," Rob called. "You there? It's me, Rob Soliz. DPD."

In the darkness a quiet, raspy voice answered, "Rob. That you?"

"Yeah, okay to come in? Got my partner Frank Pierce with me."

The voice called back. "Sure, come on in, but close the door."

They slipped inside the apartment just as a wall lamp switched on in the corner. The hair on Rob's neck stood at attention as he realized what had almost happened.

In an oversized beanbag chair sat Ben Ferris, or what was left of him. The retired cop squinted in the bright light and laid the cocked .44 Magnum beside the almost empty bottle of Jim Beam. A smile moved across the shriveled lips below his ragged Fu Manchu mustache.

"By God, it is you."

Ben struggled to extricate his skinny self from the man-eating beanbag chair. A four-day growth of gray stubble outlined his thin face, and the long ponytail had a greasy look. He stood, wobbled once, and stuck out his hand. Rob shook it.

"How's it going, Ben?"

Ben pumped Rob's hand like a rescued hostage does his rescuer. "I'm good, damn good."

Ben's grip was still strong, but his breath smelled like a cocktail lounge and bread mold. He turned to Frank. "Haven't seen you guys in years."

"Good to see you again," Frank said.

Ben ambled to the kitchen and thumbed a light switch. The hanging lamp over the dinette table flickered on. Motorcycle parts, old food containers, and stacks of newspapers littered the table. Rob glanced at the rest of living room. Little furniture, but a black Harley Davidson motorcycle sat on a blue tarp in the corner with the engine partially disassembled. Place had that old garage odor Rob remembered as a kid working in his uncle's tire shop after school.

"Pull up a chair. Don't mind the mess," Ben said, "cleaning day is tomorrow." He chuckled. "Can I get you boys something to drink?"

Frank shook his head while pulling out a chair. "We're good. Still on duty."

Ben laughed. "Being on duty never stopped us before." His brow tightened. "Hey, is this an official visit?"

"Yeah," Rob said and took a seat.

Ben cleared his throat and sat back in the chair. "What's happened?"

"Hear about the Ricardo Salazar thing the other night?" Rob asked.

Ben nodded. "Finally got what was coming to him. About time."

"That's not the whole story," Rob said. He filled Ben in on the unpublished details. When he got to the part about the Voodoo doll found beside Ricardo's corpse, Ben's forehead wrinkled.

As Rob talked, Ben fished a pack of cigarettes from his pocket and held the pack out to them. They shook their heads as he lit up. It was a short unfiltered thing with coarse, black tobacco. Some foreign brand that smelled like burning horse hair. Ben inhaled a long draw and let the smoke flow out in a narrow stream between his lips. He nodded a couple of times during the briefing. After Rob finished, Ben rolled the cigarette tip in the ashtray, already overflowing with butts, and asked, "And you believe Levern might have done it?"

Frank pursed his lips. "Not necessarily. But he does have the Voodoo reputation."

Ben laughed and slapped his leg. "That's just for show. His grand-mamma was no more of a Voodoo priestess than yours. A French Quarter whore, just like his mama."

"You know him better than anyone," Frank said. "What do you think? Could he have done it?"

Ben gazed at Frank with the same intense stare he had in his police graduation photo. "I'm not saying he couldn't do it, but I'd be surprised. Levern is more direct."

"Is Levern as heavy into the drugs as rumored?" Rob asked.

"You mean using or distribution?" Ben said.

"Distribution."

Ben took another deep drag from the cigarette. "Yes and no. Old Levern stumbled into that sweet spot between the lines. He doesn't deal in drugs per se, except a few stolen pharmaceuticals. He repre-sents most of the black drug dealers as a go-between with the Chi-cago mob. Levern takes a generous cut in exchange for keeping the gang leader's pockets full and the supply flowing up north. About the only thing he's directly involved in is the cargo hijacking." Ben walked across the room and scooped the bottle of whiskey off the floor. He pushed aside some papers on the table, found a semi-clean glass, and drained the bottle into it.

"You never made a case on him?" Frank asked.

Ben dropped his head. "Nope. Guy's too careful. Ever since that incident when he was attacked as a kid, he's been spooked. Now he keeps a lot of protection around, lots of middle men to guard and insulate him."

"Heard the feds might have a case on him," Rob said.

Ben tried a swig of Jim Beam and smacked his lips. "Don't believe everything you hear. They might have a case or indictment, but he'll walk. Levern's too smart." Ben stared at the floor a moment and appeared to lose his train of thought. He shook it off and sucked hard on the cigarette. "Yeah, Levern's thought of everything but one."

"What's that?" Rob asked.

Ben had drifted off again, staring at the floor. "What?"

"Thought of everything but one. What's the one?" Rob asked.

Ben coughed. "He forgot about Chicago. The mob has its hooks so deep in him he'll never wiggle off. They own him for as long as they want."

Frank stood as if to leave. "Thanks, that's information I can use."

Ben jumped up as Rob also rose. "You guys going already?" His baggy eyes gave him an old dog appearance.

"Yeah, we're on a mission from God," Rob said.

Ben's lips cracked into another smile. "You mean Edna?"

Rob shrugged. "One and the same."

"Terry said to tell you hello," Frank mumbled as he walked to the door.

Ben swallowed hard and the smile faded. "Tell him I miss him."

Rob wanted to give Ben what he probably longed for. The knowledge that his career had amounted to something. That he'd given up his life for something meaningfully. But no one could do that except Ben. That was the challenge every cop faced when they retired. That's what drove many of them crazy with self-doubt and self-worth.

A copper plaque hung on the inside of the front door. In Old English script was the words, "If You Ain't Police—You Ain't Shit!"

* * *

Walking back to their car, Frank recalled the reasons for Ben's early retirement. Alcohol, erratic behavior, and dereliction of duty. The same things that had collapsed his marriage.

"Thanks for saving me back there," Frank said.

"Hate to see that kind of stuff," Rob answered. "Burglar baiting is sick."

Frank chewed his lip. What would have happened if Rob hadn't been there to stop him from going in? Not the first, or probably the last time, he owed him.

"I can't believe how screwed up Ben is," Rob said. "I've seen cops fall before, but never that low."

"You just never know about the human condition," Frank said, "people conceal things they don't want to, or can't share with the world. Like the old Billy Joel song, 'The Stranger.' 'We all have a face that we hide away forever, and we take them out and show ourselves when everyone has gone.'"

Rob stared at him. "You sure that's Billy Joel? Sounds like something Elton John would sing."

Rob knew country and western music, but drop him back in the pop days of the seventies and eighties—guy didn't have a clue. Frank released a long tired breath. "No, Rob. It's Billy Joel."

"You going metaphysical on me again?" Rob asked. "We talked about that. Remember?"

Frank gritted his teeth. "Don't make me crazy before lunch."

"Speaking of that, I say we eat before seeing Levern." Rob tapped the key fob and slid into the driver's seat. "Should have figured we'd find Ben all screwed up."

"Why?" Frank asked.

"The guy worked narcotics for too many years. Everybody who works drugs or vice too long gets a little kinked and strange after a while."

Frank frowned. "Hey, I worked vice."

Rob raised his brows and his lips pressed together. "Yeah . . ."

They swung by Pappadeaux's off Northwest Highway for lunch. Rob ordered fried seafood and Frank ordered the gumbo.

"Old Ben doesn't seem convinced Levern's involved," Rob said.

"No, he doesn't."

"Levern's a crook. Could be involved. Who else brags about that Voodoo crap?" Rob asked.

Frank didn't answer. He kept turning over in his mind what Ben said. "Levern is more direct."

The food arrived and Rob crossed himself, and then made quick work of the seafood plate. Frank took a half hour to spoon down the last of the gumbo. "One thing's for sure," Frank said. "If Levern's not involved, as of now, we got no other leads."

Rob wiped his lips. "You sure know how to ruin a better than average lunch."

6

Antoine Levern's desk phone rang. Caller ID showed it was Phil from Chicago. *Shit, what does he want?*

"Antoine, how's things?"

Levern straightened up in his chair and cleared his throat. "Everything's good, Phil."

There was silence on the line a few seconds too long before Phil spoke again. "Word's out Dallas had a little trouble the other night."

Sometimes it paid to act dumb. "Trouble?"

Phil's tone changed for the worst. "Yeah, you get the paper? Have a TV, internet? Ricardo, wiseass. That's what I'm calling about."

Levern's stomach churned. Sometimes it didn't pay to act *too* dumb. "Oh, yeah, that."

"Know anything about it?"

"Why would I know something?"

"Well, I won't know until I ask, will I? Wiseass," Phil said.

Levern lowered his voice. "I didn't have anything to do with it, if that's what you're getting at. Just found out myself."

"Okay. Ricardo is New York's guy. Wouldn't want any trouble with them when things are running so smoothly."

"Yeah, sure. Don't make waves. That's what I say," Levern mumbled. He wiped a little sweat from his neck.

"Coming down for a visit tomorrow, wiseass."

Levern squirmed in the chair. *Oh, Christ. Not tomorrow.*

"Charlene still working?" Phil asked.

33

Phil liked Charlene. Best hooker in the city. Levern always fixed Phil up as a courtesy when he visited. "Yeah, just waiting for you."

"Ha, I bet," Phil replied and hung up.

Levern dropped the receiver into its cradle. Phil was one of the crazies—totally unpredictable with a hair-trigger temper. Once shot a guy for sneezing without covering his mouth. Well . . . that was the story anyway.

The elevator door opened and Keno, one of Levern's bodyguards, motioned to Tabor. He met him halfway. The guard passed him a card. Tabor marched toward Levern, eyeing the thing, a toothpick wiggling between his lips with each step.

"A cop's in the restaurant—wants to talk to you," Tabor said, holding out the card for Levern.

He shook his head and waved it away. "You know I don't talk to cops. Have them contact my attorney."

Tabor pocked the card and turned back toward the door.

Levern paused. *Why would a cop want to see him?* "Hey, let me see that?"

Tabor passed the card to Levern.

"Well, well, Detective Frank Pierce," Levern said. "Show him up . . . might be fun to chat."

* * *

Rob had never met Antoine Levern, but he knew about him. Working homicide and SWAT before coming to CIU, Rob had never crossed paths with him. As far as Rob was concerned he never wanted to meet the doper. A low-life who didn't deserve to breathe the same air as him.

When Levern's family resettled in Dallas in 2005, Frank still rode patrol as a uniformed officer. According to the story, one night Frank ran an assault on a minor call and found a local gang had jumped the new kid in town, Antoine Levern. He would have been beaten to death if Frank hadn't rolled up. As a reminder not to tread on their turf again, one of the gang members stabbed Levern through the knee cap before he fled. Against departmental policy, Frank loaded Levern in his patrol car and rushed him to the closest hospital. Levern recovered, but kept a distinctive limp as a reminder of that night.

Rob gazed around at the room. The smell of seafood and chatter of customer's conversations was deceiving. "So this is the restaurant?"

They were in the Deep Ellum part of downtown Dallas—the old warehouse district, now an entertainment Mecca—at the Cajun Crawdad on St. Louis Street. Rob stared in the mirror over the long bar and raked his hands over his high and tight Marine haircut. While old Ben slowly wasted away in his dingy apartment, Levern lived the high-life with his drug money in a three-story building with a restaurant. The rich get richer. . . .

Frank leaned against the bar facing the patrons. "Yeah, these yuppies have no idea they're dining in the restaurant of one of the biggest drug guys in the Southwest."

"He owns the whole building, doesn't he?"

Frank caught the glimpse of a cute brunette at a nearby table. Long hair, plunging neckline, and nice breasts. Her lunch companion had his back to Frank. When the guy glanced out the window, the brunette winked.

Frank grinned.

She blushed just as her guy started talking to her again.

"I said, he owns the whole building, doesn't he?" Rob repeated.

Frank kept eyeing the beauty. Half the department thought he was gay—wasn't married, never seen in public with a woman. The other half, including Rob, knew the truth. Like most unmarried cops, Frank had a lot of lady friends. Having once been a professional chef gave him an edge. He'd wine and dine them at his place, then make love for a couple of hours. Last year one of Frank's dates, after copious amounts of wine, had let it slip that Frank had a way—a technique. Rob and Carman had been married for so long; stopping at a Hardee's was a treat. And as far as making love . . .

Frank finally answered the question.

"Yup." Frank swiveled his head. "He picked up the old building on a foreclosure. Did a complete and costly renovation. First floor is the bar and restaurant. Second is where his guys hang out. And he lives on the third." Frank motioned up with his head. "Heard he bullet-proofed the windows up there. Guy's paranoid about getting whacked."

"Is it true he only has one conviction?" Rob asked. "Kinda hard to believe with his reputation."

"Uh-huh. Stole a bike as a kid in New Orleans. That's it."

It was tougher and tougher to be a successful thug every year, especially in the drug trade, but Antoine Levern had mastered it. Well . . . until recently. Word on the street was he had been indicted by a federal grand jury on a charge of conspiracy to distribute methamphetamines. Folks said the U.S. Attorney's Office had offered him a plea deal. This might work in their favor. Levern might think he could work a deal through Frank and CIU. Guy didn't deserve a deal—deserved to go down.

A large black man about the size of Fort Worth approached them. "Mr. Levern will see you now."

*　*　*

Frank and Rob followed the man into the hall behind the bar. The big guy led them into a service elevator, closed the gate, and pressed a button. Frank looked the dude over. About six-foot-eight, five inches taller than him. But he'd either once played pro ball or did some serious competitive weightlifting. Didn't do a very good job of concealing the gun under his jacket—a big automatic.

Frank had mixed emotions about seeing Levern again. Anytime you save a life, you want to believe it was worth the effort. That somehow, someway, the person you saved will help make the world a better place, or at the very least, not make it any worse. Frank couldn't say that about Levern. He'd squandered his second chance by becoming a professional criminal. Saving his life had resulted in him hurting many others.

The elevator stopped with a jarring clang on the third floor. The doors opened and the big guy slid the metal gate back before giving them a look. He shoved the toothpick to one side of his mouth and said, "I'll take those guns before you meet Mr. Levern."

Rob's eyes pinched and he took a step back. His hand dropped to his pistol and he looked up at the giant. "The hell you will."

"Hey, Antoine!" Frank yelled. "Want to call off your muscle?" His voice echoed in the cavernous room.

Laughter sounded from beyond the elevator doors. "Okay, Tabor, let 'em in. And they can keep their precious guns."

Frank hadn't seen Antoine Levern in five years, but he still had that new-kid look Frank remembered. In his early thirties now, a decade younger than Frank and Rob, he'd made the most of his time. Managed to build a first-rate drug cartel. The diamond stud in the left ear and short, spiked hair were his trademarks. He sat behind a dark oak desk, cluttered with papers. Levern stood when they entered. A wide smile crossed his lips.

"Frank."

He strolled to them, the limp still noticeable. He didn't offer to shake hands, and Frank kept his in his pockets.

"How are you?" Frank asked.

"Getting by." Levern eyed Rob. "And who's this, your driver?"

Rob frowned.

"He's my partner, Detective Soliz," Frank said.

"Come in and take a look around. No cop's ever been up here before. Drink?"

"No thanks," Rob quickly said.

"Do you have a good red?" Frank asked.

Levern smiled again. "Still the same old Frank." Levern motioned to the guy who brought them up. "Call down and order a red for me and my friend. Not that bar shit. One of the good ones from my private stock." He stared at Frank. "So what do you think?" Levern waived his arms around, gazing at the large room.

"This place is probably bigger than the whole apartment building you lived in growing up in New Orleans." Frank's voice echoed through the vastness of the renovated warehouse. Place still had a new paint smell.

Levern pointed at the far wall. "Gutted the old joint. Two stairways on each side of the elevator. Keep men on the stairwells of the second floor when I'm here. Plus a half dozen or so with me all the time. Better protection than the damn vice-president."

They walked the length of the room. Rob followed. He eyed the place and kept his arms crossed. The white concrete walls, stained floors, and dark blue support columns made the place look like an ultra-modern loft.

"Have a built-out bedroom and bath area in there." Levern pointed to a walled-up corner of the warehouse.

Rob grunted.

Levern glanced at him.

"Come on. Let's sit a spell." Levern led the way to an L-shaped leather sofa in the corner. He flopped down and massaged his knee.

"Still giving you problems?" Frank asked.

Levern hesitated before answering. "Only all the time."

No sunlight filtered through the dark smoky window tint. "Opaque glass?" Frank asked.

"Yeah," Levern said, "mirrored on the outside and bulletproof."

Rob showed a wide smile. "Playing hard to kill, huh?"

"This driver of yours has a nasty sense of humor, Frank."

"Yeah, he does stand-up in his spare time." Frank nodded toward Levern's right hand. A tattoo of a target bull's eye with a red dot in the middle decorated the back of it. "Nice."

Levern held it up eye level and admired it. "Yeah, thanks."

A waiter from the restaurant with a tray and two glasses of wine approached. Levern handed one to Frank and then claimed the other for himself.

Levern took a slow sip, his eyes on Frank. "So what do I owe the pleasure of this unexpected visit?"

Frank didn't answer at first, continuing to stroll around the area.

He stopped at a table with a tall green vase of multicolored gladiolas. He sniffed the arrangement and then sniffed the wine. He finally came to rest on the arm of the plush sofa as Levern settled deeper in the cushions. The couch smelled like sex. God only knew what the hell he'd done on that thing. Rob must have also noticed because he remained standing with his arms crossed.

Having never worked in an undercover capacity, Rob found it distasteful chumming with criminals. Frank didn't judge people too often, even criminals. He was as comfortable around the underworld as most folks are visiting their in-laws. He believed each person found a level of comfort consistent with their personality. The fact he could get close to the criminal element and not feel distasteful sometimes made him wonder . . .

Frank's plan was to put a little scare in Levern and see which way he ran. If Frank left this meeting not knowing if Levern was involved, then all he'd gotten out of the deal was a glass of wine. Frank held the wine up to the light, swirled it a couple of times, and took a sip.

"We were wondering if you'd heard about the death of Ricardo Salazar."

A grin cracked Levern's lips. "Yes—tragic."

"Yeah, I can see you're all torn up over it. Umm, this *is* the good stuff." Frank rested an arm across the top of the sofa. "We figure his demise will send some business your way."

Levern squinted. "Frank, whatever are you implying? Salazar was a notorious drug lord. How could I possibly benefit from his death?"

Frank reached over and raked his finger across the tip of Levern's nose, showing him the trace of white powder. "What's this? Sugar donuts?"

Levern wiped his nose on his sleeve. "I'm shocked you'd resort to trying to plant drugs on me, Frank."

Frank sipped his wine again, wearing his usual lackadaisical expression. "I'm sure you are."

"Besides," Levern motioned around the room. "Salazar was an

idiot. Sleeping in a residential home with only two guards—deserved to get hit."

Frank leaned forward, resting his forearms on his legs. "I'm going to pass on some information that hasn't been officially released yet, so keep it to yourself."

This was his play. If Levern was involved, he would soon know.

Levern eyed him suspiciously, as if he might be trying to set him up. "Yeah, okay." He moved a little closer.

"When we found Ricardo's body, there wasn't a mark on him," Frank said.

Levern showed no emotion. "No shit. So what killed him?"

Frank swirled the wine again, not looking at him. "That's what we're trying to figure out. You know anything?"

"Why, do you suspect me? Why should I know anything? You wearing a wire? Besides I got alibis!"

"I never said I suspected you," Frank said, "and I'm sure you do have several alibis. You could probably get twenty people to testify tomorrow that this meeting never happened. That you were out of the country playing pinochle in Piccadilly with Polish pickle poppers."

Levern didn't answer, but the corners of his mouth formed into a grin.

"Well?" Frank asked.

Levern shrugged. "Read about it in the paper, that's all. Why you asking me?"

"Oh, no reason"—Frank finished the red—"just that we found a Voodoo doll beside Ricardo, and he looked like he'd been scared to death. Emptied a magazine of .45 ACP at someone, but that didn't save him."

Levern's mouth dropped open, and he looked back and forth from Frank to Rob. "No shit, a Voodoo doll, huh?"

Frank stood and sat the empty glass on an end table. "Yeah, know anybody who deals in that sort of stuff?"

"Come on, Frank. You don't believe all that crap on the street.

About my grandma being a Voodoo priestess." Levern had a stupid grin as if it was all one big joke.

"Doesn't matter what I believe. Matters what they believe back east," Frank said.

Levern's grin twisted into a frown. "What you mean?"

"Ricardo supplied which family in New York? The Gambizi's?"

Levern broke his stare and gazed at the floor. "How should I know?"

"What do you think they're going to do when they find out one of their main suppliers got whacked in Dallas? Those guys hate to have their chain interrupted. Costs 'em money."

Levern's eyes shifted a few times, and he changed positions on the couch.

"Heard you finally ran afoul of the feds."

Levern smirked. "There's nothing to that. My lawyer says they got no case."

"Playing pinochle in Piccadilly with Polish pickle poppers?"

Levern smirked again. "Something like that."

"You're in a dark and dangerous place, Antoine," Frank said.

Levern didn't answer. He had that "little kid caught with his hand in the cookie jar" expression.

Frank sat back on the arm of the sofa. "That's two strikes against you. Now, if your pals in Chicago get the idea you might accept a plea deal from the feds, they could start wondering what you might tell about ya'll's arrangement. They could send someone down for a talk."

Levern listened and nibbled at his lower lip, but still didn't answer. He couldn't make eye contact with Frank.

"How much of their product do you supply? About 10 percent, 20 percent? How many names could you give up if the feds offered the right deal?" Frank paused for effect and nodded. "Yeah, they could send someone down. And if Gambizi makes the connection between you, the Voodoo doll, and their dead supplier, that could start *them* thinking." Frank shook his head.

"Hey, I didn't kill nobody."

"If you say so. You don't want New York and Chicago thinking too much about you, Antoine. Bad for your health. This killing creates a mess. And just like all messes, someone has to clean it up, whether they were invited to the party or not." Frank stood and dropped his hands into his pockets. You get ready for some help give me a call. I'll see what I can do, but don't wait too long."

Levern didn't answer. His look could best be described as hesitant.

"Thanks for the wine," Frank said.

*　*　*

Tabor escorted Rob and Frank back down the elevator. Rob was happy to leave. Hated guys like Levern. Guys who profited from others weaknesses.

Walking outside, Rob glanced at the sky. Dark rolling clouds had drifted in from the west. The smell of rain was in the air. Rob said, "Think he believed you?"

"Doesn't matter," Frank said, "it's the truth whether he believes it or not."

Rob hadn't been Frank's partner two weeks before he'd figured out Frank was the king of the mind game. He could get inside your head and make you believe anything by his nonchalant interviewing technique. During their first interrogation, Frank had the guy crying and begging to give a confession. Benevolent Frank had granted him absolution. Rob tried the same thing the next week and got a stink eye from the suspect for his trouble.

As they slid into the car seat, Frank said, "Levern is a drug dealer, and who knows what else. Sooner or later, the Chicago and New York bosses are going to want answers. Levern could be the fall guy whether he's responsible or not."

They didn't talk on the way to the station. Just as they pulled into the police parking garage, Rob said, "So, what now?" Rob suspected Frank had a plan, but hadn't informed him as yet.

"Levern uses us like we use him, to get inside information."

"You shared confidential investigative stuff with him. What did we get in return?"

Frank scratched his chin. "Well, what I hoped to get was confirmation he wasn't involved in Ricardo's killing. But I'm still unsure on that. Thought I'd have a better feel for him than I did."

"He's still our best suspect."

"He's our only suspect," Frank said. "Spooking him a little didn't hurt."

"I think whoever hit Ricardo is still around. A professional job by a local.

Frank thought about that a few seconds before answering. "As closed-mouth as the gangs are, we'll probably never find out. In war, truth is the first casualty."

"Think this is the start of a war?"

Frank opened his door. "We'll soon find out."

7

In the upscale restroom of Bob Banyan's Steak and Chop House in Brooklyn, Jimmy Russo stood at the urinal bracing against the wall with one hand and handling business with the other. The celebration had started earlier that afternoon after he'd signed his life over to the New York U.S. Attorney's Office. According to the plea agreement, in exchange for his cooperation he was promised protection, a new identity, and entry into the Witness Protection Program. This was his last day of freedom until after his testimony. Tomorrow morning he'd surrender himself to the U.S. Marshals and be kept in an undisclosed location.

Old man Gambizi was going down. The state and feds had wanted a piece of old Joe's ass for decades. Now they were going to get it, thanks to Jimmy. He'd worked for Gambizi for over twenty years. Never advanced enough in the organization to be a made-man, but worked as back-up for a good crew out of lower Brooklyn. Made nice money, but one mistake had cost him everything. He was a lover—a lover involved with a made-man crew member's wife. Been pounding that thing for months. He'd always kept it quiet until the guy's old lady, who must have had a psychotic episode, up and confessed to her husband about their affair. The guy came to Jimmy's house. It was a him-or-me situation. Figured the organization would understand. They didn't.

Seems you needed permission to whack a made-man. Had to go before the council for discussion first. Who had time for discussion?

Jimmy caught the guy slipping around his house and beat him to death with a nine iron. *Never was any good at golf.*

Anyway, Jimmy heard a rumor he was getting whacked, so he ran. After disappearing for a few days, he confirmed it. After that, he had nowhere to go but the feds. Jimmy had twenty plus years of dirt on Gambizi, which gave him leverage. He could take down the entire organization. Put a couple of dozen away in the next year and cause more damage than Sammy "The Bull" Gravano. Feds like that kind of stroke. Couple of 'em probably wet their pants at the thought. Or more likely enjoyed a seldom-remembered hard on. Anyway, one last night with a few trusted friends from the old neighborhood and then off to wherever.

Jimmy shook the last few drops of dew off the rose and zipped up. He meandered to the sink and washed his hands. The attendant was new. He lifted a fine linen hand towel from the rack and waited for Jimmy to finish. *Going to miss this kind of service.*

"How are you this evening, sir?" the attendant asked. "Mouthwash?"

A man who wants a good tip. "Sure why not," Jimmy said, as the attendant passed a small plastic cup of green liquid to him.

Jimmy freshened his breath, spit into the sink, and patted his lips dry. "You new here? Where's the regular guy?"

The attendant smiled. "I work the nights Fred's off."

"Yeah, right, Fred's the other guy."

Jimmy sprinkled on a little aftershave and studied himself in the mirror. He raked the hair back into place on the sides and cinched his tie. *Nice.*

The attendant held a coat brush. "You have a sprinkle of dandruff back here, sir. Shall I get it?"

"Yeah, sure."

Jimmy leaned toward the mirror to pick something black from between a front tooth. The movement from behind was so smooth and swift it looked like one motion. Before Jimmy could react, a strong grip yanked his hair and jerked him backward. A glint of silver flashed in the light, and he watched with horror in the mirror as a straight razor sliced open his neck. Must have been the shock, but he didn't feel a thing as bright red blood cascaded down the front of his blue shirt. The last sound he heard was the attendant whisper, "Joe Gambizi says bye-bye, rat!"

* * *

Joseph Gambizi had always been lucky. He'd survived being an infantry man in Korea in '52, two assassination attempts in '77 and '84, and a federal racketeering indictment in '99. Last month his doctor had declared him cancer free, and he maintained the reputation as the last "old-time Don" of the northeast crime families not dead or in prison. And all that at the young age of only eighty-six.

He gazed out his dining room window as darkness absorbed the fall foliage of the Adirondacks. Just a scarlet line on the horizon was all that was left of the day. *God, I love this place.* He'd come here for a week or two each year since buying the cabin in '63. Air always had a clean, sweet smell. He loved the leaf change—an autumn tradition.

The Gambizi family held on to traditions like most families do old silverware. Passing down crooked politicians, cops, and judges to buy favors or repay old debts. Gambizi had a lot to be thankful for. His health and his wife. His kids, not so much. Hadn't been so lucky with them—four girls and a boy. After the son was born, his wife developed an ovarian tumor. The operation was successful, but they'd had their last child. Just Joe's luck, the brat grew up stupid. Managed to get himself killed in a bar room brawl over thirty years ago. *Shit.* Still pissed him off.

The family would probably dissolve after Joe's death. None of his sons-in-law wanted anything to do with the business—all professionals—embarrassed by Joe's success. The family would likely be taken over by another one, unless his under-boss could show enough strength. Anthony Palazzo might just pull it off.

Palazzo threw another split log on the fire, closed the screen in front of the fireplace, and dusted his hands. He tugged up his charcoal gray trousers and smoothed his black turtleneck as he strolled back into the dining room. Always dressed to the nines. Palazzo rejoined Gambizi at the table and took a sip of coffee.

"I miss the old days, Tony," Gambizi said.

"The good old days or the bad old days?"

Gambizi grunted. "Both. It was simpler then, you know? We had the whole world by the tail and were too stupid to know it. Not like today. Now we have the darkies doing drive-bys and killing children. Children, Tony!" Gambizi finished his coffee. "I mean we had a better handle on things back then. We had the city cut up and each family kept to their areas. The Teamsters, the garment district, the building trades—we all knew where we stood. Not like now. Nothing but thugs trying to out-kill each other—no respect anymore. Killing causes problems."

Palazzo nodded but remained quiet. He took another sip of coffee, his eyes on Gambizi.

"What happened in Dallas? Does anyone know?"

Palazzo settled back in the chair and exhaled. "I haven't been able to get a straight answer. Ricardo got hit. That's all we know for sure. Cops are staying quiet about the details."

Gambizi watched the last traces of sun as it slipped out of sight. He folded his hands across his stomach and exhaled. "We had too much of our business tied up in him. Should have diversified years ago. What will this do to our supply?"

"Ricardo shipped about 10 percent," Palazzo said. "Some months 15. It's going to hurt until we get another supplier. He had a lot of connections. Smart enough not to share them all. Could be a while before we get them reestablished."

"How much?" Gambizi asked.

"Quarter million a month."

Gambizi nodded, looking out the window again. "If we get into the habit of letting people hit our suppliers without penalty, we're sending the wrong message. It needs to be understood that if you screw with us, you pay. Let's find out what happened down there and who's responsible."

"Old school, huh?"

Gambizi lifted his chin and nodded. "Yeah, old school."

8

Frank sat on his balcony with a glass of red and enjoyed the evening. The mid-October days grew shorter and cooler. Just enough chill in the air to make it nice to sit outside again after another scorching Dallas summer. The aroma of a neighbor grilling made his mouth water.

A redbird perched somewhere in Frank's jungle of patio plants. Its song relaxed him.

Frank didn't look back too often. His life had so many twists and turns, it didn't make any sense to try and figure them out. But something a crook told him once popped back into his head. Guy was suspected of selling porn to minors. Frank utilized an old interviewing trick he'd used dozens of times to get the guy to give it up—shifting the blame to the kids who bought the porn, rather than directly accusing the porn broker of selling it. After an hour convincing the guy he was only fulfilling what the minors really wanted, the suspect gave a full confession to the crime, and Frank filed charges on him.

Weeks later in court, the guy eyed Frank and said, "You're a bad man." Frank didn't care at the time—he'd been called a lot worse. He knew the guy had done it, and the guy knew he had done it. Tricking him into giving the confession was just good interrogating. But something about the way he said it and the look in his eyes stayed with Frank. Ever so often, something triggered the memory.

Frank didn't necessarily believe he was a bad man. He seldom swore. Considered vulgar language to be the last bastion of the uncouth,

49

uneducated, and lazy—the ones who didn't have the intelligence to use a more descriptive word. He called his parents once a week. And he always played fair with everyone. Except crooks. After the loss and injustice he'd suffered in New York, he would never play fair with them.

When Frank gave up being a chef and entered police work, he never dreamed that there would be so many rules. Everything was stacked in the crook's favor. Of course there had to be rules to stem police misconduct, but they had become so onerous it got harder to make a case every year. And that's why he didn't play fair. When Frank believed he had someone dead to right, he went in for the kill. Sometimes he skipped a few steps of acceptable investigative procedure, but he never crossed the line enough to let them get off on a technicality.

He and Rob were of the same mindset: never let the rules get in the way of a good investigation. This had landed them on Edna's lecture couch more than once. The police brass and politicians all gave lip service to the "follow the rules" mantra, but there were guys like him and Rob in every big city department. And when one of their own was in a jam, or the thing looked like a political shit bomb about to explode, they all turned to the guys who they knew would get fast results. He and Rob both had more than one official reprimand in their personal files. Higher-ups often described their method of policing with terms like "rogue" and "outlaw." Funny how no one ever suggested breaking them up or having them reassigned to other units.

Frank lived with so many regrets he cared little about whether crooks thought he was a bad man. He never tried to blackmail, frame, or intimidate anyone. That would be wrong. So why did the bad man thing keep popping back into his head?

Maybe he *was* a bad man.

The redbird flew off—probably a sign. *Time to call it a day.* Frank downed the last of the wine and fixed a light dinner of spinach salad, whole grain crackers and goat cheese, with spiced red peppers and olives on the side. His experience as a chef seemed wasted on such a meal. But he only really cooked when he had a friend over—they appreciated it. Just before taking his first bite, his cell rang. Paul Sims from Homicide.

"Frank, just thought I give you a head's up. I got a look at the M.E.'s report on Ricardo's autopsy. Guy had a bad ticker. Probably just one taco away from a major coronary event."

"That's interesting."

"Yeah, but that's not why he died," Sims said. "You remember that straight pin through the head of the doll in the closet?"

Frank picked a piece of goat cheese off the salad and popped it into his mouth. "Uh-huh."

"According to the report, Ricardo died of a cerebral hemorrhage. Had an artery pop in the brain just about where that pin was."

* * *

Wednesday morning, Frank meandered through his building's underground garage to his car. Lots of old money and yuppies—and a few nouveau riche like him—lived there. A clicking noise drifted through the air. He swiveled his head and discovered Mrs. Silverstein behind the wheel of her vintage Lincoln, staring at the gauges and grinding away at the starter.

He liked her. Most of the wealthy people in the building seemed snooty—not Mrs. Silverstein. The old girl had almost adopted him last year while he spent six weeks on medical leave after being shot, bringing food several times a week until he could manage. As thanks, he had her over about once a month for one of his gourmet meals. She enjoyed the company. Frank found value in older people—especially women. Old men had better stories, but older women had more wisdom.

Frank opened her car's passenger door and she jumped. Her expression relaxed after recognizing him.

"Having car trouble?"

"Thing won't start. I'll have to call the dealership."

"Let's see what we can do first."

Ten minutes later, after jump-starting the battery, he sent her on her way. Even with the delay, Frank still got to work before Rob. His partner usually hit the police gym about seven o'clock for weights and a round of boxing before strolling in around nine. Frank's exercise schedule took less time—a half hour of yoga at home before breakfast. Frank started the coffee pot and powered up his computer.

Terry shuffled in a few minutes later. "Did you guys talk to Ben yesterday?"

"Yeah." Frank kept typing a request into RMS, a DPD in-house search index. Five reports popped up in which a Voodoo doll had been mentioned as part of an investigation. He scanned the synopsis of each case as Terry talked.

"How's he doing?"

"Not great, but getting by."

Terry leaned closer and stared at the monitor. "What are you checking?"

Frank's fingers raced across the keyboard. "I'm running 'Voodoo doll' through the system. Nothing promising. According to the query log, Sims ran the same thing last night."

Frank's office phone rang. Kelly from the lab.

"Frank, just sent the forensic results of the stuff we found on the two gansters' clothes and sofa to Paul Sims. Copied you too."

"Thanks. What kind of stuff?"

"A fine white powder. Tested out as plant-based material. Could be some kind of bio-toxin. Won't know for sure till we have it fully tested."

"How long will that take?"

"Well, if this were frigging *CSI Miami*, about ten minutes. But since we're still in the real world . . . could be weeks. Depends on their backlog."

"You're still my hero, Kelly."

"Thanks. I'll cash that in for what it's worth," Kelly said before hanging up.

Frank looked at Terry. "Residue of some plant at the scene. All over the two guys downstairs."

Terry pursed his lips. "Umm. Say, try and play nice with Edna today. She went to bat for you guys with the sixth floor yesterday. Put herself out there—know what I mean?"

Frank nodded. "I promise. Whatever she wants, I just say, yes, ma'am."

Terry headed for his office.

A drop of blood pooled on Frank's keyboard. *Crap, wrist leaking again. Might need a stitch after all.*

Edna strolled past, still not looking too happy.

Frank patched his wrist with a Band-Aid, watching Edna through the glass wall of her office as she settled in. She could be a pain in the butt but always stood up for "her guys." He poured a cup of coffee and added two cream packs, stirred it, and walked in just as she took a seat. As she finished putting away her briefcase, he sat the cup on her desk.

"Looked like you could use this," he said.

She nodded and picked up the cup. "Thanks, Frank."

"By the way, Rob and I paid a visit to Antoine Levern yesterday."

Edna blew on her coffee and took a sip. She sat back in her chair. "The guy who's related to Carlos Marcello?"

"Well, Levern claims to be an illegitimate grandson. Kind of resembles the old boy, but who knows? He tells a different story about his family every year or so."

"Why him?" Edna asked.

"Think that toy we recovered from Ricardo's might be a Voodoo doll."

Edna crossed her legs. Her skirt rode up, revealing a little thigh. Her olive complexion and perfect white teeth took Frank back to his one and only trip abroad. That Mediterranean cruise to Italy and Greece—prettiest women in the world.

"Is Levern into that kind of thing?"

"Yeah. He supposedly has some kind of Voodoo connection in the drug community. Claims his grandma was a Voodoo priestess back in Haiti, or something. Probably just another BS story to give him extra street creds."

Edna rocked back a little more. Frank's stare shifted from her eyes, back to her legs and thigh. He quickly recovered from his Pavolvian response, but she'd caught him. Her smirk and lifted eyebrow was confirmation.

Why does she have to be my lieutenant and married?

She took another sip before asking, "Find out anything from him?"

Frank cleared his throat and shifted his stance, keeping his eyes on hers. "Not sure. He claims not to know anything about it. Not certain I believe him."

"Interesting," Edna said.

Frank turned for the door.

"Hey."

He looked back.

Edna winked. "Thanks for the java."

* * *

Rob sauntered in a few minutes before nine wearing a new cowboy cut suit. Poor Rob. Born a hundred and fifty years too late. Would have made a great Texas lawman in the mid to late eighteen hundreds. A while back he tried wearing a cowboy hat into the office. That lasted until lunch when Terry slipped up beside him and whispered, "Rodeo's over—lose the hat."

"Morning," Rob said as he draped his jacket over the back of the chair.

Frank kept typing, but mumbled something he hoped Rob would interpret as good morning. Rob hummed a country and western song under his breath while he busied himself powering up his computer and organizing his desk.

Frank stopped typing and took a long patient breath. He'd mentioned once or twice about Rob's humming—a serious distraction. Rob forgot stuff like that. Never a bad thing to remind him.

Frank scanned the websites until he found what he wanted. Rob snatched up his cup and headed to the coffee bar in the corner. Frank reached over the top of the low cubicle and turned the volume to the max on Rob's computer speakers. Then he attached the link to the email and hit send. Rob flopped back into his chair a moment later, still humming, and opened his emails.

"Hey, what's this?"

Frank stopped typing. "Huh?"

"You send me a link?"

"Yeah, something you'll like."

Rob lifted the cup to his lips as he clicked the link. Freddie Hart's voice boomed through the squad area. EASY LOVING . . . SO SEXY LOOKING! Rob jerked the cup, sprinkling his freshly starched khaki pants with coffee. As every head turned, he clawed for the volume knob. Edna gawked at him, and Terry's eyes bore down from his glass office.

Rob wiped his pants. "Carmen's going to kill me. Just got these from the cleaners."

Now Frank felt bad. Not for playing the joke, but for making poor Rob face Carmen with his newly cleaned pants stained. Girl wouldn't tolerate nasty clothes on Rob.

Edna stood at her door and motioned with her head for Frank. She reclaimed her executive leather chair as he strolled in.

"I had an idea." She opened her notebook and removed a business card. "Since the chief's office wants us working this Ricardo business with Homicide, we should get a good handle on this Voodoo thing."

Christ. Frank hated when she had ideas. It usually meant him doing twice the work for half the benefit. "Oh, yeah, what's that?"

She passed him the card. "I made an appointment for you and Rob to see a pal of mine."

Frank looked at the card. "A professor at SMU?"

"Met him at a luncheon. Would love to take his comparative religion class, but my schedule's too full this semester."

The best Frank could tell, Edna had been continually in school since she entered the first grade. Prior to joining the department, she'd earned her undergraduate degree from Texas A&M. Got a master's after becoming a cop, and now had her eye on an executive management degree from SMU.

"He might be able to shed some light on this business," Edna said. "Knows a lot about religion and things like that. You'll like him. Nice old guy."

Frank's promise to Terry still echoed in his ears, *I'll just say, yes, ma'am.* He bit back a sarcastic comment.

"Yes, ma'am." *There, playing nice.*

Back at his desk, Frank examined the card. Doctor Jonathan Plebe, Dedman College of Humanities and Sciences. Frank finished typing up yesterday's interview with Levern and sent an electronic copy to Terry and Edna.

Rob had his ear buds in, attached to the surreptitious iPod he hid under his notebook. As he typed, his lips moved and his head bobbed in time with another country-western tune. Rob had about a thousand songs on that iPod.

"We have a new mission," Frank announced. He made it a point to smile as he passed the business card over the top of the cubicle.

Rob slipped an ear bud out and read the card. "What?"

"Saddle up, cowboy. We're riding to SMU."

9

When Rob and Frank ambled into Dr. Plebe's office, an older man with bright, intelligent eyes stood and warmly greeted them. He fit Rob's expectation of a college professor. Tall and thin with an aquiline nose. The herringbone jacket and green striped bowtie added a flash of style to what otherwise would be an ordinary looking man. If Mr. Rogers had a twin, they'd just found him.

After inviting them to take a seat, he leaned on the desk and clasped his fingers. "Gentlemen, Edna tells me you have some questions about Voodoo." A quick grin swept across Plebe's lips as if he had a secret but wasn't about to share it. "Used to teach those classes myself until we got our new associate professor—expert in ancient religions and the occult."

"You, or the new professor?" Rob asked.

Plebe's brow furrowed and he opened his mouth, but caught what he was about to say. "What? Oh, yes. The new professor, I mean. Sorry. Dr. Hawkins really isn't new. Came to us years ago, but I continued teaching the ancient religion courses until recently."

Rob wanted to be anywhere else. *What a waste of time.* To make matters worse, they were doing this just to appease Edna. "We had a couple of questions. Do you have time to help us?"

Rob glanced over at Frank. From his expression it was clear he also thought this a wasted effort. After shaking hands with Plebe and sitting down, Frank hadn't said a word. He played with his jacket button while Rob made conversation.

"I'm sorry, but I should defer Voodoo questions to the true expert," Plebe said. "Much better versed in that sort of thing than I." He flashed an apologetic smile.

Rob shifted in the chair. *Christ! Why can't he just give us some BS answers to our BS questions and let us get out of here?*

Frank still hadn't spoken. He had that zoned-out look he showed when something didn't interest him. Or he already knew the answer and was listening just to be polite. Intellectuals never impressed Frank. Probably because he was one. Of all the guys in the department, Rob never figured he'd end up partnering with someone like Frank. A guy who owned more books than fishing lures.

Plebe cleared his throat and stood. "Let's take a walk down the hall. I'll introduce you." He stood, opened the door for them, and they followed.

Rob already had his mind on dinner. Carmen promised beef tips and gravy tonight—his favorite. The sooner they could ask a few stupid questions and get out, the better. Edna would be happy and they could claim victory.

As they followed the professor down the hall, photographs of distinguished looking men and women in university caps and gowns hung on the wall. Probably previous heads of the department. Having gone into the Marines right out of high school, Rob never received any higher education—unless you counted being in combat and fifteen years in the PD an education. Plebe stopped at a closed door and knocked. A female voice said, "Come."

Plebe swung the door open and they walked in. She sat at her desk with the phone pressed to her ear, her long red hair covering the receiver. She stared at them and held up one finger.

Frank touched Rob's shoulder, but he ignored him, keeping his eyes on the beauty. Best looking professor he'd ever seen.

Frank leaned his mouth to Rob's ear and whispered. "It's her, the red-haired woman from Ricardo's."

* * *

Antoine Levern stared at himself in the mirror. Shaving lather sagged from his chin as he dragged the razor down his cheek. He made sure not to get too close to his soul patch. The ladies loved that thing.

Levern never saw himself as a crook. More of a businessman. His business just happened to have a criminal slant, but supplying a demand was a very capitalist idea. Besides, he helped fund the American dream. He employed lots of people. That helped the economy, right? He finished shaving and wiped his face with a warm cloth. He smoothed the small tuft of hair just under his lip.

Frank's visit yesterday still disturbed him. Ricardo getting whacked simplified Levern's business but could complicate his life. Would New York and Chicago ask questions, or just accept it as the cost of doing business? While the Voodoo doll was a nice touch, Levern really didn't give a rat's ass about Voodoo. He'd used it before though, as device to keep his street people in line and frightened. The snake handling trick he'd learned from his grandmother. The old woman used to live on a half-rotten houseboat way back on the Tangipahoa River. He'd spent several summers there as a kid.

But being given credit for Ricardo's hit came with consequences. While it gave him standing, it also drew unwanted attention—could put a target on his back. Ricardo's friends and family, and also his New York associates, might be a problem. The New York associates had enforcers to handle disruptions in their supply chain. Might be a good idea to bring in a few more of his boys as guards for a while.

Levern splashed on aftershave and donned a black shirt. The only problem with bringing on more guys as guards—trust. Most of these characters were two-bit thugs—hired guns who'd sell you out in a minute. He needed more people he could trust, like Tabor.

Levern finished buttoning his shirt and opened the bedroom door. Tabor was waiting when Levern strolled out.

"What's on for today, boss?" Tabor asked.

Tabor had been with him since he'd arrived in Dallas. Loyal as a dog, needing only his basic needs met. He liked women and dope.

Levern made sure he got all he could handle. Having one loyal man around in a business like his was worth any price.

Levern's knee always stiffened up in the mornings. He rubbed it. "Put together a list. About three or four of our best guys. Thinking about adding a few extra security people."

Tabor gnawed the shredded toothpick and nodded. "You got problems, boss?"

"Nothing I can't handle." But Levern wasn't so sure. Until he saw which way the wind blew, he'd have to be extra careful for a while. Lot of game pieces in play. Hard to keep track of all the moving parts. Let one piece fall and. . . .

* * *

Frank may as well have told Rob he'd seen a unicorn in the room. Rob's brow creased and he frowned just as the lady hung up the phone.

"Alma, these are the gentlemen I told you about," Plebe said.

The woman stood. She was about thirty-five, nice figure, and intense green eyes to complement the flowing red hair. She extended her hand. "Hello, I'm Alma Hawkins."

Frank introduced himself and shook hands, his skin tingling as if little shocks of electricity had run up and down his back. He held her handshake a second too long and searched her eyes for something. He got nothing.

She shot a concerned look at Plebe. "Bad news," she pointed at the phone. "That was Professor Webb. His wife's been in a car accident. She's okay, but he's helping her out. He was wondering if I could cover his class—just monitoring an open book exam."

Plebe stammered apologies to Rob and Frank.

"That's not a problem. We understand," Frank said. "Perhaps I could give you a call later this afternoon?"

Dr. Hawkins smiled the kind of smile you get from a woman in a bar after asking for her phone number. "Of course." She handed him a business card from her desk. "Should finish my last class by three.

Be in my office after that until six." She eyed Plebe while gathering up a notebook and some loose papers from the desk. "I must run if I'm going to make it."

Ten minutes later on their way to lunch, Rob said, "So that's it. You've finally lost your ever loving mind."

Frank remained silent. Sometimes just giving Rob room to rant was the best course of action.

"Let me see if I got this straight," Rob said. "You're convinced that the person responsible for Ricardo's hit wasn't another gang leader who has an army of thugs working for him. Oh, no! It's a female college professor in religious studies at SMU? Does that just about cover it?"

Rob loved to simplify things. Boil them down to their basic elements.

Frank slouched in the seat with his eyes closed. "That's not what I said."

"Well, what you said means the same thing."

Frank turned and pulled the sunglasses down on his nose with his index finger. "I said the professor has more to do with Ricardo's death than Levern."

"You're always quoting statistical probabilities. What do ya' think they are here? Huh?" Before Frank could open his mouth, Rob answered his own question. "About as close to zero as it gets. You're fixating again, Charlie Brown. Edna tells you to go find the little red-haired girl, and you identify the first one you see as the suspect. What'cha going to do?"

"Interview her."

"When?" Rob asked.

"When she gets off work—after six."

"Hey, remember I have that dental thing. I might not be out till later."

Frank pushed the glasses back up and closed his eyes. "No problem, I'll handle it."

"You serious? Really going to interview her?"

"Yeah."

"I want to be there when you tell Edna." Rob snickered. "Promise you'll let me know before you walk into her office and say, 'Yes, lieutenant, I've located the missing woman. Guess what? She was hiding in plain sight all the time. And you'll never guess where. At the very place you sent us—SMU. A professor no less! Who would have thunk?'"

Rob glanced Frank's way for a reaction. Frank ignored him. The more he pushed this Dr. Hawkins thing, the more untethered from reality he appeared. Rob was right. He'd probably just put two and two together and gotten six. *No way is Dr. Hawkins the woman at the house.* Still, she was attractive. If someone had to interview an attractive university professor to satisfy Edna's Voodoo obsession, might as well be him. Since she wore no wedding ring, the game was fair.

Something still felt wrong. Frank never believed in coincidences—no cop could afford to. But every now and then, about once in a blue moon, there was a major coincidence in a case. Something happened that made you ask if the investigative fairies had floated over and dropped it square in your lap. *Is that what this is?*

Rob laughed. "Can't wait for you to tell Edna. She's going to have a cat."

"That's good," Frank replied, "she likes animals."

10

Alonzo Salazar took another drag from the joint and passed it from the backseat up to Loro in front. They'd parked but kept the old Chrysler running at the corner of Beckley and Illinois—waiting for the call.

Ricardo should have listened when Alonzo warned him. But Ricardo, being Ricardo, let his machismo get in the way of common sense. Alonzo had loved his big brother. Their mother had become so distraught at the news of his death she had to be sedated.

Well, time to put things right.

Alonzo didn't need some stupid cop telling him who killed his brother. He already knew. Only one man hated Ricardo that much—Billy Henderson. Ever since the deal between them went south last year, Billy had been making threatening noises about what he'd do to Ricardo if he got the chance. That's all the proof Alonzo needed. Time for the biker redneck to pay up.

Ricardo's death had put a kink in the business. Alonzo's brother had always played his cards close to the vest and kept the contacts to himself—his insurance against New York trying to cut him out. It would be difficult rebuilding the network and getting supply back up. But by taking care of Billy, Alonzo could avenge his brother and get points with old man Gambizi in New York.

Alonzo gazed at the traffic passing through the light, and Loro changed the radio station. Jay-Z's "Renegade" boomed through the car. Where was Henderson? He always took this way home. Alonzo glanced at his phone's clock just as it began ringing.

"Hey, turn that down."

Loro turned down the music and stared at Alonzo.

"He's coming," the voice on the other end said. "Just made the turn on Beckley."

Alonzo hung up and tapped Loro on the shoulder. "Billy's turning. Let's go."

They coasted down the street, and Alonzo let the rear passenger window down. The cool breeze felt good on his face and helped sober him up. Ahead, Billy Henderson completed the turn astride his vintage '66 hog, only about fifty yards in front of them. His long brown hair and beard danced in the wind.

Alonzo tapped Loro on the shoulder again. "Get closer or you'll lose him at the next light."

Loro closed the distance. The light changed from green to yellow as Billy made the left turn. Loro slid through just before it went to red. The clopping sound of Henderson's bike drifted in through the window, and Alonzo wiped his hands on his jeans and readied himself.

"Slow down. Don't crowd him. I want him parked. Hand me that joint."

Billy took a right into the driveway of the seventies-era house and pulled under the carport. He switched off the bike and unstraddled it. As he turned, Alonzo pushed the Car-15 out the window. Aimed. Pulled the trigger.

The bolt slammed forward with a "snap."

Misfire.

"Shit!"

Alonzo sprang from the backseat, racked another round in the chamber, and aimed again.

Billy didn't wait. He bolted for the yard gate, reaching for the 9mm in his back waistband. When he shoved the gate open, he turned and sent two shots that missed Alonzo's head by inches. Alonzo, not to be out done, squeezed the trigger again. Five rounds of .223 raced toward Billy. He ducked going into the backyard just in time. Wood from the gate splintered into a hundred pieces and showered him.

Alonzo ran up the driveway and kicked the gate open. Just then two bikers with pistols rushed out of Billy's back door into the yard. Alonzo dropped them with another dozen rounds. Billy stuck his head from around the side of the house. He fired several shots, again missing. A ricochet hit a brick, and a flying chip cut into Alonzo's neck. Assuming he'd been shot, he screamed and charged Billy, firing from the hip.

Apparently a kamikaze charge from a screaming Mexican gangster unhinged poor Billy. He scampered over the fence into his neighbor's backyard. Alonzo jumped on top of the AC unit. He leveled the assault rifle and squeezed off several more rounds. Dirt flew around Billy as he ran. Billy swung back and fired another couple of wild shots. He stumbled over a tricycle but got up and kept running. Alonzo cursed himself with every breath for missing. He jumped the side fence just as Billy jumped the front fence of his neighbor's house. Alonzo swung the weapon over the top. He had Billy in his sights as he ran across the neighbor's front yard. Alonzo pulled the trigger. But the frigging bolt had locked back. Empty.

"Shit!"

Alonzo bound over the fence and gave chase. He pulled his .357 from his pocket. Billy ran down the middle of the street with Alonzo in pursuit. They exchanged shots, with neither coming close to the other. Dogs barked, people fled, and cars stopped—except one.

The sound of its engine revving up behind him sent waves of panic through Alonzo. He jerked his head around and, realizing the danger, dove to the left. The car, going forty-five miles an hour, hit Billy and ran him slap over. After dragging him another thirty yards, it backed up and Billy rolled out, his neck completely twisted. He lay on his stomach, but his dead eyes stared at the sky. Half his long hair had been scalped off and hung by a small piece of hide. His clothes were tattered, and where he'd been dragged, blood stained the pavement.

Alonzo shuddered with disgust. Looked like the Predator had skinned him.

With sirens screaming in the distance, Alonzo ran to the vehicle that killed Billy.

Loro smiled from behind the steering wheel. That impish look, with the streaked green, blue, and yellow hair, and a joint hanging from the corner of his mouth. Alonzo hopped in beside him.

"You are one crazy parrot."

11

Rob and Frank coasted up to Sarge's. They hadn't eaten there in almost a week. In Rob's opinion, going a week without grabbing a bite from their favorite lunch place was unconscionable.

When Sergeant Jimmy Bielstein retired from the Dallas Police Department five years ago, he'd followed his dream. Sunk half his retirement into a hole-in-the-wall space around the corner from the bus station downtown. After a year's work, Sarge's was open for business. Sarge, as everyone called him, ran the place with his wife, Jan. Because of its proximity to the Lew Sterrett Criminal Justice Center and the downtown courts, it got a lot of lawyer, prosecutor, and plainclothes cop business.

It was a great bar, but Sarge also made sandwiches all day, every day, and they were the best. Always used Honey Baked Hams. The other draw, the Cokes. Being an old vice cop, Sarge figured having a drink with lunch helped take the edge off the day and made you more productive. He had a standing rule. If you ordered a Coke, you got Coke. If you requested a cherry Coke, a shot of bourbon found its way into the glass. Order a vanilla Coke, and somehow vodka appeared. Plainclothes cops on duty could order only one, and uniforms weren't allowed any. Although the worst kept secret since Elton John came out, no one asked any questions. Just playing along seemed like the best plan.

A couple of minutes past eleven, they strolled in and Rob spotted his old homicide pal, Paul Sims. He already had a sandwich in one hand and a Coke of unknown origin in the other.

"Hey guys, join me," Sims said, motioning with his head.

They grabbed a couple of stools beside him. Jan looked up from her prep work slicing up lemons. "What will you have?"

"The usual," Rob answered, which meant two ham sandwiches and two cherry Cokes. God, his mouth was already watering.

Sims wiped a dab of Dijon mustard off his lip with the napkin. "Getting ready to shoot you two a call." He took another big bite, filling his mouth with so much sandwich he couldn't talk.

"Why?" Rob asked. He wanted Sims to say he'd already solved the thing. Something about the way this case was heading gave Rob an uncomfortable feeling in the pit of his belly. The sooner it was over the better.

Sims chewed a second and took a sip of Coke. "Guess who just got hit?"

Rob shrugged. "I give up. Madonna? Oprah? Doctor Phil?"

"Billy Henderson," Sims said. "Couple of Mexicans ran him over like a scum-sucking dog right in front of his house. Figure some of Ricardo's people were behind it. They hated each other." Sims pulled the crust from a slice of bread and dropped it on his plate. "Before getting run down, Henderson and an unknown suspect had a running gun battle down the street. Bullets hit a house and several cars in the neighborhood. That should piss off the brass."

Rob grunted. *Yeah, that would piss off everyone. Gang violence spilling into quiet neighborhoods always did.*

"Anything else on the Ricardo killing?" Frank asked.

Sims stopped chewing. "Waiting on forensics."

Sarge stepped from the men's room around the corner. He'd just turned sixty-six, but looked ten years younger. The thick blond hair on the big guy gave him a Viking look. Even though he was retired, Sarge always knew what went on in the department before the chief.

"Hey, how's the case going?"

"Still working it," Rob replied.

They got their sandwiches and Cokes. Everyone ate in silence, watching the early news on the TV over the bar. Reporters were interviewing terrorized neighbors in Henderson's neighborhood.

Sims finished his food first. "Hey, Frank. I did get one piece of information you might be interested in." He dropped the napkin on the empty plate and stood. "Finally able to interview the two gangster bodyguards at Ricardo's place. Both said they were watching porn on TV when the door opened and something hit them in the face like confetti. One caught a glimpse of a red-haired woman traipsing up the stairs. Next thing he knew he woke up in the ambulance. Guess you didn't imagine her after all."

Sims laid a ten on the bar and released a huge belch. "Thanks, Sarge."

"Hard to believe they didn't bother locking the doors at Ricardo's," Rob said.

Sims fished a piece of candy from his pocket and popped it into his mouth. "According to them, the doors were locked—front and back. You guys said they were unlocked when you arrived, right?"

Frank sat his Coke down and half turned. "Yeah, I went in the back and Rob through the front—both unlocked."

Sims shrugged then walked toward the door. Over his shoulder he mumbled. "Guess the redhead unlocked 'em. Wonder who gave her the key?"

Frank picked at the sandwich—didn't seem hungry. He gazed at his plate without blinking. He'd drifted off again, his mind doing a walk-about, probably trying to sort through the puzzle. Rob didn't understand these trances. But to Frank they were like a nap. After each one he usually came back a little stronger with something profound to say. After a couple of minutes Frank spoke.

"Been pondering what you said on the way here," Frank said. "If Edna got wind of my suspicions about Dr. Hawkins being the red-haired woman, she *would* freak out. I'll know more after the interview. I suppose I could have been mistaken, but I'd have bet a month's pay."

Rob nodded. Well, nothing all that profound here, but Rob understood. Frank had a reputation of thinking too much. Cops are trained to act. Not Frank. His mind wouldn't allow it.

Movement from the bar mirror caught Rob's attention. A forty-something black woman strolled through the front door.

Oh, hell, Vivian!

Vivian Johnson showed up about once a week looking for her husband, Detective J.T. Johnson. Their marriage was a country-western song—"Good Hearted Woman in Love with a Good Timing Man." Rob had known J.T. since they worked SWAT together years ago. He was a handsome fellow. As most people age, they sag a bit in the face and put on a few pounds, especially around the middle. Not J.T. The detective had a little graying on the sides but was slimmer and better looking with each passing year. *Bastard.*

"Uh-oh," Sarge said.

Frank froze his hands on his cherry Coke and frowned while eying Vivian in the bar mirror. "Everyone remain perfectly still."

Vivian's presence wouldn't ordinarily have disturbed the earth's orbit, but today was different. Her husband sat in one of the rear booths with his new girlfriend. He had a different one every month or so—kind of hard to keep up with. Today he was so enthralled by their conversation, holding her hand across the table, he'd not noticed his wife enter.

Vivian wobbled passed Rob and Frank. Rob caught a strong whiff of liquor breath as she scanned the bar stools near them and turned her attention to the back booths. She knew J.T. played around and made a hobby of trying to catch him every chance she got. But she had a different look today—a disturbed, crazy look.

"This won't be pretty," Frank whispered.

As he got the words out, she spotted J.T. He chose that exact moment to look up. His smile disappeared and he straightened in the booth, dropping the woman's hand like it was a venomous snake. The young lady, probably wondering what had happened, turned around. When she and Vivian locked eyes, that lit the fuse.

"You son of a bitch!" Vivian screamed.

As the drama played out, everyone froze. Frank had been right—not going to be pretty.

J.T. stood and held out his hands in the stop position. His mouth was open, ready to explain.

Vivian wasn't having any of that. She'd decided to escalate a little . . . well, a lot. Staggering backward a step or two, she opened her purse and scratched around in it for something. Tears flowed down her cheeks and muted curses drifted from her lips. When she pulled out the gun, everyone went to ground. The lawyers, closest to the front and back doors, bolted outside carrying their drinks with them. The cops at the bar vaulted over it to the cover of the other side. Other patrons in nearby booths dove for the floor.

J.T.'s mouth moved in an explanation, but no words came out. His eyes were opened so wide you'd have thought the daughter of Satan had come calling.

Vivian staggered forward waving the pistol at him—crying as if she'd lost her best friend.

Everyone in the place knew about their problems, and while cops made up almost half the crowd, not one pulled their weapon. Nobody wanted to kill another cop's wife—bad luck. Especially when J.T. was the one who needed shooting. He'd been messing around on that poor girl since the day they'd said "I do."

Complete silence filled the small bar as Vivian closed the distance.

J.T., probably feeling the breeze from the wings of the angel of death hovering over him, dropped his hands and bolted into the men's room to his left. His date followed. That's when the first shot rang out. In the small narrow space it sounded like a cannon going off. Bottles on the bar rattled. Rob had just his eyes above the top of the bar. *Oh, hell.*

Sarge hunkered down with the rest behind the bar and yelled, "Don't hit the mirror!"

Frank sat behind the bar with his back against the wall. Somehow in the confusion he'd managed to retrieve his Coke and bourbon before jumping over. He sipped it and didn't appear too concerned. He gave Rob a "so what" look.

Rob bugged his eyes at Frank in a show of displeasure because of Frank's lack of worry.

Rob peeked over the top of the bar again as Vivian approached the men's room door. Her hand shook and she whimpered soft sounds. She was so unsteady on the high heels she might topple over any minute. Must have realized this, because she kicked them off as she aimed at the door.

Sarge began dialing his cell.

"Who ya calling?" Rob asked.

"Who do you think? The police!"

Rob snatched the phone from Sarge as the next shot sounded. Vivian swayed, emitting more curses with each breath. As gun smoke filled the air, she screamed something about J.T.'s two-timing ways. She aimed down the sights and squeezed off another round into the door. Rob looked at Frank. He stared back and held up three fingers.

Someone in the back screamed, "Stay down J.T. She means to kill you for sure this time."

Rob spoke into the phone as the nine-one-one operator answered. "There's a shooting in progress at Sarge's. Send units, but don't attempt to enter. Detectives are on the scene, and we'll handle it."

Rob handed Sarge back his phone and said, "If the uniforms bust in, they'll smoke her. They don't understand the situation."

Vivian appeared to have trouble cocking the pistol but somehow managed it. The fourth shot drilled into the men's room door. During a brief pause in the action, a couple of other patrons took the opportunity to slip out.

Sarge grumbled, "I'm going to have to replace that damn door."

Vivian again took aim and fired. Then she bent at the waist, resting her hands on her knees, and wails of crying filled the place.

Frank registered the event with five fingers. He stood and sat his empty glass on the bar. Rob joined him and they paced toward

Vivian. She didn't notice them at first. Eyes clouded with tears and head down, she mumbled incoherently. When Rob and Frank were about ten feet away, she raised the pistol, pointed it in their direction, and cocked it. Her lips still moved, but nothing came out.

They stopped. Rob raised his hands. "What? You're going to shoot us, now?" he asked.

Vivian cut loose with another bout of crying. Sirens wailed in the distance. The uniforms would be here any second. If they didn't get the word not to come in, Vivian would be dead soon. Uniforms hate people with guns—makes 'em nervous. Vivian getting shot wasn't acceptable.

Frank held back so as to not crowd her. Rob took one careful step at a time. He extended his hand.

"Give me the gun."

She cried and wiped her nose with her free hand but kept the pistol trained on him. "Stay, back!" she screamed. The gun was cocked and ready. Her shoulders shook with each sob and her mascara-streaked cheek gave her a wild look. Rob glanced out the front door. The first patrol car pulled up, lights still flashing. Sirens screamed in the distance. Soon the parking lot would be full of police.

Rob moved closer, motioning with his palm. "Vivian, for God's sake give me the pistol."

Frank must have realized the danger, because he marched to the door and put his badge up to the glass for the arriving officers to see—effectively blocking their view of what was going on inside, giving Rob a chance.

"Come on—the gun, right here," Rob held out his hand palm up, moving his fingers back and forth.

J.T., never a good one for timing, stuck his head out of the men's room door. When Vivian glimpsed him, she swung the pistol in his direction and pulled the trigger—*snap*.

Rob rushed her and wrestled it from her grip. Unarmed, she collapsed into a pitiful heap, sprawling on the floor, bawling. Rob gently lifted her and let her cry a few seconds on his shoulder before walking her to the door. Frank opened it for the uniforms and they escorted her to the waiting patrol car.

Patron's heads began popping up like moles in a yard. Sarge poured a shot of vodka and strolled around the bar. He downed the glass and said, "That's either the bravest, or stupidest thing I've seen since leaving the force."

"Both," Frank said, walking back to the bar.

Rob meandered to the men's room and said, "Don't shoot, J.T., I'm coming in." With that he pushed open the splintered door and stuck his head inside. "It's safe to come out." Rob walked back to the bar.

Sarge's hand still shook as he poured another drink. "You guys took a big chance."

Frank picked up his glass, crunched the remaining ice, and then slammed it back down on the bar. "Not that big. Chief's Special .38. Only holds five rounds."

Most of the customers stuck around and finished their lunch. Sarge tried to make amends by offering everyone who'd witnessed the drama a drink on the house. Most everybody knew that weird things sometimes happened at Sarge's. But that was the charm of the place. If you preferred less excitement, there were dozens of other places to eat and drink.

When Rob and Frank strolled back into CIU, Terry motioned them into his office. "Did you hear? Billy Henderson just got killed. Shot up the whole damn neighborhood. The sixth floor has called a supervisor's conference."

"We heard," Rob said. The incident with Vivian had unsettled Rob more than he realized. Watching a woman try and kill her husband sent Rob to thinking about Carmen. She'd never hurt herself. Would she? He'd tried calling and texting, but got no response. Hopefully just taking a nap. Just in case, he'd leave early today.

Terry reached for a file on his desk and flipped it open. "Read your report, Frank—the interview with Levern."

Frank didn't respond, moving his feet shoulder width apart and crossing his arms.

Terry cleared his throat. "Anyway, it sounds like you're not sure if he's involved." He lowered his gaze back to the report. "So, any ideas?"

Frank shrugged. "I'm working on a couple of angles. Interviewing a professor later about that Voodoo stuff. Might get a lead on what to look for."

"Is that the interview Edna set up at SMU?"

"Yeah." Frank cracked a grin. "I said, 'yes ma'am.' No arguments."

Rob and Frank meandered back to their cubes and Frank checked his email. After about twenty minutes, he shut down his computer and grabbed his jacket. He had the kind of smirk he showed when he was up to something.

"Cover for me. I've got to get ready for the interview this evening."

Rob pulled up his sleeve and eyed his watch. If he questioned Frank about where he was going he might find out things he'd rather not know—what the hell. "It's only 12:45. The interview isn't until after six. Where you going?" Frank never left early—usually the last guy out.

Frank adjusted the collar of his jacket and headed for the door. "Picking up supplies."

"Supplies? From where?"

"Central Market," Frank said as he strolled out.

Carmen drifted back into Rob's mind. He glanced around the squad area. Terry and Edna were both on the phone not paying attention to what was happening. No one appeared to notice Frank's departure. Without drawing attention, Rob powered off his computer, grabbed his jacket, and headed for the door. *Time to check on his wife.*

12

Antoine Levern stared out the limo window as the driver made the turn into Rochester Park in South Dallas. Some folks called it William Blair Jr. Park, but all his associates used the old name. Everyone loved this place—a favorite among gang members. They felt safe here. Plenty of wide open spaces. Most hung out there during their teen years. A place to meet friends, have a little barbecue and some beers.

Levern didn't like taking chances, especially when it involved meetings with gang leaders. Bad things had happened in the past when too many of those guys got in the same place at the same time. Just like in all gangs, old rivalries, grudges, and vendettas often reared their ugly heads. But he felt he couldn't afford to let what Frank told him hit the street without an explanation.

Of the twenty-five black gangs operating in Dallas, Levern represented twenty-three. All the variations of Crips, Bloods, and a dozen other fringe groups had aligned themselves into a loose confederation. Levern set up deals with Chicago, Pittsburgh, and Baltimore, which made everyone more money. His five percent broker fee also made him rich. But keeping the groups' trust remained a full-time job. In this business, your street creds meant everything. Let them begin to fray, and your shit got real flakey real fast. That's why this assembly had been called.

For today's meeting, everyone had agreed only two persons would accompany each leader. If you didn't set a limit, over a hundred idiots would show up with enough hardware to launch a revolution. One stupid move and a high body count could be the result. Not a lot of trust among these guys.

Levern selected his best driver and Tabor to back him up. The limo circled behind the pond levee and the line of vehicles came into view. Twenty-three cars waited, parked in a ragged row. No one had gotten out of their rides. Levern's driver parked at the end of the line and Levern touched the .45 in his waistband. Small comfort with a crowd this big, but better than nothing.

He eyed Tabor. "Stay in the car and keep your eyes open. This won't take long."

Tabor nodded and the sound of the safety clicking off the MP-5 machine gun in his lap echoed through the limo.

Levern slid out of the backseat and jerked down the lapels of his knee-length leather coat. A cool, soft breeze drifted across the meadow. The tall prairie grass on the levee swayed back and forth like ocean waves. The clouds kept the temperature down and threatened rain later this evening.

Doors opened, and the other gang leaders stepped out. Levern nodded at them and walked toward a stand of trees about forty yards down the hill. No one spoke or greeted each other. Guns bulged from under shirts, sweaters, and jackets. Most guys kept their hands in their coat pockets. No need asking what they were holding. Levern glanced over his shoulder a couple of times before he made it to the tree line. Now that everyone stood equal, the meeting could begin. The group formed two rows in a half circle as Levern spoke.

"I appreciate you all coming." He strolled around with his hands in his pockets like a teacher. "You've heard about Ricardo." He scanned their faces. "Anybody want to claim it?"

No one spoke. A couple lit cigarettes and a few gazed at the other leaders.

Levern continued. "Okay, I need to—"

"Heard Henderson got hit today. Bet Ricardo's boys were behind that," Lemarcus said. Lemarcus ran a fringe gang, the Cliff Manor Gangsters.

Several other leaders nodded and grunted in agreement.

Levern stopped walking and eyed Lemarcus. "Something's going on you need to know. I got this from a guy who's in the loop. Apparently a Voodoo doll looking thing was left beside Ricardo's body."

The group studied Levern with suspicious eyes. A few whispers ensued.

"I'm telling you this so that when you hear it later, you'll know the truth. It wasn't me."

No one uttered a word. Several shuffled and glanced to the guy to their left and right.

"But we need to find out who's behind it," Levern said. "Last thing I want is some sucker popping a cap on my ass for something I didn't do." There—that sounded convincing.

"You're the only one who cares—I don't give a shit," the leader of Cuzz Texas said.

Levern hated Jaylen. He didn't give a damn about anything. Never saw the big picture. Levern stared him down. "Well, you better give a shit." He looked at the group and pointed. "You all should. Killing's bad for business. Keep your eyes and ears open. Watch your backs. Anyone with information pass it on to me. I have a way to check it out." *Frank won't let me down.* "Any questions?"

Everyone gawked at him.

"Okay, meeting's over." Levern turned and walked toward the levee where the cars were parked as the crowd followed. Halfway back, a muffled shot rang out from the parking area. Everyone except Levern jerked out their guns and stared at each other.

Levern held out his hands. "Hey, you guys chill. Just relax."

That idea held for about two seconds before everyone ran toward the vehicles. Levern had been afraid of this. Putting this many fools together wasn't a good move. This could end badly.

As they got closer, a commotion drew them toward a black Chevy.

Tabor's booming laugh drifted from the small group of drivers already assembled around the car.

Levern gasped for air as he ran up. "What happened?"

Tabor slid his pistol back into his holster. "Sammy's driver was screwing around with his piece. Shot his foot."

Levern shook his head in disgust. He really needed to associate himself with a better class of people.

*   *   *

Frank hadn't been able to get Dr. Alma Hawkins out of his head since meeting her that morning. A beauty—most likely divorced. The long red hair, fair skin, and curve of the nose was the same profile he saw walking onto Ricardo's porch that night. But Rob nailed it. Didn't make any sense—no connection. What Paul Sims said at lunch only added to the mystery. "If it was her, who gave her the keys to the place?"

Frank swung into the basement residence parking garage and unloaded his groceries. Alma would be back in her office soon. He'd give her a call and set up the interview. By his calculations, his plan had a 90 percent chance. Something in her eyes and smile told him she might just take him up on a dinner invitation. If he'd miscalculated, he could get another complaint out of the deal. Having a subject matter expert as a dinner guest wasn't exactly SOP. But it was a chance worth taking. Something about her intrigued him. Some might call this unethical, but Frank didn't care. *Maybe I am a bad man.* His curiosity was aroused. Either she was or wasn't a suspect. Either she would or would not be interested in a more intimate relationship. Either way, he had to know.

Frank unloaded the groceries and cinched his chef's apron around his waist. The apron held a special place in Frank's heart. He always wore it when he cooked for guests. It was awarded to him by the restaurant the year they won the James Beard Award. Frank sipped a glass of red as he washed the beef and cut it into half inch cubes. Then he diced the onions and sautéd them in extra virgin olive oil in the stew pot. Just as they took on that glossy look, he added the beef cubes and cooked them until they browned. After adding the fresh garlic and paprika, he poured in enough warm water to cover the meat and let the stew braise. Frank loved the smell of braising meat. Couldn't wait to serve it to Alma.

Distant thunder rumbled over the horizon. Frank took his wine to the balcony and had a seat. Dark clouds rolled across the Dallas skyline, and the smell of rain filled the air. It was already three thirty, so he dug out Alma's card. There was no doubt in Frank's mind that what he was about to do was unprofessional. And no one had to tell him that in these politically correct times it was also bad. But Frank lived by a different credo. In every decision he made, he always asked himself the same two questions: is it illegal or morally wrong? If the answer was no—he charged ahead. This had landed him on Edna's lecture couch more than once. He always took the butt chewing with as much good humor as possible.

He called the number on the business card. She answered on the first ring.

"Dr. Hawkins?"

"Yes."

"Detective Pierce here. Hope I didn't disturb you. Wondering if we could get together on that Voodoo thing this evening? My supervisor is really pushing it."

A short hesitation. Like maybe the call surprised her.

"Sure, I'll be here till six," she said.

"Actually, since you're doing me this favor, the least I could do is buy you dinner." Frank held his breath waiting for a response.

Another hesitation—a longer one this time.

"That's very thoughtful, but you don't have to do that."

Frank continued. "It would be my pleasure. Will you please join me?"

"Do you have a place in mind?"

Yes! "Seems like a good evening for Hungarian goulash. I know where we can get the best in town."

"Sounds good. What time?"

Frank took a slow sip of wine before saying, "Seven okay?"

"I can do that. What's the name and address of the place?"

"The Tower on McKinney." Frank gave her his condo's address.

"Is that uptown?"

"Yeah."

"Okay, see you at seven," she said.

Frank disconnected. With the first part of the plan in motion, he pondered how he'd handle the second. When in doubt, open another bottle of red. Frank cut up the tomatoes and green peppers while sampling the new wine. Another clap of thunder and lightning flash as a light rain started. Yeah, a perfect night for goulash. Frank walked to the sliding glass patio door. He eased it open, and a cool breeze flowed in. He loved the sound and smell of rain splashing on the concrete.

By six-thirty Frank had showered, finished cooking, and decanted the wine. He picked a few slices of cucumber from the salad and tasted them before popping the salad into the refrigerator. Next, he put on some mellow jazz. He wasn't surprised when she called. Would have been surprised if she didn't.

Her voice had a confused sound. "Detective Pierce. I must be turned around. I'm at that address, but I don't believe it's a restaurant."

"Park in the visitor's section—I'll come down and meet you," Frank said.

He hung up before she could answer. Grabbing an umbrella, he ran for the elevator. He managed to arrive just as she stepped out of her car. The popping sound of rain drops echoed under the umbrella as he held it over her. She had a look he couldn't read.

"Nasty night, huh?"

She closed the car door and her eyes narrowed. "Yes, very nasty." Her gaze drifted up the tall building.

Frank escorted her to the awning at the front of the building where the suited doorman swung the door open for them. "Good evening, Mr. Pierce. Ma'am." He performed a slight bow.

"Good evening, Ralph," Frank said.

Stepping into the plush, dark paneled lobby the man at the desk smiled and nodded. "Mr. Pierce."

"Evening, Jerry."

Alma whispered, "You're well known here. Where's the restaurant?"

"Follow me." Frank stepped into the elevator and pressed the up button.

*   *   *

Alma wasn't 100 percent certain until Detective Pierce stepped off the elevator into a hall of doors. When he unlocked the condo door and she walked in, the smell of stewing meat confirmed her suspicions. *I've been had.*

She should be angry, but instead she was curious. What did he have up his sleeve? She'd withhold judgment until she could figure it out.

"Let me take that coat," he said.

She allowed him to slip the jacket from her shoulders as she eyed the expensive loft. No sign of a woman's presence. "Is this your home?"

"Yes."

He flashed that boyish smile she found attractive. A handsome man. Not a rugged kind of handsome, but nice-looking. His soft features indicated a sensitive person. Someone of culture—a thinker. The kind of guy she'd date if she was interested. He hung her jacket in a coat closet as she strolled around the room past a wall of windows and a long bookcase with hundreds of books. She scanned the titles. *He certainly has eclectic taste.* She stopped to admire the well-appointed kitchen—expensive appliances.

Alma said, "I never expected when you invited me to dinner it would be at your house. Your wife"—she looked around and raised a brow—"must be furious. A guest for dinner without a day's notice?"

Frank meandered into the kitchen, joining her. He lifted the lid on the pot and gave it a stir. "I'm not married."

Alma almost demanded her coat be returned so she could make a show of storming out. "You know, Detective Pierce, doing stuff like this is going to get you your very own hash tag."

He looked up with an innocent expression and grinned. "A good one?"

She shook her head.

Frank held his hands up in surrender. "This is an interview and dinner, not an interrogation. You're free to go at any time."

He'd called her bluff quicker than she'd expected. Didn't try to apologize. Didn't offer a cute explanation. *What was his game?* She set her jaw and gave him her most intimating stare. "I thought we were going to dine at the best goulash place in town?"

He flashed that sexy smile again before picking up a wine decanter. "This is the best. I make it myself. One of my specialties when I was a professional chef in New York. Not many Texans appreciate it as much as New Yorkers—thought you might." He held up the decanter. "May I pour you a glass?"

Alma did a double take. Did he just say professional chef? Whatever he was cooking smelled fantastic. "You were a chef in New York?"

He poured red wine from the wide mouth decanter into two glasses. "Yeah, go figure. From chef to cop."

She relaxed when he handed her the glass. Either the best bullshitter in Dallas or telling the truth. Besides, who would make up a story like that?

"Make yourself at home," Frank said, "I need to finish up a couple of things. We'll eat at the bar, if you don't mind. Haven't really rushed into buying much furniture."

He busied himself with the meal and she looked around some more, paying careful attention this time. The place must have cost a fortune. Where did a policeman get the kind of money to live in an upscale building like this? When he said not much furniture, he wasn't joking—only a sofa. The wall of windows overlooking the sparkling night lights of downtown Dallas held center stage. Rain dripped off the edge of the balcony roof onto the patio plants. A rich earthy smell wafted through the open patio door. She sauntered back to the white bookcase. Nothing was organized. Books on every topic lined the shelves. It took up an entire wall.

"You read a lot?" she gazed at several titles and brushed the books with her fingers as she strolled past.

"Yeah. You?" He stirred the pot again and sprinkled in a little salt.

"Ha! That's all I seem to do every day. Mostly essays from my students, but I also have to scan the latest research papers."

Frank didn't answer. He fiddled with the pot, adding a sprinkle of this and a dash of that, stirring and tasting it after he added each ingredient. *Yeah, he's a thinker.* She sipped the wine. *Um, delicious red.*

Alma worked her way back to the kitchen and eyed the appliances again. She'd once priced a Vulcan refrigerator. He had one *and* a freezer.

He uncovered the two bowls of cucumber salad and placed them on the bar, then strained the noodles. His movements were fluid, no wasted effort, as if years of muscle memory guided his hands. Alma started believing he might just be a chef.

Frank glanced in her direction. "Hope you like your goulash served over noodles. Could have used potatoes, but it felt like a noodle night." He nodded to the rain dripping on the balcony.

Alma sat on a barstool. Professional chef, big time reader, great wine selector. *Is he straight?*

He wiped his hands on a kitchen towel, stepped back and smiled. "I think that's everything." Frank joined her at the bar. She tasted the goulash.

"This is delicious." Yeah, a professional chef. But this left her more confused.

He wiped his lips before answering. "Glad you like it. Told you— the best in Dallas."

* * *

Frank wasn't much of a socializer. Never could think of much to say—except to gorgeous women. But he had to be careful here—real careful. Why had he invited her? What role did she play? Suspect? Subject matter expert? Future lover? Until he sorted it out he'd best keep a professional distance. They dined, he charmed her, and the small talk stayed light.

Alma rested an elbow on the bar and sipped the wine. "May I ask a personal question?"

"Go ahead," he said. She had a curious expression. Something between intrigue and doubt.

"Do all detectives live in half-million-dollar lofts uptown?" Her green eyes showed a feline quality. The corners of her mouth cracked a smile.

He sat his glass down. "Only the ones whose grandparents left them a large trust." Frank gazed in all directions and held his hands up. "I blew the whole thing on a nice home."

She didn't exactly smile. Her expression still confused him. He couldn't tell if she believed him or not. That expression could be read in a dozen different ways.

Alma held out her glass and he refilled it. She studied him a moment as one might study a complex math problem. "You're not like other cops, are you?"

A blush raced to Frank's cheeks. "No, I guess I'm not."

After dinner they sat on the sofa and shared another glass of red. Frank had been with dozens of women. Each had a special appeal. Something about their expressions, or words they chose, or sense of humor let Frank know when they were interested in a closer relationship. He didn't get any of these tells from Alma.

She kept a cool professionalism during dinner, but sitting with him on the sofa, she appeared more relaxed. He'd tried convincing himself that she had no involvement in the case, but the vision of her—or someone who looked like her—entering Ricardo's house stayed in the back of his mind. It was time to get down to business. He'd soon know if she was involved.

"I suppose you've heard about the gang leader's death?" Frank asked.

She tilted her head to the side. "Yes, read about it—terrible. Do you investigate that sort of thing?"

"Not ordinarily. We have another unit that handles that. But my unit is looking into it because this dead guy had a Voodoo-like doll lying beside him. Hoping you might give us some insight into profiling who could be responsible."

That sounded innocent enough. Always start with a leading open-ended question. Let the person fill in the details, then ask it another way and check for inaccuracies.

Alma raked the red hair over her shoulder. "A photo of the thing would be helpful."

"Thought you might say that."

He'd been waiting for this all evening. Frank pulled the picture from his pocket and handed it to her. If she was involved, something would register in her expression. The twitch of an eye, nose wrinkling, something. . . .

She casually studied it a moment before passing it back. Frank got nothing—no reaction at all. *Weird.*

She took a short sip of wine and relaxed back in the soft cushion. "There are many types of Voodoo. Almost every continent has some version of the backwoods practice. They may call it other things, but the basic principle is the same. The three main ones we hear about in the U.S. are West African, Haitian, and Louisianan. While they have a lot in common, they all have peculiarities that separate them."

Alma reached for the photo again and pointed. "For instance, I'd say the stitching and overall construction of this doll is more characteristic of Louisiana." She stared at the photo a moment longer and shook her head. "But it's unusual, being found near a dead person and in Dallas."

She took another sip of wine and handed the photo back to Frank. Probably her professor's stare—waiting for the question that begged an answer.

Okay, he'd bite. "Why is it unusual?"

She shrugged. "The original purpose of Voodoo dolls is to focus spiritual energy in a positive way to help a person. Not harm them."

Frank never heard that before. Everyone knew Voodoo dolls were meant to harm someone—not help them. "I didn't know that."

Alma's glistening white teeth showed through the parted full lips. "It's true. For people who believe in that sort of thing, Voodoo has a strong spiritual pull. The doll is just a tool for focusing meditation, prayers, and magic spells. There are instances where it's used for harm, but most of that is Hollywood stuff—not real. Voodoo's a religion."

This wasn't working the way Frank had hoped. He eyed the photo. "So that doesn't help me narrow down who we're looking for." Frank allowed disappointment to lace his words. "From your description it sounds like it's a firm 'maybe' or 'maybe not.'"

She laughed.

He liked her laugh.

"Sorry, I couldn't be of more help. Afraid you wasted a great dinner on me."

"Oh, I wouldn't say wasted."

"I'd like to ask you a question," she said.

Frank knew that look—mischievous. When a woman had that look and asked a question, better be ready for anything.

"Okay."

She leaned closer. A whiff of floral perfume drifted his way. "What made you so sure I'd accept your dinner invitation?"

Frank hesitated. Was this a come-on? Never met a woman so hard to read. Better play it safe. "Well . . . you looked hungry."

She sat upright and smirked. "Now that could be taken in a number of ways, Detective Pierce."

"No one calls me Detective Pierce. I'm Frank."

She grinned. "And I'm Alma." She glanced down and said, "Oh, you're bleeding."

Frank followed her gaze. He'd laid his arm on his Dockers and a small red spot had appeared. "Crap."

"Here, let me have a look," she said.

"It's just a scratch from work."

She pealed the Band-Aid off. "You might need a stitch. Have any peroxide?"

"Yeah."

"Get it and another Band-Aid and I'll fix you up."

"That's all right. I—"

"Shush. Do what I said. Doctor's orders."

He found the peroxide and Band-Aid box in the medicine cabinet. She waited at the kitchen sink.

"Hold your arm here."

He held his arm over the drain and she poured a little peroxide over it, dabbing around the edges with a clean paper towel. She unscrewed the cap from a small brown bottle and held it over his wrist.

"What's that?" Frank asked.

"I carry a little in my purse all the time. Best thing in the world." She poured a few drops of the syrupy, yellowish liquid over the wound and applied the new Band-Aid. "There you go. Don't remove it until tomorrow."

He examined her work. "You *are* a doctor."

"Ph. D., not M.D.," she reminded him. Alma looked at her watch. "It's late. I have an early class tomorrow."

"I'll walk you down." Frank helped her with her coat and they headed to the elevator. The rain had stopped and a heavy mist enveloped the parking area. Reminded Frank of the final scene in *Casablanca*. "*Here's looking at you, kid.*"

She opened her car door and turned around to face him. "Thank you for dinner. Hope it wasn't a disappointment. Sorry I wasn't much help."

Frank wanted to kiss her, but he wasn't getting any of the signs or signals he figured he should. She did have a glint in her eyes that probably meant something, but darn if he could decode it. "No disappointment on my part," he said, "I had a great time. Perhaps we could do it again."

She cocked her head and showed a half grin. "I'd like that."

* * *

Driving through the foggy night, Frank stayed on Alma's mind all the way home. Something about him excited a passion, an old hunger she hadn't felt in years. She didn't understand it and couldn't explain it, but it was there.

She parked in her back driveway and gazed across the street at the lake. The thick swirling fog gave it a magical, surreal look. The high clouds broke just enough for the moon to cast an eerie yellow glow across the water. Turning up her collar, Alma paced to the back door. Something moved in the darkness and she jumped. She snapped her head around and heard it again.

"Okay, you guys. Come on out."

Slowly they eased into the dim glow of the back porch light— little apparitions who always greeted her when returning home. Two raccoons, a squirrel, and a rabbit. She bent down and scratched each behind the ears. Alma knew what they wanted.

"Sorry I'm so late getting home, guys." She unlocked the back door and reached inside on the kitchen counter, grabbing a handful of raw peanuts from the bowl. She tossed them on the ground and the animals scurried to get their share.

"Now, no fighting. There's plenty for everyone." She flipped on the kitchen light as she closed and locked the door. Alma peeked through the curtains. Beemer and Goff, the two raccoons, were getting the lion's share, as usual.

She dropped her keys on the counter and stared at the silent kitchen. Her home had a loneliness, an emptiness since Clare died. Alma hadn't dated anyone in almost a year. Was this her attraction to Frank? Loneliness? She strolled to her bedroom, dropping her coat on the chair. *I could start over.* She didn't need another man in her life—not now—perhaps not ever, but another child . . .

Alma undressed and readied herself for bed. Frank could be the one, but he might not call. Probably had lots of other lovers. But before she made a final decision, she wanted to know him better. The next move should be hers. She'd put her plan in motion tomorrow.

She opened her purse and removed the bloody Band-Aid from Frank's wrist. She'd stashed it in a tissue after sending him for the peroxide. Unfolding it on top of her dresser, she left it to dry.

13

Joseph Gambizi always loved a good cigar after dinner. He lounged back in the recliner and drew in the smoke. A full-bodied maduro was probably good for digestion. His doctors disagreed, but what did they know? He'd already outlived a dozen of them. Probably outlive the current ones.

The shadow of one of his guards passed the large window, bundled up against the Adirondack's night chill. The crackling of the fireplace and smell of birch logs burning took the Don back to happier times—times when there was more hope, when his future was ahead of him.

"I thought your doctor told you to give those up?" Tony Palazzo said.

Palazzo didn't smoke, so he didn't understand what a good Dominican meant. Gambizi rolled off some ash into the tray. "I'm self-medicating," he said, and took another long draw. "Ever get any word from Dallas?"

"Yeah, I got word."

Gambizi waited for the bad news by taking another pull and slowly releasing the smoke.

"Got a call earlier. Rumor is a local punk, a darkie, ordered the hit on Ricardo."

Gambizi nodded. "Why?"

"Looks like he wanted a bigger slice of the pie . . . Ricardo's slice."

"Does this darkie have a name?"

"Antoine Levern."

Gambizi considered the answer. "Never heard of him. Must be small time." This might just be the excuse he'd been waiting for. Good time to make the pitch to his underboss. He leaned forward. "Tony, do you trust me?"

Palazzo frowned and shrugged. "What kind of question is that? Of course I trust you, Godfather."

Gambizi eased back into the chair. "I know my time's short. I can't continue leading this family forever. I've groomed you to take over, but you haven't proven yourself to the other families yet. They don't respect you." Gambizi eyed the younger man. "There's a fine line between respect and fear. I'd always prefer respect, but if I can't get that, I'll settle for fear. If they ever stop fearing you—you're done."

Palazzo lowered his head without answering.

"You're my right-hand guy, Tony. My choice to succeed me, but you have to show some strength—some back bone. I've not allowed you to do that in the past. That's on me, but we need to fix that right now. This is the perfect opportunity for you to gain respect. To show strength."

"I'm not sure I understand," Palazzo said.

"I want you to let the word leak out that you're in charge of settling the Ricardo score. I want the darkie's organization taken down— everyone—scorched earth. When this gets out, the other families won't screw with you when I'm gone. You'll have their respect."

Gambizi understood this went against Palazzo's nature. Tony liked to keep things quiet, settle scores behind the scenes.

Palazzo grimaced. "You sure that's the kind of message we want to send? Taking down a whole organization seems a bit much. Besides, that Levern guy is a supplier for Chicago. Take his organization down and we mess with their business. Could be trouble."

Gambizi pointed the cigar at him. "Mark my words: if we don't do it, if we don't send a hard message, how long do you think you're going to last before one of the other families makes a move on you after I'm gone? Huh? I'll tell you. You'll go to my funeral one day and your own in less than a week. Is that what you want?" Gambizi pulled in more smoke, letting Palazzo think about that awhile.

Palazzo lowered his eyes. "I defer to you. I'll get the boys working on it.

"I don't want our people involved."

"Why?"

"You instill fear because of the unknown," Gambizi said. "If we use our people, everyone knows how we operate, so they take precautions. They lay on more protection. No, we need someone who they can't protect against."

"You have someone in mind?"

Gambizi rolled the tip of the cigar in the ash tray again and looked up. "Jesse."

"Jesse doesn't work cheap."

"I don't want cheap. I want the best. Consider it an investment for the future."

14

Antoine Levern had always operated on the theory that being too obvious and drawing unwanted attention wasn't smart. Keeping a low profile was good insurance against fed involvement. Oh, he knew they'd like to nail his hide to their wall, but there were just too many other fish that were easier to catch. Levern kept his core organization small. Only the most trusted were allowed full access.

Several of his old New Orleans cronies had found their way to Dallas and ran crews in North Texas. He trusted them up to a point, but most were small-minded crooks who would drop a dime on him in a minute if the feds squeezed hard enough.

Levern pushed away from the table and wiped his mouth on his sleeve. He'd not eaten half his breakfast. Meetings like the one he was going to left him with little appetite.

Tabor strolled up rolling a toothpick between his lips. "Car's ready."

Levern didn't have to do much he didn't want to. But occasionally issues popped up and he'd have to smooth them over. Beating issues back into submission took up more time each year. This morning his problem was Phil, a representative of the Chicago Outfit, who received the majority of Levern's cargo thefts.

A good truck driver could cover the eight hundred miles from Dallas to Chicago in fourteen hours. Pharmaceuticals were what the Outfit wanted, and Levern had a connection that guaranteed a steady supply. Within twenty-four hours of stealing the truck, he could have the money in his account and forget about it. The sweetest and safest enterprise he ran.

Levern slid the .45 off the table and fitted it into his waistband. He pulled the sweater down and Tabor helped him with his black leather jacket.

"Let's go," Levern said.

Phil liked to stay at the Omni in downtown Dallas. Always got a suite with a view. Fifteen minutes later, Levern sat with him as Phil poured coffee for them.

"Antoine, you're looking well."

Phil glanced at the new tattoo of the bull's eye on the back of Levern's right hand.

"Very nice. Something new?"

Phil always started with a compliment before letting you have it. He'd been a wise guy in the old days—still one of DiFrinzo's right-hand men—a capo. They called him Phil "The Actor" because of his good looks. Tall, urbane, with distinguished gray hair combed straight back. He always smelled like he just left the barber's chair—some hundred dollar a bottle cologne. Yeah, he probably could have been an actor.

Phil wasn't wearing a jacket. The starched pin-striped shirt and red silk tie signaled his status. He played with his gold cuff links and offered his best smile. All straight, white teeth.

"Everyone's very pleased with the last shipments," Phil said. "Your product line is impressive."

Levern grinned. Damn right it was impressive. He was one of the best money makers Chicago had. But Levern knew where this compliment shit was going. The guy always dug a little deeper with each visit—find out a little more about his contacts. He'd love to cut Levern out. No middle man meant a higher profit margin. Time to screw with his mind a little.

"Yeah, well things are looking a little shaky with my main supplier," Levern said. "Don't know if I can continue to fill the orders if he drops out. Might have to try and find someone to take up the slack."

A frown crossed Phil's chicken lips. "Shaky?"

"Yeah, shaky."

"That's unfortunate. We were looking to increase our orders."

"What do you need?"

"More hydrocodone, oxycodone, and meperidine. Any of the opioids. We also could use additional antibiotics. Demand is sky-rocketing." Phil lit a cigarette with a gold lighter and tossed it back on the table.

Levern nodded and showed what he hoped might be a very circumspective look. "I'm working on a couple of deals. Let you know if anything pans out." Keeping Phil and Chicago a little off balance wasn't a bad thing. Just a little more insurance against being replaced or whacked.

Phil shifted and eyed him with a fatherly expression. "There is another matter."

Levern never liked it when Phil started a sentence with those words. Nothing good ever came after that.

"Some are a little worried about your discretion."

"Say what?"

"They feel that whacking Ricardo was unnecessary and danger-ous. Raises your profile too much."

Levern threw up both hands and his voice rose. "Whoa! Hold on right there. I didn't have shit to do with that. Ricardo got hit, but it wasn't me."

Phil gave him that condescending look he hated.

"And just your good fortune that you'll be the recipient of most of his business?"

"I didn't do the guy! Yeah, I'll get a share of his business, but so will others!"

Phil ran his hand over the tablecloth smoothing out a crease. "The Voodoo doll thing wasn't particularly wise either. Whacking a guy for business is one thing. Leaving a calling card like that—stupid."

Levern wanted to bitch slap him. He leaped to his feet. "I didn't do it! Are you freaking deaf?"

He realized his mistake immediately. The muscle guarding the door let his hand drift a little closer to his piece. Phil stayed cool, but his expression had darkened. The cold gray eyes took on an appearance Levern hadn't seen before—a dead glare. Phil turned to the second muscle in the corner and motioned for him. Phil nodded toward Levern. "The hand."

The muscle screwed a pistol into Levern's left ear and dropped his meaty grip on Levern's wrist, locking his hand in place on the table.

Levern struggled a couple of seconds before Phil whispered, "Don't move, Antoine."

In slow motion, Phil flicked the ash off his cigarette and lowered the hot tip onto the red dot in the middle of Levern's new tattoo. A burning flesh stench and sizzling sound followed. It felt like someone drilling a hole into the back of his hand. Levern gritted his teeth and shook with pain, but didn't let out a cry. The pistol stayed pressed against his ear.

Phil removed the cigarette and dropped the smoldering butt into the ashtray. "Well done, Antoine. Shall we start again?"

Levern had forgotten the cardinal rule when dealing with Phil. Always respect the man. Never raise your voice and never question what he said or threaten him.

"Now, sit back and relax," Phil said. He spoke just above a whisper and motioned to the muscle to release Levern.

Levern gawked at his hand. A throbbing black smudge was all that remained of his bull's eye. He flexed his fingers a couple of times and slid the injured hand under the table into his lap.

Phil picked off a piece of lent from his trouser leg and locked eyes with Levern. "If that's the answer you want me to take back to Chicago, of course I will. But if it's true, it sounds to me like you have someone who's trying to implicate you in something that could prove dangerous in the long run."

Phil opened the thick envelope lying on the table. He thumbed through the stack of hundreds and passed it to Levern.

"A little token of our appreciation. Use some of that to buy information on who's behind the Ricardo killing. If you're being set up, that could affect us all. You understand—bad for business. Especially if you get killed. Huh?"

Levern stood, but didn't answer. Tabor waited outside, leaning against the hall wall. Levern slipped his burned hand into his coat pocket as he marched past. "Let's go."

What Phil said echoed in Levern's ears. The truth hung out there like a dead guy at a dinner table. If this had been a setup, they'd done it right. He might just make some inquiries. As with all things criminal—someone, somewhere, knew something.

* * *

"Jesus H. Christ." Rob stumbled behind Frank into the rubble of the trailer house. Why hadn't it caught fire? Blood stains marred the carpet in a Picasso splatter near the scorch mark of the explosion. A familiar odor wafted past Rob's nostrils—burned phosphates. That stench always brought back bad memories of dark days in Iraq. Days when someone got hurt, or worse.

Paul Sims, who had called them to the scene, stood outside talking to Kelly from the forensics team.

"What do you make of it?" Frank asked. He squatted and poked something on the floor with a coat hanger.

"Some kind of explosive device. Maybe homemade. Pipe bomb, I'd guess," Rob answered.

Frank stood and dusted his hands. They made their way out the front door and strolled beside Sims, who'd just finished a phone call. Kelly scribbled something in his notebook. Streaks of smut and dirt covered his white Tyvek suit, and his dust mask sat perched on his forehead. He'd drawn a large, red set of lips on the front.

"How many killed?" Frank asked.

Sims popped another M&M into his mouth. "Only Arne. He'd just got home, according to witnesses."

Arne Weaver headed up the local chapter of the Aryan Brotherhood.

"Anybody see anything?" Rob asked.

Sims thumbed through his notes. "Nope. A little girl said the sound of a car accelerating down the street preceded the explosion. She was riding her bike past the trailer when it exploded. Got showered with flying glass. Few cuts and bruises. Nothing serious."

"Why was a kid riding a bike? Shouldn't she be in school?" Rob asked.

Sims grunted. "Home schooled. Mother said the kid was out playing while she fixed lunch."

Frank stuck his hands in his pockets and craned his neck, taking in the denizens of the trailer park as they gawked at them. Rob had worked with Frank so long he could read his partner's thoughts as he stared back at the group. *A collection of white trash, working poor, and highly uneducated.* Rob never told Frank that most of his relatives lived in places this bad or worst. Growing up, Rob had been lucky. His parents at least had a small house.

Sims dropped his pen in his jacket. "Oh, I almost forgot. About the Salazar case. They finally finished forensics on the bullets they picked out of Ricardo's bedroom wall. All fired by the .45 found beside him." Sims popped another M&M. "Don't know what in the hell he thought he was shooting at, but he didn't hit anything but a wall."

Rob strolled around the trailer with his hands in his pockets. He bent down and looked underneath the trailer a couple of times, but saw nothing interesting. When he came back, Frank had his trademark *I'm bored* expression glued on tight. He looked at Rob. "Ready to go?"

On the way downtown, Rob thought out loud. "I don't get it. Three gang leaders in as many days. Is this a war?"

Frank brooded in the passenger seat. He hadn't said a word since leaving the trailer. He glanced at Rob. "Yup, Edna was right, but what kind of war?"

"Huh?"

"A gang war, or a war on gangs?"

"I don't follow."

"It all depends on who's killing who. This kind of random violence doesn't make any sense. There's no common dominator among these losers, and honestly, the world's better off without them. We don't have a real pattern yet."

"So you think someone's killing off gangsters for fun?" Rob asked.

"Not enough information to say that. Probably just killing off each other. But if some vigilante is doing it, he's playing in a rough league."

"So you were telling me about the interview with Dr. Hawkins before Sims called," Rob said. "How did it go?"

Frank slouched a little lower in the seat and yawned. "We talked over dinner. I don't believe she's involved."

Rob perked up. "Dinner, huh. Where did you go?"

"I cooked."

Rob shot him a look. "She spent the night?"

Frank showed the face he reserved for dullards. "Of course not." He extended to the full slouch riding position, resting his knees on the dash. "Only dinner."

Had Frank just gone weird again? Rob couldn't tell. Frank taking an interest in some woman wasn't unusual. Taking an interest in a woman who was a professor was. Was it a business or pleasure thing with Frank? "Talk about the Voodoo doll?"

"Yeah, she said it was unusual for a Voodoo doll to be left at the scene of a death. Said they were used for helping people, not hurting them."

Rob changed the subject. "Want to have some lunch?"

Frank shrugged. "Okay, but fried chicken today."

Frank's phone rang.

"This is Pierce." He looked over at Rob, "Yeah, we were just discussing it. Okay, we'll meet you there." He disconnected.

"Who was that?"

"Ford."

"What's up?"

"Has some info he doesn't want to share on the phone. We're meeting him at the Northwest Highway Humperdinks for lunch."

Rob laughed. "Humperdinks—big surprise."

* * *

As they pulled into the parking lot, Ford stood near the entrance and waved. Frank liked him. They'd worked a case together a few years ago. David Ford was an FBI agent assigned to the Dallas Division—organized crime squad. Athletic build, black hair combed straight back, and dark blue eyes. Every straight woman in Dallas wanted a piece of him.

They greeted each other and ambled inside. If it wasn't for Ford, this Humperdink's location would have closed years ago. It was close to the FBI office and had better than average chow. Ford ate there almost every day. Always ordered the same thing—a big green salad with grilled chicken strips on top. After they were seated and placed their drink orders, Ford grabbed a menu off the table. This was perhaps the most ridiculous part about dining with him. A ritual he insisted on. Must provide him with a small amount of comfort in an ever-changing world. If Frank had to eat the same thing everyday he'd need to be fitted for a straightjacket.

"What have you guys been up to?" Ford asked as he scanned the menu he'd memorized three years earlier.

"Trying to keep a lid on this gang war," Rob replied. "Another one got hit today."

Ford tossed the menu back on the table and laid his forearms on it. "Yeah, I heard. Got something that might interest you." He glanced around, dropped his voice, and leaned forward. "A possible contract on one of your gangsters."

"Who?" Frank asked. For heaven's sake, don't let it be Levern.

"Antoine Levern."

"Where did this come from?" Rob whispered.

The waiter brought the drinks and smiled. "Be right back and get your orders," he said.

Ford allowed him to get halfway across the room before saying, "Federal wiretap. Can't tell you who the target is, but we found out about it from a call Tony Palazzo made last night."

"Who's Palazzo?" Frank asked.

"Underboss to the Gambizi crime family. Heir apparent when old man Joe Gambizi kicks the bucket."

"So it's definitely a hit?" Rob asked.

"Sounds like it," Ford said. "They didn't go into a lot of detail on a line they figured might be tapped. Palazzo only said they had a problem in Dallas. Sending someone down to handle it."

No one needed to tell Frank this was the game changer they'd all dreaded. Sending down an enforcer was a power play. New York was serious and willing to put all their chips on the table with a hit man to back it up. "Did they say who?" Frank asked.

"Jesse."

"Who's that?" Rob said.

"Didn't give a last name, just Jesse," Ford answered. "We checked the family roster. No one by that name is an enforcer for them." Ford shrugged. "For that matter, nobody by that name in the whole organization."

"What do you figure? An outside contract?" Rob asked.

"Either that or a new player."

"I know you've probably already checked," Frank said, "but are there any contract killers named Jesse in the bureau's system?"

Ford grinned. "Yeah, two. One's doing thirty to life in Joliet for a double homicide, and the other's in a Mississippi hospice, dying of prostate cancer."

"Plan on warning Levern?" Rob asked.

Ford shook his head. "Nope. If they play in that street, they should expect to get hit sooner or later. Won't compromise a good tap for a crook."

The rules were clear, but that didn't stop Frank from feeling sorry for Levern. "Any time frame?" Frank asked.

Ford raised his eyebrows. "The hit's on. Could be any time. Only Jesse knows when."

"Hey, Frank, you're losing your Band-Aid," Rob said.

Crap, not that again. It sagged, about to fall off. Frank saved it the trouble and peeled it back. He stared at his wrist so long Rob asked, "What's wrong?"

Frank didn't answer immediately. A small quiver in his stomach—this wasn't possible. His mind whirled for an answer. The cut had closed up—no more bleeding and oozing. Still a little swelling and redness, but at least 50 percent better than yesterday.

"So you got a stitch?" Rob asked.

"No."

Ford bent forward, trying to see.

Rob pointed at Frank's wrist. "Got a nasty gash the other night—needed a stitch. Looks better. I can't even see where they stitched it."

Frank continued staring at his wrist and mumbled, "Didn't get a stitch."

The waiter took their orders and Ford and Rob shot the bull until the food arrived, but Frank didn't join in. His mind drifted back to last night. The conversation over his kitchen sink with Alma. *"Carry a little in my purse all the time. Best thing in the world."*

* * *

Levern dipped his garlic bread in the shrimp étouffée and scooped a mouthful of soup. He seldom ate downstairs at the restaurant. Took most of his meals in his third floor digs, away from the crowd. Today he hadn't felt like eating alone. Sometimes he enjoyed watching others dine, listening to the voices blend together into one contentious conversation, getting louder and louder until it became a subtle roar. Place was getting more popular. Already a line at the door for lunch. The buzz about his star chef had grown since the restaurant won the Best Cajun Cooking award from *D Magazine* last year. Maurice Sontau had also left New Orleans after Katrina. When

Levern opened the place, he cut Maurice in on the action and never regretted his decision. A head chef could make or break a joint. Besides it was a great cover for what went on upstairs. Easier to launder drug money when you had a legitimate business on the side.

Tabor leaned closer and whispered, "Hey, boss. Someone's making eyes at you."

"Who's that?"

Tabor motioned with his head. "Blonde by the window, eating alone."

Levern scanned the room and found her in the corner. Short blonde hair, nice face, and no wedding band. Sort of an all-American girl look.

"Want me to ask her to join you?" Tabor asked.

Levern took the last bite, dabbed his lips, and dropped the napkin on the table. "I have a better idea."

The blonde kept her eyes on him as he limped toward her with Tabor. She grinned and lowered her head demurely as he approached. She'd almost finished the oyster po'boy and fries.

Levern put on his best smile. "Enjoying your lunch?" Not a very original pickup line, but he'd had success with it in the past.

She giggled, blush rushing up her neck. "Sure am."

"It's on the house, baby."

Her eyes pinched. "Seriously, you're buying my meal? Why?"

"Like your looks, besides, I own the joint. Can give away all the meals I want."

She raked a loose strand of hair behind her ear and bit her lip. "No kidding, you really own the place?"

"Sure do." Levern stood a little taller. "Love to show you around sometime." He leaned on the table and scribbled a date and his initials on one of his business cards. He called them his pickup cards. Best investment he ever made. He handed it to her.

When she took it, her soft finger brushed his. He got a rise.

"How about right now?" Levern asked. "It's just upstairs."

She frowned and the sweet lips formed a pout. "Oh, I wish I could, but"—she checked her watch—"I have to get back to work."

"Well, you got a free lunch. Just show that to the waiter. You can have that tour anytime—just call." He pointed over his shoulder. "If I'm not available ask for Tabor," Levern showed his full teeth smile. "He'll get the message to me."

She grinned and lifted the card, reading the front. "Thank you . . . Mr. Levern."

He held out his hand and she shook it. "You can call me Antoine," he said, "and what's your name, my dear?"

She tilted her head and winked. "I'm Jesse."

15

Jesse left the restaurant and drove to back to the Extended Stay America Hotel on Greenville Avenue. She'd just arrived this morning and hadn't bothered to unpack. When a job required several days or longer, she always chose a place like this—more privacy, few kids, and a staff who treated you more like a long-term tenant than a guest. Just like her car, the Extended Stay America was plain. High class hotels and expensive cars drew attention. Harder to blend in. More easily remembered later if a cop asked around.

Jesse parked the ten-year-old white Toyota and unlocked the trunk. Removing the long cardboard tube, she scanned the parking lot. Tucking the tube under her arm, she unlocked her door and ducked inside.

Jesse lived by a few basic rules. Never fly—she drove everywhere. The tools of her trade didn't mix well with TSA screenings. Never use a credit card—traveler's checks or cash only. She kept a special bag for her dozen TracFones—burners she used once and then destroyed. Never use your own computer—the complimentary desktop at the business center in the hotel was good enough. In the digital age it was impossible to travel and remain completely invisible, but she didn't make it easy to track her movements. For the most part, unless someone got lucky, she was invisible.

Jesse had wanted to meet Antoine Levern. Gauge him—see what he was like. Pretty much as she'd figured. Cocky, self-confident, and arrogant. All those things made him predictable. All those things made him vulnerable.

She opened the cardboard tube on one end and slid the M-24 sniper rifle onto the bed. She shucked her blouse, bra, and pants, slipped on an oversized tee shirt and sat on a chair to thumb through the briefing material she'd received on Levern and his outfit. Levern wasn't a gang leader per se. More of an agent to the gangs, representing the Chicago mob.

She poured herself a little scotch over ice and considered Tony Palazzo's words yesterday. "Gambizi wanted to make a statement—send a message." She'd accepted contracts from the families before. They were business men, paid well, and in cash. This would be the biggest of her career. *My career?* She took a long swallow and let that sink in for a moment.

The choices we make in life define us.

Her dad said that to her once. But more often than not circumstances do as well. If her dad were still alive she'd be in another place—not doing this. He'd always been so sure of her. That she'd make something of herself. That she'd do great things in life. As a kid, all she'd ever wanted was to please him. What would he think of her choices? How ashamed would he be to call her his daughter? She still recalled the excitement of their first hunt.

Jesse had just turned six the week before. She stared out the pickup truck window at the featureless landscape around Laramie, Wyoming. The fresh coffee aroma filled the cab. Her dad drank a lot of coffee. He was a good dad. His warm, reassuring touch could calm her from a bad dream and encourage her when she had doubts.

"How's the collection going?" he asked.

Jesse had received a stamp collector starter kit as a birthday present. "Okay, I guess."

"I bet you'll find something rare in that stack of stamps that came with the kit. Maybe an Inverted Airmail."

If she did, they'd all be rich. Those drew over $40,000, according to the booklet.

"So you sure you're up for this?" he asked.

He had one hand on the wheel and held a McDonald's cup with the other. Steam rose from the top, and he blew on it before taking another sip. His smile told her he was kidding about being up for today. He kidded a lot. Not like her humorless mother who never smiled—never kidded.

"Uh-huh," she replied. She stroked the head of Buddy, the family beagle on the seat between them. He let out a dog sigh and nuzzled a little closer. The heater was busted in the old truck again, and the morning chill made Jesse shiver. In a quiet voice she said, "What's it like?"

Her dad shifted his gaze from the road to her. "What?"

"To shoot something?" If anyone would know it was him. He'd hunted all his life and downed elk, deer, and anything else to put meat on the table.

He didn't answer at first. His lips pulled tight and he stared straight ahead. Finally he said, "It's kinda like a game."

She studied his face, but it gave nothing away. "Game?"

"Yeah, the animals know humans are dangerous. And we know that they know. So we try for some advantage. We have to outsmart them—a game."

She wasn't satisfied with the answer. She stared out the window as a herd of cattle grazed in the cool September morning. "Why didn't Mama come?"

Her dad frowned and shook his head before taking another sip. He didn't make eye contact. "She's not a hunter, like us." He reached over and goosed her until she giggled. Buddy hardly moved, only releasing another lazy sigh.

There were things Jesse didn't understand. Things about her mom and dad that were never discussed. Like why they hadn't slept in the same room for the last year, why her mom never smiled or, for that matter, hardly even spoke to her dad. Why her mother sat in her bedroom with no lights on when Jesse and her dad watched TV or played cards. Her mother rocked for hours in that old chair, humming some song from long ago. She wasn't a happy person. She loved Jesse, in her own way, but her daddy never held back, as if all the love and attention he couldn't give Mama, he showered on her.

She had looked forward to this day for months, but her nervousness made her scared. Scared she'd mess up. She eyed her dad. He'd wanted a son so bad that that when she came along he named her Jesse, spelling it the same way a boy's name was spelled. That's what Mama told her. He'd turned his girl into a first-rate tomboy.

If daddy wasn't working, he spent every moment with her. Taught her how to fish, skin animals, and stalk prey. After much pleading, her mother finally relented and allowed him to teach her to shoot for her fifth birthday. The day she held a rifle for the first time, something happened she couldn't explain. Something about the feel of the cool metal and slick wood stock sent chills through her. It wasn't much of a rifle. A one-shot .22 with iron sights. But that feeling stayed with her each time she handled it. Did everyone feel that way?

Most days, after her dad picked Jesse up from kindergarten, they'd set up targets and shoot. At first, the expectation of a sudden explosion so near her face made Jesse flinch before pulling the trigger. Her dad helped her to relax and explained that if she knew when the shot would come, she'd always flinch—and miss. She must become the master of the surprise shot. A slow, even squeeze of the trigger that caused the rifle to shoot by itself without jerking the trigger.

By the end of the school year she'd learned all the basics. That summer she'd improved so much that her dad entered her in the kids' target shoot at the county fair. When they placed the trophy in her hand, it was the proudest day of her life, and her dad's. No one so young had ever claimed that prize. Her picture appeared in the paper days later. She kept a copy tacked up on her bedroom wall. Her achievement. Something she did on her own.

Jesse rummaged through her suitcase and took out the folder. She opened it and smiled. This relaxed her, made her feel like being back home. She fitted the jeweler's glass in her right eye socket, slipped on the sheer cotton gloves, and picked up the tweezers. She ran her fingers across the stamps. Yeah, she'd screwed up, but the truth always won out. She downed the last of the drink before getting to work on her collection.

16

Frank and Rob meandered back into CIU just as Terry stepped from Edna's office.

"Guess what?" Frank said.

Terry stopped in midstride. "I give up."

Frank didn't have a delicate way to say this so he just blurted it out. "There's a contract on Levern out of New York."

Terry blanched and spun around, directing him and Rob into Edna's office.

"Well, shit!" Edna exclaimed after hearing about their lunch with Ford. "Nothing on this Jesse guy?"

"Nope," Rob said.

She glanced at Terry. "Do we have a responsibility to warn Levern?"

Terry shook his head. "Regular folks would get a warning, but if we divulge information that screws up a federal wire for a crook, we'll never hear from Ford again."

Edna tapped her pen on the desk a few seconds, her gaze thoughtful. "The chief's office is going crazy about these killings, doesn't matter that it's drug dealers. A gang war is still a gang war. That child getting hurt when the trailer exploded only makes a bad situation worse. If Levern gets whacked, that'll just torque things up another notch."

Frank and Rob went back in their cubicles. Frank didn't like stuff he couldn't explain. He stared at his wrist again and rubbed it. If you dug deep enough there was always a reasonable explanation for anything. He took the magnifying glass and scanned it. The soreness had almost disappeared. What did Alma put on it?

"What'cha doing?" Rob craned his neck watching him.

"Nothing."

"What did you do to that thing? It looks 100 percent better. Figured you'd need a stitch."

"I put something on it," Frank mumbled. *Carry a little in my purse all the time.*

Frank wasn't sure where he came down on things like ESP and other supernatural phenomenon. Might have some valid aspects. Probably not.

But what happened next caused him to rethink his position. As he pondered last night with Alma his cell rang—it was her.

"Frank, I just wanted to tell you how much I enjoyed last evening. You're a great cook. Thank you again."

"You're welcome."

Her voice took on a smoky sexy tone. "In fact, it got better as the night went on."

What does she mean by that? He must have waited a little too long to reply, because she said, "Hello . . . still there?"

Frank came awake. "Yeah, sure. I enjoyed it too."

Now the hesitation came from her end of the line. Frank waited.

"So . . . I wondered if you'd join me for dinner tonight?" she asked. "Have a roast."

Frank wanted to see her again. In fact, he'd planned to give her a call in a few days and suggest another dinner date. She'd beat him to it. Did that mean something?

His chest tightened. "Yeah, sure. That would be great. Can I bring anything?"

"A bottle of that delicious red."

"Give me your address."

Frank hung around the office late. Nothing to do but kill time until he drove to Alma's. The rest of the unit had cleared out. In the quiet of the empty squad room, his mind drifted back to that night at Ricardo's. That's what kicked off this gang war—the hit on Ricardo. With all that had happened since, that single fact had gotten lost. Frank still had too many unanswered questions about that night. Waiting for forensics was like watching the first part of a mini-series, and three months later seeing part two. What rendered the two guards unconscious? A plant-based substance? Who killed Ricardo? Why was he killed? If Alma wasn't the redhead, who was?

Frank doodled on the notepad and got into his full slouch position. Tomorrow he would deconstruct the whole Ricardo killing piece by piece. If his death wasn't just a coincidence, what did that mean? Still, a feeling he was missing something nagged him. Something as big as Dallas and he just couldn't see it.

Edna startled him sticking her head from her office. "Going to sleep there tonight?"

"Just thinking." Frank blew his nose.

She strolled out with her briefcase, switching off her light. "Why are your eyes so red?"

"High pollen count today."

Edna opened her purse and dropped a couple of gel tabs on his desk. "Try these. The grass pollen this time of year does a number on me too. These are the only things that work. They're prescription."

Frank scooped them up. "Thanks."

She sat on the edge of his desk. Frank always enjoyed it when just the two of them were alone in the office. That's when the real Edna came out. He loved the real Edna.

"I want you to contact Levern."

He tried reading her neutral expression while tearing open the allergy tabs package.

"Let him know his life might be in danger—no details. Just put him on his guard."

"Why do that for a crook?" Frank asked. He was happy she'd decided to do it but still wanted an explanation.

She stared at the floor for a moment, her lips becoming tight lines. "I have enough rotten memories for a lifetime from when I worked uniform." She looked up. "Don't want to carry around any extra baggage." Her expression softened.

Frank popped the tabs in his mouth and took a swallow of water from his bottle. He had saved a half dozen lives in his police career. When he thought of Levern, his mind automatically defaulted to that night when he rolled up on the young black kid bleeding and almost dead. To save a life was to give another a second chance. Sometimes he thought it would have been better if Levern had just died. But he didn't. Frank wanted to believe that everyone could find redemption—even him. He still didn't want to give up on Levern—not yet.

"I understand," Frank said. "Thanks, Edna."

She nodded as she turned to go.

He left five minutes later and swung by a liquor store to pick up the wine. The mid-October sunset was the best he'd seen—a broad streak of orange, red, and yellow across the western sky. He always put himself in position to view sunrises and sunsets. Rob said he was weird, but for Frank, it was necessary. Perhaps even spiritual. He drew energy from the sun. Call it a vitamin D thing or whatever. Nikola Tesla believed it. Days without sunlight sent Frank into a Seasonal Affective Disorder spiral during which he'd go for hours and never utter a word. Couldn't survive in the Pacific Northwest. When these bouts happened, everyone gave him space.

Alma said she lived near White Rock Lake. Just before sunset he turned on West Lawther. Bikers, dog walkers, and joggers crowded the hike-and-bike trail that circled the lake. He scanned the million-dollar homes. Pretty nice neighborhood for a university professor. Before he got to Jackson Point, he found the address and swung into the drive beside the house.

As he stared at the place, a sense of déjà vu swept over him. He gazed at the small, natural stone cottage with the white picket fence and yard overflowing with wild flowers.

He had been here before.

*   *   *

Jesse adjusted the scope tighter on her target's head. She stood under an ancient oak, behind a junkyard fence in southeast Dallas. This dirt alley between the fence of the junkyard and the fence of the homes to the south offered the perfect shooting location. Her car was parked a few feet away with the back passenger's door open. The shadows of the tree camouflaged her from a distance. The rifle stock rested on the fence, and filtered sunlight painted a dim shadow of the rifle's suppressor on the grass. Early morning and early evening shots were the best. The sun could be used to highlight or blind the target. She shifted to a more comfortable standing position and studied him pacing behind the hip-hop club, talking on his cell.

According to an old *Texas Monthly* article, her target ran the local chapter of the Crips—one of Levern's associates. He wore a wife-beater tee shirt and baggy black cargo shorts. He motioned with his hands when he spoke. *Probably trying to cut another dope deal.* Jesse moved the scope to the right and took slow, even breaths. A couple of his guys stood by the club's back door watching their boss rattle on. They looked bored, as if they wished they were any-where else.

Jesse moved the scope back to the target. He was in his mid-twenties, maybe late twenties. He lit a cigarette and laughed, unaware of how close he was to death.

That's what people do. They go about their lives never thinking about death. Then one day it comes calling, and they all want more time.

Death didn't bother Jesse. The thought of it actually warmed and consoled her. She'd lost so many people in this life. So many she'd loved and who loved her, the idea of joining them in the final great adventure calmed her.

Jesse ranged the distance at a little over seven hundred yards—easy shot. But she liked her targets stationary. Leading a target from this distance could be tricky, especially with the cross breeze—she could wait.

*   *   *

Her dad made her understand that getting the kill on the first shot was the most important thing a hunter could do. That day when she was a kid shooting in Uncle Bill's pasture changed everything.

The bump of the cattle guard signaled they'd arrived. Her uncle's half-mile-long dirt road led to the house and barn. It looked like an island in a vast sea of pasture. They drove past dozens of Black Angus grazing on either side. When her dad stopped, Uncle Bill came out to meet them. He shook hands with her dad, and she gave her favorite uncle a hug. Buddy sprang from the truck and greeted Uncle Bill's dog, Skeet. While Uncle Bill and her dad visited, Jesse ran inside to see what Aunt Janet had made. After milk and chocolate chip cookies, they left her aunt at the house to make lunch and drove to a back pasture. Jesse had been there many times. Her dad made the drive about once a month to visit his brother and shoot prairie dogs. Uncle Bill had several colonies living in a ten-acre stretch.

They unloaded the equipment from the pickup, and her dad rolled an old quilt onto the ground. Jesse always loved the grassy smell of the back pasture—a rich fresh scent. Back there, away from the road and the house, only the wind, sky, and lush green grass remained. She'd spent many hours sitting on the tailgate, watching her dad and Uncle Bill shoot the little hole-dwelling critters. Today it was her turn. She licked dry lips and rubbed her hands down the legs of her jeans.

"Okay, Sis." Dad always called her Sis when she was on the range. His way of helping her relax and focus. "You know how it works. Pick your target and stay on it. Don't shoot when it's moving. Wait for it to settle down."

Uncle Bill stood in the bed of the truck with a pair of binoculars glued to his eyes. He scanned from left to right. "Lordy, lordy, never seen 'em so thick." He jumped to the ground and pointed. "The most are over there, just this side of that little rise on the left."

Her dad adjusted the quilt and an old sand bag for the rifle rest. He held the .22 while she dropped to the prone shooting position. Even after the snack, her stomach felt hollow, her mouth so dry she couldn't even spit.

Her dad checked the .22 and made sure the bolt cycled properly. Uncle Bill leaned against the tailgate of the old Ford and sampled the pint of whiskey he kept hidden from Aunt Janet. He screwed the cap back on and folded his arms. All eyes were on her, and the excited, nervous feeling wouldn't go away. She'd never experienced this on the shooting range.

Jesse took a deep breath as her dad slipped a bullet into the chamber. He closed the bolt, winked, and took a knee, handing her the rifle.

"Keep your finger off the trigger while you select your target," he said. "Once you have him, cock it, and ease your finger into the trigger guard."

Her sick-looking smile must have given her away because he patted her back. "You'll be fine—just remember what we talked about."

She lowered her gaze to adjust the sight picture. Keeping the top of the front sight level and between the rear sight, she scanned the landscape looking for a suitable target. Her eye picked up movement to the left. Jesse zeroed in on the prairie dog. Without taking her eyes off him, she cocked the rifle. She took a breath and released half as the front sight became crystal clear on the thing's head. Her finger moved to the trigger and she jerked it. The shot went wild to the right. A puff of dirt rose behind the critter. She dropped her head and her heart sank.

"That's okay," her dad whispered and stroked her hair. "Take a minute and relax."

How could she relax? Her stomach was so twisted and knotted she felt like she'd throw up.

Her dad spoke in low comforting tones. "This isn't like target shooting. It's different. When you're getting ready to end a life, it feels different than just poking a hole through a piece of paper. It's more serious."

He didn't say anything for a minute or two but kept his big warm hand on her shoulder as a comfort. He leaned closer and said, "When you're ready try it again. Eject the case."

Jesse swallowed hard and slid the bolt to the rear. The empty case flew out to the right. Her dad held another bullet and she took it, catching a glimpse of him. He gave her a reassuring nod.

She slipped the bullet into the breach. Slid the bolt closed. Found another target, cocked the rifle, and adjusted her sight picture again. This one was closer. She squeezed the trigger, but just before the shot, for some reason, closed both eyes. Another wild miss. She'd forgotten everything she'd been taught the past year. What was so easy at shooting contest and in their backyard now became impossible.

Jesse lowered her head to the rifle's stock. Warm tears skated down her cheeks onto the cold metal. She'd never felt so worthless. She'd let her dad down. She'd let herself down. Her silent cry broke out into a full bawl. Her tiny shoulders heaving at the anger and humiliation she felt. That rock solid hand gently stroked her hair. When she turned toward him, he was lying beside her with a mischievous grin.

"I'm sorry," she said. She wiped her tears on her sleeve, but they were soon replaced with others.

"I know what your problem is," he said. "Wanna know?"

She sniffled and nodded.

"You're just overthinking. Remember, Sis, shooting is only 50 percent physical—the other 50 is mental. I have just the remedy—works every time." His confident reassurance could always relax her. He could figure out anything. He reached into his jacket and came out with a piece of peppermint candy, rolled in clear plastic. He opened it and gave it to her.

"Pop that under your tongue and let it melt. Concentrate on the taste and not your nervousness. It'll calm you down. Peppermint has that quality."

Jesse tried swallowing, but there was nothing to swallow. She took the candy and eased it under her tongue. Her dad loved peppermint. Kept some on him all the time. He reloaded the rifle and handed it to her. She lowered it across the sandbag and looked down the barrel at the front sight. A fat prairie dog scurried from one burrow to another. Her heart pounded.

"Which one are you aiming at?" her dad asked.

She replied in a whisper. "The big one running. Waiting for him to stop."

"No, not that one."

"Huh?"

He pointed in the distance. "See that rock thirty yards behind him?"

"Uh-huh."

"Shoot that skinny one to the right of the rock."

Panic rose in her voice. "Are you kidding?"

His hand rested in the middle of her back. "No, you can take him, Sis."

A smaller target farther out? The candy melted and filled her mouth with sweetness. She calmed down and shut out the thought of distance, allowing her year-long training to take over. She cocked the rifle, and her finger slipped into the trigger guard. The critter craned its neck and stood on his hind legs, looking at another prairie dog. She had the sites tight on him but hesitated. Thoughts drifted through her head about his friends and family and how much they'd miss him. Her breath came in pants, and her hand was so sweaty it slipped on the stock.

Her dad whispered, "Just relax, Sis, don't think about it. It doesn't matter. You're in control and have the power if you want it. If you don't, someone else will take it—it's just a game."

A quiet calm settled upon her again. Her vision sharpened. The sight alignment and sight picture was perfect. She took one final breath, let half out, and in slow motion squeezed the trigger. The furry thing's head exploded.

"Holy shit!" Uncle Bill exclaimed. "Pardon my French." He held the bottle in one hand and binoculars in the other. He took a quick swig. He stared at her with his mouth open. "Jess, you hit the head. A ninety-yard head shot! I can't even do that."

The soft pat on her shoulder filled her with pride. But another feeling, much more intense also raced through her. Something she didn't feel shooting targets. Too young to understand, she only knew she wanted more. Jesse racked back the bolt and the cartridge case sailed out. She gazed at the box of shells her dad held.

"May I have another?"

Ten years later, she won the regional marksmanship tournament, and a year after that, the state. Jesse never again felt the hesitation and doubt she'd experienced that first day. She became an expert tracker and hunter, bagging something bigger every season from unbelievable distances. Her only regret—the humiliation her dad would feel if he knew about her life choices. He was an honest but poor man. A man of honor and great pride in his only child. He was probably rolling in his grave right now.

*　*　*

Jesse pulled herself back to the here and now. Her target looked like he was about to present himself for the perfect shot.

Never taking her eyes from the scope, she reached in her pocket and her nimble fingers unwrapped the peppermint. She popped it in her mouth and let it slide beneath her tongue. She maintained her even breathing pattern. In . . . out . . . in . . . out.

Don't hold your breath until just before the shot.

The gangster slowed his pace, turning directly toward her. He stopped and she put the crosshairs between his eyes. Her finger tightened on the trigger. He whirled around and walked in a different direction, still jabbering away on the cell. He stopped again and she tightened again. He laughed and leaned back against the white cinder block building. As his shoulders touch the wall, she completed her trigger squeeze.

The rifle made little sound—a small whistle. The wall behind the target speckled red, and he dropped straight down. His two buds were still in conversation at the other end of the building. She swung the rifle in their direction. It would be so easy—bam, bam. She pulled her gaze away from the sight. Not part of the contract. Only Levern's lieutenants—not the humps.

One noticed what happened and pointed. He yelled something and they raced to their fallen boss. Jesse slowly racked the spent shell from the rifle and pocketed it. She glanced around before returning to her car and slipping the rifle into the large cardboard tube on the back floorboard.

A rustling sound drifted through the air. Jesse snapped her head to the left. She strained her ears listening to hear it again—nothing. The wind sometimes played sound tricks in trees. She removed the Teddy bear, diaper bag, and blanket from the baby seat and tossed them on the tube. One last scan of the junkyard and the trees, and Jesse backed out of the shadows of the ancient oak and disappeared into the maze of back streets.

* * *

Frank opened the wooden gate and strolled on the flagstone path through a garden that looked like it belonged in the English countryside. The various plant colors and textures blended into a relaxing palette that spilled over the walkway, touching Frank's cuffs as he walked to the steps of the porch. Bees, hummingbirds, and butterflies flittered from one plant to the other. *Strange.*

Shouldn't they have flown south already?

When Frank's foot touched the first step, something happened. He felt intoxicated—light-headed. A state of peace, bliss, and happiness swept over him. He paused and did a gut check, leaning on the rail.

What the . . . ?

It wasn't like he never felt this way before, but it usually took a couple of bottles of red to get him there. What was going on?

To the left of the front door hung a Texas Historical Commission marker. Frank leaned a hand against the wall and read the inscription. The house had been constructed in 1910. One of the first around the new Dallas Lake.

Yeah, I know this place.

Frank knocked and Alma answered the door wearing a tight white sweater and dark blue skirt. Her red hair flowed over her shoulders. She looked great.

"You found the place," she said.

Frank handed her the wine. "I'm a detective."

Her warm inviting smile drew him across the threshold. "Yes, you are. Come in."

She looked different from yesterday. Couldn't quite put his finger on it. A few years younger? She'd changed her hair, which gave her a more sexy appearance.

"Roast still has a half hour. Want to relax in the garden?"

"Let's open the wine first," Frank said. Something touched his leg. He stared at the tabby rubbing its cheek against his pants.

"Don't mind Maggie. She's just saying hello." Alma led the way through the living room. It was just as he remembered—all antique furniture. A mismatch of early American, Colonial and English. Probably not one piece less than a hundred years old. Lace curtains hung from the windows, and soft Persian rugs covered the dark, hardwood floor. The only out of place furnishing was the wall-mounted big screen TV. Everything else was right out of a museum.

"You know I've been here before," Frank said.

Alma stopped as they entered the kitchen. Her mouth fell open and she stepped away from him. "You have?"

Frank had seen that expression a hundred times. Right after a long interrogation when the suspect realizes they're trapped and the only way out is to confess. He gazed in all directions. "Yeah, about sixteen years ago when I first moved to Dallas."

Alma's shoulders relaxed, but she held her breath. "Pray tell?"

Frank took the wine from her and picked up an opener from the counter. As he attacked the cork, he explained. "When I first moved here I was looking for something to do one Saturday and signed up for a tour of homes. Helped to familiarize myself with different parts of the city before becoming a police officer."

She leaned back against the counter and crossed her arms. The way she stared at him, never blinking, made Frank wonder.

In a defensive voice she said, "I didn't live here then."

He pulled the cork from the bottle before setting it on the counter. "The tour guide said the owner was in Ireland or Scotland for the summer, I can't remember. But I always remembered 'The Cottage by the Lake.' Had sort of a romantic ring."

Frank studied Alma. Besides looking different, she acted different. He couldn't care less. He felt wonderful. Why overthink a beautiful evening with a beautiful woman?

Alma's eyes shifted and finally met his before she asked, "So how long ago was that again?"

"Like I said, fifteen or sixteen years." He poured her a glass and then him.

"I think you're a romantic for going on a tour and remembering something from that long ago."

Her smile had a seductive quality. She held the glass in those delicate fingers, and for no particular reason, Frank found that it excited him. Alma sipped the wine, never taking her mesmerizing green eyes off him.

"My aunt lived here then," Alma said. "Died a few years ago and left the house to me."

"Wish I had an aunt like that."

She laughed. "You did. Except it was a grandparent who left you a big trust. Come on." She opened the kitchen door and grabbed his hand. They stepped outside.

A giant bald cypress shaded the small side yard, giving it an enchanted, magical feel. A cool breeze swept around the house as evening shadows closed in. Her long hair fluttered in the wind, and she looked like one of those story-book princesses you read about as a kid. They strolled down the mulch garden path past green gnomes peeking around rocks. Crystals and gem stones littered the base of shrubs. When they turned the corner, Frank gazed at the expansive backyard—one huge garden. Her place was as beautiful as the Dallas Arboretum, which was on the opposite side of the lake.

"My God," he exclaimed.

"Let's take the tour," she said.

Alma led him past trees, beds of herbs, around plantings of colorful flowers, and under arbors of wisteria and grape. Bird houses and feeders hung from a dozen tree limbs. Colorful birds flitted from one tree to another and their songs blended into a strange eerie melody. She stopped at a sun dial in the middle of a large paved-stone star.

"Who takes care of all this?" he asked.

"I have a gardener help me with the heavy things, but I do a lot of it."

Frank was so relaxed and comfortable he could have slept right there on the stone path. The stress of the investigation had disappeared, and he was totally at ease—like being home—only better. Something strange was going on, but Frank enjoyed himself too much to care.

"Oh, dear," she said, and handed Frank her glass. She ambled to a rabbit limping across the path. Alma bent over and examined its hind leg. The animal didn't attempt to flee.

Frank picked up a small metal donkey decoration from a flower bed. He gazed at the piece of yard art and at the tight skirt stretched across Alma's back side as she bent over.

"There," she said, "you just had a sticker—all gone, now."

As the bunny hopped into the bushes, Frank said, "Nice ass."

Alma jerked her head in his direction and he held up the metal donkey. "Never saw one like this before." He allowed a smile to crack the corners of his mouth.

She grinned, lifted a brow, and stood, sauntering beside him. She took back her glass and sipped it before saying, "So you're an expert on asses now?"

"Know a good one when I see it."

She nuzzled next to him and put her hand behind his head. Their eyes met and his lips touched hers. The kiss lasted a long time. Exploring each other's mouths. This totally surprised Frank. He hadn't expected she'd make the first move. This evening was going better than he could have anticipated. Dizziness enveloped him and he stumbled backward.

"Whoa." She steadied him and they laughed. "Let's have dinner," she said.

She took his hand again and led him through the maze of plants. They passed a circle of mushrooms on the way back to the cottage. He motioned at them.

"Those are growing weird—never seen that before."

She playfully chuckled. "It's a fairy ring."

The explanation confused Frank, but he didn't care enough to follow up. The sun had almost set, and the long shadows of evening danced on the path like playful little spirits. In the back of the house stood a lush eight-foot yellow rose bush. The top snaked above the roof and ran along the gutter. The last fleeing rays of sun illuminated it, and it appeared to shine. Frank stopped and sucked in its sweet fragrance.

"That's magnificent," he said.

Alma wrapped an arm around his waist. "It's my favorite. The Yellow Rose of Texas." She grabbed his hand. "Come on, dinner's almost ready."

Walking back into the house, the fragrant garden smell was replaced with the aroma of cooking meat. She popped the garlic bread into the oven while he poured more wine.

"I meant to ask you," he said, "what did you put on my wrist?"

Her forehead crinkled. "What's wrong?"

"Nothing." He held it up for her to see. "It did the trick—look." He peeled back his shirt sleeve for her examination.

She rubbed her finger across it. "Does that hurt?"

Frank shook his head. "Not a bit. What was that stuff?"

"Just a little something I whipped up. Want 'a see?"

Alma led him to a room off the kitchen, a little smaller, but packed from floor to ceiling. On a half dozen shelves there were labeled bottles of crushed powders, salves, oils, and extracts. An ancient, wooden counter surrounded the room with the shelves above it.

"What's all this?" Frank read the labels as he walked past—Wolf's bane, Frankincense, Milk Thistle . . .

She strolled to the counter, turned, and leaned back. "I'm an herbalist. What I treated you with was all plant-based substances. Nothing but herbs and plants from my garden. A little aloe gel, comfrey leaf oil, and chickweed salve." She winked. "Nothing that would hurt you."

They had more wine with dinner and chatted about everything from gardening to cooking. Frank always considered his roast recipe second to none, but what Alma served collapsed that notion. She had peach cobbler for dessert—best he ever had. He helped clear the table.

"I want that roast and cobbler recipe," Frank said.

Alma released a nervous laugh. "I have to admit I was worried all evening about cooking for a professional chef. Never did that before. Living alone, I'm afraid my cooking skills have deteriorated."

"It's like riding a bicycle," Frank said.

Alma put on some light jazz and kicked off her flats. She held out her arms and Frank folded into them. They slow danced in the living room to old John Coltrane and Mary Lou Williams's songs. Her perfume had a mysterious floral fragrance he'd never encountered. Frank still found it hard to believe—the perfect evening with the perfect woman. They laughed, joked, and exchanged soft kisses as the evening rolled on. While swaying to the music, she laid her head on his shoulder and caressed his back.

"I wasn't sure I should invite you to dinner," she whispered.

"Why?"

She gazed into his eyes. "I don't know . . . I . . . I wasn't sure if you would find it too forward, me asking you over. We hardly know each other."

Frank found her candor absolutely endearing. "I'm happy you did. I wanted to see you again. Just wasn't sure how to ask."

She laid her head back on his shoulder. Frank could have danced with her all evening. She floated over the floor gracefully, as if she were part of him.

Massaging the back of his neck, she said just above a whisper, "I find you terribly attractive."

Nothing she could have said would have turned Frank on more. She pushed her pelvis closer and held him tighter.

Frank was about to explode. She must have felt him getting harder. As she pushed closer, the beating of Frank's heart resonated through his skull like a base drum. He couldn't take much more. How did he miss all the signs the other night when he had her over for dinner? They must have been there. Had to be if she felt this way about him. Something was very weird here, but in Frank's condition he couldn't have cared less. *Never overthink a good thing.*

After almost an hour, she reached up and gave him a deep, wet kiss, her tongue exploring every corner of his mouth. He ran his hand up her sweater and deftly unhooked her bra with two fingers. She broke the embrace and her hungry eyes studied his for a moment before taking his hand and leading him to the bedroom.

They undressed each other between long kisses. Her breath came in pants as he laid her on the bed.

"Lie on your stomach," he whispered.

Alma rolled over and arched her back, sliding partway up onto her knees.

Frank eased between her legs.

A gasp of delight escaped her lips.

He was gentle. Being better endowed than most men, he moved slowly while massaging her back until she relaxed. When he picked up the pace, her climax came in spasmodic waves.

On her hands and knees, she cried out in pleasure and leaned back against him, taking him all in. After a minute, her breathing slowed, and she rolled from his embrace. She came back up on her hands and knees, facing him. Tilting her head, she studied him like a cat does a mouse before dinner. Her eyes narrowed, and the intense stare frightened Frank a little. Alma kissed him and said, "Now it's my turn. Lie on your back."

For over an hour Frank experienced sensations he'd never felt. He considered himself a specialist in the art of physical love, but Alma existed in a class all her own. Frank climaxed over and over—a feat he'd not accomplished since youth. He was exhausted; catching his breath, he stroked her breast as she cuddled beside him. He drifted into a shallow, dream-like sleep.

Frank woke to the sound of running water. He lifted his head and gazed through the bathroom door. The shower turned off and Alma stepped out, drying herself. He pulled himself out of bed and staggered on weakened legs to the bath. She dropped the towel to the floor and nuzzled close, nibbling at his lower lip.

"Ready for another go?" she teased, wrapping her arms around his neck.

He gazed in the mirror at her perfect bottom, a small Celtic tattoo inked at the panty line of her back. "You've drained me—nothing left." He moaned.

Her voice took on a lyrical quality as she whispered, "Good, that's what I wanted—every drop."

Something about the way she said it sounded odd, but with his mind in a fog, he didn't give it another thought. He patted her behind. "I've got to go."

She kissed him before saying, "I know."

Walking out of the gate into the fresh air, Frank's mind cleared for the first time that evening. *What just happened?* He drove home staring at the full moon with all kinds of thoughts, ideas, and questions. It was as if his mind's email had gone down for a few hours and now the box filled up with delayed messages. *Have I been drugged?*

* * *

Alma slipped on a robe to see Frank out. She paced back to the bedroom, removed the hidden photograph of Clare from her dresser drawer, and returned it to her nightstand. After gazing at it for several seconds, she touched the tip of her finger to her lips and then pressed it on the photo. She prepared what she needed for the ritual and opened her *Book of Shadows*, refreshing her memory as to the wording. Minutes later with all the lights out, Alma stood behind the half circle of five red candles glowing from the floor, the full moon spilling light through her window. She dropped the robe and sat cross-legged in the half circle. In the pewter saucer she sprinkled sea salt and dried yellow rose petals. Unwrapping the Band-Aid from the tissue, she draped it over the salt and petals. She'd cut away the adhesive parts, leaving only the blood-soaked gauze center.

Alma sprinkled dried lemon verbena, three drops of lavender oil, and crumbled seven dried jasmine leaves over the gauze. She closed her eyes and spoke in Gaelic, whispering the ancient Druid fertility prayer. She struck the match and laid the flame under the little pile in the saucer. The smoke lazily rose and she leaned over it, washing herself in its *magick*. She waved it under her arms, over her face, and massaged her breast in the sweet fragrance, repeating the prayer in whispered tones over and over until only the last smoldering whiffs drifted into the air.

17

Friday morning Rob and Frank sat in Levern's restaurant eating breakfast. Rob passed up his workout in favor of joining Frank. Homemade biscuits, saw mill gravy, grits, and an omelet had an appeal the gym couldn't offer. Rob had to admit, for a doper, Levern served a first rate meal. Frank seemed tired, or maybe just distracted. They waited for Levern and chatted about Leon, the gang banger who got snipped the day before behind the hip-hop club.

"Blew his head plum off," Rob said, as Frank started to take a bite.

Frank grimaced, sat his fork down, and took a sip of coffee instead. "Any info on the shooter?"

Rob shrugged. "Nope, a rifle, that's all we know so far. Forensics is still working it."

"No one saw or heard anything? Find a shell casing?"

Rob scooped the last of the omelet into his mouth. "Nothing." He wiped his lips and gazed over Frank's shoulder at Levern strolling up. "Sleepy head's here."

"About time. I called him an hour ago," Frank mumbled.

Levern pulled a chair out and sat beside Frank. "Sorry it took me so long. Didn't realize you guys were just around the corner."

Levern had droopy eyes—as if he'd had too little sleep or too much coke. He wore a Band-Aid over his tattoo on the back of his hand.

He smirked at Rob. "What are you looking at?"

Rob sat back and sipped his coffee. He hated this guy more every time they met. "A doper." Rob slapped his hand over his mouth. "Oops, did I say that out loud?"

Levern grinned and nodded. "Yeah, well, we've all got a part to play." He wiped his face with both hands and yawned.

"What did you hear about Leon?" Frank asked.

Levern helped himself to their pot of coffee, adding two sugars. "I didn't hear nothing until this morning. Some asshole called and woke me up."

"You talking about me?" Frank asked.

"Naw, man—some other asshole—guy I know called about three o'clock."

"Remember how our last visit was kind of unofficial?" Frank asked.

Levern's brow wrinkled. "Yeah."

"Well, this one's officially unofficial."

"What you talking about?"

Frank motioned and Levern edged closer.

Frank whispered. "There's a contract on you."

Levern jerked back like he'd been slapped. "On me?"

Rob couldn't resist grinning. "On you."

Levern looked from one to the other in disbelief. A stupid smile broke out. "Naw."

Frank said, "Listen, I know what I'm talking about. Can't tell you how I know, or anything that would do you any good, but take extra precautions. There's a professional involved."

Levern jumped up, knocking over his chair as his voice rose. "What did I do—why me?"

Every head in the restaurant turned at the commotion.

"Your number finally came up, Levern," Rob said letting another smile spread across his lips.

Frank waited as Levern picked up his chair and reclaimed his seat. "They think you did Ricardo."

"They . . . they. Who's they?"

Neither Frank nor Rob answered.

Levern's eyes shifted from one to the other. It took him about five seconds to figure it out. "It's New York, right? Ricardo worked for New York. It's got to be New York."

"Just be careful," Frank said.

"Or not," Rob chimed in. "Shouldn't have killed Ricardo."

Levern yelled, "I didn't kill him!"

The hum of conversation from the several dozen diners stopped, and all eyes shifted back to him. Tabor walked toward them. Levern caught the movement and waved him back.

"At this point it doesn't matter," Frank whispered. "The contract's set."

Levern took a couple of deep breaths and nodded like a bobble-head doll. "Okay," he said, "if that's how it's going to be." A dark expression swept over him. "If you hear anything else, you'll let me know, won't you?"

Frank and Rob stood and pulled out their wallets. "I'll let you know," Frank said.

"Hey, breakfast is on me," Levern said.

"No, thanks," Rob threw a wad of cash on the table.

Frank did the same. "Watch yourself."

Walking to the car, Frank had a slight limp.

"What's wrong?" Rob asked. "Career-ending yoga injury?"

"Think I pulled a groin muscle."

Rob tapped the key fob, and both door locks snapped open. "Like I told you, that type of Eastern meditating crap isn't what real Americans do."

They slid into their seats.

"I didn't do it exercising. Had a date last night."

Rob loved hearing about Frank's sexual escapades. Reminded him of his and Carmen's early marriage years. "Okay, so it's a career-ending sex injury. Anyone I know?"

Frank assumed the full slouch position and slid his sunglasses on. "Dr. Hawkins."

Rob had already shifted into gear, and the car was easing forward. He slammed on the brakes. "Whoa! You shitting me?"

Frank stared ahead. "She made us dinner and . . ."

Rob leaned closer. "Yeah, go on."

Frank rolled his head toward him. "And we had a nice time."

Rob decided on a different tactic. "You know if Edna gets wind of this, she'll have a cow."

Frank stared back. "I thought Edna only had cats. Haven't we already discussed this? Besides, I don't intend to tell her. And I can't imagine Dr. Hawkins saying anything. So that just leaves you. You telling her? Want to join our cabal?"

Rob huffed. "I'd never say anything."

But Frank already knew that. He showed one of his rare grins. "I know. Let's get to work."

*   *   *

While Rob drove to the station, Frank thought about Alma. Being single for so long gave him perspective. His short marriage was nice while it lasted, but the loss and pain he felt later wasn't something he ever wanted to experience again. Never wanted another long-lasting relationship that made him emotionally vulnerable or dependent on another. The call girls he dated didn't want that kind of relationship either. But something about Alma had awoken a feeling in Frank he hadn't felt in a long time. A good feeling he still remembered from long ago. Wonder why she wasn't married? . . .

They parked in the employee garage and crossed over the third-floor walkway. When they strolled into the Criminal Intelligence Unit, half the cubicles were empty. Lots of CIU guys met Terry for breakfast at the end of the week to catch him up on their investigations—Terry's way of staying close to the troops. Edna stuck her head out of her door.

"Talk to Levern?"

"Yeah," Frank said. "Now I'm even more convinced he had nothing to do with Ricardo."

"Then who did it?"

Frank leaned a hand against her door frame. She smelled good this morning. "Somehow it all goes back to that night. The Voodoo doll and all that other stuff—that's the key." He ran his hand through his hair and shook his head. "But there's no clear connection."

Frank hadn't had many cases with this many loose ends and no direct links. The tabby bolting from Ricardo's, herbs and plants at Alma's, plant-based substance rendering the guards unconscious. . . .

"I know you, Frank. You'll come up with some reasonable explanation. By the way, did the professor at SMU offer any help?"

Frank hadn't mentioned Alma or their meeting to Edna. Still too many unanswered questions there. He shrugged. "Not much."

She whirled around and strolled toward her desk. "Keep thinking, Frank. It'll come to you."

Frank dropped his coat over the back of his chair and grimaced as he eased into it. The groin pain took his mind back to Alma. A snicker drifted from Rob's cubicle. He eyed Frank and chuckled again at his discomfort. Frank ignored him. Alma would call or text sooner or later. What would he tell her? He still had a lot of questions about last night.

He absentmindedly pecked on the computer keyboard and pulled up Google Earth. Typing in Alma's address, he drummed his fingers, waiting for the image to load. Frank tightened the magnification on the "Cottage by the Lake." Something caught his eye in the backyard. He scrolled to the garden, and as he zoomed in, his gut tightened. Frank sat up and put his face inches from the screen, staring into the sea of green plants at something he would never have noticed at ground level. The paving stone circle with the sun dial in the middle of the Texas star—was it a Texas star or a pentagram?

18

Jesse sat in her hotel room and stared down the barrel of the M-24 sniper rifle. She held a penlight and illuminated the barrel from the breach end—spotless. She laid it aside and dipped an old toothbrush in solvent before giving the bolt a good cleaning. Jesse loved cleaning her weapon. The sweet smell of the solvent, the softness of the cleaning patches, and the feeling of total control. She wiped the bolt with a clean rag and applied a light coat of oil before reinserting it into the rifle. She racked it several times and squeezed the trigger. The snap bounced off the walls. After slipping the rifle back into its cardboard tube and hiding it under the bed, she flopped down in the chair.

Restless, she peeked through the blinds. No one was in the pool area. She slipped into her one piece, and five minutes later she stretched out on a lounge chair by the pool.

The bright October sun warmed her. She closed her eyes and her mind drifted back to her first visit to Texas. When she enlisted in the U.S. Air Force at eighteen, she never imagined doing *this* seven years later.

On a hot July morning in San Antonio, the bus load of new recruits arrived at Lackland Air Force Base to the screams of the training instructors. Nervous chatter from the young men and women was quickly suppressed by the people in Smokey Bear hats, which they called campaign hats, and everyone was ordered to assemble beside the bus. As the yelling continued, Jesse followed the others to form up in ranks. Her stomach churned with doubt.

Did I volunteer for this?

"This is the sorriest looking mob I've ever laid eyes on," one training instructor screamed. Hat low on his forehead, starched uniform, and broad shoulders. Intimidating as hell. Jesse pulled in an uneasy breath as she kept her eyes facing forward and stood at attention.

This might not have been a good idea after all.

The eight-and-a-half-week basic military training course challenged them all, but something unexpected happened to Jesse after a couple of weeks. She discovered she enjoyed it. With her tomboy upbringing, she'd done more than just keep up with the physical challenges. She excelled.

The fourth week they began weapons training. Days of orientations, demonstrations, maintenance and upkeep of the M-16. Finally, they marched to the rifle range for their first day of actual shooting.

From the tower, the range officer spoke into the mic, her voice booming from the speakers. "Is the firing line clear?" She paused while half a dozen instructors paced behind the shooters on the line, making sure all rifles were pointed down range and no one had a live weapon. Yells of "clear" sounded up and down the firing line as each instructor did a visual examination of the airmen's weapons. Jesse and twenty-three others stood in the cement encased holes with their M-16s lying on the ground. The hot Texas' sun had dried the black clay, and it cracked around this glorified sauna. The concrete radiated heat until the air blistered. No wind, only the stench of sweat.

After what seemed like minutes, the range officer said, "The firing line is clear. Shooters! Pick up your weapons and insert a magazine."

The echo of two-dozen twenty-round magazines being slapped in place floated down the line. Jesse licked her lips, that old nervousness slipping back into her stomach.

"Shooters, charge your weapons!"

Jesse hooked her index and middle finger over the charging handle and pulled straight back. She released it and the bolt slammed the bullet into the breach. *I should have drunk more water.* She wasn't used to this heat. She glanced, ensuring no one was watching, and slipped the small piece of peppermint under her tongue.

"Shooters! The line is hot. Watch your targets."

Jesse took in a slow breath and licked her parched lips. *It's kinda like a game.*

This first qualification round was to identify shooter deficiencies. Was the airman holding the weapon properly? Were they using their sites correctly? Were they squeezing the trigger and not jerking it? A hundred yards down range, her paper bull's-eye rested on a large piece of cardboard encased in a metal frame. The training instructors would check the shot patterns and decide how to fix the mistakes. The shooters had been instructed to only fire one shot and wait for the range officer's order to fire the next. Jesse looked down the barrel and the front site came into sharp focus.

"Fire," the range officer said.

Shots rang out on her left and right. Jesse slowly squeezed off her round and waited.

It took several seconds for everyone to fire their first shot. This went on until they had expended the twenty rounds in each magazine. The heat was unbearable. Waiting between each round caused the exercise to go on forever.

"Shooters! Clear your weapons."

Jesse kept the rifle pointed down range, and like they'd been taught, pushed the magazine release button. The empty magazine dropped on her boot. She re-cocked the rifle, locked the bolt in place, and checked the breach before moving the selector switch to safe. From over her shoulder an instructor said, "You're clear," and tapped the top of her helmet before proceeding to the shooter to her right.

"Shooters! Ground your weapons and come to attention."

Ten minutes later, Jesse's group rested under the shade of a tin roof shed behind the shooting range while the second group fired.

She took long gulps of water. God, she'd never been this hot in her life. Was all of Texas like this?

From the direction of the tower, two training instructors marched toward her group, one carrying a rolled up paper target. They'd been scoring them while the second group shot.

"Who the hell's Wilcox?" he bellowed. He didn't look happy, and he was the biggest.

Jesse slowly stood, her stomach in knots.

"You Wilcox?"

"Yes, Training Instructor," she croaked.

He motioned. "Get your butt over here."

Jesse paced toward the two burly men—afraid to make eye contact. Other recruits gawked in lurid fascination. A hushed murmur rose from the crowd.

"You want to explain this?" He unrolled the target with a silver dollar–sized hole drilled through the "ten" ring.

"Is that mine?"

"Damn right it is." Beads of sweat rolled down his black face, giving it a shine.

She looked at the T.I. and shrugged. "I did the best I could."

The older T.I. fought a grin and turned away. The younger one lit into her. He put his face inches from hers and screamed, "Do you expect me to frigging believe you put all the rounds into a hole this size from a hundred yards?"

The older T.I.'s shoulders shook from silent laughter as he faced the opposite direction.

"Yes, Training Instructor."

"We'll see about that," he screamed. "When this group is off the line—you're up next—get ready." The T.I.s marched back to the range tower. Laughter sounded again from the older one.

Jesse ambled over to the waiting recruits, who all had a slack-jawed look.

"Did you really put them all in the ten?" one asked.

Fifteen minutes later, Jesse again stood in her firing pit waiting for the range officer's instructions. This time a T.I. stood on each side of her. She'd slipped her piece of peppermint under her tongue moments before, while in the latrine. One T.I. had a set of binoculars and the other a spotter scope. She was the lone shooter. She willed herself to relax. *It's kinda like a game.*

After firing her twenty rounds, the older training instructor with the scope mumbled, "Holy shit!"

They dismissed her to the rest area while they scored the target.

After about fifteen minutes, the range officer, a young female lieutenant, trooped toward her followed by the two male T.I.s. The airmen all jumped to attention.

"Wilcox!" the lieutenant yelled.

Jesse stepped forward and came to attention, chin up, eyes straight. "Yes, ma'am."

The lieutenant's expression softened. "At ease, shooters. Gather around." She addressed the group. "I want you people to see what happens when God bestows a gift." She unrolled Jesse's target and held it up for them. Laughter echoed under the shed. Jesse had used her rounds to shoot a happy face in the "ten" ring. The range officer rolled it back up.

"Okay, firing group one: back on the line. Let's see who can beat Wilcox." She gave Jesse a quick wink and marched back to the tower.

The memory caused Jesse to smile. She stretched on the lounger and readjusted the shoulder strap on her bathing suit. Until two days ago, she hadn't returned to Texas after her time at Lackland. Most of her work kept her east of the Mississippi. Staying in one place too long wasn't the way she rolled. People in her line of work who stayed in one place too long could get tracked by some hot shot cop. This Dallas job would keep her here much longer than she liked, but the money was too good to pass up. New York wanted to send a loud and clear message to this Levern guy. But at fifty grand a pop, even old man Gambizi would tire of that after a while.

The pool gate creaked and Jesse opened an eye. A pasty mid-forties man, looking like he was eight months pregnant, eyed her. Of the dozen other lounges around the pool, he made a beeline for the one closest to her. He spread his towel out and flopped down. The lounge sagged.

Why do I always attract the jerks?

He popped the tab on a can of beer and took a sip while reaching for his pack of cigarettes. Lighting up, smoke drifted past her nose and stunk up the fresh morning air. He eyed her as he opened his book. After a few minutes of ignoring her, Mr. Cool made his pitch.

"Weather's a lot nicer here than back home."

Jesse glanced his way. A satisfied smile covered his stupid face. Sort of a "made you look" expression.

She ignored him and turned back to the sun.

"So, you here on business?"

She stared at him again. *Okay, you asked for it.* Jesse sat up and pushed out her chest. His eyes took in the cleavage.

"Yes, and you?"

"Oh, yeah. Work for Trinity Masonry and Concrete in Duluth—bidding on a project."

His wide, jerk-like smile almost made her regret what she intended to do. Jesse leaned forward and licked her lips. "Bet it gets lonely on the road, doesn't it?"

He beamed. "You bet 'cha."

She batted her eyes. "Like some company?"

His mouth gaped. "Sure."

She motioned at the beer. "Got another one of those?"

He struggled to free himself from the lounge. "Sure do. Be right back."

She waited until he was out of sight, then dropped the cigarette into the beer can, tossed his towel into the pool, and picked up his book on the way out of the gate. As she rounded the corner of her building, she dropped it into the garbage can.

Asshole.

* * *

Frank and Rob spent the rest of the morning on the piles of paper-work that littered their desk. Frank couldn't concentrate. Alma lurked in the shadows of his conscience. He checked his phone for texts—nothing. Usually didn't take women this long to contact him. Strange.

Rob's eyebrows drew together as he stared at his monitor. He pinched the skin at his throat, deep in thought, or worry. Hard to tell with Rob. With his wife's medical problems, worry was a real possibility. A few minutes later he stretched and ran his hands down his face, a signal he would demand food soon.

Frank had been in police work a long time, but still hadn't fig-ured out the whole *eating thing* cops held so dear. Frank enjoyed going out once a week for a bite, but most days he preferred to just eat a sandwich or some homemade soup at his desk. Never had much of an appetite. Probably the reason he couldn't gain any weight. But every cop he knew lived for going out with a colleague for lunch. Something about escaping the office and dining together drove them to find a familiar place and relax for a meal. Probably why Sarge's bar was so popular.

"Ready for lunch?" Rob asked.

"Sure."

Rob bounced up with a relieved expression. "Great idea. Sarge's?"

"Why not."

They got to Sarge's early, before all the parking spots were gone. As they approached the entrance, they met Detective Paul Sims, about to go in. He took the last bite of an ice cream sandwich, wadded up the wrapper and tossed it in the garbage can by the door.

"Early desert?" Rob asked.

Sims licked his pudgy fingers. "Appetizer."

Frank held the door for Sims. "We need to talk," he said.

Sarge sat a tray of clean glasses behind the bar and spotted them. "You guys grab a seat."

Frank headed for a rear booth. Something about the familiar beer and bar smells always relaxed Frank when he strolled through the door of Sarge's.

My own private Cheers.

Rob and Frank settled into one side of the booth and Sims slid into the other. Sarge meandered over. His bushy blond hair was a tangled mess this morning.

"Never thanked you guys for what you did for Vivian," Sarge said.

Franked eyed the new men's room door. "Get J.T. to chip in for that?"

"Gave him a choice. Lifetime suspension or new door."

No one wanted to be suspended from Sarge's. It was the only sane place left in the city for police to drink and grab a bite of lunch.

Sarge threw the bar towel over his shoulder. "Anyway, I appreciate the help. Lunch is on the house."

"What about me?" Sims asked.

Sarge snorted. "Didn't see you do anything but gobble down your food and leave."

"Two of the usual," Rob said.

"Me too," Sims chimed in.

"Only a bowl of soup for me today," Frank corrected.

At Frank's urging, Sarge had added a new item to his lunch menu. Since Sarge only used Honey Baked Ham to make his sandwiches, Frank, being a former chef, suggested he take the leftover bones from the hams, add a few pounds of beans and chopped onions then drop everything into a giant slow-cooker overnight and make soup. Soup and sandwiches. Sarge was always looking for a way to save a buck, so he latched onto the idea. Always sold out—no waste.

Frank asked Sims, "Anything new?"

"Nope. But I can tell you this. Whoever popped that banger last night wasn't another banger."

Sarge's wife Jill delivered their drinks.

Frank leaned closer. "So how do you figure?"

Sims gulped half his cherry Coke in one swallow. "That was a professional hit."

"What makes you think that?" Rob asked.

"Bangers don't shoot from that distance," Sims said. "They favor assault rifles and pistols. The closer the better. The two bangers that were behind the building when their boss got whacked didn't see or hear a thing except the thud of their boss's head vaporizing."

Frank didn't want to tell Sims what the FBI said, so he did the next best thing. "Who would hire someone like that?"

Sims shrugged again, swirling the Coke in his glass. "Someone with money. You do a kill that clean—it costs."

Sarge delivered the sandwiches and Frank's soup and then headed back to the bar.

"The guys in Ricardo's house that night saw a woman," Frank said.

Sims grinned. "Your mysterious red head?"

"Yeah."

"Only one of the mopes saw her—didn't get a very good look. The other was out cold before he knew what hit him."

"Still got them in jail?" Frank asked.

Sims took a big bite of sandwich and held up a finger. After a few seconds of chewing, he said, "Yeah, both held on warrants in Lew Sterrett."

"Mind if we talk to the one who saw the woman?" Frank asked.

"Suit yourself, but better take Rob."

"Why?" Rob asked.

"Cause the guy claims not to *habla* English too good. Probably a waste of time. Don't think he knows any more than he told us."

19

An hour later in CIU, Rob stuck his head over the top of the cubicle to check on Frank. He'd been on his computer since they'd gotten back from lunch, working nonstop. Guy hadn't said a word.

Rob had been checking the NCIC indices relating to known suspects who used rifles. Whoever this Dallas shooter was had a cool head and a perfect aim. Reminded Rob of a guy in his Marine platoon—Corporal Lee. The guy would sit in a sniper's hide for days, hardly moving, waiting for the perfect shot. When he pulled the trigger, there was always a dead body found the next day with a hole poked through the head.

Rob stretched and glanced at Frank. He didn't look up as he used his mouse to fit the last photo into its little square on the lineup sheet.

"Okay, check me on this." Frank pushed back in the chair and propped his feet on his desk.

"Huh?"

"I'm just thinking out loud," Frank said. "Correct me if I stray off course."

"Go ahead."

"So, Ricardo gets hit and everything points to Levern."

"With you so far."

Frank showed his "don't patronize me face," and continued, "Anyway, then all hell breaks loose when other gang leaders start getting whacked."

Rob nodded.

"We get word through a federal wire there's a contract on Levern—some guy named Jesse—a professional."

"Yup."

"And now another gang leader's been killed by, what Sims describes as, a professional. Time for a come to Jesus meeting, I'd say."

Rob stood and put on his jacket. "And so you want to interview the gangster from Ricardo's place again. The one who supposedly saw the woman. But this time see if he can pick her out of a lineup."

"You know me so well." Frank hit the print button, grabbed his jacket, and slid the lineup sheet into his notebook. On the way out, he had that old excited look he got when he thought they were at a turning point on a big case.

Rob eyed him. When he got this way, the goofy smile wasn't far behind.

Yup, there it is.

* * *

Frank and Rob waited in the interview room at Lew Sterrett. The Dallas County Jail had that familiar smell that comes with housing criminals. One part body odor, one part fear, and one part Lysol. Frank hated it. The Spartan furnishing of the small white room, plus the long wait to pull a prisoner from his holding cell, was aggravating. Frank fidgeted with anticipation.

"Guy's name is David Juan," Frank read from the arrest report.

Rob did a double take. "You're making that up."

"Nope, see for yourself," he handed the report to Rob.

Just then the door opened and a sheriff's deputy hauled in Juan. He was early twenties, short, with a shaved head. Tattoos ran the length of each arm, and neck. The spit hood gave his head a honey-combed appearance. Sort of a space-alien look.

The deputy sat him in the chair across the desk from them. "Wanna keep the cuffs on?"

"We'll try it without them," Rob said.

"He'll spit without the hood and cuffs," the deputy warned.

"Take them off for now—we'll let you know," Rob said.

The deputy grinned and removed the handcuffs. Juan jerked the spit hood off and glared at the deputy. He had that hard demeanor you get from hanging around a gang too long.

Juan's lips formed into a spit pose.

The deputy raised his hand. "You spit—I hit."

Juan swallowed and sulked back into the chair. He turned to Frank and Rob.

"Be outside if you need anything," the deputy said, before closing the door.

"*Si tu me escupes, te arrepentiras,*" Rob told Juan.

Speaking Spanish fluently wasn't Frank's forté, but he could follow it well enough. Juan had been warned: if he spit at them, he would come to regret it.

Juan answered with only a nod. His squinty eyes shifted back and forth from Rob to Frank, never blinking.

Frank laid out the photo lineup sheet he'd printed—all red-headed women. He tapped the sheet. "Ask him if any of these are the woman he saw at Ricardo's house that night."

Rob rattled off Frank's question in Spanish, also tapping the lineup sheet.

Juan leaned over as if to examine the photos, but instead, spit on Rob's lapel. Just as a smile crossed Juan's lips, Rob slapped it off. Juan crashed onto the floor. The chair fell on top of him.

Frank yawned and didn't move—no need. Rob would handle it. Guy hated to be disrespected—especially by other Latinos. Rob was a proud man, and a proud Mexican-American. He wanted all Latinos to succeed. When he encountered one who he believed gave the race a bad rap, it really pissed him off. And when one ignored or insulted him, he wasn't above a good attitude adjustment.

The door busted open and the deputy looked in. Juan slumped

on the floor; the red outline of four fingers spread across his left cheek and a drop of blood forming in the corner of his mouth.

The deputy grinned and looked from Rob to Frank. "Everything okay in here?"

Rob smiled and rubbed his hands down the side of his trousers. "Fell off his chair. We're fine, thanks."

The deputy nodded and retreated as Rob wiped the spit off his suit. His smile faded as he stood over Juan. In Spanish he spoke in low threatening tones. Rob's eyes did that thing when he got really angry. They became two black holes drilled into his face. If you looked close enough, you could see your own death.

"Do it again and you'll be swallowing those front teeth," Rob said.

The banger's lips and chin trembled and he lowered his head.

"Okay, let's try once more." Rob stuck the photo lineup to the guy's face. "Do any of these women look like the one you saw at Ricardo's house?" Rob's tone was so threatening that Frank almost confessed.

Juan flashed a hateful look and didn't answer.

"Okay, have it your way," Rob said. He had an evil expression as he pointed at Juan. "Do you know what's going to happen when we walk out of here?"

Juan looked back and forth from Frank to Rob, but still said nothing.

"So, let me tell you." Yeah, the son-of-Satan grin set the right mood. "When we walk out I'm going to put my arm around your shoulder," Rob said, "and in Spanish say, thanks, that really helped us identify them. We'll have you out of here in no time."

Juan's eyes widened.

"And do you know what's going to happen after that?" Rob asked. "Sometime tonight, or maybe tomorrow night after the story gets circulated, you'll receive a visit from some gang members. They'll have something sharp. So, what do you think they'll cut off? Your tongue or something more important?"

Juan swallowed hard and his shoulders tightened.

Rob stuck the photo lineup back to his face. "Last chance. See any of these women at the house that night?"

Juan thought a second and nodded. He laid his finger on the fifth photo—the one of Dr. Alma Hawkins.

20

Rob got home that Friday evening a few minutes after six. As usual, the start of the weekend traffic made the drive to Mesquite just a little more challenging. He dropped his keys in the tray on the table and listened. The house was dark and quiet except for muffled voices coming from the family room. He sniffed—no sign of cooking.

Rob followed the sound around the corner and found Carmen lying on the couch watching the evening news. Only the fading light through the blinds outlined her body under a blanket. At first he believed she was sleeping, but the closer he got, the more apparent it became that her dark brown eyes were open. He squatted down in front of her.

"Hey."

"Hey, yourself." A quick grin moved across her lips.

The place had a stale, musty odor. Rob gently raked her black hair to one side and gave her a kiss. "You feel okay, babe?"

"Just tired—no energy."

Rob looked around the room. "Eaten anything today?"

Her eyes narrowed and the lids fluttered a second. "I think I ate lunch."

Rob stroked her back. "Can I get you anything?"

She shook her head. "Nuh-uh."

He made his way into the kitchen. A pile of dirty breakfast dishes lay in the sink. No sign of any lunch dishes. He checked the daily pill box he'd bought her. All four pills of today's medication were still there. He exhaled and his fist tightened. Didn't know whether to be angry with him or her. She should have remembered. But he'd been so busy he hadn't thought to call and remind her. *Shit.*

He shook out three pills and poured a glass of water. She sat up as he approached. "You forgot, again," he said, holding out the pills.

She gave her scolded puppy look. "Sorry." She downed the pills with one gulp of water.

Rob flopped on the couch and she snuggled closer, laying her head on his chest. No one spoke for several minutes, but Rob's mind ran a hundred miles a second. Would the depression ever stop? Would the doctors ever find the right combination of medications? *Would Carmen ever remember to take them?*

After a half hour, his stomach rumbling gave him an idea. Going out wasn't an option, he didn't want to leave her alone and get takeout, and they both hated delivered pizza for dinner. "Hey, what say I boil a few hot dogs, toast some buns, and dig out the diced onions and relish? I could open a can of chili and it would be just like an evening at the ball park."

"Umm, sounds delicious."

Rob shifted to stand, but Carmen held him tight around his waist. "Can we just lie here a few more minutes?"

"Sure, babe." For her, he would stay there forever.

21

Saturday morning, Frank did his yoga routine in his living room. The early morning sun outlined his lean body in shadow on the floor. Good way to check your form without using a mirror.

After a half hour, he made coffee. Frank took his coffee two ways. At the office and restaurants—black. But at home, when he had time to fuss over it and get it just right—*café au lait*. Frank loved the simplicity of the French press. He ground the fresh beans and added them to the press, followed by a large cup of almost boiling water. He took another cup of whole milk and set it on the stove—low heat. Five minutes later he pressed the coffee and added the milk with a tablespoon of unprocessed sugar.

He sat on the balcony wearing a robe over his gym shorts and watched a plane on final to DFW. Alma popped back into his mind. Actually, since the gangster picked her out of the lineup yesterday, she'd never really left. If Ricardo's killing was the instigating event that kicked off the whole gang war, what did that have to do with Alma? If Frank had been wrong about seeing her at Ricardo's, why did the gangster pick her out of the lineup? Just how many coincidences would he tolerate in this case before throwing the bullshit flag? There had to be a link between a prestigious university professor and a notorious drug gang leader.

Frank ate breakfast, showered, and spent an hour in Central Market. His chef's eye picked out the freshest produce and the best cuts of meat. And of course, he took advantage of every sample. A lazy guy could make the most of this; if he showed up at a different Central Market for each meal and ate all the samples offered, he'd never have to cook again.

By the time Frank left, he was too full for lunch. He popped everything into his refrigerator except the steak. When he'd called Debbie a few days ago and asked her to dinner, it went without saying she'd want Yucatan pork steak.

Debbie was one of the high-end call girls he dated. Of all the women he knew, she was the most like him. They talked for hours about her studies at the university, where she was pursuing a master's in Medieval European history. She wanted to be a professor someday, but didn't have the funds. Figured out that with a face and body like hers, she was literally sitting on a gold mine. When she wasn't in class, she turned thousand-dollar tricks for out-of-town businessmen. Her moniker was *Debbie loves Dallas.*

She got plenty of attention, but sometimes, all she wanted was someone to talk to. Treat her like a lady. Cook a delicious meal and give her a full-body massage. She reciprocated with favors. Should have been a contortionist.

Frank mixed the grapefruit, orange, and lime juices with four minced scallions and two ground jalapenos. He washed the steaks, poured the marinade over the meat, and covered it with Saran Wrap before setting it into the refrigerator. Settled on his sofa, he opened the laptop browser, intending to check his Gmail. Instead, he typed in the word "witch" into Google.

The screen filled with more references to witches, witchcraft, and Wicca than Frank had expected. Who knew? Witches were big! Sorcery was one of the few things Frank knew little about. Never wanted to know. He'd read books on every topic that he believed might help him someday in police investigations. Witches never made the cut—superstition and fantasy that had no bearing on modern life. After reading for a couple of hours, Frank had to reassess his belief. Much more relevant today than he'd figured. Was that really a pentagram in Alma's backyard, or just a star?

There were a few things that especially drew Frank's attention. The first was the description of the "Green Witch." An herbalist, healer, wise woman. Lover of nature and plants, and has a special relationship with all animals. The second, the description of a witch's familiar: a demon or spirit that takes the shape of an animal. A servant the witch can command to do her bidding. Frank's thoughts defaulted back to that night at Ricardo's—the tabby bolting from his bedroom. Alma's tabby rubbing its cheek on his pant's leg when he visited her.

The only common dominator between the various types of witches appeared to be their Grimoire, or *Book of Shadows*. A Wicca book of religious texts and magical rituals.

He checked the clock. *Crap.* He'd been reading all afternoon. Debbie would be here in a couple of hours.

An hour and a half hour later, Frank had straightened up the place, decanted a bottle of red, and taken a shower. He shaved extra close for Debbie. Girl wouldn't tolerate stubble.

Debbie was a down-to-earth person and didn't like fancy things like most girls in her profession. Born and raised in Weatherford, she attended college in Fort Worth and worked in Dallas. Frank had tried all the fancy foods on her. She didn't care for French, wasn't especially taken by Mediterranean, and hated Asian. Her taste ran simple—the stuff she grew up with living on her family ranch.

Frank had just put the new potatoes to boil, turned the yellow squash and onions on low simmer, and poured his first glass of red when the doorbell rang.

Debbie was barely five feet tall, and she wore a short, purple, strapless dress that showed off her ample bosom. Her long amber hair fell loosely around her bare shoulders.

She stood on her toes, wrapped her arms around Frank's neck, and kissed him long and hard before coming up for air. The naughty grin cracked the corners of her mouth.

"Thanks, I really needed that," she whispered.

Frank closed the door. "You need a drink."

Debbie tossed her clutch on the sofa and sniffed. "Umm. Something smells good."

Frank had his back to her as he poured another glass of red. The warmth of her hands sliding up his un-tucked Polo startled him. She massaged his chest and laid her cheek against his back.

"My week's been so crazy, Franklin. I couldn't wait for tonight," she said.

Frank expected this. Many of his lady friends used him as a sounding board for complaints and ideas. They viewed coming over as a cathartic experience. He never argued, never judged, and always comforted them. She was the only one who insisted on calling him by his Christian name—Franklin. He wished she'd stop—reminded him of his mom. He turned and handed her the wine. "Just relax, babe. Put yourself in my hands tonight."

She took a sip. "That's my plan."

Frank had preheated the grill and taken the pork steaks out of the refrigerator an hour earlier. He slipped his chef's apron over his head and carried the meat onto the patio. As he laid each piece on the red-hot grill, a sweet, smoky sizzle rose into the air.

Debbie loved the patio hammock. And, like a few others, it was her favorite place to make love. There was something about doing the wild thing twenty stories above the city, in an ocean of plants with all the lights out, gazing at the stars and planes lining up for a landing, that appealed to her. Frank did his best to dissuade it. Getting too old for that type of behavior. Besides, did insurance even cover an injury from that? He seared the steaks on each side, poured marinade over them, and lowered the temperature.

The aroma caused Debbie's eyes to glaze over.

"So, how's school?" He settled himself in a lounger a few feet from the grill.

Debbie stretched in the hammock. "All good. Finishing my master's this semester."

"That's great," he said. He paused a few seconds, deciding on whether to ask the next question. "I was wondering . . . in your medieval history classes, have you studied witches?"

She laughed. "What an unusual question." Her brow pinched. "How much wine did you have before I arrived?"

Frank held up his glass. "This is the first. Scout's honor." He crossed all the fingers on his left hand, making sure she saw.

She giggled. "You're a hoot."

Frank eyed her. "No, seriously. I'm curious."

Debbie took a sip of red. "So I assume you're asking about supposedly real witches as opposed to the legendary Hansel and Gretel type."

"Yup." Frank relaxed back into the chair.

She flashed him a skeptical look. "Medieval history is filled with witches. The *Malleus Maileficarum* written in 1486 by two monks was basically a witch hunter's guide. England, Germany, France, Scotland, all cited it for murdering hundreds of people—mostly women. Joan of Arc was probably the most famous."

She paused to take another long sip, wiping off what dribbled down her chin. Frank always dribbled when he tried drinking in that wretched hammock. This, to his way of thinking, was another excellent reason to toss the thing in the trash.

Debbie's information pretty much lined up with what he'd been reading all afternoon.

"But the biggest blow to witches happened long before that," she said. "The *Malleus Maileficarum* just legalized it. The death knell was the rise of Christianity."

Frank's mind had drifted. He sat a little straighter and said, "Huh?"

Debbie looked over the rim of the glass and took another long swallow. The wine had relaxed her. All the tension in her face and body had faded away as the sweet warmth of the grape took hold.

"The Druids were the religious leaders of the Celts." Debbie raked a loose hair from her eyes. "The first members of the Druid priesthood were all women. When Christianity was introduced into the British Isles, the Celts moved out of sight—into the caves and woods. They were a very spiritual people, and not as sexually repressed as their Christian neighbors."

Frank kept listening as he turned the steaks and added the last of marinade. "You sure know a lot about witches."

Debbie kicked her legs over each side of the hammock, resting her toes on the concrete. A sliver of white thong showed under the short dress.

Yeah, she's relaxed.

She released a sensual groan and focused on him. "Do we have to keep talking about this?"

"Just finish your thought. The pork still needs a few minutes."

She finished her glass before her thought and held it out to him. He refilled it and took his seat.

"Anyway, I edited a dissertation for a friend of mine. *The Demise of Sorcery in the Christian Age.* Used to edit lots of dissertations and term papers for extra money," she said, slurring her last few words. She got this way faster than anyone Frank knew. One or two glasses and she'd hit her limit.

"I believe you ended on sexual repression," Frank said.

She nodded and a goofy grin spread across her lips. She took another long swallow. "Yeah." She spoke slowly, concentrating on each word. "Sexuality was encouraged in their religion. Fertility was prized. A gal with two or three youngins was paid a higher dowry than virgins."

Frank grimaced. *Oh, no.* Debbie had slipped from her cosmopolitan ways back into the full Texas twang and Southern slang. He'd better get some food in her fast.

"So," she continued, "as Christianity grew, Celtic paganism retreated. The Christians managed to reduce the Druid priesthood to an instrument of the devil—witches and sorceries." She slurred her words again, giggled and wiggled a finger in his direction. "And that's how you took down a competitive religion in the old days." Debbie hiccupped, put a hand to her mouth, and sat up. "Can we eat now?"

Frank drained the squash, poured the sautéed onions and butter over the potatoes, and popped the buttered French bread in the oven while he let the steaks rest. Debbie helped herself to another glass of red. If she kept this up, her slurring would become so pronounced that she may as well be speaking in tongues. When her back was turned, Frank hid the wine. They dined on the small patio table listening to Van Morrison sing "Moondance" as the sun set. Debbie sobered up a little more with each bite. Frank took the dishes to the kitchen and filled the dishwasher while she excused herself to the bathroom. He'd had made a pecan pie and bought a pint of Blue Bell ice cream for the occasion. He slid the pie into the oven to warm it up.

A noise from behind drew his attention to the hall. Debbie had shucked the dress and wore nothing but the white thong. Frank turned off the oven and meandered to her. She was more sober now, and when she kissed him, the mint taste of his bathroom mouthwash tingled his lips. She stepped back and ran her palm over his cheeks and chin.

"Did you shave extra close?" she whispered. Her hand dropped down to the front of the thong.

"Sure did."

She smirked. "Devil," and led him to the hammock.

* * *

Rob relaxed in his favorite recliner in the living room. He had a mini-cooler packed with ice and beer on one side of the chair and a small trash can on the other. He dropped the empty beer can into the trash and retrieved a new one from the icy water in the cooler. Popping the top, he took an extra long swallow.

It wasn't fair. It wasn't fair what happened to him and Carmen. They'd been married over twenty years. Their kids had left for college and now they were officially empty-nesters. This should have been their best years since falling in love back in high school. They had the time and money to travel, see the world, and act like irresponsible teenagers again. They could make love every night and walk around the house naked if they wanted—except for one thing.

Carmen's clinical depression.

Every time the doctors believed they had a good handle on the problem, Carmen would slip back into a full-blown episode. The drugs were the sticking point. They assured him when they found the right pharmaceutical combination, all would be well. They'd been saying that for the last two years. Some days, Carmen walked around like a zombie, so medicated she didn't know whether to fix breakfast or dinner.

Rob turned up the volume on the movie a little. Really didn't need to. He'd seen *Lonesome Dove* so many times he could read the actors' lips. He and Carmen had lain on the sofa until she went to bed an hour ago. He held her and they watched the movie in her favorite spoon position. He loved her so much. Why . . . why couldn't they have a normal life? She hardly spoke when she went into a tailspin like this. Her silence hurt him more that her crying. And there was plenty of that. No matter what, he intended to see this through. He just needed to hold on a little longer.

Rob torqued the volume another notch and took a sip of beer. His favorite part of the movie was coming up, that part where Captain Woodrow Call says, "I hate rude behavior in a man. Won't tolerate it." *Yeah, I should have been a Texas Ranger. Those were the good old days.*

Rob couldn't help from feeling guilty. Carmen was the one hurting, and all he could do was cry in his beer because he wanted their life to be more normal. At work he kept up a good front. Frank knew Carmen had problems, but Rob hadn't said a word about the latest round. No use putting any more stress on his partner than necessary. Rob would show up for work Monday morning and wouldn't say a word about Carmen. Then he and Frank would solve this sniper case. He believed that. He had to believe that. Man has to believe in something.

* * *

Sunday morning Frank cracked his eyes open and gazed at a foot. That was one of the trade-offs of having Debbie over—restless sleeper. She'd pull covers, change positions, and stretch herself across the entire bed. Not bad if you're used to sleeping with a spider monkey. Frank didn't mind being awoken a half dozen times. A night with Debbie was worth no sleep.

He unwound himself from the tangled, twisted sheets and got up. After slipping on a pair of gym shorts, he headed to the living room. Halfway through his yoga routine Debbie tiptoed into the kitchen and started the coffee. By the time he finished, she handed him a cup.

"Didn't really understand our conversation last night," she said, taking a sip. "Witches? Really?"

Frank kept his answer short. "Just curious, that's all."

They dropped the subject and enjoyed the rest of the morning on the balcony. After lunch, she headed back to Fort Worth, and Frank spent the afternoon and evening reading his suspense/thriller novel. Anything to keep his mind off the case, Alma, and witches. After the harrowing night, Frank hit the sack early. He'd fallen into a deep sleep by ten o'clock.

22

Monday morning, Frank got up and did his yoga with the first rays of the sun illuminating his living room. He needed to dig into Alma's business a little deeper, and her home was the best place to start. Had to wait for her to go to work, so he piddled around his house for a couple of hours until traffic settled. The thought occurred to him that he may have compromised himself by his intimate affair with her. But was she really a suspect? Probably not. Perhaps he should have been more bothered by the prospect, but it really didn't trouble him at all.

Strange. Maybe I am a bad man.

About nine o'clock he called CIU and told them he'd be in later—running out a lead. Frank drove to Alma's. No car in the driveway and no movement in the windows. He pulled in back and gazed around, listening. All quiet. He wandered through the lush garden. An intoxicating flower fragrance filled the air as he headed toward the pergola. Something had happened to him the night he came to dinner. Something strange, yet wonderful. Everything seemed so perfect that evening. Her lips were sweeter, the wine richer, and the sex had left him with an exhausted ecstasy. Had he been drugged? No, not drugged—enchanted. That was the only term that could describe it. *Enchanted.*

There was something about the garden that didn't occur to him at the time. Many of the plants seemed unfamiliar. While he'd never admitted it to his fellow cops, Frank was a plant person. Most police enjoyed fishing, hunting, and playing with some kind of ball. Frank liked plants. The feel, colors, and varying textures of a well kept garden filled him with joy. Not a very macho thing for a big city cop. But he never cared what others thought. He had a very *laissez-faire* attitude about most things. A long time ago he'd decided not to judge—lest he be judged.

He enjoyed going to the Dallas Arboretum twice a year. Every spring and fall he'd spend the day walking around the grounds admiring the plantings. He never asked anyone to join him because he didn't want to be rushed. For hours he'd sit watching a stream meander through a grove of ferns, and just think. On his patio he'd created a private forest of potted plants and hanging baskets. He was well versed in most plants native to Dallas and Texas, but some of Alma's stumped him. Something nagged at the back of his mind that this was important.

He opened his camera app and took pictures of a dozen trees, shrubs, and flowers he'd never seen before. Behind him, the sound of shrill giggling floated in the air. He snapped his head around, looking for the source—it stopped. He lowered the phone and scanned the area, then strolled in the direction of the laughter, his foot bumping a brightly colored gnome along the path. It tumbled over. Frank set it back in place and another round of giggling sounded from behind him. When he spun around, his heart almost stopped. Along the path he'd just traveled were three additional gnomes, blocking the way. Frank's skin tingled and his stomach twisted. He wasn't alone. He drew his gun and listened for movement. More giggling— from every direction. Dozens of voices formed a chorus that became louder every second. The air seemed alive with electricity and energy, as if something would explode. Frank took the short way back to the rear of the cottage, keeping a wary eye on who might be following. As he approached the back door, the cat he'd seen the night he came to Alma's, the one that looked like the cat at Ricardo's, raised its back, bared its teeth, and hissed.

Frank bolted awake and stared at his bedroom ceiling. *A dream . . .*

a stupid dream. His eyes widened at the apparition at the foot of his bed. It was Alma, dressed in a ghostly white Druid robe with the hood partially covering her head. Her red hair bloomed from around the edges of the hood, yellow rose petals lay sprinkled throughout her long red curls. Her eyes had a stern look, and her index finger rested against her lips. She didn't speak, but a *shushing* sound resonated from her lips.

Frank rolled over and grabbed his mini-flashlight from the night stand. He turned back and switched on the beam. In the one second he took his eyes off the apparition, it had vanished. Frank turned on the table lamp and searched the whole condo—nothing.

As he laid his head back on his pillow, he woke up for real. Focusing on the same dark ceiling again, he tried to catch his breath, his pulse pounding in his head. He turned the lamp on. The flashlight hadn't been moved. Had he just dreamed about having a dream? He stood and ran a hand down his face and searched the condo—nothing. The doors remained locked and bolted.

Get a grip, Frank . . . a big grip.

Already four fifteen in the morning. May as well start the day.

As he worked out, showered, and ate breakfast, the dream stayed with him. What was the apparition trying to tell him? To be quiet, not to tell something to someone, or just be careful what you say? She'd appeared to him when he'd been snooping around her garden. Actually, that wasn't a bad idea—looking around Alma's while she was at work.

He called CIU and told Terry he'd be in later—checking out a lead. Frank kept pinching himself and doing other things to cause discomfort to make sure he wasn't dreaming again. *Is this how schizophrenia starts?*

He spent a couple of hours killing time, waiting until he was sure Alma had left home. His piddling consisted of exactly the same actions he'd taken in the dream. It was disconcerting, a Bill Murray, *Groundhog Day* moment. At nine o'clock he opened his door to leave, making sure to pinch himself before stepping out. He searched his pocket for his car keys. *Crap, where are they?* Frank traipsed back into his bedroom and scooped the keys off the dresser. As he turned back to the door, something caught his eye in the shadows at the foot of the bed, half hidden by the covers. Frank's breath caught. *No, that couldn't be possible.*

A yellow rose petal?

Frank stopped breathing as he approached the object. The pulse in his head pounded when he slowly bent down to retrieve it. As he focused in the dim light, he released the breath.

A Post-it Note.

∗   ∗   ∗

Paul Sims took the elevator to the first floor and rushed down the hall. He tilted the Cracker Jack box to his mouth, crunching as he walked. When he marched into the Youth Division, Detective Jeanine Crawley met him.

"Where is he?" Sims asked, his head on a swivel.

She got in step with him. "Interview room two."

"You're not jerking my chain are you? Did he really say that?"

She gave him the look. "I told you what exactly what he told me."

Sims tilted the box one last time and dropped it in a garbage can outside the interview room. He turned back to Crawley. "Does he have a record? Is there an attorney in there with him?"

"Paul, he's only seven years old, for God's sake." She handed Sims the folder and he scanned the preliminary interview report.

"Oh. Yeah," he said, and shook his head. *Naw, this isn't possible.* "I still don't believe it."

Crawley posted her fist on her hips. "Some thanks I get. The second I heard the story I thought of your investigation. His mom says the kid has a touch of autism. She's pretty upset, so be cool. You know how you are."

Sims shifted his gaze from her to the doorknob and tucked the folder under his arm. Opening the door, a young woman with short brown hair sat beside the child, stroking the back of his head.

Someone had given him a box of orange juice, and he slurped it through a straw. He barely noticed Sims entering.

"Good afternoon. I'm Detective Paul Sims," he said, shaking the woman's hand.

Her tense shoulders relaxed a little. "Hello, I'm Bea Harper." She pulled a loose strand of brown hair behind her ear and eyed Sims with a cautioned stare.

Sims smiled and bent lower. "And who do we have here?"

The kid disengaged his lips from the straw long enough to say, "Ronnie."

The little guy had freckles and a Dennis the Menace wild cowlick in back that stood straight up.

"Hello, Ronnie," Sims shook the small hand. "Can we talk for a few minutes?"

This time the kid only nodded, preferring to finish the juice and not waste time answering.

Sims sat across from the woman and child and opened the folder.

"I would have come down sooner," Mrs. Harper said, "but to tell you the truth I really didn't believe him. That is, not until I heard about that man being shot just down the street."

Sims grinned. "That's okay. You're here now." He shifted in the chair and leaned closer to the kid. "Ronnie, can you tell me in your own words what you saw?"

Ronnie nodded. "Uh-huh."

Sims fished his pen out and waited. The kid just stared at him. After several seconds, Sims said, "Okay . . . so what did you see? From the beginning. Don't leave anything out."

A playful look enveloped the small, impish face, and he handed his empty orange juice box to his mother.

"I was in my ship looking for the enemy when I saw her."

Sims cocked an eyebrow. "Whoa, you were where?"

Mrs. Harper stroked the child's head again and grinned. "He has a vivid imagination—too many movies. His ship is a tree in our backyard. Likes to climb it and play pirate."

Sims winked. "Gotcha."

Ronnie cupped his hands like he was holding a spy glass. "So anyway, me and Captain Jack Sparrow were scanning the seas when we saw her."

"Her? Who's her?" Sims asked.

Ronnie gave him a sour look. Probably hated being interrupted. "The lady."

"Oh, okay—the lady." Sims nodded in agreement.

Ronnie positioned his hands again. "She leaned against the back fence of that place they have the old cars."

Mrs. Harper said, "Jacob's Spare Car Parts is behind our house. Lots of wrecked and salvaged cars there."

Sims recorded it in his notebook.

Ronnie leaned in closer and his eyes grew wide. "She had one of those guns like the American Sniper used. Long, with a thing on the end."

Sims took a breath and sat back. His mouth went dry. "Go on."

Ronnie was in his own world now. His little eyes glistening, reliving the glory of the day. He repositioned his hands, like holding a rifle, and closed one eye as he aimed the imaginary weapon at Sims. "And POW, she shot it."

Sims jumped involuntarily. He was afraid to ask, but did. "What did she shoot?"

Ronnie shrugged. "Don't know. Couldn't see that far."

Sims checked Mrs. Harper's address in Detective Crawley's notes. Just a few blocks from where the banger got splattered against the back of the club. He glanced up, and Ronnie had this look of expectation.

"So . . . you saw her actually pull the trigger?" Sims asked.

"Yup." Ronnie smiled.

"I should have come down sooner, but when he told me I thought he was only goofing off." Mrs. Harper sat on the edge of her chair, wringing her hands.

Ronnie's brow tightened as he turned to his mom. "I don't goof off."

"Did it make a loud noise?" Sims asked. "You know, when she shot."

"Nuh-uh, like I said, it had one of those things on the front of the gun."

"A suppressor?"

Ronnie squinted. "A what?"

"You know, a silencer, so it wouldn't make any noise."

The kid nodded and flashed another smile. "Yeah, right."

Sims patted the kid on the shoulder. "Think you'd better tell me what this lady looked like. How old?"

Ronnie shrugged. "I don't know."

"Older or younger than your mom."

"About the same."

"Hair?"

"Yes."

"Yes, what?"

"Yes, she had hair," Ronnie said, crossing his arms.

His innocent expression almost made Sims laugh. He repositioned in the seat. This would take longer than he thought.

Forty-five minutes later, Detective Sims reviewed the notes as the kid and his mom walked out. Now this made no sense. Nothing the little guy said was believable, except the part about the rifle and leaning against the fence. The part about the short-haired blonde lady, nice dress, and Sunday go-to-meeting shoes, which Ronnie's mother interrupted to mean "high heels," sounded made-up. But there were other things in the kid's eyewitness account that made Sims wonder.

Frank described a redhead at Ricardo's house. Now a blonde was involved. Wig, or dyed her hair? Frank and Rob would love this.

23

Alma Hawkins smiled at Dr. Plebe sitting across from her in her office. He was a kindly old soul, but he got on her nerves. He prattled on and on about the new guidelines in the religious studies department, and she quickly tired of listening, so she just nodded. If he wasn't such a good mentor and hadn't been such a comfort after Clare's death, she would have blown him off. In those dark days after burying her daughter, Alma had told him things about herself . . . things she now regretted having shared.

". . . and the degree hours are all out of balance," he said. "Don't you think?"

Alma hadn't heard a word he'd just said. She showed her best serious look and nodded. "Absolutely."

He nodded back. "That's just what I told them."

She touched a stack of papers on her desk and made a show of checking her watch. "I really must get to these. Only have two hours."

His brow relaxed. "Of course, I understand." He rose. "Thanks for the talk."

After he left, she pulled the papers in front of her and her computer chimed. She opened the browser and logged onto her home alarm system. With hidden cameras on the front and back porch equipped with motion detectors, she got a notification anytime someone walked up.

She studied the figure for a moment. Well, well, well . . . wonder what Detective Frank Pierce wants?

Alma had thought about him a couple of times since their tryst. Best lover she ever had. Shame she didn't want a man in her life at the moment. He would be a nice pet to keep around.

Frank cupped his hands over the front door window and put his face against it. Moments later his reflection showed in the rear window.

Yes, a shame. But she'd gotten what she needed from him. Her hand rested on her stomach, and she took in a long satisfied breath.

Her plans didn't include staying in Dallas, anyway. Always planned to move on. Staying in one place too long came with hazards. She already had Dartmouth wooing her to relocate. A more northern exposure would be better.

Frank stepped back from the door and swung his head toward the back garden. Alma leaned closer to the monitor. What was he doing? He took out his cell phone and strolled down the garden path. She considered driving home to confront him but changed her mind. Better try and figure out what he was up to first.

* * *

"Bullshit!" Rob said and tossed the report on Sims' desk.

Sims sat back in his chair, twisted a piece of taffy out of the wrapper, and popped it into his mouth. "That's what I thought when I heard it."

Frank read the report for the second time, his mind calculating how something like this could be. He flipped back and forth from one page to the other. Was it Alma? Wearing a blonde wig?

"So do you believe him?" Rob asked.

Sims chewed a couple of times and swallowed. "Story sounds good, until you get to the part about the dressed-up blonde with a silenced rifle." Sims grinned and popped another piece of taffy.

Rob looked over at Frank.

Frank laid the report on the desk. The last thing he needed was a new wrinkle in the investigation. "Congratulations, Sims. You just took a complicated case and made it more complicated."

Sims licked the tips of his fingers. "Don't quite know how to handle this. Any ideas? Can't say I want to buy in on the theory of a hit man who is a hit woman, especially one who dresses up to kill people."

When Sims said "hit man," Rob focused on the desk and didn't look up.

Frank cleared his throat. "What I'm about to tell you is on the Q.T. We received information about a contract on Antoine Levern out of New York. Came from a confidential federal source."

Sims' spine stiffened. "Go on."

"All we have is a name. Jesse," Rob said. "That's the one with the contract."

Sims frowned. "So when were you going to tell me about this?"

Rob hung his head again. "Federal wire tap, Sims. We were keeping it in CIU until we got a confirmation."

Frank stood. "It was only a rumor, but now . . ."

"Now it's real," Sims finished the sentence.

"Yeah," Frank admitted.

"So, is this thing the kid saw a B.S. story, or what?" Sims asked.

"It sounds B.S. except the part about her pocketing the empty shell case," Frank said. "That's not a detail a seven-year-old would understand, or make up, unless he actually watched it happen."

"My thinking exactly," Sims agreed. "If this kid is making this up, he's wasting his time in second grade. He should be writing scripts for Hollywood."

"So do we start looking for a blonde with a rifle, and forget about the redhead?" Rob asked.

Frank stared morosely at the desk and his voice was a whisper. "That's not the question." He met eyes with Sims and Rob. "The question is: how are they related?"

* * *

"A female shooter? Is that what you just said?" Edna asked. She sat behind her desk and rapidly clicked her pen—an aggravating habit that made Rob crave a dip of Copenhagen. Rob had lost the coin flip, which meant he had to tell her about what Sims just told them minutes earlier. Rob had lost a lot of flips lately. He was starting to wonder if Frank was somehow cheating.

Frank lounged in the full slouch at the other end of the lecture sofa and remained silent. Rob was convinced Frank wouldn't show the kid the photo lineup he'd shown the gangster the other day. To do that would entail explaining why he'd included a SMU professor as a suspect. Terry sat in his usual chair, pursing his lips and shaking his head.

"Never heard that one before," Terry said. "But that part about pocketing the shell case has me concerned."

Rob didn't reply.

Edna broke the stalemate. "Okay, for the sake of argument, let's say there was a woman who did the shooting. A woman with short blonde hair." Edna rested her elbows on the desk and leaned forward. "We already have one woman with long red hair. If the kid is correct, is it the same woman? Has to be. Based on precedent, it's unusual for there to be two women as suspects in a murder investigation." She glanced at Terry for confirmation.

He nodded, but it was a tentative nod.

"You guys making any progress on identifying the red head?" she asked. She looked back and forth from Rob to Frank. When neither answered, she said, "My gut tells me if *we* can identify and locate the red head, *we* could figure this out."

When Edna used the word "we" that way, Rob took it to mean, "Get off your asses and find her." Frank still hadn't spoken. He sank deeper into Edna's couch.

"Okay, guys, let's go," Terry said, and stood. He led the way back to Frank and Rob's cubes. Terry leaned against Frank's desk and glanced over his shoulder at the glass wall separating Edna's office from the main area. Edna was on the phone, scribbling something on a notepad.

Terry leaned closer and whispered, "Stay focused on the woman at Ricardo's. We have no way of knowing if these two things are related, or if there even is a blonde with a rifle. Kid's mother said he watched too many movies. Let Sims follow up on that lead. That's homicide's job anyway. If we go off in several directions, we'll be chasing our tails and not get anything accomplished. Okay?"

Terry was right, as usual. He'd been around long enough, seen lots of weird shit. He knew how to keep an investigation focused. That was the key. Drill deep into it and see what popped out. But to Rob, this one had a serious problem: the deeper they drilled, the more confusing it became.

A loud clap of thunder sounded outside. Rob jumped, although Frank remained perfectly still and mute. He probably wasn't convinced but didn't want to get into a pissing contest with Edna or Terry over which woman was which. In the years Rob had worked with Frank, his partner had never seemed swayed much by popular opinion. His gift was seeing clues that everyone else saw, but didn't recognize. Frank's eyes always gave his thoughts away if you knew what to look for. Rob studied them. He didn't like what he saw.

Edna rushed out of her office. "Breaking news. Channel Eight just reported what appears to be another gang shooting. Two cars racing down the LBJ Freeway exchanging shots. Hit a car driven by a woman with three kids."

"Oh, hell," Terry mumbled.

Edna's cheeks were red. "Higgins has called a meeting on the sixth floor."

The look on Edna's face reminded Rob of the look death row inmates showed when taking their final walk. She headed for the door. Frank lowered his head and let out a long slow breath. No one could help her now.

24

Antoine Levern sat in his recliner and stared out his third-floor window at the afternoon thunder shower. Sheets of rain drifted over downtown and the dark clouds whirled. Whirling and spinning out of control, just like his life. He had spread around all the money Phil left, plus twice that much of his own, but all his feelers had come back dry. No idea who put the hit on him, or who had the contract, or who blew Leon's head off behind the club the other night. Not even Frank had come up with anything. Antoine accepted the fact he'd done enough bad things in his life that if a hit man whacked him, it would only be poetic justice. But that didn't make it any easier. And this time, he hadn't actually done anything wrong. He was innocent.

"Need anything, Boss?" Tabor asked, walking up.

Levern shook his head. "You got the new guys squared away?"

"Yeah, two stay in the parking lot all the time, keeping an eye on who's coming in. The other two are downstairs, backing up the ones in the restaurant stairwells."

"Think that's enough?"

"More than enough," Tabor said. "It would take an army to get in here."

Levern sucked in a deep shattering breath. "It's not an army I'm worried about—just one guy with a rifle."

Tabor shrugged and chewed a toothpick. "Think you should be sitting beside that window then?"

Levern stretched his leg and touched the glass with the toe of his shoe. "Bullet proof, and reflects out. No one can see in."

Tabor shrugged again and dropped his hands in his pockets. "Okay, call if you need something." He meandered toward the stairwell.

"Hey," Levern said, "you know one day you'll have your own gang. Might even take over from me when I retire. I won't do this forever."

A knowing grin swept across Tabor's face. "Yeah, Boss. I know—someday."

"Thanks. You're the only one I can really count on. The rest are just punks."

Tabor shuffled his feet and removed the toothpick from his mouth. "That's all I want right now—to learn from you."

After he left, Levern pushed against the window with his toe again and frowned. He stood and slid his chair back into a shadow and settled down, staring at the wet buildings across the skyline. If someone were after him, someone he couldn't get to first, he couldn't let his guard down. Whoever it was wasn't known to the community. Usually, after spreading around a few thousand on the street, he could find out anything. It wasn't working this time. He felt as if some monster was crawling toward him and he kept blasting it, but it just kept coming.

Levern checked his watch. Almost dinner time, but he wasn't hungry. He'd started losing his appetite after Frank's visit. Being a prisoner in your own home wasn't something Levern had ever considered. He'd sit here awhile longer and enjoy the rain.

He rose and switched off the lights in the room, and then walked back to the chair.

* * *

Jesse wrapped herself in the towel and switched on the hair dryer. She fluffed her hair which was bobbed to her chin, with her spare hand and stared in the mirror. Another clap of thunder shook the building. She strolled into her bedroom and gazed out her window at the storm. Sheets of rain blew sideways across the hotel parking lot. She liked the rain.

Pouring a couple of fingers of bourbon, she plopped down in a chair and watched the lightning streak across the sky. Jesse picked up the pile of papers and looked at the names. An explosion of thunder rumbled in the distance, and rain fell so hard cars had to pull over on the street. On a night just like this, not that long ago, she'd learned her own secret. Nothing had been the same since.

* * *

March 2009

The thunder shook Glen's old Chevy truck, the hard rain sounding like a stampede on the roof. Under the camper shell in back, she sat astraddle of him. They were both naked. The smell of old diesel rags mixed with his aftershave lingered in the air as she rocked back and forth, feeling the pleasure wash over her like a great hot wave. He lay on his back panting, both hands caressing her breast. When her climax came, she screamed and fell on him. He took her in his embrace, and they didn't move for a long time.

God, I love him so much.

Another thunder bolt that sounded like an explosion rattled the truck. He moved his hands to her butt and squeezed. With the cold front passing through, the night had a chill. She grabbed the blanket and pulled it over them.

Glen let out a groan. From the outline of his face, she was sure he was smiling. He always had that grin right after. In two months they'd graduate from high school. Glen had taught her about passion and sex. They'd hunted together and been lovers for the last year. Rumor around town had it he was in the market for a ring.

She cuddled closer. "What time are you leaving tomorrow?"

He nuzzled her neck and kissed her ear lobe. "About sun up."

"Wish I were going with you."

"Me too."

"Will I see you when you get back Sunday?" she whispered.

He squeezed her butt again and his pelvis pushed up. One last wave coarsed through her, and she shook.

"I'll see you Sunday night," he said.

She kissed him hard, holding his face in her hands. "I love you."

"I love you," he whispered.

She'd been putting off asking him a question, but now seemed right. She raked his hair from his face and kissed his nose. "When you shoot something, how do you feel?"

"Huh?"

"You know, that second you pull the trigger, how do you feel?"

He laughed. "I don't know. How am I supposed to feel? If I'm on the target range and nail the ten ring, I feel damn good."

Jesse phrased it another way. "No, that's not what I'm talking about. I'm not talking about shooting paper—I'm talking about shooting something alive."

He laughed again. "Well, I feel good if I make a clean shot and drop the animal. Is that what you mean?"

Of course, it wasn't. What she couldn't tell him was that her feelings were *so* different. Shooting prairie dogs that day at Uncle Bill's had been the tip off. When she pulled the trigger, it gave her a thrill. She loved it—looked forward to experiencing it again.

The next day she slept late and helped her mom around the house. Just another ordinary Saturday. Her mother promised to teach her how to make stuffed cabbage—one of Glen's favorites. About lunch, a sheriff's department patrol car pulled into the driveway. Jesse leaned closer to the window as Deputy Rogers got out and walked to the door. Before he could knock, she opened it. His brow wrinkled and he cleared his throat. He removed his hat and hesitated, not letting his eyes meet hers. It was at that exact moment—she knew. He didn't have to explain. Her legs weakened and she leaned against the door frame.

"Jesse, we just got word. Glen was reported killed earlier this morning—DWI on the wrong side of the road hit him up north." The deputy's mouth continued to move, but Jesse couldn't hear the words over the loud roar in her head. Her mind went blank. Her limbs went numb. She clung to the frame, but her legs no longer supported her. She sank to the floor. All her dreams and future destroyed with just a half dozen words. Her soul seemed to leave her body, and she didn't want to live.

Jesse took the last swallow of bourbon and gazed again at the rain-soaked parking lot. The memory was an old one she seldom had anymore, but when it snuck up on her it left her with a hollow, used-up feeling.

*   *   *

Frank was in a full funk this Tuesday morning and hadn't moved in an hour. Rob was sure rigor mortis would soon set in. These semi-catatonic episodes were nothing to be concerned about, but they only added fuel to his colleagues' opinion that Frank could be a bit strange. Rob knew different—he was *very* strange. Frank stared at the blank computer monitor with an empty expression. Who could blame him? This case drove everyone a little crazy. Sims's revelation about the kid who witnessed the hit had probably been the tipping point.

But Rob knew what bothered Frank most. He thought he'd witnessed Dr. Alma Hawkins enter Ricardo's house, and a banger inside had made a positive identification on her. But it was useless information without something else—motive. No connection between her and Ricardo. No one saw her attack him, and no forensic evidence linked her to being there. Because he died an apparent natural death, there was also no murder weapon. All this only went to confirm what Rob knew from the first day of the investigation—case was screwed up. Never should have gotten involved.

Rob went back to work on his report. A half hour later Frank grunted, moved from his slouch position, and sat up straight.

"I need a cherry Coke," Frank said.

When they walked into Sarge's, the man himself was at the bar, in the middle of one of his long stories to a group of D.A. investigators. He acknowledged Rob and Frank with a wave as they sauntered to the last two stools on the end. A big round of laughter barreled from the investigators and Sarge strolled over.

"What'll it be boys?"

"Whiskey for me and my men," Rob said, and slapped his palm on the bar.

Sarge stink eyed him. "Rob, Frank is rubbing off on you more every day. You two need new partners."

"The usual," Frank mumbled.

Sarge shot him a glance. "What's with him?"

Rob said, "No luck on the case. We may have a woman sniper to contend with now."

Sarge's mouth fell open. "Huh?"

Sarge had worked vice his last few years before retirement and had supervised Frank when he worked there. He also saved Frank's life the day he got stabbed. They had this father/son thing going. Frank even wore his hair in the same surfer style as Sarge.

Sarge fixed their Cokes and slid them to the pair. "Sounds more messed up every time I hear it. The media's been having a field day. In every paper—on every channel," Sarge said. "Glad I'm retired."

"Thanks for the reminder," Rob said.

Frank sipped his Coke. "Sarge, you hunt, correct?"

Sarge made a swipe with the towel at some crumbs on the bar. "Yup, every season."

Frank shifted his stare to Rob. "And you hunt?"

"Sure."

Frank studied his glass, running his finger around the top. "So how hard is it to make the shot this shooter made? You know, from a hunter's perspective?" He looked from Rob to Sarge.

Rob shrugged. "That's a tough shot no matter how you slice it."

Sarge said. "Most deer hunters won't even try a shot over one or two hundred yards."

Frank thumbed through his pocket notebook. "If we can believe the kid in the tree, forensics made it a little over seven hundred yards."

Sarge released a low whistle. "And hit the banger between the eyes?"

"Yes," Frank said.

Sarge shot a glance at Rob. He cleared his throat. "You don't get that good from hunting deer. And you don't stay that good unless you practice a lot, or received some kind of special training. Lose your edge pretty quick. That's why hunters brush up on their shooting and re-adjust their scopes at the start of each season."

Frank took a slow drink and sat the glass on the bar. "And where does someone get that kind of special training?"

"Military," Rob said.

"Or police," Sarge added.

Frank sat back and interlaced his fingers. "I'm betting military. And not just an M-16 trained grunt, but a sniper with a special rifle and scope."

Rob shook his head. "Our military doesn't train women as snipers—only guys."

Frank thought a moment, staring at the bar. "So if we did train women, who'd maintain the records?"

Rob shrugged again.

"Good luck trying to find that out," Sarge said, taking another swipe at the crumbs on the bar. His wife Jan handed Rob and Frank their sandwiches. "Even if there is one, bet you can't get them to release that kind of info. They'll probably think you're nuts."

Rob nodded. "Yeah, the army has a school at Benning, and the Corps runs its Scout Sniper School at three or four locations around the country. Doubt any of them will just open up their files for us. Besides, like I said, we don't train women as snipers."

Frank tore a piece of crust from the bread and popped it into his mouth. "Bet I know someone who could get that information."

* * *

There's something about the smell of an old, abandoned house. Jesse lifted her nose and sucked in the odor. Especially one vacated years ago with windows broken out and a leaking roof. The combination of mold, bird crap, and rotting wood impales itself in your olfactory memory. Like the smell of death, it's something you never forget.

Jesse set her foot on the top step of the staircase and examined the dim hall. Filtered light floated through the mildew-stained curtains onto the wall and floor. The cooing of some bird drifted down from above. The inner ceiling had collapsed in places, and the water-stained wooden floor showed evidence of rot. Birds had crapped everywhere. Little white caps on the floor, long dried, outlined their comings and goings.

Jesse's training guided her. *Before utilizing a dwelling for a sniper roost, ensure the structure is secure.* She carried the long cardboard tube under one arm and in the other hand, her most trusted compact pistol—a silenced Ruger 22/45. When discharged, the .22 with the AAC suppressor sounded like a sneeze.

Jesse bent at the knees, silently placing the tube carrying her rifle to the floor. She'd already checked the rooms downstairs and now began a systematic search of the upper floor. She cleared each room using a dynamic entry—quickly bursting in and scanning from left to right with her pistol in the combat shooter position. She checked all the rooms and retrieved her cardboard tube from the hall.

Jesse had an idea of what room she wanted—the one facing northwest. According to her calculations, that gave the best line of sight to the target. She studied the room—nasty. Place stunk. Some critter with fur had built a nest in the corner behind a broken-down cardboard box. Twigs, pieces of paper, and strips of cloth—probably a rat. Droppings were scattered around the nest. In the opposite corner lay an old mattress. Cigarette burns and butts outlined the edges. Several empty rubber packs, together with the same number of used rubbers lay on the floor. But the nastiest thing was an old tampon at the foot of the mattress. Empty beer cans, malt liquor bottles, and whisky bottles littered the place. *Party on, baby.*

She needed a stool or table of some kind. She'd seen a small wooden card table in the room next door. After dragging it into her sniper position and setting it about eight feet from the window, she found an old crate with a faded picture of a bag of oranges on the side and adjusted it behind the table.

She sat. *Perfect height.*

Jesse unpacked the rifle from the tube and extended the Harris bipod at the front. Once she'd positioned it on the table, she strolled to the window. All the panes were broken out but two. Jagged pieces of sharp glass outlined the frame. Staying out of sight, she wiggled the pieces of broken glass until they lifted out. There was no curtain on this window, but shooting from eight feet deep in a room with no light made her invisible to anyone outside.

Jesse uncapped the front and rear scope covers and made an adjustment, bringing the target location into sharp focus. She approached the window once more. A clump of leaves from a tree in the backyard lazily swayed in the breeze. Less than a five-mile-per-hour crosswind. Shouldn't be a big factor, but she'd check it again later. With the pre-shot preparations complete, Jesse checked her watch. He would arrive soon. Time to go to work.

She repositioned herself behind the rifle and gazed through the scope to check the elevation. From her oversized purse she pulled out the range finger and brought the target location into focus. She ranged the distance. Almost nine hundred yards.

When Jesse had first arrived in Dallas, she already had the background info on most of her targets. Old man Gambizi wanted her to go to work rather than screw off doing research. At the prices she charged, she understood why. Still, she'd taken a couple of days to do surveillance on the first few targets to get an idea of where they'd be at certain times. Creatures of habit make it so much easier.

This guy always arrived at six o'clock at the dry cleaners to pick up a young woman—his sister, or more probably, his girlfriend. There were a half dozen open places to park in the lot, but he always chose one of two handicapped spaces near the door. It couldn't have been better. By choosing those spaces, he silhouetted himself perfectly against the sun as it completed its descent in the western sky. All she had to do was make the shot before the woman got in the car.

As Jesse waited, a feeling of doubt washed over her, that little voice that always whispered to her. She'd not felt comfortable at her hotel lately. She'd been a fool letting her temper take control of her at the pool that day with Mr. Minnesota. *Never stand out. Never draw attention to yourself.* Probably time for a new place. Something on the other side of town. Or in another town, perhaps.

Less than ten minutes later, he wheeled into the parking lot in a vintage gold Cadillac—STS. He backed into the closest handicap space and slammed it into park, keeping watch on the cleaner's front door from his side mirror.

Jesse popped a peppermint under her tongue, checked the wind once more, and racked a round into the chamber. She took a deep breath. As she slowly released it, her finger eased back on the trigger, taking up the slack until the rifle fired. She caught him between the temple and ear. He dropped into the seat and the bullet kept going, blasting out the passenger window. A second later the door to the dry cleaners opened and the young woman bounced out, lighting a cigarette. She strolled to the passenger door and started to get in. Her mouth opened into a silent scream, and the cigarette fell from her lips. She backed away from the car and her purse slipped from her arm. People ran out of the cleaners to the woman, who had collapsed in the parking lot.

Jesse had seen enough. She quickly packed up her equipment and headed toward the staircase. When she was halfway down, she glanced at the front door. After clearing the room earlier, she had blocked the door with an old chair. The chair now sat against the wall, a good six feet from the door.

Never heard it open.

Head turning from side to side, she held her breath—listening. Jesse took the silenced pistol from her purse and allowed the purse strap to slide off her shoulder. She eased down the last few steps before silently sitting the cardboard tube with the rifle on the floor. Breathing in slow, shallow breaths, she strained to hear any sound. But it wasn't a sound that gave him away. It was the smell. To her right, from around the corner, came the pungent odor of marijuana.

Jesse moved to the other corner, peeking around it quickly. All clear. She walked through the old dining room into the kitchen. Someone cleared their throat from the other room and she stopped. Keeping the pistol in the combat shooter position, she eased around the corner. He had his back to her. The gangster crouched low to the floor with an automatic pistol in his right hand. He took a last drag on the joint and dropped it on the mildewed carpet.

The sound of distant sirens drifted through the room. Probably ambulance and police heading to the dry cleaners. Jesse took a step, keeping her eyes on the guy. Her foot bumped something beside the fireplace. He looked over his shoulder and caught sight of her. His eyes widened and he spun around. The guy's gun hand came up toward Jesse as she fired. His unexpected movement caused her to miscalculate. The bullet entered just below the left eye. The guy's head slung back as she fired again. The second one hit him in the forehead, and he went limp, falling to the floor.

Jesse moved farther into the room to check him. The next thing she knew something crashed into her from behind. Falling to the floor, she landed on her right side with her pistol underneath her. Another gangster.

The kid grappled with her, slamming her head back into the floor so hard she saw stars. He was young but larger than her. She struggled against him, but it was only a matter of time before he'd win. She pushed his snarling face away from her with her left hand, her right hand and the gun still trapped beneath her. Jesse released the gun and wiggled her hand free. She ran her thumb around her waistband until it found the tactical knife clipped to her pants. She yanked it out while releasing the switch blade.

The kid struck her with his fist in the side of the head just before she jabbed the knife hard into his neck and shoved him to the side.

She was numb from the strike. Jesse lay there unable to move as the gangster clutched his throat and rolled on the floor. A gurgling sound filled the room and blood oozed between his fingers.

After a minute, she pushed farther away from the dying man. *God, I hate using that thing.* Her head throbbed and she spent a moment catching her breath and watching the death throes. He was just a kid, really.

When he stopped moving, she pulled the knife from his neck and cleaned it on an old rag.

Funny, when you stick a knife into someone, they seldom pull it out. It's as if they accept it as part of their bodies. Like pulling it out might end things sooner. People must have crazy thoughts just before dying.

Jesse had long ago stopped attaching emotion to her work. Doing that was crazy. She'd refused contracts before because she didn't believe the targets needed killing, but once the contract was accepted, she carried it out with military precision. Being judge, jury, and executioner suited her. Just like her dad had said. *"If you don't take the power, someone else will."*

No one was as good as her, and she didn't intend to give up one ounce of power. The thought had once crossed her mind that she might be a functioning sociopath, but she quickly dismissed the idea. Crazy thoughts like that could get you killed.

Jesse collected her tube and purse and then headed for the door. From the peephole she watched another gangster leaning against her car parked on the street. Was he with the other guys? She gazed again at the gang-banger as he bent down to put his face against her passenger window. It wouldn't be long before the investigators arrived at the dry cleaners crime scene. Once they decided the shot originated from another place, they'd fan out in an organized search grid looking for the shooter's location. This was the trouble operating in an urban area; you needed someone to watch your six. Doing it alone in a city was ill advised. Doing it in a city in a combat zone—suicide.

Jesse needed to get out of there. The gangster turned toward the house and studied it a few seconds. She laid her equipment on the floor, removed her jacket, blouse, and bra, and opened the door. The guy was still staring at the house when she stepped into the open threshold. His jaw dropped and she smiled, motioning him with her index finger. He looked from one side to the other before strutting up the walk. Jesse picked up the silenced pistol and stepped around the corner before he came in. As the door creaked open and the sound of footsteps drifted through the room, she popped her head around the corner and grinned at him. When he advanced toward her, she shot him between the eyes.

25

Early the next morning Frank and Rob rolled up to the old house where the gangster bodies had been discovered the night before. Rob noted a marked patrol car, a CSU van, and Paul Sims's unmarked car parked along the curb.

Clouds threatened rain again, and a cool north wind made it a good morning for a jacket. Frank was asleep, as usual. Guy took every opportunity to grab a nap.

"Hey, we're here," Rob said.

Frank pulled himself to a seated position and yawned. "Already?"

Rob grabbed his cup of coffee as he got out. Frank snatched up his cup, got out, and did a back stretch against the top of the car.

"I have something you need to put in your Directive to Physician's folder," Rob said as he walked to Frank's side of the car.

Frank took a sip and stared at the house. "What's that?"

Rob led the way up the cracked and overgrown sidewalk. He glanced back over his shoulder as they walked. "Make sure you specify that before they embalm you, they ensure you're not just asleep."

Frank didn't answer.

A uniform officer stood cross-armed at the door. Rob flashed his I.D.; Frank flashed his Shrek donkey smile. The team inside was breaking down the crime scene. All the bodies removed. All the forensic work done. They'd started twelve hours earlier. Paul Sims's voice led Rob around the corner into the old living room.

"Hey, Sims. This your scene?" Rob asked.

Sims disconnected from the call, took the last bite of Twinkie, and strolled toward them. "No, thank God. Edwards got this one. He just went home. Been here all night. Thought I'd stop by for a look. What a mess."

Frank squatted down and examined a blood stain.

"What the hell happened?" Rob asked.

Sims shook his head. "That's what they've been trying to figure out."

Kelly stepped from around the corner, still dressed in his white crime scene Tyvek overalls. He peeled off a blue Latex glove. "Thought I heard your voice," he said to Rob.

"Can you explain this?" Rob asked.

Kelly shrugged. "Gang massacre. That's what they're calling it."

"But who killed who?" Rob asked.

"Whom," Frank said.

Rob shot him a look. "Whatever."

Kelly said, "Still not sure. Found one here," Kelly pointed where Frank had squatted, "and two more around the corner in the den." Kelly motioned and led the way through the dilapidated old kitchen. It had all the charm of a filthy version of *The Addams Family* home.

Rob sniffed. The smells of animals mixed with mold and the metallic odor of blood still hung thick in the air. Frank's sensitive nose had already started twitching. He hated nasty crime scenes. The smells seldom bothered Rob except for bodies that had putrefied. Kelly stopped at the area where the kitchen ended and the den began. He pointed at the floor.

"Appears there was some kind of struggle there. Dead guy had a puncture wound in the neck—knife probably. We didn't find one, so the killer probably took it with him." Kelly wiggled his finger at the fireplace. "Other dead guy was over there. Two bullets to the head. Small caliber. Most likely a .22, same as the guy around the corner."

"Anybody see or hear anything?" Frank asked.

"Talked to Edwards before he left. Lady across the street noticed an older model white sedan parked on the curb in front of the house earlier," Sims said.

"Make? Model?" Rob asked.

"Said all cars look alike to her." Sims grunted. "Anyway, she never saw the driver, but noticed two of the local gangsters go into the house while the car was there. Never saw them leave. When her husband came home from work, she sent him over to check it out. Found the first dead guy and called the police."

Frank slid his hands in his pockets and circled the room. He stopped occasionally and squatted, studying the scene from different angles.

Rob studied him. What's he looking at?

"But that's not the most interesting part," Kelly said.

Frank had been staring at the two blood stains. He turned his head. "Oh, yeah?"

"Yeah." Sims motioned for them to follow, and he led them through the den and up the stairs.

Frank's expression contorted and his nose looked like it would wiggle off his face with every step. The animal feces and mildew stench was stronger up there. Sims led them to a corner bedroom and they followed him inside.

Rob saw it immediately. "Holy shit," he exclaimed.

"What?" Frank asked.

Rob walked to the table and orange crate turned on end. He stood behind the table, bent down, and looked out the window with the broken panes. "Son of a bitch." He looked back at Sims.

Frank stared at the table and crate. "Is this—?"

Rob finished his sentence. "The sniper nest used to kill that gang banger at the dry cleaners yesterday." He squatted down and studied the new footprints on the dusty floor. He traced it them his finger. *Woman's five, maybe a six.* Small—very small. Smaller than Carmen's. Had he screwed up the other day when he made the patent statement about the military not training women as snipers? He hadn't been in the military for sixteen years. Things were changing fast. Things changed now in sixteen months.

Frank strolled to the window and gazed toward the northwest. "Well, I'll be darned."

"And check this out," Sims said. He put his toe on scratch marks in the dust and grime. "Drug the table from another room."

An hour later when Rob and Frank walked into CIU, Edna wasn't in her office. Rob was relieved. There had been so little progress and so many loose ends he didn't want Edna interrogating them just now. Rather find a live roach in his Copenhagen can than face her. He marched to the coffee pot and poured a cup as Terry strolled over and met Frank at his cube.

"Make it out to the house?"

"Yup," Frank said.

"Bad as I've heard?"

"Worse." Frank hung his jacket on the back of his chair and took his seat.

Rob said, "Real blood bath, Terry. The upper floor of the house was most probably used by the shooter in that dry cleaner snipe."

Terry grimaced. "What exactly went down out there? Does anyone know?"

"Not yet," Rob said.

"Edna's in a meeting. Everyone's catching hell over this gang killing. The woman and kids getting shot was the last straw. Brass is trying to figure out how to explain the up tic in gang violence to the press," Terry said, before turning back to his office.

Frank wiggled into his slouch position and stared at some point about a million miles away. He'd drifted into "silent mode" again. Guy seemed to have lost his mojo. Usually didn't take this long for him to come up with a theory. It might be a crazy theory, but he usually had one.

Rob logged on to his computer and googled female snipers in U.S. military. After scanning the postings, he came to the conclusion he'd been both right and wrong. "Hey, Frank."

Frank didn't look at him, but grunted. "Huh?"

"I was wrong."

Frank slowly turned his head. "About what?"

"Women being trained as snipers by the military."

Frank seemed to come alive. He sat up straighter. "You mean we do?"

"Not in the traditional sense, but the Air Force trains females as snipers for base security operations in combat areas like Iraq and Afghanistan. The footprints at the house this morning were too small for a man."

Frank stared at him and pulled at his lower lip with his thumb and index finger. "Interesting."

Rob wished he'd never opened his mouth at Sarge's that day about the military not training women as snipers. In a criminal investigation the only thing worse than no information was bad information.

Twenty minutes later, Edna rushed in, went straight to her office, and closed the door. She had the look of someone who'd just had a big bite taken out of their butt by a supervisor, probably Higgins. She spent the rest of the morning on the phone. From her expression it was clear she wanted to be anywhere else.

Around lunch Rob glanced at Frank. He'd drifted off again into the mental hinterlands. Rob walked down Lamar Street to Off the Bone Bar-B-Q and ate a pulled pork sandwich. When he meandered back into CIU Frank was gone. Computer off, jacket missing, and chair scooted under his desk.

* * *

Frank parked at White Rock Lake and stared at the blue water and trees on the opposite shore. Alma's house was around the next corner. He didn't plan to go there, but just being in close proximity helped him think. It all began with her on the front porch of Ricardo's that night. Everything that had happened since was a derivative of that. The connection was loose, but the ends had started to fuse together. Frank had been meaning to pay his friend Dana a visit since taking the photos of Alma's garden. This seemed like the perfect time.

As Frank drove, he pondered Dr. Alma Hawkins. He hadn't been with a woman in years who, after spending the night with him, hadn't called him back within a day or two—except Alma. Was it his ego or curiosity that drove him to want to see her again? A little of both. Or possibly something else. He liked her. He liked her a lot.

Ten minutes later, he sauntered through the aisles of plants at Dana's Garden Center. He shopped there for the best herbs and patio plants. Dana, who was an American Horticulture Society Master Gardner, had been married to Fred Sweeney, Frank's old partner when he was still in uniform. Even after Fred's early death from a heart attack, Frank still checked in on Dana every couple of weeks.

He found her squatted over a five gallon Texas Mountain Laurel, scratching in the dirt around the edge of the pot.

"No one looks better dirty than you, lady."

Dana snapped her head up and a broad smile followed. She was almost ten years Frank's junior. She stood, dusted her gloves on her jeans, and gave him a hug. "Hi, Frank. What brings you out during the week? Never see you except on Saturday or Sunday."

Frank pulled out his iPhone.

"Got something I need advice on. Been thinking about some new plantings for the patio." He opened the phone to photos and scrolled to the first picture he took in Alma's garden. "Not familiar with these plants. Can you tell me if you carry them?"

Dana stripped off the dirty gloves and slipped on a pair of cheaters that hung around her neck. She examined the photos, scrolling her finger across the screen. Her expression changed from serious to a smirk as she moved from photo to photo. She handed the phone back to Frank.

"Okay, you've had your little joke for today. Now, what do you really want?"

He held up the phone. "I want to buy some of these plants."

She frowned. "You're kidding, right?"

"No, absolutely serious."

She snatched the phone back and moved her finger across the screen again, eying each plant. "So were you on vacation in New Hampshire or Nova Scotia when you took these?"

Frank didn't answer.

Her eyes moved from the phone and she stared at him. "Well?"

"Neither."

She continued scrolling. "You won't find any of these around here. They won't grow. Texas summers are too hot. These are zone two, three, and four plants." She pointed at the first one. "Frosted Violet Euchre. The farthest south it can survive is zone six. We're in zone eight." She moved her finger and a blue flower appeared. "And this here. Monkshood, grows in mountain meadows. Some folks call it Wolf's Bane—never survive a Dallas summer. And this." She scrolled to a green shrub with red berries. "Bearberry. A sub-alpine that's native to Canada." Her eyes narrowed and she moved her finger across the time and date at the top of each photo. She readjusted her reading glasses, and her jaw went slack. "These were taken recently. Where?"

"Near White Rock Lake."

She handed him the phone. "That's not possible. It's a joke, right? They're artificial."

Frank scrolled back to the Monkshood. Using thumb and index finger he enlarged the shot and pointed to the photo. "Butterflies don't feed on artificial flowers.

26

When Frank walked back into CIU, Rob was rushing out, slipping on his jacket.

"Hey," Rob said, "just about to call you—let's go!"

"What's up?" Frank's spirits rose. Was this the break he'd been hoping for?

"Come on. I'll explain on the way."

They trotted over the third-floor walkway to the parking garage. As Rob ran he stuck a pinch of Copenhagen in his lip.

"What's the hurry?" Frank asked.

"Call just came in. Sniper in downtown parking garage just shot a black guy getting out of his car."

"Do they have them in custody?"

"Nope, active shooter," Rob said, unlocking the car.

Rob jumped behind the wheel, spit into a plastic cup already half full, and sat it back on the dash.

"You need to give that up," Frank said. How people could put that stinky stuff in their mouths still baffled him.

Rob slammed the car into reverse. "Doesn't hurt you one way or another." He braked and shifted into drive. The cup of brown spit slid off the dash and dumped into Frank's lap. Rob's lips flattened. "Sorry about that." He burned rubber out of the garage.

Frank cleaned his pants with a napkin, gagging with bile rising in his throat with each wipe. "Who called it in?"

Rob swung onto Lamar and hit the grill lights and siren. "Sims called me—don't know who called him."

"Where are we going?"

"Thanksgiving Tower—1601 Elm."

Frank dreaded this. Bad memories of July 2016 rushed back—the last time a sniper shot anyone in downtown Dallas. Rob and Frank had been there, working the intel side of the event. Five officers were killed during a rally and march.

Texas lawmen take a dim view of snipers in general. But after killing five brother officers and wounding seven more, the Dallas Police Bomb Squad rigged one of their robots with a homemade bomb and blew the guy up. First time in U.S. history something like that was done—killing a suspect with a remote bomb.

A six-block perimeter had been established. Television, radio, and social media warned downtown workers to remain inside and away from windows. As usual, the faces of hundreds pressed up against window panes in every building. A SWAT command post was set up at the corner of North Griffin and Commerce. Rob and Frank parked behind the Federal Building, badged their way through the perimeter, and approached the black SWAT war wagon. Paul Sims leaned against the truck, popping Gummy Bears into his mouth. SWAT Lieutenant Carl Gunn had one foot propped on the back step of the vehicle and leaned his elbow on his leg. He had a street map of downtown Dallas spread on the floor of the truck and spoke into a mic.

". . . and let me know when you're ready to execute."

A voice on the radio answered, "Will do."

Rob and Frank nudged beside Sims, keeping the bulk of the armored vehicle between them and the shooter in the parking garage.

"What do we have?" Rob asked.

Sims pointed over his shoulder. "Unknown suspect on the third or fourth floor of the garage shot a guy near a car on the street."

"Was the guy a gang-banger?" Rob asked.

Sims shrugged and popped another bear in his mouth. "No idea. Ambulance did a load and go before he could be interviewed. Have detectives at the hospital now trying to get a story out of him. Witnesses reported seeing the shooter, and uniforms have secured the building. Been evacuating occupants for the past fifteen minutes. SWAT's about to assault the garage."

Lt. Gunn stared at the threesome. "What the hell are you guys doing inside my perimeter?"

"Hey, Lieutenant," Rob said. "Think this shooter might be the one we're after?"

Gunn scowled. "Try not to get shot. I have enough on my plate just about now."

A voice from the radio said, "Evacuation complete. Ready to commence assault."

Gunn spoke into the radio, "Sergeant Burns, the operation is yours."

"How many teams?" Rob asked.

Gunn removed his cap and drew his hand across the short gray stubble. "Three. One will move up the ramp and the other two will take the stairwells. If he's up there, we'll get him."

"If it's a 'he,'" Frank mumbled. About a dozen thoughts raced through Frank's mind, causing a mental roadblock. Was it Jesse? Could they have gotten that lucky? Did she seriously miscalculate and get trapped this time?

About five minutes later, a volley of weapons fire echoed through the downtown canyons. Rob, Frank, Sims, and Gunn exchanged glances.

"Shooter down!" Sergeant Burns' voice yelled over the radio. "Requesting an ambulance to the third floor. Clearing the upper floors."

Gunn grabbed the mic. "Copy. One down. Request ambulance, clearing upper floors." He and Sims huddled near the back of the truck.

Rob bumped Frank's arm and motioned with his head. They

strolled down Commerce until they got to North Akard and hooked a left. On their way to the garage, they ran into SWAT guys, in full battle dress, filing out of the building.

Frank held up his badge. "Where's the shooter?"

One of the officers removed his helmet, wiping sweat from his brow. He motioned with his hand. "Third floor on the west side—DOA."

Rob and Frank went up the west-side stairs and badged their way past another SWAT officer. The scream of the ambulance's siren died as it pulled up below. Huddled around a body on the concrete were four SWAT members and Sergeant Burns. As Rob and Frank approached, the officers parted. On the cold garage floor, curled in the fetal position, with blood pooling around his back, lay Alonzo Salazar—Ricardo Salazar's little brother.

*　*　*

At four o'clock in the afternoon, Antoine Levern still lounged in his pajamas in his dark living room and snorted another line of coke. He'd taped black paper over all his bullet-proof windows, blocking out any view or light. He rubbed his nose, coughed, and listened to the radio news report of the downtown shooting. *Crazy-ass people. Fools killing each other.*

Something stunk. Even through the coke-clogged nose, Levern smelt it. He sniffed under each armpit. Oh, yeah. Skipped the shower last night. He ran his hand over the stubble on his cheeks. Needed a shave. Maybe tomorrow. Not going out today anyway. In fact, for the time being, Levern had no intention to go out again, period. Too dangerous on the street. With one of his guys being dropped almost every day by this sniper, going out was insane. Besides, he hadn't felt well in a few days—wanted to sleep all the time.

A knock on his door and Tabor stuck his head in. He shifted the toothpick to the side of his mouth and said, "Boss, you still eating dinner in tonight?"

"Yeah, why?"

Tabor grinned. "Have plans if you're not going anywhere."

"Lady plans?"

"Yeah. A hot one."

"Go ahead. Have fun."

"Thanks." Tabor closed the door.

Levern laughed to himself. Guy was such a geek. Most awkward dude around women he'd ever seen. Never been able to keep a woman, much less a hot one. Wondered what his definition of hot was, anyway?

* * *

After work, Rob and Frank sauntered into Sarge's just as the place was starting to get crowded. Sarge always played country and western music after five o'clock. His wife, Jill, waved them to the rear booths where Sarge leaned on a table talking to Paul Sims. Sims had a small package of pretzels and snacked on them with his beer.

Frank really needed a drink. Not a good day.

"Hey, guys," Sarge said, "the usual?"

"Yup," Frank answered.

Sarge remembered thousands of drink preferences. Because "the usual" at twelve noon for someone wasn't always "the usual" for the same guy at five o'clock. When Sarge was Frank's supervisor in Vice years ago, he had the worst memory of any cop Frank knew, but he always recalled what everyone on the squad liked to drink. Probably found his true calling by retiring and opening his own place.

Paul Sims downed the rest of his beer while Rob and Frank slid into the booth. Sims had called this meeting to bring them up to speed on the downtown sniper incident.

Rob stared at Sims as he opened his notebook and slowly turned the pages. Frank almost laughed watching Rob's fingers drum the table. His partner didn't have a lot of patience with slow, fat people. Finally, Sims cleared his throat and looked up.

"Okay, so some of our information was wrong." He paused a moment before continuing. "The guy that Alonzo Salazar shot this afternoon wasn't black as first reported—he was a dark-skinned Hispanic."

Sarge arrived, shoving beer and red wine toward the trio and collecting Sims's dirty glass.

Sims emptied the crumbs from the pretzel bag into his mouth and took a sip of his new beer.

Rob's left knee had a nervous bounce, getting ready to propel him across the table if Sims didn't hurry up.

"We sent detectives to interview the guy Salazar shot. He's still in the hospital. They also interviewed Salazar's mother," Sims said. "Starting to look like just a domestic incident. Guy was messing around with Salazar's old lady. Dude said Salazar had been following him. Figured he try something sooner or later. The mother said Alonzo was fascinated by the sniper shootings—all he talked about."

Sims leaned back. "He must have squirreled out and figured he had the perfect opportunity to off the guy and make it look like another sniper shooting. Uniforms sealed off the garage exits sooner than he'd figured, and he got himself trapped. Don't think it really has much to do with our primary case."

Rob's knee stopped bouncing and he took a long swallow of beer.

Frank's disappointment deepened. He'd hope this would crack the case, or at least point them in a direction that might pay off. He'd not told Rob about his strange visit to Alma's or the impossible plants she grew. Frank would keep that as his personal investigation for now. The gangster's identification of her wouldn't hold up in court without additional evidence. Who'd take a crook's word over an attractive lady Ph.D.?

"So that's it?" Rob asked.

Sims grinned. "There are a couple of other things." He flipped a few pages in his notebook and took another swig of beer, obviously in no hurry to finish his dissertation.

Rob's right eye started up with that tic, waiting for Sims to casually turn one page after another. When Rob's knee started bouncing again, Frank laid a hand on his arm.

"Oh, yeah. Here it is," Sims said and took another slow sip.

"Well, what the heck is it?" Frank blurted out.

"That kid I interviewed," Sims said, "he might not have been making up the story about the blonde lady sniper after all. Forensics hasn't finished analyzing all the stuff from the gangster massacre at the old house yet, but they called and said they'd found an anomaly." Sims checked his notes again. "All the hairs in the house are from black people except one. Found it at the site of the scuffle—an eight and three-sixteenths–inch blonde Caucasian hair. Can't see how it moves the ball for us, but it adds credence to the kid's story. Guys don't usually wear their hair that long." He glanced at Frank. "Well, most guys. You two turned up anything new?"

Frank sipped the red. "Rob and I think the sniper is probably a woman."

Sims sat back in the booth. "Because of the long hair?"

"That and the size of the footprints upstairs," Rob said.

"Forensics had a couple of questions about them too," Sims said.

Frank raked his hair away from his eyes. "You said there was a couple of other things."

"Oh, yeah." Sims flipped a page. "Got a measurement on that shot from the old house to the dry cleaner parking lot. They make it close to nine hundred yards."

"No way," Rob said. "That's over half a mile."

Frank sat motionless. Half a mile? His mind drifted to Levern. How do you protect yourself from someone that good?

An uncomfortable silence descended around the table. Finally, Sims finished his beer in one long gulp. He stood and stared at Rob and Frank.

"Any chance of going back to that federal source to get more info about this sniper?"

Rob stared at him. "It's not that kind of source, Sims."

"Figures. I can tell you this much. If we don't get a break soon, the sixth floor will come unglued. Everyone from the mayor's office to the governor is calling, wanting an update." Sims waddled toward the door without saying good-bye.

Frank didn't say good-bye either. But one thing was for sure. Sims was right on this one: the sixth floor was looking for someone to come down hard on. Sims and Homicide was number one in their sights. CIU and Edna weren't far behind.

Rob took a sip of beer and stared into the glass. "The other day you said you might have a contact who could pull records from sniper schools."

Frank nodded. "Yeah, well not so much a contact. More like a relative."

"Relative?"

Frank downed half the red. "An uncle." Christ, he hated the thought of calling him.

Rob shrugged. "You going to talk to him? Because if you are, there's not a better time. Not everyone can shoot from nine hundred yards and nail a guy in the head."

"I called and left a voice message the other day. Hasn't called me back." Frank had hoped it wouldn't be necessary to call his relative again. Uncle Clyde was his dad's youngest brother. Asking favors from the old SOB turned Frank's stomach. Pushing sixty, he was scheduled to retire the first of next year. Frank had asked him for a favor in the past, but the guy was such an asshole about it Frank dreaded the thought of asking again.

Rob stayed for another round, but Frank just wanted to get to a familiar place and be quiet for a while. His patio was his oasis, the place where ideas popped into his head with little effort. He parked in his assigned space and walked to the elevators. Someone had apparently just taken both up, so it took a few seconds for one to return to the basement. The elevator arrived and Frank stepped inside and pressed his floor.

When it opened, the sight of poor Mrs. Silverstein fumbling with her door key, while holding her oversized purse and juggling a bag of groceries, brought a smile to Frank's face. The old girl always tried to do too much with too few hands. He rushed to her aid.

"Let me help."

She jerked her head in his direction, dropping her purse. "Oh, dear," she exclaimed.

He took the groceries as she pushed her door open.

She sighed. "Thank God for you, Frank. You always show up when I need help the most."

"My pleasure."

He bent down and picked up a tube of lipstick, a notepad, and book that had spilled from the purse. When he picked up the book he stared at the cover, unable to move. His breath caught and that old tingle raced down his spine. *That's it!*

"Frank . . . Frank?"

He looked up. "I'm sorry, what?"

"I said would you like to read the book? We discussed it at my book club this week. I'm finished, if you want to borrow it." She showed the sweet smile he loved.

Frank handed it back and shook his head. "No, thank you. Have all the information I need from the cover."

A perplexed expression raced across her face and she nodded.

An hour later, Frank had finished a light dinner, showered, and was relaxing on his balcony. He gazed around at the lush plants and stared at the Dallas skyline. Twinkling lights filled the sky. He broke the seal on a bottle of red and screwed the opener into the cork. After drinking a couple of glasses, Frank did what had to be done. He called his uncle again. The guy was an arrogant prick who knew it all, but he did have access to military records. He'd made the Air Force a career. His current assignment—NORTHCOM in Colorado Springs.

After the usual pleasantries, Frank told him what he needed.

His uncle cleared his throat. "Frank, this might take some doing. I'd have to call in a bunch of favors. Even if I can manage it—no telling how long it might take."

"I'll wait," Frank said.

"Okay, I'll start the ball rolling. Call you when I get something. Oh, by the way, my birthday's next week."

Frank released a long breath. *Here it comes.* "Still drink Glenlivet 21?"

"Well, that's mighty generous of you, nephew."

"No problem," Frank said. "Happy birthday." *There goes two hundred bucks, plus shipping.*

As Frank disconnected, a disturbed calm washed over him. He poured another glass. He'd always considered himself an educated and somewhat refined man. He wasn't prejudiced or opinionated. But the idea of a witch in Dallas wasn't just absurd—it was silly. Only ignorant peasants in the Middle Ages and tribesmen in undeveloped countries could take such things seriously. The idea he even entertained such thoughts made Frank question his own ability to think and reason reliably. All these crazy dreams and unexplained happenings had him wondering just who was in control of the case. He was on the verge of dropping the whole witch idea when he helped Mrs. Silverstein with her spilled purse. Then he saw the cover photo on her book. It was of a young woman with long, fiery red hair, and sparkling green eyes. She wore a golden Druid triangle necklace and a low-cut dress. She held a candle and had an inquisitive expression. The book's title—*The Celtic Witch.*

27

Thursday morning, Frank began his research into Dr. Alma Hawkins as soon as he got to work. A Google search revealed about what he'd expected. Her academic credentials were impressive. Bachelor's in religious studies from University of South Carolina. Master's from Columbia and Ph.D. from Cambridge. Moved around a lot. Taught for a dozen years at several universities on the East Coast. Yup, moving every few years. Why? Serious professors all go for tenure. Being able to put down roots in an academic community was what they lived for. But not Alma.

Frank scanned social media and found nothing. Her background was sketchy at best. Several Alma Hawkins existed around the country. Even with her Texas driver's license number and date of birth, the search was confusing. And he found something very odd—few photos of her existed. Yearbooks from schools where she'd attended or taught all showed "Photo Not Available" below her name. And as far as Frank could tell, she'd been born an adult. Little about her existed before the age of twenty-five.

He slouched in his chair and massaged his temple. Rob strolled in, fresh from his workout.

"Morning," Rob said.

Frank kept his stare on the computer monitor. "Morning."

"We still have the squad meeting at ten?"

Frank pulled at the skin on his neck. "Huh?"

"Meeting at ten still on?"

"I guess."

Rob flopped down and switched on his computer.

"Hey, I'm checking on someone and not much is coming up," Frank said. "Any suggestions?"

"Start with the residence and work back from there."

Frank perked up. *Why didn't I think of that?* He typed the street address for "Cottage on the Lake" into Google. The search engine filled several pages. Frank scanned each article looking for clues. House constructed in 1910. Photos of construction on the new dam and planting trees along the future lakeside. Grand opening of the lake and proclamation by mayor's office. He scrolled down the articles and found an obscure mention about the natural stone cottage being the first home constructed around Dallas's new reservoir and future water supply. The grainy photo didn't look anything like the current place. Not one plant in sight.

There was a fuzzy picture of the owner and his wife. Frank zeroed in on the couple. Mr. and Mrs. Ezra Pullings. Frank leaned to within inches of the monitor. The man was tall and refined. He wore a stylish suite and fedora, sporting a thin, well-trimmed beard. Frank sucked in a quick breath and enlarged the photo, making it even more grainy and obscure. The woman in the photo looked like Alma. It didn't just resemble her, it *was* her.

Frank read the article about how the couple had moved from up north to open a clothing store in Dallas. They'd finished construction of their new home only days before the lake's grand opening. Nothing about Mrs. Pullings in the article. Frank cleaned up the grainy photo as much as he could before hitting the print button. He studied it the rest of the morning. So many bizarre thoughts went through his mind, but being an intelligent pragmatist, he didn't want to believe them.

About five to twelve, Edna rushed up to Frank's desk. "I need a favor."

When Edna got excited or anxious, a flush rushed up her neck and cheeks, giving her a glow. Frank always found it attractive.

"Sure—name it," he said.

"Dr. Plebe, from SMU, will be here in a few minutes. We have a lunch date planned. He's going to advise me on some spring classes."

Frank sat a little straighter. "Okay?"

Edna's gaze darted back to her office. "So, Higgins just rang and wants to start a conference call." She glanced at her watch. "In two minutes. I need someone to meet Plebe in the lobby and babysit him until I can get off this damn call."

From the corner of his eye Frank caught a smirk from Rob.

"Sure, Edna, no problem." Frank stood and slipped on his jacket.

"I really appreciate it. He knows you. Just stall him."

"Will do."

"I'll wait," Rob said.

"Go ahead and eat. I'll grab something later," Frank mumbled before heading for the door.

Frank took the stairs down. Just as he got to the ground floor, the professor walked through the glass doors into the lobby. Frank called his name. The professor turned with a surprised expression.

Frank extended his hand. "Good morning, Dr. Plebe."

"Detective Pierce, isn't it?"

"Yes, sir. Edna . . . that is Lieutenant Crawford sends her regards, but she's been unavoidable detained. She wondered if you could wait a few minutes."

The old professor nodded. "I suppose so. Will she be long?" He eyed his watch.

"No, sir."

Actually, Frank was happy to be alone with the guy. Might get a few more insights into Alma Hawkins.

"Dr. Plebe, let's have a seat." Frank directed him to a couple of chairs away from the others.

"Was Dr. Hawkins able to answer your questions regarding Voodoo?"

"Oh, yes. Very helpful," Frank said. He needed to be careful how he handled this. One slip and he'd give it all away. "How long has she been at the university?"

Plebe said, "A little over five years."

"Well, she certainly is well versed."

Frank's cell rang, Edna calling.

"Frank, did you find him?"

"Yeah, having a nice chat."

"Tell him I'll be right down."

"Will do."

Frank dropped his cell in his pocket. "The lieutenant will be down directly." He leaned a little closer. *Time to move in for the kill.* "Just curious," Frank said, "is Dr. Hawkins a Wiccan?"

A curious smile crossed Plebe's lips. "How did you know?"

"I didn't until now."

"Oh, goodness," Plebe said. His brow pinched and he leaned back before placing his hand over his heart. "Perhaps I shouldn't have said anything." He cleared his throat. "You'll not mention my indiscretion to her I hope. I'm not certain how it would be perceived. A Wiccan teaching religious studies at a Christian university."

"Of course not—our secret."

Plebe looked down. "She entrusted that bit of information to me after her daughter's death. Poor thing went through a bad period." His voice cracked and he looked Frank in the eyes. "That's when we became friends." He shrugged. "A shoulder to cry on."

"She had a daughter?"

"Yes, a beautiful thirteen-year-old girl. Died in January."

The elevator door opened to his left and Edna came strutting out, all smiles, making a beeline for them.

Frank had time for one last question. "How did she die?"

Plebe also noticed Edna approaching. He stood and waved. "I'm sorry what did you say?"

Frank stepped closer, whispering. "How did she die?"

Plebe frowned and shook his head. "A drug reaction from the food at a friend's party."

Edna walked up and shook hands with Plebe. "I'm so sorry to keep you waiting. Last-minute call. I hope Frank kept you amused?"

The professor grinned. "Yes, we had a lovely chat."

"Let's get going," Edna said. "I want to pick your brain on a couple of things." As she turned, she whispered, "Thanks, Frank. I owe you."

"My pleasure." It was his pleasure. Plebe's revelation about Alma's daughter revived an old memory.

Frank raced back to his desk and pulled up the report. It was as he recalled. January 28 in North Dallas, several kids became ill at a birthday party—one died. Food poisoning was first suspected, but the Dallas Health Department soon narrowed down the source of the trouble. An unknown drug having hallucinogenic qualities had been introduced to the punch. Frank quickly scanned the reports. The police had received a tip about Ricardo Salazar, and he was questioned. He denied selling the drug and lawyered up. Attorney got him off using a loophole. Frank sped through report after report until he discovered what he wanted.

The dead girl was Clara Hawkins. Only child of Dr. Alma Hawkins, professor of Religious Studies at SMU.

Frank sat back in his chair and eyed the last line of the report for a long time. An old, disturbing memory surfaced. A memory that took him back seventeen years ago when he lived in New York. A memory he'd tried to purge from his conscience.

28

Jesse walked into her bedroom while slipping on her blouse. She was tired. In the last few days she'd taken down another three gang leaders in Levern's circle.

The TV showed a stock photo of Bagram Airfield in Afghanistan, reporting on the deaths of two Afghan Security Troops from a rocket attack near a gate. Jesse stopped and stared at the TV. *I know that gate.* How many hours in freezing cold or stifling summer heat had she manned the sniper tower beside it? How many hours had the harsh winds dried her lips and skin? She lay on the bed and gazed at the TV.

The place of my greatest accomplishment and greatest failure.

* * *

July 2012

Jesse took the last few steps at a trot before stepping into the shade of the fifty-foot sniper tower. Mark was already there, bullshitting with the guys. Their laughter drifted down as she climbed the stairs. She stepped inside and dropped her pack. The day guys had already gathered their equipment for the shift change. Sweat rings outlined their under arms, back, and chest. As always, the floor and everything in the tower had a fine layer of dust, but the view was spectacular. The old town of Bagram lay straight ahead, and the mountains rose up in the distance.

"Hey, Jess," Mark said.

She had been paired with Mark for the last two months. Arriving at Bagram in February, she'd first worked with a veteran base sniper. She and Mark had attended sniper school together, almost a year ago.

"Hey, Mark." She tossed her pack in the corner. Each two-person sniper team consisted of a shooter and spotter. They spent eight hours in "the box," as they referred to the towers near each base entrance. It was the most miserable assignment on post. Constructed of wood and fortified steel plates, it was the coldest place in the winter and hottest in the summer. A two-foot opening on all sides allowed super-heated or super-freezing air to blow through, and the driving rain soaked them.

Jesse removed her helmet and took a peek through the high-powered binoculars mounted on a tripod. She scanned Disney Road, leading from the base to the old town. Today she was the shooter and Mark was the spotter. They switched off each day.

"Sit rep?" she asked.

The shooter from the day shift grunted. "Nothing of any significance. Reaper 5 depart at 0500. Afghan outer perimeter security stops by every few hours. Nothing on the ops sheet."

The other team slung their packs and rifles over their shoulders and departed down the stairs. Mark keyed the radio.

"Ops, this is Disney Gate, radio check."

"Disney, you're five by five, how me?"

"You're five by, out."

Mark had already ditched his helmet and camo shirt for a soft cap and tee shirt. Jesse did the same, checking the thermometer—104 degrees.

"Going to be a hot afternoon." She eased into the chair and readied her M-24 sniper rifle. She worked the bolt several times and snapped the trigger on an empty chamber. Jesse loaded the magazine with five 7.62 × 51 mm rounds and inserted it into the rifle. She rested it on the sandbag with the muzzle pointing down the road. Checking the scope, she insured it was still property aligned.

Mark fished a cold bottle of water from his cooler and eyed her. After taking a long swallow, he said, "I'm getting married."

Jesse cocked her head. "Oh, really? When did all this happen?"

Mark leaned against the far wall, propping his feet on his pack. "Proposed before coming to work today—she accepted."

Jesse had long suspected Mark of being an incurable romantic. He read books, listened to classic music, and seldom joined in the camp goings-on. He'd always been the perfect gentleman around her, never making lewd comments or asking suggestive questions. That was more than she could say for most of the rest. His girl back home, Tara, seemed to be the only thing on his mind lately. He spoke of her often.

Jesse sat the rifle down and looked his way. "I'm happy for you. Congratulations."

"You got anyone back home, Jess?"

As she fitted the radio earpiece into her left ear, she smiled to herself. It was well known that young, single, and attractive females had their pick of male companionship on base. She'd never spoke of a romantic relationship back home and had spurned all attempts since arriving in the country. A few whispered that maybe girls were her preference. What no one realized was she had a sizzling liaison going on with the sexiest guy she'd ever met. They kept their romance secret, because that sort of thing was frowned on. They both wanted a career in the Air Force, and being obvious wasn't anything but trouble for career airmen.

Jesse stood and grabbed the ops clipboard before answering. "No, don't have anyone back home." She didn't meet eyes with him, but kept her concentration on the clipboard, flipping through the old ops orders.

He dropped the subject and took up position behind the spotter's binoculars, checking off the fire points. She slid back into her chair and stared down the miles of perimeter wall wrapped at the top with razor wire. She lived on the six-square-mile base with forty thousand other people, the largest town she'd ever resided in. All wanted to go home—back to their loved ones. Not her. She had nothing to return to. In the distance the sound of a C-17 Globemaster accelerating for takeoff filled the air.

After basic training, they'd approached her about applying for counter-sniper school. She'd been accepted to one of the last few slots. The only female in the class, it took all the physical and mental endurance she had to finish the course. She'd graduated as the class "top shot." A short vacation home followed before being deployed to Afghanistan as the new fire team member of the 822nd Security Forces Squadron. Her mom and dad had been so proud. And she was proud of herself. Nineteen years old and starting a new career with a bright future. But she felt so hollow inside. Like some part of her heart was still dead from Glen's loss.

Meeting Clive had helped. She'd never met a more handsome man. Dark wavy hair, tall, and all muscles. Saying he'd swept her off her feet sounded like such a cliché, but it was true. She'd never had sex half that good with Glen. Clive stirred some primitive, uninhabited emotions she didn't realize she had. He was reckless, daring, and the devil-be-dammed attitude made him perfect for Reaper.

Reaper was part of the 755th Expeditionary Security Forces Squadron. The security of Bagram Air Base was their responsibility. They worked twelve-hour shifts patrolling the 180-square-mile security zone outside the wire. If there was trouble brewing, the twenty airmen of Reaper usually encountered it before it could affect the base.

Clive's voice came over the radio. "Ops, this is Reaper 5. We're trailing what appears to be an Afghan Security Forces truck driving slowly through the old market. It's on the main street that intersects Disney. Thing is riddled with bullet holes. Could we get an aerostat on it?"

"Reaper 5, this is Ops. We'll make it happen."

Mark leaned in closer to the binoculars, staring in the direction of the old market. "Can't see it yet. Still in town behind buildings."

Jesse scoped her rifle in that direction. The aerostat surveillance balloon might give them a better idea of what was going on.

Mark switched on the TV as Jesse glanced in his direction. The thing flickered and an overhead view of the downtown area flashed on the screen. People strolled through the old market with its dozens of booths, selling everything from raw lamb to rugs. The vehicle hadn't shown itself yet, still probably weaving through the narrow streets. A moment later, the aerostat operator zoomed in and put the camera on the truck. Clive's Bradley Fighting Vehicle followed about 100 meters to the rear.

"That thing's been shot to hell," Mark said. "The Afghan's would never use it. They'd get a replacement."

Jesse kept her eye to the rifle scope, waiting for the truck to break out into the open. She gnawed her lower lip. Mark was right. The Afghans would turn a vehicle in for replacement if it had a flat tire. They'd never drive that piece of crap.

"Reaper 5, this is Ops. We're putting up a Kiowa to check it out. Maintain a safe distance."

Jesse's stomach twisted. Maintain a safe distance was right. The last time something like this happened, the truck had over eight hundred pounds of explosives. When it detonated, it left a crater the size of an Olympic swimming pool.

"Ops, this is Reaper 5. No time. We just made the turn onto Disney Road. Permission to interdict?"

"Reaper 5, this is Ops. Stand by."

Just then the vehicle came into view in Jesse's rifle scope.

Mark keyed the mike. "Ops, this is Disney Gate. Vehicle on Disney road approaching our position—approximately 500 meters out. Do they have clearance to approach the gate?"

Silence filled the tower as Jesse and Mark waited for an answer. Finally Ops said, "Wait one . . . we'll attempt to contact."

Jesse tried swallowing but her throat was too dry. Any vehicle approaching the air base was required to notify Ops and receive clearance before entering the 500 meter exclusion zone. The Afghan

Security Forces patrolling the perimeter and stationed just outside each gate never gave the regulation much notice. Each ASF commander pretty much did as they liked without regard to what their American guest wanted.

A few seconds later, Ops broke their silence. "Disney Gate, unable to establish contact. Deploying ASF to interdict."

Jesse zeroed in on the driver side window of the suspect vehicle—poetic justice. The ASF were stationed below her tower on the other side of the wall. They'd better hurry. The truck was almost within the 300 meter kill zone. Any uncleared vehicle entering that area was subject to being fired on. Jesse glanced over the edge of the tower at the ASF guys standing around. One of their armored personnel carriers should be heading that way by now, but they just sat there.

"Truck approaching kill zone, Jess," Mark said, keeping his eyes glued to the high-powered range-finding binoculars. "I make it at 400 meters."

Jesse pressed her eye tighter to the scope, and her fingers found the candy in her pocket. She unwrapped it and popped the peppermint into her mouth as she watched the mysterious vehicle draw nearer to the gate.

Clive's voice crackled through her earpiece. "Ops, this is Reaper 5, we're going to interdict that vehicle approaching Disney Gate."

Jesse kept the scope on the truck, sucking the life out of the candy. All markings on the vehicle looked genuine. It was a two-and-a-half ton Afghan standard transport with two occupants in the front.

"Reaper 5. You are cleared to interdict. ASF not responding," Ops said.

A cold feeling invaded Jesse. *This isn't going down right.* Too much wrong. Too many coincidences—a set up. As Clive's armored car closed the distance, the truck hit the gas. It entered the 300 meter kill zone as Jesse worked the bolt, slamming a round into the breech. She said, "Mark, request permission to engage." Jesse's full concentration remained on the truck. She kept the crosshairs centered on the blurred figure behind the wheel, but her mind also was with Clive in the scout vehicle racing to catch it. Beads of sweat wormed down her cheeks, tickling her neck. The sweet taste of peppermint filled her mouth, and she relaxed, again focusing on the approaching target.

"Ops, this is Disney Gate," Mark said. "Target in kill zone, request permission to engage?"

"Stand by," the voice said.

Jesse had been blessed with a cool head and sharp eye. A rope or heavy black string flopped in the wind from the passenger's window leading to the back of the truck . . . a wire!

Clive's Bradley Fighting Vehicle was going its full thirty-five miles per hour and then some, catching up to the truck.

"Mark," she yelled. "Request permission to engage!"

Mark relayed the request to Ops, but there was no reply. The sun was at that angle reflecting off the truck's windshield that made it impossible to get a clear picture of the occupants. All Jesse could make out were the outlines of two men. The Afghan forces outside the gate scattered. She took two deep breaths and slowly exhaled through her nose as her finger tightened on the trigger. If she fired without approval from Ops, it would be hell to pay. Especially if it was some new Afghan driver behind the wheel.

Screw it!

Jesse fired, shattering the truck's front windshield on the driver's side. She worked the bolt, got back on target, and fired again just as Ops signaled the all clear to engage. Automatic weapons from the base, as well as the 25mm chain gun on Clive's vehicle, let loose as she racked the bolt the third time and fired. Machine-gun bullets tore through the speeding truck and peppered the ground, sending up little puffs of dust as the truck began to weave off the road toward the ditch. Her last shot drove through the cab as a bright orange flash and deafening explosion followed. The hard concussion raced through the air in a visible wave and slammed into the tower.

The whole structure shuddered as she and Mark were knocked

back off their stools against the wall. Jesse's ears throbbed. She opened her eyes to a cloud of dust blowing through the tower's openings. The stink of cordite filled the air. Something warm and wet in her right eye made it difficult to see.

"You okay, Mark?" she asked.

He sat up and touched his face and ran a hand over his head. In a hesitant voice he said, "I . . . I think so. Jess! You're bleeding."

Jesse touched her right eye and stared at her hand. Blood covered her fingers.

Mark crawled to her and held her head, staring at her face, a mask of fear distorting his handsome features. "Can you see?"

Jesse nodded. "I think it was just the rifle scope. Must have blown back and nicked my eye during the explosion." Jesse stood and slapped a handkerchief over her bloody eye. As the view cleared, a black and orange mushroom rose from the area where the truck had vaporized. A cloud of smoke and dust drifted over Clive's armored Bradley. It had been blown sideways and rested less than fifty meters behind.

Jesse stuck the earpiece back in her ear and keyed the radio. "Reaper 5, status?"

She held her breath as tense moments past and ops also attempted to raise the stricken Bradley.

Jesse shook, the adrenaline kicking in. *God . . . not Clive too.*

Mark found the binoculars in the corner and focused them on the Bradley. "No movement," he whispered.

Jesse scratched around and located her rifle. Using her only good eye, she aimed it at the Bradley. No hatches opened. No radio transmission. The Bradley's tires were on fire. A wave of dizziness hit her and she slumped, her knees so weak they no longer supported her. She couldn't take losing—

A scratchy radio transmission filled her earpiece. It was Clive's voice that said, "Reaper 5, we're down, but not out. Nice shooting, Disney Gate."

Jesse dropped the rifle and fell back on her butt. She laid her face in her hands and shook. She didn't want to cry, but all the stress and emotion bubbled up into tears that burned the cut on her eyelid. Mark wrapped his arms around her, and she rested her head on his chest, crying like she'd cried at Glen's funeral.

It took several days to complete the investigation of how insurgents made off with an Afghan truck, loaded it with explosives, and got so close to the base. Engineers determined the blast was equal to almost two tons of high explosives. It took days to repair the crater in the road. Jesse actions, engaging the vehicle before being officially cleared, were conveniently swept under the carpet. The Air Force just happened to be in the market for a new hero. The fact she was an attractive female made it an added bonus. Jesse had no illusions—Clive and the chain gun in the Bradley probably had more to do with stopping the truck than she. But his radio transmission came to be the definitive last word on the subject. *"Nice shooting, Disney Gate."*

Stars & Stripes ran a feature article on her. She was named Outstanding Airman of the Year, received the Purple Heart, Combat Action Medal, Achievement Medal, and several lesser medals and awards. She was the person to know on base—a celebrity in her own right. They pressured her into accepting an offer to return stateside several months early to help with recruiting. Magazines, newspapers, and morning shows all wanted to interview the "Hero of Bagram."

Two days before she was scheduled to fly out, a full bird colonel walked in on her and Clive screwing like two dogs in heat in the back of the gym late one night. Their punishment was fair, but not good. As the subordinate to Clive, she would be allowed an honorable discharge and Clive would get a general. Any attempt to challenge the decision would result in immediate court martial. Of course they had accepted the ruling. What choice did they have?

It felt good to be on top for a while. But that made the fall even worse. Jesse was disgraced and humiliated—from hero to heel in record time. Again she faced an uncertain future. What to do with the rest of her life?

At least she still had Clive. She came to be more psychologically dependent on as him as the weeks passed.

In the lonely hotel room, Jesse kept her eyes on the TV. Clive had been her rock, and nothing he could have done would cause her to let go. Not even when he asked her to help him kill a man.

29

As Anthony Palazzo sat at his desk and thumbed through the papers, a grimace twisted his face. Son of a bitch! Jesse *had* been busy. She'd whacked over a half dozen guys in Dallas. He'd give her credit, she was good. Too good. Because the Godfather insisted on using her instead of their own enforcers, she'd racked up over a quarter of a million in fees. After every hit, she'd confirm the money had been wired into her Cayman bank account before she'd go after another one.

Palazzo slammed the folder shut. This could end up costing more than the loss of Ricardo Salazar. Palazzo understood Gambizi's rationale for using her, but enough was enough. All the Dallas papers reported on the vigilante sniper targeting drug dealers. The cops were going nuts and now the feds were even snooping around. Drawing so much attention wasn't smart. By Palazzo's way of thinking, they'd made their point to the other families. It was time to put an end to this. Whack the Levern guy and call it finished. He'd almost convinced the Godfather to either suspend Jesse's contract or at least let some of their enforcers finish it. One last try should do it.

Forty minutes later, Mrs. Shaw, Gambizi's housekeeper, led Palazzo down the dark hall of the nineteenth-century Manhattan Beach home Joseph Gambizi had occupied for the last fifty-two years. One of the organization's boys always stood in the hall leading to the Godfather's office. Palazzo nodded to the guy. His street name was

"Eddie the Eyes," because his stare could melt steel. Crazy-ass eyes that spooked most folks—black as Satan.

"Is he in his office?" Palazzo asked, without breaking stride. Maybe the Godfather would see the logic behind using family resources.

Eddie marched beside him to the door at the end of the corridor. "Went in a couple of hours ago."

Palazzo knocked twice before entering and found Joseph Gambizi slumped in his executive leather chair. The old Don stared up into space through lifeless eyes, like a man trying to get a glimpse of heaven. Eddie rushed to him and checked his pulse. Palazzo had seen enough dead guys to know when it was too late. They called an ambulance and Palazzo covered the Godfather with a blanket from the sofa. A sick feeling rumbled in his stomach. Palazzo sat on the couch and gazed at the far wall.

Eddie poured a drink from the crystal decanter. He walked it over to Palazzo and shoved it into his hand. No one spoke for a couple of minutes. Palazzo sipped the whiskey and Eddie leaned against the door frame with his arms crossed. After a moment he cleared his throat.

When Palazzo looked up Eddie said, "What are your orders, Godfather?"

Three days later, Joseph Gambizi was laid to rest at the Old Calvary Cemetery in Queens. Tony Palazzo stood graveside with the family and held the hand of Gina, Gambizi's wife of over sixty years. It was a mild day with low clouds and a light breeze. Palazzo pulled in a slow breath and took in the view. The heads of the other crime families, wearing serious expressions and dark suits, had assembled on the opposite side of the grave. At forty-four, Palazzo was the youngest of the group. Most of those old men standing a few feet away had hemorrhoids older than him.

At the conclusion of the service, the priest blessed the coffin and those in attendance. One at a time, each head of a crime family approached the casket, laid a single red rose on top, nodded to Palazzo and Gina, and stepped back in line.

Burying Joe was the easy part. Palazzo didn't look forward to attending the meeting after the funeral. He'd called it, but it still sent chills through him.

He gave Gina a hug and handed her off to one of her daughters before nodding to the men with the dour faces a few yards away. A reception was scheduled at the church for friends and family. Palazzo would not attend. The crime family leaders would meet at Joseph Gambizi's house in a half hour. Palazzo had played every psychological card he had. Making sure he was seen holding Gina's hand graveside was the first. The second was scheduling the meeting in Gambizi's home. And the third, making sure it was in Gambizi's own office with Palazzo sitting behind the Godfather's desk.

He'd heard no rumors from his spies about the other families conspiring against him, but he recalled Gambizi's words that night in the cabin. *"You'll go to my funeral one day and your own in less than a week."*

A half hour later, he sat behind Gambizi's desk and waited. They trickled in one by one, and soon the most dangerous group of men in New York formed a half circle in front of his desk. He'd met them all before, but having them in one room this close felt like swimming with a school of great whites.

The maids served each man his drink of choice and then quickly retreated. Palazzo sat with his back straight and eyed each Don. "I called this meeting to clear the air and make sure you all know where I stand." Under the desk he wiped the sweat from his hands and touched the automatic pistol in the holster glued to the underside of the desk.

"In the past there's been bad blood between some of you and the Gambizi family."

No one said a word, but several of the men nodded.

"But I want you to know," Palazzo continued, "that I'm willing to put all that behind us. I'm Gambizi's chosen successor. And you know me as a serious man of my word. It's my hope that we can get along. Start a new relationship, free of all the misunderstandings that plagued Joe these last few years." Palazzo's throat was so dry he found it difficult to talk. He licked his lips and tried swallowing.

"If anyone has anything to say I'd be happy to listen."

No one spoke for perhaps ten seconds. A few sipped their drinks, a couple smoked, and everyone waited for something to happen. Finally Giuseppe Morello stood. Palazzo had never cared for the guy. Gambizi said to never trust him. Morello headed up the Genovese crime family and went by the name Bobo. At five-foot-seven, he was short in comparison to the other Dons, dark complected. His sixty years only showed by a little graying on the sides of his short black hair.

"Don Palazzo, I want to thank you for calling this meeting. It's been a long time coming."

Palazzo relaxed a little and released a breath. By Bobo using the term "Don," he had acknowledged Palazzo's right to lead the Gambizi family. *Good sign.*

Bobo looked around at the other family leaders. "I have to admit a few of us have had concerns of late. Joseph Gambizi was an old man—a hard man. We all respected him, but he grew up in bad times." Bobo shrugged. "God only knows what things he had to endure in the past. But times have changed. The way we do business has changed." He waived his hand at the other men. "We all do things different now. We're more interested in making money and staying out of prison than acquiring new territory." He laughed and several others who'd served time did as well. "But as I was saying, speaking for myself." Bobo laid his hand over his heart. "I welcome this peace offering from you." He sat down and crossed his legs.

This was going better than Palazzo could have expected. He glanced at the other men's expressions and couldn't get a read on any of them. Winning over a big fish like Bobo should have broken the ice for the others, but everyone remained silent. Palazzo waited a few more moments for someone else to speak. Perhaps he should throw down the gauntlet. He stood and said, "Thank you, Don Morello for your endorsement. I look forward to working with you."

He eyed the others. A knot had formed in the back of Palazzo's neck and signaled the beginnings of a headache. "Anyone have anything else to say before we adjourn the meeting?" Palazzo didn't like this. Getting one endorsement out of five wasn't good. He released a breath and calculated how many seconds he needed to pull the pistol under the desk if things went tits up. The leaders of the Bonanno, Colombo, Gambino, and Lucchese families sat mute.

Palazzo's mouth was so parched his tongue felt like sand. He reached for his glass of water. As he took a sip, his eye caught movement from one of the family leaders to the left. Angelo Armone from the Bonanno family nodded to Bobo. When they stood, it startled Palazzo and he flinched, spilling a few drops of water on the desk.

Palazzo figured they'd have guns in their hands, but instead they wore broad smiles. Nobody had to tell him what they were thinking as he wiped up the water with a napkin. Yeah, they'd spooked the hell out of him.

"Don Palazzo," Bobo said, "you speak of this new beginning, of clearing the air." He looked at the others. "If we're to work together, we need to understand that anything one does affects us all."

Next to him, Armone nodded.

Palazzo returned his glass to the desk. "I understand this, Don Morello, and I intend to do my part."

Finally, Armone spoke up. "If what you say is true, then a small gesture would go a long way to help seal this new deal."

Palazzo couldn't believe it. Did he just say *seal this new deal?* That meant they were ready to accept him into the club. The only question—what kind of gesture?

Palazzo motioned for the two men to sit. He leaned back in the leather chair and put on what he hoped was his most serious face. "What kind of gesture did you have in mind?" Palazzo was ready to offer anything to insure he'd have their backing as the new Godfather. The seconds felt like hours waiting for them to answer.

"This business you set in motion needs to stop," Bobo said.

Palazzo wasn't sure what he meant, but the other family leaders all nodded. They'd probably already discussed it among themselves. Best to let them clarify it.

"None of us deny you your right to defend your people and territory," Bobo said. He eyed the others. "We'd do the same, but enough is enough. If you want to snuff this darkie in Dallas, so be it. But the problem we're having is with Chicago. All this killing has interrupted their supply. The last thing we need is a war, especially over this."

Elation and relief washed over Palazzo. These guys wanted the same thing he did—to terminate Jesse's contract. But one thing old Joe taught him was to never appear to give in too easily. Time for a little drama. Palazzo stared at the group and counted to himself slowly. When he reached fifteen, he asked, "So correct me if I'm wrong. But if I call off the enforcer in Dallas, you'll give me your backing as the new Don?"

Bobo and Armone said, "Yes," at the same time. The other three also nodded.

Palazzo had won his victory and it hadn't cost him a dime. He'd send word to Jesse to whack Levern and end the contract. Everyone was a winner—especially him. He stood and raised his glass.

"Consider it done."

30

"**A**re you nuts?" Rob asked. Frank had come up with some weird theories in the past and most were right on target, but Rob couldn't believe what he was hearing. Was the guy having a breakdown?

Frank slumped in the passenger seat and shrugged. "I laid it out for you. Make up your own mind."

"A witch? Tell me you're joking." Rob kept driving but eyed the photo from 1910 Frank held. "Sure, this looks a little like her, but I look like my uncle Jose too. He's not me, and I'm not him."

"Okay, for the record, I never said she was a witch," Frank said. "There's just a lot of things that are hard to explain, that's all. It's not just the photo—it's everything." Frank slid it back into his folder.

Frank had that look that said "I'm not backing down from this. No matter what you say." Rob figured any argument he put up, Frank had a counterargument ready to knock it down. Best to humor him and see where it went.

"Okay, for the sake of argument, let's say you're right. Where do you go with it? A priest, an exorcist, Edna?"

Frank shot him the look again but didn't reply. Then he turned and stared out the windshield. This only confirmed what Rob already knew. There was no place to go with it.

Rob took a left into the parking lot of Levern's restaurant. "Why are we here?"

Frank opened the passenger door. "Levern wanted to see us."

"You mean he wants to see you?"

"You rather sit in the car?"

Rob didn't fully understood why Frank got along with the punk. Probably went back to Frank saving Levern's life when he was a kid. Rob put drug dealers just one notch below murders. He hated them all.

"You'll need someone to back up your skinny ass in that nest of vipers," Rob said, sliding from behind the wheel. He caught a quick grin from Frank.

When they entered the Cajun Crawdad, the big guy they'd met at their last meeting with Levern was waiting for them at the door.

"Tabor, right?" Frank asked.

"This way." Tabor stepped around the corner into the elevator landing.

They followed him into the elevator and he hit the up button. No one spoke. Rob hated this place. Good spot for a cop to disappear and never be heard from again. The elevator stopped with a jolt and the doors opened to Levern's loft. None of the lights were on. Tabor didn't get off but motioned for them to exit.

Tiny slivers of light crept around thick black paper taped on all the windows. The place had a claustrophobic feel, as if the walls might collapse at any moment. Frank acted like he didn't have a care in the world. Rob unsnapped his holster and kept his hand near his piece.

"You need to have your partner relax, Frank."

They turned toward the voice. From the shadows, Levern limped into the small pool of light slashing from the elevator across the floor. It had been about a week since they'd last seen him. His hair looked like a dirty mop, and his eyes had sunken into their sockets, giving him a drugged out appearance. He wore no shirt and his pants sagged.

Frank surveyed him. "You look like hell."

Levern raked his fingers through the hair and across his scruffy face. "Yeah, well I haven't felt good lately." He strolled closer, rubbing the back of his neck and stared at the floor. "Think I'd like to make a deal," he mumbled.

"What kind of deal?" Frank asked.

Levern glanced at Rob. "I might be able to help the police with a few things."

Frank shook his head. "What kind of things?"

Levern looked away into the darkness, shoving his hands in his pockets. He again lowered his head and said just above a whisper, "You know. Pass on some information."

With a bit of humor in his voice, Rob asked, "You want to be a snitch?"

Levern's mouth contorted like he eaten a pickle. "Naw . . . well, you know."

"What's going on?" Frank asked.

Levern became animated, waving his hands. His voice warbled. "I want to know what I'd have to do to get police protection."

"You're scared," Frank said.

Rob almost felt sorry for Levern. Every day another gang leader had been whacked. One sitting in his car, one in his living room, and the last one standing in front of a strip joint. Always the same—a high-powered rifle, which no one heard. To say there was true terror in the gang community was an understatement. Everyone realized this wasn't a local thug. This enforcer had been brought in for an express purpose.

"Damn right I'm scared!" Levern shouted. "My people are dropping all over the place. You'd be scared too."

"You have more security than the governor," Rob said.

Levern talked fast, waving away Rob's comment. "I'm alone up here except for Tabor."

"Why?" Frank asked.

"Because the word is whoever's whacking my boys has someone on the inside of my organization. Knows where they'll be, knows the best way to get to them. I've cut almost all my bodyguards loose."

"You don't trust your own criminals to protect you anymore?" Rob laughed.

"You think something's funny here?" Levern's hands formed into tight fists.

"Just relax," Frank said. "If you have some information you'd like to pass on, I'll send it up. But don't expect a quid pro quo."

Levern's brow furrowed. "Say what?"

"They won't protect you unless you have a lot to give up. You'd have to spill everything. If you have good enough stuff, we might get you into witness protection, but that's the fed's decision—not ours."

Levern limped to his desk chair and sat. Even in the shadows, Rob couldn't help but see his eyes had misted. Levern put a finger against his lips and turned from their stares. In a quiet voice, laced with emotion, he asked, "When are you cops going to catch this guy? When the dude killed all your pals at the Black Lives Matter march, you had *him* in a couple of hours."

"Yeah, well, this one's smarter. This one doesn't have a death wish. A professional," Frank said.

Levern glared at Frank. "Of all the people in this city, I only trust you and Tabor." Tears trickled down his cheeks.

"Levern, you have lots of money," Rob said. "Retire! Get the hell out of town. Take Tabor on an around-the-world cruise. This thing will blow over sooner or later. Once you're no longer in charge, they'll forget all about the hit. You won't be in a position of power anymore." He turned to Frank for support, but Frank remained silent.

"Right, Frank?" Rob asked.

A frown swept across Frank's lips. "Maybe . . . maybe not. Never can tell about those Mafioso types. They have that honor thing. Gives them crazy ideas."

"So that's it?" Levern asked.

"Sorry, can't make any promises without seeing the merchandise," Frank said.

"Thanks for nothing," Levern mumbled under his breath, staring in the opposite direction.

Frank turned and pushed the button on the wall. The grinding sound of the elevator filled the room.

"Put together a list of what information you have and I'll pass it up," Frank said.

When they got back to the car, Rob asked, "You really think New York would come after him if he made a run for it?"

"Yeah, I do."

31

Alma rolled over, switched off the alarm clock, and lay staring into the darkness. Her life was routine—on autopilot. Up at five—coffee, news, and breakfast by six. Shower, hair, and make-up by seven. At her office between seven thirty and seven forty-five. When Clare was alive, her life had meaning. A new challenge each day—something to look forward to. Now the house had a cold, lonely feeling. A home of sad memories and a sweet little ghost.

No one needed to tell Alma she was due for a change. Word came yesterday about her application to Dartmouth. The department head was elated and wanted her for the spring semester. The applicant interview was only a formality. Her credentials carried a lot of weight. Showing up pregnant, with no husband, wasn't really what she'd planned, but the people in Hanover were a liberal, forgiving lot. She'd give her notice to SMU today. Dr. Plebe would be devastated, but Alma didn't care. Every day in Dallas caused her sprits to sink a little lower.

She'd already contacted a Celtic-based coven in Hanover, and being a third degree, she'd been accepted as the thirteenth member. At the moment, it was a cold comfort. Many in the Wicca religion believed their witchcraft got real results, but Alma understood they were probably just fooling themselves. Long ago, and after years of experimentation with spells, Alma resigned herself to being a witch in spirit and beliefs only. The practice helped her cope with things she couldn't change. Some things were too difficult to face without some spiritual help. She covered her face with her hands. After a moment she slowly drew her hands down and rested them on her chest.

Life would be so much easier if I were a real witch.

There was much to do and little time. Give notice, travel to New Hampshire for the interview, and put the house on the market. Alma backed the car out of her drive and enjoyed the view of the lake as she drove to work. She would miss some things about Dallas. The mild winters, the Mexican food and barbecue, and her year-round garden. But the sad memories of her time there with her daughter outweighed all that. She took a right and glanced in her rear mirror as she made the turn. She thought she recognized the driver two cars back. Just a profile, but she was pretty sure.

Frank Pierce, why are you following me?

* * *

Rob glared at Frank. "You're fixating again. You actually followed her to work?"

Frank slouched in his office chair, staring over the partition at Rob. He couldn't blame him for the remark. He was fixating, but at least he realized it.

"Yeah."

"Did she see you?"

Frank shrugged. "Don't think so . . . well, maybe."

"Don't we have enough shit on our plates?" Rob leaned closer and lowered his voice. "First she's a suspect, and then not a suspect. Then she's a witch, and then she's not a witch. Now you're following her—you're fixating. Stop it."

Frank turned back to his computer.

Rob kept eying him like he expected an explanation.

Frank didn't answer.

Rob shook his head and marched to the coffee bar for a refill. Frank needed to put the whole business of Alma behind him, but he'd become much more emotionally involved than he wanted. Something about her lured his concentration away from everything else. Rob was right. Frank needed to invest all his attention on Jesse. The gangster had probably just made a lucky guess and pointed to Alma in the photo lineup.

Edna stalked out of her office and threw up her hands. "Well, the chief is barking mad. The feds have opened an investigation and the national press reports live each night from Dallas. They said it's becoming a bigger murder capital than Chicago."

Everyone stared at her. No one uttered a word.

Edna took in a couple of deep breaths and grimaced before a frown swept across her mouth. She swallowed, and after another glance around the squad room, retreated back to her office.

The whole mess ate at Frank. He'd never been a social butterfly, but the last week he had become even more reclusive. He and Rob had gone to every gang-related homicide but still had no good leads. They'd sent emails and had canvassed all the hotels in the Dallas/Ft. Worth Metroplex in the hopes Jesse had registered under her own name.

Frank's frustration was reflected by the arrangement of his desk. A couple of dozen sticky-notes hung from the monitor and the sides of his cubicle. A link analysis chart, showing Ricardo's murder at the top, had colored lines drawn every which way and looked like a demented spider's web. Yeah, he was fixating again. But on the wrong person.

Rob wanted Mexican food, so Frank agreed to go to South Oak Cliff. Go figure, a black neighborhood had Rob's favorite Mexican restaurant. Rob ordered a plate of tacos and Frank just had a bowl of tortilla soup.

When they got back to the police garage, Rob said, "Let me have your keys." He held out his hand.

"Huh?" Frank said.

"I think I left a pair of sunglasses in your car a while back. Been looking for them everywhere."

Frank shrugged and tossed him the keys. He couldn't even recall the last time Rob had been in his car.

"I'll see you upstairs," Rob said.

*　*　*

Frank dropped into his chair and rubbed his eyes again. Damn allergies.

Edna walked by on the way to Terry's office. "You look awful."

"Grass pollen, again."

"Did those prescription gel tabs work the other day?"

"Yeah, dried me right up."

Edna whirled back to her office. She soon returned and dropped two more on his desk. "Take them. Your eyes look like you've been on a three-day drunk."

She still had a pissed off look. Frank had come through for her so many times in the past he didn't want her to think he'd lost his touch. She sat on the edge of his desk and eyed the notes and crazy spider web he'd created. A quick grin cracked the corners of her mouth.

Never taking his eyes off her, Frank popped the tabs and washed them down with a swallow of water.

Edna leaned in closer. Her scent filled his nostrils. In a whisper she asked, "Where are we on this, Frank?"

He understood what she wanted. Some assurance he'd take care of it. That he would soon figure it out. That her position was secure with Higgins and the chief.

More than one detective's gaze fell on them. The lieutenant never strolled out and sat on a guy's desk.

Frank didn't want to lie, but what should he tell her? None of his explanations would do anything but cause her more pain. He leaned closer on one arm and spoke in a quiet voice. "I'm almost there, Edna. Just a little more time. Waiting for a source to get back to me." The heat from her body radiated around him, and his breathing and pulse increased.

She pursed her lips and nodded. Her hand slipped to his arm and gave a squeeze. "Don't wait too long, Frank. Fix this ASAP."

32

Jesse finished lunch on her outside table of the Italian restaurant in Lower Greenville. The sun ducked behind the clouds every few minutes, making the wind a bit cooler. The sweet smell from the bakery down the street tempted her—chocolate chip cookies were her favorite. Could they make them as good as Aunt Janet? Crispy on the outside, chewy on the inside. Hers were the best.

Jesse sipped her second latte while thumbing through *The Stamp Collectors Bible*. She couldn't concentrate. Her mind kept drifting, trying to think like Anthony Palazzo. She had no illusions—he wasn't her biggest fan. Maybe he didn't like women, or just women doing traditional men's jobs. Either way, as the new Godfather, he'd decide how long she'd remain in Dallas. She kinda enjoyed the place. The only problem—the targets were wise to her M.O. The days of picking them off like cherries from a tree were over.

No one strolled or sauntered anymore. The cool shuffle had been replaced by the sprint. People ran to their cars, got behind their tinted windows, and drove crazy speeds to avoid being shot. The days of outside meetings had long passed. Sitting in a car and cutting up a deal might have deadly consequences. With everyone skittish, she needed a new way to get to them. When she got the go-ahead to take out Levern, he'd be the easiest. She'd already made a serious investment that was sure to pay off.

No matter how it went down, Dallas was her last job. She'd saved enough to get out. Start a new life out west. Wyoming, Montana, or maybe Idaho. Buy a place and settle down. She could start a hunting guide business. Live in a cabin on a lake or beside a clear mountain stream. Were these real dreams or just fantasies? She didn't know. She knew one thing for certain: what life she had left, she wasn't going to live it like this.

Jesse slept well at night with the ghosts of people she'd killed. They all needed killing. Her conscience was clear. She wasn't afraid of facing God's judgment. But when she died and saw her daddy again, what would he think about her life? She'd gone against every principle he'd lived by—broken every rule, every commandment. That's what she regretted. That was her biggest fear. Facing the old man and explaining her life choices to him. A life of shame.

If she'd never met Clive, she wouldn't be in this situation. But at the time he seemed like the answer to all her prayers and dreams.

* * *

September 2012

After being drummed out of the Air Force, Jesse went home. She'd put together an elaborate lie about how she'd been sent stateside to help out in recruiting. It felt good to be home. She needed a sense of family.

Her dad made her retell the story of taking out the explosives truck every chance he got. But Jesse couldn't look into her dad's face every day and live the lie. The stress of the charade became heavier as time went on. Her salvation came when Clive called.

Clive was a New Jersey native. He'd also gone home after leaving the Air Force. Hearing his voice again was like a breath of much-needed oxygen.

"Hey, Jess. How's it going?"

Jesse's heart swelled with love. "We're all good. How are you?"

"I'm great. Got a new job and moved into my own place. So you have any plans?"

Jesse didn't answer for a few seconds. Her mind whirled, thinking about what to say. Before she could answer, Clive said, "I love you, Jess. Come and be with me."

Jesse covered her mouth with her palm, and warm tears formed in her eyes, clouding her vision. It sounded better than a marriage proposal.

Jesse said good-bye to her parents and flew to New Jersey. Clive met her at the airport. He'd let his beard grow. The black mane that outlined his face gave him an exotic, sexy appearance. She ran and leapt into his arms. Their kiss was like a hot relaxing bath she never wanted to leave.

That weekend he showed her New York. They got a room at the Plaza, slept late, and walked across the street to Central Park. They visited SoHo, the 9/11 Museum, and had lunch at a Manhattan deli. That night they saw *Annie* on Broadway. Jesse was in love. Not just with Clive, but also New York.

Sunday afternoon they checked out and drove to his apartment in Elizabeth, New Jersey. It was on Front Street, and Clive's balcony overlooked the river.

Clive took her in his arms. "I have to work for a couple of hours tonight."

"Work? On a Sunday night? Who works on Sunday night?"

Clive released her and moved back a few paces. "I do. It's my job."

Jesse hadn't asked anything about Clive's work. "What exactly do you do?"

Clive grinned. "I'm like a bodyguard for a guy who does collections."

Jesse laughed. "You work for a collection agency?"

Clive lowered his gaze. "Naw, just the guy who does the collections."

Jesse thought the whole thing was weird.

A few days later, Clive asked for her help.

"Jess," Clive said, as he wiped pizza crumbs from his lips, "I could use your help tonight on one of my collections."

Jesse never expected this. Had no idea what help she could be.

Something felt wrong. Clive wore an expression she'd seen before, the same expression he showed in Afghanistan when he and the Reapers were about to go into a hot insurgent area.

"What can I do?"

Clive walked to the other side of the room. "I work for what's known as a high-risk collection group. The reason I'm paid so well and work so little is because we only go after collections where a certain amount of danger is involved."

Jesse didn't like the sound of this but still didn't fully understand what he meant. Something was screwed up somewhere. "You can't just take them to court for the money?"

Clive shook his head. "It's not that kind of deal. They make high-risk loans to high-risk clients. The guy I protect, Michael Calabrezie, is the collector. He works for the main company; I'm just a contract employee."

"Is this what people call a loan shark operation?" Jesse asked.

"Yeah, I guess so," Clive said, "I know they charge sky-high interest rates."

"Is this the kind of work you want to make a career of?"

"No way." Clive waved away the suggestion. "I'm looking for something else."

"What do you need me to do?"

Clive strolled to the closet and removed a rolled up blanket. Unwrapping it, a familiar shape came into view—an M-24 sniper rifle. Clive held up the brand new rifle and scope.

"Still remember how to use one of these?"

"Why would I need that?"

We're collecting from some Puerto Ricans tonight. Rule of thumb is: never collect from a Puerto Rican without backup."

Jesse didn't want to say yes and she didn't want to say no. *Oh, God. Why is he even asking me?* Every fiber of her being screamed—NO! But her heart said yes. If she allowed something bad to happen to Clive when she could have prevented it, she wouldn't be able to live with herself.

"I'll do it just this once, but don't ever ask me again," she whispered. "Okay?"

"Can I get you anything else, miss?" the waitress asked.

Jesse shook the memory away and looked up at her. "No, thank you."

The waitress collected her plate and cup and turned to tend to a guest at the adjoining table. A bout of fatigue swept over Jesse. Her whole body felt heavy and lethargic, what her dad used to call the melancholy blues. She smiled at the thought. She needed something to cheer her up.

After dropping a twenty on the table, she collected her book and strolled toward the bakery.

* * *

Frank was deep into administrative paperwork when Rob strolled into the office. He tossed Frank's keys on his desk.

"Sunglasses aren't in your car," Rob said. "Must have dropped them somewhere."

Rob had a worried expression, and Frank blamed himself. With all his speculation about Alma, he'd kept Rob off balance every day about something weird happening. Rob didn't like weird. When Frank drifted too far off course, Rob was the anchor who kept him grounded in reality.

Frank began to feel a little giddy, relaxed, and light-headed. As five o'clock neared, his phone rang—Uncle Clyde.

"Got something I could use?" Frank asked.

A sarcastic voice answered. "That's what I like about you, nephew. No 'how are you?' No 'how's Aunt Wanda?' No 'kiss my ass,' or nothing. Straight to business."

Frank gritted his teeth and took a long breath before asking, "So how's Aunt Wanda?"

Clyde laughed. "She's fine. Thanks for asking. Ready to talk?"

Frank sighed, grabbed a pen, and slid a notepad closer. "You have something?"

Clyde's voice lowered a notch. "I'm sending you an email. Not sure if this is the person you're looking for, but she's the only female sniper named Jesse on record."

"Can you give me a thumbnail right now?"

"Served in Afghanistan. Got just about every metal and award the Air Force has except one."

"Oh, yeah?"

"Yeah. Got an early out with an honorable discharge, but no good conduct metal—go figure."

"What do you think?"

"Must have been a disciplinary issue. Nothing in the report, but the copy I got is only a summary. I've included all her identifiers and a photo in the email."

"When will you send it?" Frank asked.

"Just did."

"You're the best."

"I'll expect a box Padron's for Christmas. I like the Maduro 7000's." The line went dead.

There goes another $250!

Frank reviewed the email, and after showing it to Rob, they strolled into Edna's office. Frank was still light-headed. He staggered a little as they walked in. *What was wrong?* Terry met them there. One look at Edna's face told Frank this might not have been a good idea. Perhaps waiting until tomorrow would have been better. Any time you came at Edna with new information at the end of the day, you never knew how she'd take it. The sixth floor had been riding her like a cheap mule, and from her demeanor it was clear she'd had just about enough. Even Terry, as mild mannered as he was, showed signs of fraying.

Edna read the email and kept pushing hair from her face. Her tight bun had begun to unravel and now resembled a long-haired cat that had been tumble-dried on delicate cycle. When she looked up, her brow knitted.

"So there might really be a woman sniper." Edna studied the

photo of the young blonde woman in Air Force dress blues. "We know anything about her?"

"No, hadn't checked. Figured I'd run it past you first. Looks like our best lead though," Frank said.

Edna raked more hair behind her ear and looked at Terry, handing him the photo.

"I wouldn't have believed it, but it's starting to look like she's our suspect," Terry said. "You run this past Sims yet?"

"Nope, just got it," Frank said.

Terry passed the photo back to Edna. "Okay," he looked at Rob, "put Sims and Homicide in the loop and let's find out all that's out there on this Jesse woman. Send out a BOLO with this photo to all the hotel and police agencies in the Metroplex. Be sure to Photoshop out the uniform—just the face. Say wanted for questioning only."

"Speaking of woman, any luck on the red head?" Edna asked.

Frank had a great argument put together explaining how Dr. Alma Hawkins was responsible for Ricardo's death, her revenge for the part he played in her daughter's death. Instead, Frank sat mute. From Edna's expression all she needed was a small push to send her over the edge. That would probably do it.

Frank broke eye contact and lowered his head. "No."

"Any chance this Jesse is the same woman that went into Ricardo's that night? You know, wearing a disguise?" Terry asked.

"Not likely," Rob spoke up. "Too many differences."

Frank was grateful no one asked about the differences. That would have led to an area he didn't want to go to just now.

Edna smirked at Frank. "So now you have two women to find. Shouldn't be hard for you."

It would have been fair to say that Edna's last comment dripped with sarcasm. Frank ignored her and turned to Terry.

"Come on guys," Terry said and led them back to his office.

Frank was so relaxed he didn't care what Terry had to say.

"Grab a seat," Terry closed his door and settled behind his desk. "Got a call from the Sheriff's office." His eyes drifted from Rob to

Frank and then back to Rob. "They got a complaint from one of the Mexican gangsters arrested at Ricardo's. Seems a couple of DPD detectives interviewed and roughed him up a little. Claims it was the Hispanic detective who smacked him." Terry kept his eyes on Rob. "Know anything about that?"

Rob stared back. "He was a spitter, Terry."

Terry turned to Frank.

Frank shrugged. "Gangster was wearing a spit hood when they brought him in. Someone must have tried talking to him with it off is all I can figure. You know how cops hate being spit on."

Terry's eyes narrowed. He slowly nodded. "Look, guys. We can't do that kind of stuff."

Rob leaned forward. The skin had bunched around his eyes and he shot Terry a pained look. "But he was a spitter."

Terry ran his hands down his face. "You know, guys," he whispered, the weariness seeping into his words. "This isn't the old days. Too many cameras recording everything. Too many cell phone videos. It's a dangerous world on the streets. Know what I mean?"

Rob didn't answer, but broke eye contact.

"I'll fade the heat one last time . . . one last time," Terry said with a sigh.

This was one of Terry's favorite go-to lines. He'd faded the heat one last time about a half dozen times this year already.

Terry's gaze landed on Frank. "I don't believe for a second you haven't gotten anywhere on the red head. I'm not sure what you're holding back, but if it blows up, you don't want it going off in your face. Neither I nor Edna can help you if that happens. Know what I mean?"

Terry also liked saying, "Know what I mean?" It was another one of his verbal tics.

Frank sat up in the chair. "I know, Terry. I just want to be sure. That's all."

When Rob and Frank got back to their cubicles, Rob plopped into his chair and woke up his computer, his jaw was set so firm that the muscles in his neck bulged. He didn't get angry too often, but when he did it took a while to cool down. From his posture and expression, it might take a little longer this time. He didn't just touch the keyboard, but assaulted it as he banged each key.

"Hey, you okay?" Frank whispered.

Rob didn't look his way, only nodded.

Frank was a poor consoler, but he gave it a shot. "Talk to me, Rob."

For perhaps ten seconds Rob didn't move. Didn't even breathe. He'd stopped typing and drilled a hole in his monitor with his stare. He finally released a breath and looked at Frank.

"Growing up as a kid, I was the smallest of the group. There was a gang of older—bigger—boys who used to pick on me and my friends." Rob no longer spoke to Frank, but talked to the floor. "Anyway, they liked to stroll past and spit on us. My friends got to where when they saw them coming they'd run. I never ran. I stood my ground and they always spit on me." Rob looked up and flashed a sad grin. "And then I came out swinging. Managed to land a good punch on at least one of them before they beat me to a pulp. My friends asked why I never ran. I couldn't . . . that was the reason. I had just as much right on that street as anyone. Why should I run?"

"And so you took the beatings?"

Rob's lips cracked into another grin. "Yeah, not all that smart. But we can't let people disrespect us for just doing our jobs. We have just as much right to make a living as the next guy. It's bad enough they assault, shoot, and try to kill us. If we allow them to disrespect us, we're not men and don't deserve to carry a badge. I may lose my job someday, but I'll never let them spit on me without consequence."

Frank understood. Probably why Rob started lifting weights in the Marines and took up boxing when he joined the police department.

Frank's cell rang and he answered it.

"Kelly here. Thought you'd want to know we were able to isolate and identify most of that white powder stuff found at Ricardo's."

Frank grabbed a pen. "What was it?"

"Combination of natural sedative and psychedelic plants ground up into a powder as fine as talc. Valerian, Belladonna, Kava, and Kratom. Plus a couple more we've not been able to identify yet. I'm emailing the full analysis to you and Sims."

"These plants, do they grow in Dallas?"

"Yeah, some do, but not all. Not all even common to the U.S."

Alma's garden and herb collection. "Thanks, Kelly," Frank said and dropped the phone into his pocket. He checked his watch—five o'clock. He tilted his head from side to side, stretching his neck, and then glanced at Rob, who was busy working on the BOLO. "Shoot Sims a call about the Jesse email." Frank put on his jacket and powered off his computer.

"You splitting?" Rob asked.

Frank adjusted his coat collar. "Yeah."

Frank just didn't feel quite right—almost drunk. As a matter of fact, the exact same way he felt when he'd gone to Alma's house for dinner the other day. What was going—Wait. The gel tabs! He'd taken the gel tabs Edna gave him just before going to Alma's. He hadn't been enchanted. He'd been drugged. And the yellow rose "petal" at the foot of his bed. Had he'd spun himself up into believing Alma was a witch based on false premises?

His brain was mush. A few hours to recharge and refresh for tomorrow, that's what he needed. Put everything case related out of his mind. He grabbed a cup of coffee to go—needed to sober up. As he stepped into the parking garage, Major Higgins walked toward his car. Frank slowed his stride. He wasn't one of Higgins favorite people for a number of reasons. Most of Frank's official reprimands had originated from Higgins's office. Best to let him leave first.

Frank tiptoed to his city car, silently unlocked it, and eased into the cover of the driver's seat. Good, foiled the old SOB again. Frank cranked his car and the siren screamed the *Hi-Low* wail. The echo chamber of the garage amplified the sound about a dozen times. Frank spilled the whole cup of coffee down his leg as he scratched at the knob to turn it off. When he looked up, he met eyes with Higgins driving past, and he didn't have on his happy face. Come to think of it—he didn't even own one.

Frank leaned his head against the steering wheel. *Thanks a lot, Rob.*

When Frank got home he tried to relax. Took a hot shower, ate dinner, and sipped wine on the patio. He picked up the note pad he always kept near. He'd settle this once and for all. One last thing to ponder. He doodled out a list of reasons Levern was or was not involved. The *was* side started with the leaving of the Voodoo doll as the scene of Ricardo's death. The *was not* side started with Ben telling them it wasn't Levern's style—he was more direct. But the biggest reason that Frank believed Levern wasn't involved was Alma's daughter. To his way of thinking, there could be only one suspect in Ricardo's death—Alma.

33

When Rob strolled into the office Wednesday morning, Frank was hard at work on the computer. Neither mentioned the siren incident. It was understood by cops that what goes around, comes around. Rob sometimes felt bad about punishing Frank with a life lesson, but never bad enough not to do it again when called for. About eleven o'clock Frank gazed over the top of the cubicle.

"I just got an email from Ford," Frank said. "He wants to do lunch."

Rob really didn't want to eat at Humperdinks today. His mouth watered for a cherry Coke and ham sandwich at Sarge's. But Ford always had something important, so what the hell.

Frank led the way into Humperdinks with Rob bringing up the rear. They found Ford at a table by a window. As usual, he was studying the menu like a physics student cramming for finals.

As they took their seats, Ford said, "Think I might try something different today."

"We discovered some information about that enforcer, Jesse," Rob said. He ran down to Ford what he'd found out. "I sent out a BOLO yesterday."

Ford shoved the menu back into the holder. "You have good sources. Thought you'd want to know that the U.S. Attorney's Office gave us a call this morning. A guy who works for Antoine Levern is ready to give him up."

Rob scooted his chair closer. "No shit?"

"Yup. Says he can put old Levern away."

"And who is this guy?" Frank asked.

"Benny Fontenot. Runs the cargo hijacking for Levern. Been with him from the start."

"Why his sudden interest in giving up Levern?" Rob asked.

Ford picked up the menu again and thumbed through it like he might have missed something. He dropped it back into the holder before answering. "Says he's scared Levern's going to kill him. Wants to make a deal."

"So what's the AUSA thinking?" Frank asked.

"They're going for it. Guy's coming to our office. We'll put him on the box to confirm what he says before opening a full investigation. Pretty sure Levern will be indicted before too long. Is he still a suspect in the Ricardo killing?"

Rob glanced at Frank. Didn't know what he felt about that. He'd let him field that question.

"Not really," Frank said.

"Since Levern's already under one indictment, the bond will be outrageous for this one. That should get his attention," Ford said. "Either way he's going down. If the New York enforcer doesn't get him, the feds will."

Rob didn't know whether he should take satisfaction or feel sorry for Levern. He hated the guy, but anytime someone's world came crashing down around them Rob felt their pain. His experience with Carmen had taught him humility.

*　*　*

The next morning, Rob picked up Frank at his place. He'd dropped his city car at the garage for service and needed a ride in to work. Rob didn't care if he missed his workout this morning. He'd spent a few extra minutes helping Carmen with breakfast and the dishes before leaving to pick up Frank.

As they backed out of the parking lot, Frank's cell rang. After a brief exchange, he straightened up from his slouch position. "Are you sure it's her?" He paused and gave Rob a loaded look. "What's your address? Okay, be there in a few minutes."

He disconnected and turned to Rob. "Extended Stay America hotel on Greenville. Manager has information on a girl fitting Jesse's description."

When they pulled up in the hotel's parking lot, Rob's head was on a swivel. The Extended Stay America was an older property at Greenville and Loop 635. Not expensive—rooms under a hundred bucks a night. The manager was a short guy in his sixties. His wild Einstein-like gray hair and bushy gray mustache made him look more like a cartoon character than a man.

"You William Sexton?" Frank asked.

The guy extended his hand. "Shane, everyone calls me Shane."

Rob and Frank displayed their credentials. Rob held out a copy of the BOLO alert with Jesse's photo. "Tell us what you know about this woman."

Shane reached under the counter and produced a brown envelope. As he opened it, he said, "Received your email a week ago about the person named Jesse. Didn't make the connection until I received the BOLO with her picture yesterday. Yeah, she was here."

"Was?" Frank asked.

Shane emptied the envelope's contents on the counter. Several sheets of paper slid out and a DVD. "Checked out a few days ago."

The sound of those six words dropped Rob's spirits into a deep, dark pit. When were they going to catch a break on this one? "How long was she here?" Rob asked.

"Little over a week. Maybe ten days. Left real sudden. Didn't give any notice. Still had a couple days left on her payment."

"What kind of payment?"

"She paid in advance—cash. Twelve days."

Frank took notes. He stopped writing and asked, "That seem a little unusual? Someone paying in cash."

Shane laughed. "I asked her about it. Said her credit cards kept getting hacked, so she stopped using them. Only deals in cash now. Guess it makes sense. Hard to hack cash."

"Can we see her registration information?" Rob asked.

"Figured as much." Shane picked through the sheets of paper before handing over the registration card.

Frank craned his neck over Rob's shoulder for a glimpse. "Linda Honeycutt? That's the name she was registered under?"

"Yeah. Is that her real name?"

"Still trying to figure it all out," Rob mumbled and pointed to the vehicle description for Frank.

"This says she drove a white 2009 Toyota Avalon with Texas tags," Frank said. "Is this tag number correct? Did you compare it to her car's tags?"

Shane shrugged. "No reason to. It was a white older model Toyota though. Can't remember if it was an Avalon or not."

"How did she act when she was here? Any trouble? Say or do anything that seemed strange?" Rob asked.

"No, not really," Shane said. "Quiet—kept to herself. Pretty little thing. Never met a commercial architect before, especially one that was a lady."

Frank moved closer. "She told you she was a commercial architect?"

"Yeah, she was unloading her car one day and had this long cardboard tube. Almost dropped it and her bag trying to carry them both. Asked her if I could help, and she said, 'No, thanks,' she was used to it, being a commercial architect and all."

Rob shot Frank a look then asked, "How long was the tube?"

Shane spread his hands. "Oh, about four feet or so. What's she done?"

Neither Rob nor Frank answered.

Shane crossed his arms. "Please don't tell me that cash she laid on me was counterfeit. Please. I can't eat that much."

"Relax," Rob said. "There's no problem with the money."

"Thank God. Can't trust credit cards or cash any more. Don't know what this world's coming to."

"Find or notice anything unusual in the room when she left?" Rob asked.

Shane shifted from one foot to the other and crinkled his brow. "No, can't say as we did."

"Have any video of her, or her car from the hotel cameras?" Frank asked.

Shane grinned. "Figured you'd want that too." He turned and picked up the DVD off the counter. "Burned you a copy of her coming through the lobby."

"Would you recognize her if you saw her again?" Frank asked.

"Sure. Like I said, she was attractive. An all-American girl look."

"Let's take a look at that DVD," Frank said.

Shane popped it into his office computer and the video came to life. The image of Jesse marching through the front doors of the lobby splayed across the monitor—the same woman in the photo Uncle Clyde had sent.

Frank pointed to the monitor and turned to Shane. "We need you to make a definitive identification for the record." Frank tapped the hotel registration printout. "Are you certain that's the woman you knew as Linda Honeycutt who drove this car?"

"Yup, that's her," Shane said. "I'm a damn good detective," he beamed, "almost became a policeman myself."

Rob knew guys like Shane. Every cop did. Those who *almost* became a policeman. When asked why, they shrugged, smiled, and said something like, "Just never got around to it" or "had a better opportunity come up." They never said, "Too much drug use, domestic violence, or theft." No, they always had an excuse for why they didn't do—according to them—what they were born to do.

After getting a signed statement, Rob slipped Shane a card. "If she shows back up or you remember anything else, give us a call." Rob and Frank turned toward the door.

Shane accepted the card, his lips pursed as if he wanted to say something.

"Was there anything else?" Frank asked.

Shane looked into the distance and mumbled, "There was one thing that seemed strange."

Rob was halfway out the door but stopped at Shane's next words.

"Her room had a funny smell."

"Funny?" Rob asked.

"Yeah," Shane muttered, "like some kind of solvent or lubricant."

*　*　*

On the way to CIU, Frank called Sims and briefed him on what they'd discovered. When they walked into the office, he was gnawing on a chunk of peanut brittle. Sims handed Frank the registration results from his check on the license plates of Jesse's white Toyota.

Frank studied the attached stolen Texas license plate report filed ten days ago by some guy named Robert Biggs. Jesse wasn't going to make it easy. Driving a nondescript older car with stolen tags. Staying in low-end hotels. Paying in cash. This girl was so far below the radar she was invisible. It took guts to drive around with stolen license tags knowing she could be discovered anytime someone cared enough to check. Lots of guts and confidence. Thing was, she never gave anyone cause to suspect her. Jesse was a chameleon who dwelled in the shadows and only emerged long enough to kill. Able to present herself as anyone, at anytime, and blend in anywhere.

"I'll see you guys later," Sims said. "Going to show the photo of Jesse to the kid in the tree—see if he can identify her." On his way out he dropped the candy wrapper on the floor, missing the trash can by a foot.

"Was the Avalon hers, or a rental?" Frank asked.

"Had to be hers," Rob said. "Who leases ten-year-old Toyotas?"

With a photo and vehicle description, most crimes could be solved. Just flood the TV channels and social media and wait for the calls to roll in. Usually got their man in a day or two. But they weren't going to be able to use that tool yet.

During the Dallas Police sniping incident in 2016 when five officers were killed, the department had posted the photo of a man on all the news services and named him as a possible suspect. As it turned out, they had the wrong guy. No one wanted to accuse another innocent person and put it out there on the news in Texas. With so many citizens carrying weapons, some go-getter might decide to make a citizen's arrest. It had happened before.

Edna had already told them the chief's office wouldn't use TV and social media until they'd confirmed Jesse was the sniper. They needed something concrete, just in case the information was wrong.

Frank's desk phone rang.

"Guess what?" Paul Sims said.

It wasn't even lunch and Frank was already tired, his head throbbed, and he wasn't in the mood for guessing games. "I give up. Discovered you could eat just one Lay's potato chip?"

The line was quiet for a moment before Sims' solemn voice said, "Frank, that's very ungenerous of you."

Frank exhaled. "Sorry. What?"

Sims cleared his throat. "Just got a call from the feds. They're checking that hair we found in the old house for DNA against Jesse from her military medical records."

"Thanks," Frank said. The case had reached that tipping point. They always do. That point when there was enough evidence to question someone, but not quite enough to arrest them. The only question now, which direction would it tip. And of course, where was Jesse?

34

Jesse had spent Thursday morning following the tricked-out yellow Dodge Charger all over South Dallas. As it made several stops, the driver always took precautions not to get sniped, either parking in someone's garage or under some type of overhang. Jesse didn't care. Being adaptable and versatile was something her dad and the military had drilled into her. *Have patience . . . wait for the target to present itself. Don't rush or crowd it. It'll come.*

Jesse glanced from the printout on her car seat to the Charger owned by Jaylen Martin, leader of Cuzz Texas. He might be a little more challenging than she'd thought. Just then, he darted out of the house and trotted to the tin-covered parking area in back. Slamming the vehicle into reverse, he burned rubber out the driveway and fishtailed down the street.

Jesse followed. Jaylen drove for ten minutes, making four or five turns, and then pulled into the two-story parking garage of some medical facility off Gaston Avenue. Interesting. A doctor's appointment or just another meeting? Jesse cruised past the entrance, noting the Charger turning left into the covered garage. What to do? Would he stay there long enough, or was this just another quick stop before taking off again? She'd bet he intended to stay. He'd been on his cell since leaving the house. Probably another meeting.

The guy was such a dork. If you googled low-class gang leader, Jaylen's photo would probably pop up. He had the complete look. Baggy Adidas joggers hanging off his hips, wearing some foreign military-type field jacket, and his hair in dreadlocks to his shoulders.

Jesse circled the building and drove into the same entrance. She turned left and scanned the rows of cars and trucks. Following the signs, she took a right leading up to the second floor. There it was—parked in a dark corner on her left. Another car was parked beside it, and two heads appeared through the back windshield of Jaylen's ride.

Yup, another meeting.

Jesse drove past and parked about a dozen spaces farther down, closer to the elevator landing. Today she wore a short, frilly pink dress with a plunging neckline and ruffles. She reached into the backseat and picked up the infant doll wrapped in blankets. Jesse checked the parking lot before removing the pistol from her purse. She screwed the silencer onto the barrel and then slipped the pistol under the doll, letting the drooping blanket cover it. She popped a piece of peppermint under her tongue and took a long, deep cleansing breath.

A woman holding the hand of a small boy exited the elevator and walked toward her as Jesse covered the doll's face with the blanket and cuddled it closer. As the woman walked past, a knowing smile crossed her lips.

"Is it a boy or girl?" she asked.

Jesse rocked the doll and smiled back, whispering, "A little girl."

"Aww," the woman said, her brow creased, and kept walking.

Jesse reached into the backseat and pulled the diaper bag from the floorboard. She waited for the woman to leave and took one final look around before walking at a fast clip toward the Charger parked at the back wall. Only the clicking of her high heels echoed through the garage as she closed the distance. The two heads were bobbing, and some rap song drifted from the car's closed windows. The sound of a vehicle heading up the ramp caused Jesse to slow her pace. She took long even breaths, relaxing her grip on the pistol. *Not too tight.* The car drove past and parked at a space around the corner. The brake lights of the Charger flickered on. Jaylen resting his foot on the pedal. Jesse stopped beside the driver's window.

Jaylen had turned away and was staring at the passenger when Jesse bent down, making sure a little breast spilled over the edge of the loose neckline. The look on the passenger's face was funny. His jaw dropped and he said something, causing Jaylen to jerk his head in her direction. She needed the window down, so with her free hand she gave the sign for "roll down your window." There was a large caliber automatic near the gear shift between the two guys.

Better make my first shot count.

Jaylen rolled down the driver's window and eyed her. He broke into a naughty smile and asked, "What do we have here?"

Jesse had practiced this shot before, but it had been a long time. Keeping the doll's head lined up with the target was key. The closer, the better.

Jesse smiled and put the doll's head about two feet from Jaylen's face. "Excuse me," she said, "but do you gentlemen know if—" That's when she pulled the trigger twice. The sneezing sound from the silencer didn't even alarm the passenger at first. Jaylen's head jerked to the side, a tiny hole appearing just below the right eye and another in the center of the forehead. It took about three seconds for the passenger's grin to morph into a grimace. He reached for the pistol. Jaylen lolled forward, blocking Jesse's shot. She took a quick step to the left and lined the doll's head up as the passenger grabbed the large automatic. She squeezed the trigger three times. All the rounds found her target's face. His hand relaxed and the pistol fell to the floorboard.

Jesse released a breath as the growling of a diesel truck wheeling up the ramp drifted through the garage. Without hurrying, she casually strolled back to her car. The end of the blanket smoldered from the heat of the shots. A burning cloth odor floated past her nostrils as she smothered the smoking blanket with her hand. The truck passed her and parked on the left. Jesse made a show of buckling the doll into the baby seat until the truck's driver got to the elevator.

Pulling out of the garage into the sunlight, Jesse thumbed through the sheets in her folder. Something familiar about the passenger stirred a memory. As she turned onto Gaston Avenue she found the photo of Lemarcus Murray—leader of the Cliff Manor Gangsters. *What do ya know. Two for one.* These idiots were so easy.

Jesse worked her way out of downtown. As she passed through the city of Irving, her TracFone rang. The only person who had its number was Tony Palazzo in New York. Good, she was just about to call him.

It wasn't Palazzo.

"We want the contract concluded as of today," an unfamiliar voice said. That was the prearranged code for, kill Levern and get out of town. *So that's that. Time to finish it.*

"I understand," she said. "Scratch Cuzz Texas and the Cliff Manor Gangsters." Then she added, "and make my deposit."

There was a short pause before the voice answered, "Will do."

Jesse went over her plan as she drove west on Highway 114. She'd already planted the seed, now it was time for the harvest.

35

Frank and Rob had just returned from a satisfying lunch at Sarge's. The newest tragedy was still in the news. The sixteen-year-old sister of a gang member was killed the night before when someone did a drive-by and sprayed the house with automatic weapons fire. It angered Frank that so many young lives were being affected by this moronic violence. Some, like this sixteen year old, would never get to experience life past high school. All because a bunch of idiots were acting out some movie fantasy and firing indiscriminately into neighborhoods. That was the problem with gang violence. There were no frontlines—no safe place to retreat when you were beaten. All danger all the time. Stupid!

Frank's desk phone rang. For a couple of seconds he considered not answering it. After the third ring he picked it up. It was Sims.

"Just got word," Sims said, "two more gang leaders found murdered in a parking garage off Gaston. I'm heading over there. Want to meet me?"

Rob reared back in his chair relaxing after the meal. He tapped his Copenhagen box a couple of times before removing the lid and getting a pinch of snuff. After tucking it inside his lower lip, he dusted his fingers on his pants and replaced the lid.

"Sure," Frank said, "give me the address."

Frank hung up as Edna marched by. She'd spent as much time on the sixth floor in staff meetings as in her CIU office—hadn't smiled in over a week. He hated being the one that made her day worse, but she had to know.

"Found two more dead off Gaston," Frank said.

Edna stopped walking but didn't turn around immediately. Her shoulders slumped. She looked back at him with a blank expression—that despondent battle-weary look soldiers get after too much combat. Her commanding voice had left her. Speaking just above a whisper she asked, "Civilians or gangsters?"

"Gangsters," Frank said.

Edna's forehead creased. "You'd better check it out." Without another word she made a beeline for her office.

Rob stood and grabbed his jacket off the back of his chair. "Ready?"

Frank slipped on his jacket and strolled toward the door. He gazed back across the squad room into Edna's office. Her elbows rested on the desk and her hands covered her face, hiding the thousand-yard stare.

When Frank and Rob badged their way past the patrol officer at the entrance to the Gaston garage, Frank remarked, "Happy we finished lunch before getting this call."

Marked units lined both sides of the street, and uniform officers scurried in and out of the garage. Yellow evidence tape blocked the up-ramp.

"Jesus, a double homicide," Rob said, before ducking under the tape.

Frank followed close behind. His energy level had dropped a little more each day. Walking up the concrete ramp to the second floor was like climbing a mountain. "A double today, a triple last week. If this keeps up, Jesse will solve Dallas's gang problem by herself."

They turned right and a gaggle of uniforms and CSI techs in white Tyvek suits were taking photographs and collecting evidence. Sims noticed them and meandered over, eating a hot dog. The bun had almost dissolved in a glob of mustard and ketchup. Diced onions and relish dripping off Sims' fingers completed the disgusting scene. One look at the mess caused Frank's stomach to turn. Sims licked his fat fingers as he approached.

"You guys want to take a look? Kelly's just about finished with the photos—pretty nasty."

Rob's face contorted. "Is that your lunch?"

Sims popped the last of the hot dog into his mouth and nodded. "Yeah. Just getting ready to talk to the building security guy. Want a look at what the cameras picked up."

Frank gazed at the upper corners of the garage. Security cameras were mounted on each side. "Should have got something."

As they walked to the security office, Sims said, "By the way, the kid picked Jesse out of a photo lineup. Positive it was her with the rifle at the fence the day the first gangster was killed."

"That's a good break," Rob said.

Frank was ready to push Edna and Terry for a full news release complete with photos. If the security camera footage from the garage was what he expected, they might just go along with it.

The building's director of security was a man named Gerald Gold, an old guy with tufts of gray hair outlining his bald shining head. His suit probably cost a hundred bucks. He was one of those weasel men. His gestures and facial expressions reminded Frank why he never wanted a pet in the house.

Gold slinked his skinny frame behind his cluttered desk in the basement-level office. His bright red tongue fluttered in and out, raking his equally red upper lip as he searched the computer registry for the security camera menu. He tapped a key, looked up with a satisfied expression, and spun the monitor so everyone could get a good look.

"Here's what we have."

Frank and Rob edged closer to the monitor. Sims leaned against the far wall, his eyes taking on that sleepy look you get after lunch.

The video was in color, and Gold ran it in reverse, starting from when the bodies were discovered two hours ago by one of his patrol officers. Gold tapped the reverse key a couple of times, but nothing much happened. A dozen cars and trucks entered or departed the garage. Just before Frank got bored, Gold tapped the key again. That's when Frank saw her.

"Stop, that's her," Frank said.

"Who?" Gold asked, tapping another key.

"Our suspect," Sims said. He pushed off the wall and stuck his head between Frank and Rob's, inches from the monitor. "Keep reversing it slowly, very slowly."

Gold grunted and pecked a couple of keys before the video started again. "Are you saying that woman with the baby is your suspect? The one who killed those two guys?"

No one answered as they watched the young blonde mother cuddle her infant. She made sure her head was always lowered toward the bundle she carried in her arms, never looking up to give the cameras a direct face shot, but it was Jesse. When she got to the car, she leaned down for a moment, apparently talking to the gang leaders. The camera angle was such that you couldn't see the guys seated in the car—just Jesse standing at the driver's window.

"I've seen enough," Sims said. "Run it forward. I want to get a better look at her car."

Gold grunted again and ran the video forward. As the woman buckled the child into the Toyota, Frank said, "No doubt about it." He pointed at the monitor. "We'll need a copy of that."

An hour later in CIU, Frank and Rob finished showing the video to Terry. He blew out a breath and eyed them. "She's changed tactics. No more shooting from a half mile out. She's right up in their faces. That takes some nerve."

Rob had helped himself to a cup of Terry's special Costa Rica blend he always kept perking on his credenza. He took a sip and said, "She's got plenty of that. A hunter with the element of surprise on her side. She'll always get the first shot."

"And our problem is we're always two moves behind her," Frank added. "Sims talked to the kid in the tree. He ID'd Jesse as the one at the back fence that day. We have her at two crime scenes now, Terry. We don't have to wait for the hair DNA anymore. Plaster her face all over the papers and evening news. Someone knows where she is. All we need is to show the public who we're looking for and they'll do the rest."

Terry just stared at him, but his eyes twitched. That was a sign he was considering the idea.

"I'll talk to Edna and push it," Terry said, "but understand the sixth floor wants to wait for proof." Terry motioned at the TV. "I don't know if this will satisfy them. It doesn't actually show her shooting anyone. The two guys aren't even in the video. All you see is her leaning down at the car with what appears to be a baby in her arms."

Frank stood and raised his voice. "If millionaires in Highland Park were being whacked as fast as crooks in South Dallas, I expect it would satisfy them."

Terry did a waving down motion with his hand. "Relax, Frank. I'm on your side. Edna's in another meeting. When she gets out we'll run this up the flagpole, see if anybody wants to salute it."

"Thanks, Terry," Frank said.

Walking back to their cubicles, Rob sighed. "If they release it, we'd better have a good plan in place when the calls start rolling in."

"I'm not sure it really matters." Frank plopped into his chair. He had a disgusted frown. "Anything we could think of, Jesse has probably already considered and made a counter plan."

36

Jesse finished her shower and put on her makeup. She seldom dressed up—her comfort zone didn't demand it—but she needed to look especially hot tonight. Until she had to leave, she kept on her tee shirt and shorts. No use putting on the dress until later in the evening.

She strolled through the empty house and into the kitchen and poured two fingers of bourbon. Even walking barefoot, there was an echo in a place with no furniture. The old wooded floors creaked and the A.C. unit had a rattle.

After moving from the hotel, she wanted a place out of the way. A place not just out of Dallas, but out of Dallas County. Somewhere she could stay for as long as the contract lasted without drawing too much attention. She'd perused the papers and found this little house for rent just a few blocks off Main Street in the old residential area of Grapevine.

Grapevine had everything she needed—a historic downtown that was a tourist destination with enough strangers meandering around to hide her. She'd rented the 1930's era home for a year, using one of her false identities.

She kept the silenced .22 where she could reach it at a moment's notice. It used to be Clive's. He'd given it to her their last night together.

* * *

November 2012

"Here, Jess," Clive said. "Hang onto this for me." He handed her the pistol.

"You won't need it tonight?"

"No. Taking a bigger one."

At two fifteen the next morning a late model silver Cadillac waited for them in the parking lot.

Jesse tossed her gear in and she and Clive slid into the backseat.

Clive introduced the two guys. Pauli, the passenger, and Rick, the driver. When they pulled up to the gate and chain link fence, Pauli jumped out and unlocked it. As they drove through the dark, a lighted area came into view up ahead. The warehouse had bright lights atop tall metal polls in the storage yard.

Rick collected a briefcase from the trunk as Jesse grabbed her gear.

She motioned toward the warehouse's roof. "Is there a way to get up there?"

"Yeah," Pauli said. "I'll go with you."

She and Pauli found a metal ladder affixed to the left of the office door. Jesse slung her rifle case and equipment bag over her back and scampered up the ladder. Pauli followed. They walked to the other side of the flat roof, dodging pipes, wires, and HVAC units along the way. Jesse unpacked her gear. Clive and Rick sat on a pile of pallets just below.

A half hour later, Pauli called a number on his cell. "They're coming," he said.

Jesse snapped her head in the direction of his gaze. A set of headlights followed the winding road through the woods. She slipped a piece of candy under tongue and got ready.

The panel van stopped about ten feet from Clive and Rick. The passenger got out and strolled over to them.

Rick handed the briefcase to the Puerto Rican guy. Jesse kept the crosshairs on the guy as he opened it. The thing was filled with hundreds, each bundle wrapped with a paper strap. He thumbed through a few bundles and smiled.

Wait a minute. Aren't they there to collect money? Why is Rick giving them money? They're paying for something.

The passenger marched back to the van. He picked up a cardboard box containing quart-sized plastic zipper bags of something. He carried it back to Rick and sat it on the ground. Looked like New Jersey beach sand. Rick unzipped one and stuck his finger into the bag. He tasted it and nodded.

Jesse's throat went dry—a drug deal.

Staying close to the side of the van in the shadows, two other guys carrying shotguns had slipped out the back doors while Clive and Rick were distracted.

"It's a rip-off," Pauli screamed.

Leaning over the edge of the roof, he emptied his pistol at the two guys by the van. Clive pulled his .45 and shot the Puerto Rican standing beside him. One guy near the van fell, but the other charged and fired at Rick and Clive. Rick dropped to the ground as the guy pumped another round into the shotgun and fired again. Jesse pulled the trigger and the Puerto Rican tumbled backward.

Clive was down and not moving. The van tried veering around the bodies, but still managed to run over a couple.

"Get that son of a bitch!" Pauli screamed.

Jesse dashed across the roof, jumping the wires and pipes she'd maneuvered around earlier. When she reached the opposite side, she knelt and swung her rifle over the low wall. As the van raced around the warehouse, she put the crosshairs on the driver's head and squeezed the trigger. The van drifted to the right and crashed into a concrete barrier.

"Well, I'll be damned," Pauli whispered over Jesse's shoulder, "you hit him."

Jesse let the rifle drop from her grip and tried standing. The adrenaline rush came on so fast her knees buckled. She stumbled to the ladder, taking one rung at a time. Numbness set in as she walked toward Clive. *He isn't dead . . . can't be dead.*

Blood covered every fiber of the front of Clive's sweater. A gaping hole in his chest from the shotgun blast turned her stomach. Tears filled Jesse's eyes. She finally lost it and dropped on Clive and wept. Time stopped. The next thing she recalled was Pauli leaning over Rick, searching his pockets. The Cadillac sat a few feet away with the trunk open and engine running. Pauli grabbed Rick's wallet and gun and tossed them in the trunk. He heaved the box of drugs on top of the gun and wallet.

Pauli ran to Clive and reached into his back pocket, finding his wallet. Pauli snatched it and trotted to the car, tossing the wallet and Clive's .45 in the trunk before closing it. "Come on. Let's go."

Warm blood covered Jesse's hand and cheek. She caressed Clive's forehead and shouted. "You can't just leave him here."

Pauli ran back to her, took her arms in his strong grip, and gave her a hard shake. "If you want to stick around and explain this go ahead." Without giving her a chance to consider, he pulled her to her feet and drug her to the car. On the way out, he stopped at the crashed van and retrieved the briefcase filled with hundreds.

A half hour later back at Clive's, Pauli led her up the stairs to the apartment. He took her to the bathroom and said, "Get cleaned up. We're leaving in ten minutes."

After changing, Jesse opened the bathroom door to find Pauli searching all the drawers in the dresser.

"What are you doing?"

"Cleaning this place of everything that's connected to me and my boss. Pack your stuff. You won't be coming back. Anything with your name on it—take it."

Jesse packed a few clothes and Clive's .22 in a suitcase and left with Pauli. She didn't ask any more questions. She'd run out of energy. Pauli took her to his home, gave her a shot of whisky, and tucked her into bed.

Over the next few days she became his lover. As trust built, Pauli filled her in. He, Rick, and Clive worked for the De Cavalcante crime family. The incident that night was a straight drug deal gone south.

Jesse's heart sank. Clive knew it all along . . . he'd lied.

Her involvement with Pauli lasted almost a month, until she got the call from her mother. Her father had died at work from a massive stroke. The funeral would be in two days.

After the funeral, Jesse returned to New Jersey. A couple of days later, she moved into a place of her own after Pauli gave her an envelope with $11,000—the money the organization owed Clive. Before she moved out, Pauli said to call him if she needed work. "We always need someone who shoots as well as you."

On her own and alone, Jesse made a decision. She wouldn't return home or work as a waitress in some greasy spoon in New Jersey. Her heart had hardened. She had a skill only a dozen others could claim in the country, and she intended to use it.

The memory made Jesse a little melancholy. She finished off the bourbon and gazed at the empty living room. The laughter of children playing in the neighbor's yard put a smile on her face. This house in Grapevine might just be her first and last shot at living a life in suburbia. She checked her watch, time to finish getting ready.

37

Alma was tired. Thursdays always were her longest days. All she wanted was a glass of wine, a walk through her garden, and a hot lavender bath. The dark clouds smelled of rain, and the light mist that streaked her windshield on the drive home would probable nix the garden walk. She hoped not. It was relaxing for people like her.

She swung into her driveway and parked in back. On her walk to the rear of the house, none of her favorites came out to greet her. *Strange. Never missed a day before.* Alma unlocked the back door and turned to disarm the alarm panel on the kitchen wall. It showed all green. Had she neglected to arm it? A scraping sound drifted from around the corner, like something being drug across the floor. She cautiously eased through the kitchen and peaked into her herb room.

Frank sat on a stool with a glass of wine thumbing through a book. She recognized it immediately. He must have heard her, because he looked up and matter-of-factly said, "Hi, Alma."

She didn't answer, glancing in all directions to see if he was alone. Better play this cool until she knew what was going on. Frank's snooping around her house and following her to work had caused her to wonder. She allowed a smile to cross her lips as she strolled into the room.

After calmly setting her purse on a counter, she asked, "Frank, whatever are you doing here?"

He stared at her with that boyish grin and took a sip of wine.

"Waiting for you." He lifted the bottle and poured an extra glass half full. "Will you join me?" He pushed the glass across the counter and smirked.

She reached for it just as a loud clap of thunder echoed through the cottage. She jumped and almost knocked it over. Her hand shook as she brought it to her lips. "Why are you here, Frank?" She was sure she wouldn't like his answer.

Frank kept reading the journal, turning page after page. He didn't look up, but said, "Just catching up on my reading."

"Oh, I see," Alma said. *Not getting anywhere with this.* Time for a different approach. "Would you mind terribly if I changed into something more comfortable?"

He stopped reading. "I think that would be a great idea. We have a few things to discuss. Might as well be as comfortable as possible."

Frank's casual attitude disturbed her. He knew something. Something so big he had no fear of her calling for help.

"Well, I'll just be a minute."

"Don't rush," he said. "I'm enjoying reading your grimoire."

Her stomach twisted. He knew.

Frank cast a hard stare at her. "Or do you call it your Book of Shadows?"

Alma shivered. He'd figured it out. She'd underestimated him. Clever, very clever. She blushed and turned for the bedroom. "I won't be long."

*   *   *

By the time Alma made it back into the herb room, Frank had his case laid out on the counter. He felt pretty good about it. Not much to argue over.

She strolled in wearing a long, see-through beige robe. She wore no bra and the red lace thong panties outlined her perfect hips.

"May I have some more wine?" she asked, holding out her glass.

"Sure. You bought it," Frank said, and poured some for both of them. She looked great.

She eyed the stack of papers and bottles of dried herbs on the table. "You have something to show me, Frank?" A command, not a question.

She'd regained her confidence while changing. *Time for the mind games.* Frank touched each herb bottle and recited the name— "Valerian, Belladonna, Kava, and Kratom. Pretty powerful stuff, wouldn't you say?"

She didn't answer but ran her hand down the robe. When she let go of the cloth, a fist formed.

"Before we get started, I need to know something." Frank sat back and crossed his arms. "Because if the answer is yes, then we'd better do this interview at the station." The frightened doubt in her eyes confirmed he'd set the right tone.

She swallowed and broke eye contact. "What do you want to know?" Her voice was only a weak whisper.

Frank leaned on the counter, resting his forearms. "Can you turn me into a toad if you want?" He didn't know what to expect in reply to his flippant question.

Alma's whole face sagged. Her eyes took on a sadness Frank hadn't seen before. She sat the glass on the counter and just stared at him.

"I'll take that as no, then."

She was a statue—her jaw set.

"Okay, here's what I have. What I can present to a D.A. tomorrow. I'm giving you a chance to explain. Do I need to read you your rights, or do you watch all the cop shows like everyone else?"

She lifted her chin, her face pale. "I know my rights."

Frank opened his folder. Time for the accusations she'd deny and have to explain. Throw her off her game a little. He laid the copy of the old newspaper story from 1910 on the counter, pushing it toward her. "You've lived here before, haven't you?"

She gazed at the old photo, bit her lip, and remained quiet.

"You were Mrs. Pullings back then, huh?"

Alma waved away the comment. "Don't be ridiculous. That was my great-aunt."

Frank lifted the photo. "Remarkable resemblance. Don't you think?"

She kept her expression neutral but didn't answer.

"Have another photo to show you," he said. "Well, six to be exact." He laid the photo lineup on the table.

Her brow wrinkled as she stared at it and then at Frank.

"Showed this to one of the gang-bangers at Ricardo's house the night you paid him a visit. The night you planted that silly Voodoo doll to throw us off the scent." Frank pointed to the initials and date from a few days ago, just under Alma's photo. "Guy gave us a positive I.D. on you. Said he looked around and you blew something in his face. Did the same to the other gangster. Last thing he remembered until the ambulance attendants woke him up."

She took a long, slow breath. The areola on her breast had reddened as they talked, and the nipples were erect. Amazingly, Frank found this both exciting and disturbing. Come to think of it, she never did answer that question about the toad.

"I neglected to tell you Rob and I were sitting down the street watching Ricardo's house the night you came calling. I saw you there."

Alma's eyes shifted from side to side as if she considered making a break. A weak grin spread across her lips.

The last newspaper clipping changed everything. Frank expected it would. When he slid it across the counter, tears formed in her eyes and her lower lip trembled. With just her fingertips, she slowly brushed the photo of her deceased daughter and stepped back. She placed a hand over her eyes. Her sobs quickly turned to loud crying and she dropped to her knees, wailing like only a mother could for a dead child.

He eased over to her and took a knee. A tinge of embarrassment and shame filled him, but he kept a straight face and even voice as he said, "I know all about Ricardo's involvement in your daughter's death. I know they let him off for lack of evidence. And I know how you must feel."

Alma kept crying, shaking her head. When she looked up, her

eyes were red and scornful. "How could you possibly know how I feel?" she whispered. "Have you ever lost a child?" She wiped her face and leaned her head against the counter.

Frank handed her his handkerchief. "Yes. I lost my unborn child and her mother. They were murdered in New York."

Until that moment, only Rob knew of Frank's loss. He'd never discussed it with anyone else. Not anyone's business. For close to twenty years, Frank had lived with the notion he, too, could have had a normal family life if not for some criminals. Leaving New York and changing professions was the only way he could cope with the memories.

She dried her eyes and Frank helped her to her feet. Her hands were cold—ice cold. The areola had gone back to a normal color. As she stood, she embraced him, laying her head on his shoulder. Neither spoke nor moved for several seconds.

When she broke the embrace, she asked, "What are you going to do?"

This had been on Frank's mind for days. Levern had thrown away his chance at redemption. Frank cared deeply for Alma, but did she also deserve a second chance? *Everyone deserved a second chance.* He shrugged. "I'm a cop. What should I do?"

Alma turned and crossed the room. She stood beside a chair and gripped it, watching Frank. Her bedroom hair and the fading light from the windows silhouetting that perfect figure through the robe was enough to scramble Frank's judgment.

"Are you saying the world would be a better place with Ricardo Salazar in it?" she asked.

Frank had no defense for such an argument. "You started a gang war. Over a dozen people have been killed. Some just innocent bystanders."

Looking down at the chair, she ran her fingers across the material for a moment. When she looked up, she said, "My question is the same. Do you believe the world would be a better place with any of those murderers in it? How many more lives have to be ruined? How many more children have to die? How many more parents have to mourn?"

He nodded, but didn't answer. This was her time to talk.

"I'll not stand by and allow someone to destroy my life," she said. "I'm happy Ricardo is dead. I'd kill him again if I could!" Alma lowered her head, staring at her hands. She looked up and met his gaze. "What are *you* going to do?" she asked.

Frank didn't answer for a few seconds. Was he a bad man? He'd held the power of life and death, of freedom and incarceration for many years. He'd taken lives and put people behind bars. Is that what Alma deserved?

Finally he answered, "Nothing."

"Really?"

"Really." Every time Frank had thought about Alma losing her daughter, his mind drifted back to his dead wife and child. Sheep set upon by wolves. He'd solved the case. Identified the culprit. But now he elected to exercise one of the oldest axioms in law enforcement— not to pursue it.

Frank knew in his heart that after his wife and child's death if he'd had the power to take revenge, he would have jumped at the chance. Fortune or possibly fate never allowed him that chance. But Alma's loss was fresh. The wound deep and raw. She'd planned it for almost a year before she struck. He still didn't know how she did it. Really didn't want to. Yeah, he might be a bad man, but he could live with that.

"I do have one question," Frank said.

The look of anticipation on her face made him wonder . . .

Frank smiled, and in a joking manner asked, "How old *are* you?" This had been on his mind for several days—ever since he saw the photo of Mrs. Pullings in 1910 and wondered about her resemblance to Alma.

Alma released a breath. "Frank, you should know better than to ask a question like that to a woman." She approached him. The long sheer robe seemed to float in the air. "Besides, what difference does age make unless we're discussing wine or cheese?" The smile formed again on her full inviting lips and she drew closer laying her hands on his lapels.

She looked different somehow. Frank couldn't put his finger on it, but different. Somehow more vulnerable. More lonely. More in need of someone to love her.

"Should have expected that kind of answer," he said. "You understand you can't stay around Dallas. If I put it together, sooner or later, someone else might."

She glanced out the window and exhaled. "I know. I've made plans."

"Don't tell me," Frank said. "It's best if you keep that to yourself. Just get to a place where it's hard for a Texas cop to drive by for an interview."

She turned back to him. "Are you busy tonight?"

Frank shrugged again. "No."

She embraced him and caressed his face. Her hands were hot. "Please stay," she whispered.

When she'd embraced him moments earlier, she wore a perfume with a sweet floral fragrance. Frank's deceased wife, Carly, had worn only one perfume for as long as they had been together—Obsession for Women, by Calvin Klein. It had a spicy, exotic smell. It could have been Frank's imagination, but he swore that same delicate scent now filled his nostrils.

* * *

Jesse and the man lay naked in his bed. She snuggled closer and played with his thick, black chest hair. "So, will you do it?"

He groaned a noncommittal groan. He was always like that after she satisfied him.

She let her fingers drift below his navel and he chuckled, pushing them away. "No more—I'm done."

"But I want more," she cooed. "That's why I want you to take me there."

He let out a long breath, started to say something, but stopped. "I don't know, maybe."

"I can handle two at a time. You could even take pictures if you like."

He looked at her and frowned. "Why would I want to take pictures of something like that?"

"Some guys like to."

"You've done it with two guys before?"

"Sure," Jesse said, "I just get warmed up with the first. Takes the second to really satisfy me."

He gave her a slack-jawed stare. "You're joking?"

"No, I always like two. So will you do it?" she asked. "We could all meet tomorrow night."

"Okay, I'll ask. Never tried a threesome before."

"It's called a *ménage a trois*," Jesse said. "It's a French expression."

Tabor laughed. "Then he'll love it. Antoine's a Coon-ass—likes everything French."

38

Rob finished his workout and strolled into CIU a couple of minutes past nine on Friday morning. He didn't stop at his cubicle or speak to Frank, but headed straight to the coffee pot. After pouring a cup, he thumbed through a couple of new notices on the bulletin board as he tried the first sip. When he turned around, Frank stood directly behind him. Rob jumped and hot coffee spilled on his hand and shirt cuff.

"Shit. Why you sneaking up on me?"

"I wasn't sneaking."

Rob shook the coffee from his fingers and dabbed his shirt with a paper towel. "Carmen's going to kill me."

Frank leaned closer and lowered his voice. "We need to talk."

Rob wasn't sure he wanted to know what Frank had to say. Every time he said, "we need to talk," something bad always happened, or they'd wind up sitting on Edna's couch explaining how things went a little sideways.

"About what?" Rob asked.

Frank grabbed his elbow and walked toward the door. "Let's take a walk."

They strolled into the hall and Frank ran down what happened between him and Alma the night before.

Rob had been willing to believe anything Frank told him, but this pushed things over the top. The thought that Frank's mind had slipped a little too far from reality became a real concern. Rob didn't understand how Frank had allowed himself to become so embroiled with this woman. Just Frank's luck to pick someone like Alma. And this ongoing belief she could be a witch only strengthened Rob's belief he might have to plan an intervention soon if things didn't straighten out on their own. For now, probably best to humor him and listen to his explanation.

"So, she confessed to killing Ricardo?" Rob asked.

"Well, not in so many words. But it was clear she did it."

"Wait a minute. Either she did or she didn't. Which is it?"

"She did."

"She said the words, 'I killed him'?"

Frank shook his head. "Not exactly."

"Okay, forget that. She told you she was a real witch?"

Frank grimaced. "Not exactly, but her meaning was clear. She has no magic powers, if that's what you mean."

Rob leaned against the wall and smirked before taking another sip of coffee. "So she really didn't give up anything."

"You kind of had to be there."

"Apparently. You stay the night?"

Frank lowered his gaze.

"Figures. So what do we do now? I assume our search for the mysterious red head is over. Don't suppose you intend to tell Edna or Terry."

Frank looked up and shook his head. "No."

Rob was relieved. As least that was one conversation he wouldn't be required to sit through. "Do me a favor."

"What?"

"Don't ever tell this story to anyone. If they wrap your skinny ass up in a straight jacket and haul you away, I'll have to find another partner."

Frank didn't answer but lifted a brow.

Rob marched back toward the door leading to CIU mumbling, "Dark Cloud" under his breath.

He and Frank caught up on reports while they waited for the

next call to meet Sims at the scene of another homicide. By eleven, the call hadn't come, so when Rob suggested Sarge's for lunch, he got no objection from Frank. It was the end of the week. They always ate there then. Everyone seemed in a more cheery upbeat mood on Friday.

Sarge's wife waived as they walked in. The place was so noisy that Jan just motioned to her right. They took the last two stools at the end of the bar. Friday lunches were always the most popular. Everybody wanted to escape the office and get a head start on the weekend. Sarge listened to a D.A. relate a plea deal he'd just cinched as Jan strolled over to Frank. "Wondering when you guys would get here."

Frank took out a nickel and slapped it on the bar. "Fill 'er up!"

Jan stared at it and grinned. "Only thing you can buy with that around here is a pine float."

Frank's eye's pinched. "Pine Float? Fine, let's try one."

Jan returned a few seconds later with a toothpick floating in a glass of water. She scooped the nickel into her pocket. "Now, what do you really want?"

Rob laughed. Yeah, she'd lived with Sarge a little too long. "We'll have the usual."

Sarge meandered over a few minutes later with their drinks. "Hey, guys."

Rob drank half his Coke in one swallow.

Frank leaned on the bar with his elbows and slowly sipped his.

"Ever make a firm connection to that sniper woman and the garage killings?" Sarge asked.

Frank kept his voice low. "We have a video of her there and at a hotel off Greenville."

"No shit?" Sarge smiled. "So when does it hit the news?"

"Waiting on the sixth floor," Rob said. "They don't want to release her photo until they are 100 percent sure."

Sarge took a swipe at a crumb on the bar with the towel and muttered, "Never can make up their minds on the sixth floor."

He hadn't finished the last syllable when the noon news announced a breaking story on the TV above the bar. A photo of Jesse flashed on the screen together with her name and a description of her car.

Rob punched Frank. "Look."

The anchorman said, "This just in. Dallas police have issued a 'be-on-the-look-out' for this woman in connection with the string of recent sniper shootings."

Everyone stopped talking and gawked at the TV. The bar was quieter than a library. The report continued for another minute with the anchor giving background information regarding the snipings.

Frank sighed. "They finally did it."

* * *

When Jesse turned on the noon news on her drive back from Grape-vine Mills Mall, the last thing she expected to hear was her name. She took her eyes off the road and stared at the car radio a couple of seconds. Impossible! How had they made the connection? She'd done everything to plan. Fake identifications, only used burner phones, wore gloves and wiped prints.

She gripped the steering wheel until her knuckles turned white. None of that mattered anymore—they had her name and photo now. Jesse always had a contingence plan, just in case.

She'd already packed for her night drive to the East Coast. The only question that remained was, leave now, or complete the contract. Leaving was the only sane thing to do. Jesse mentally went over her options. They had her name and photo, but she had other names and disguises.

Jesse drove directly to her rental house in Grapevine. She still had a little time. After she'd parked the Toyota in the one-car garage and closed it, she hurriedly switched out the license plates for another set she'd liberated earlier from an old Ford. She rushed inside, grabbed her suitcase, and raked the toiletries from the sink into a grocery bag. A quick search of each room ensured she'd left nothing that could further compromise her.

Her stomach churned with nervous excitement. She'd taken big chances in the past that had paid off. Because of rules and adminis-trative procedures, cops were usually slow to understand and act on hot information. Jesse's motto had always been that of the British Special Air Service, *Qui audet adipiscitur*, Who Dares Wins.

She'd decided. Taking out Levern was a bonus payment—one hundred thousand. The thought of completing the contract under these circumstances should have filled her with anxiety and fear. But strangely it was the opposite. The excitement of pushing the envelope to the very edge and beyond kicked in an adrenaline high. A pleasing warmth pulsated through her body. She could do this. She was the best there was. Only one consideration—had Tabor or Levern been tipped off? One phone call to Tabor just before she arrived tonight would tell her everything. If he knew, she would hear it in his voice and she'd just keep driving east. Either way, by this time tomorrow she'd be safe at home.

She needed a place to lay low and get dressed for this evening—some local hotel would do. Jesse tossed all the bags in her trunk and pulled out the cardboard box tucked in the back. Opening it, she removed the wig and fitted it onto her head. *Haven't been in this thing for a while.* Since her car had new plates, she needed a new look as well. Everyone would be looking for a short-haired blonde woman. Jesse pushed a strand of hair deeper under the wig and slipped on a pair of dark sunglasses. She raked her fingers through the new shoulder-length do and mused,

I look damn good as a redhead.

* * *

After lunch Rob and Frank returned to the P.D. One look at the front and Rob wanted to turn around and head back to Sarge's. Three remote TV trucks sprouting a dozen antennas were parked on Lamar Street. Reporters and camera crews jockeyed for a better live shot at the entrance to police headquarters. Rob grabbed his Copenhagen can and took an extra big pinch.

"Circus is back in town," Rob said.

Frank didn't answer, but a soft snore escaped his lips. He'd achieved the full slouch sleeping mode in record time.

Terry and Edna were both out of the office—probably another meeting. At five o'clock Rob stood and slipped on his jacket as Frank's phone rang.

"Hold on," Frank said, "I'm putting you on speaker."

It was Sims. "Guess what, guys? Just got a call from Grapevine P.D. They have a lady in their office who recognized the photo on the news."

"You mean Jesse?" Frank asked.

"Yeah."

"Where did she see her?"

"Rented her a house in Grapevine last week."

39

Antoine Levern had stayed up until 3:00 a.m. playing *Mass Effect Andromeda* and doing a line or two of coke every few hours. Helped him keep his edge—made him a better gamer. He finally got up in the early afternoon and ordered breakfast from the restaurant. As he finished, Tabor walked in.

"Hey, Boss. Feeling better?"

Tabor didn't have to explain. Levern understand what he meant. The once dapper Antoine Levern, man about town, had become a Howard Hughes-like recluse. Not sleeping well, no appetite, going days without bathing or even brushing his teeth.

"Yeah . . . I'm good," Levern said.

Tabor wore an expression Levern knew well. He had something uncomfortable to discuss. Levern waited, but Tabor just stared at him with both hands in his pocket. "Was there anything we needed to talk about?" Levern asked.

Tabor lowered his gaze and removed the toothpick from his mouth. "Well, I have a confession."

Levern hated anybody leading off with that as their first words. "What happened?"

"My new girlfriend is someone you know."

Levern shook his head. "What does that mean? So she's someone I know. So what?"

Tabor sucked in a deep breath. "You know that blonde we met in the restaurant a couple of weeks back?"

Levern sat back and grinned. "You dog! You're screwing the gal I gave the free lunch to?"

Tabor nodded. "She called last week and we talked. Told her you wasn't feeling too good—wasn't seeing people." He shrugged. "Asked me to take her out."

Levern smiled and shook his head. "Hell, I thought it was something big." He placed his right hand over his heart and bowed his head. "Go ahead. Have a little fun with my blessing."

"Yeah, well, that's what I wanted to talk to you about. Seems she likes having fun with a crowd. Wanted me to ask if you'd join us in a *ménage* a something or other tonight."

"*Ménage a trois?*" Levern asked.

Tabor nodded. "Yeah, that's what it's called."

Levern leaned forward and clasped his hands together. "Let me get this straight. That sweet little thing wants to do both of us at the same time?"

"That's what she said."

Levern had to go far back in his memory to pull out the last time he'd been in a *ménage a trois*. There had been good whiskey, good coke, and two good looking women. Never did two guys on a gal before. Might be fun. Besides, he was due for a little R & R. "Sure, tell her I'm in."

"Tonight?"

Levern ran his hand over his four-day stubble. "Why not? Gives me a reason to clean up."

* * *

Frank, Rob, and Sims parked about fifty yards down the street and waited for Grapevine P.D. to take the lead. Antsy as hell, Frank couldn't sit still. He wanted this to end right here, right now, tonight. Sims snacked on a Tootsie Roll and had a look of anticipation.

The SWAT battlewagon roared to life and charged. When it skidded to a stop, a half dozen tactical officers dressed in black ran to the front and back doors of the rental. Less than five minutes later Frank got the all-clear call. By the time they marched through the front door, the Grapevine detectives were standing around looking at each other with hangdog expressions.

"What?" Rob asked.

"Place is cleaned out," one said. "We'll get the team over here to try and lift some prints, but whoever was here is long gone."

Frank didn't say a word. He didn't have to. He looked at Rob, shook his head, and walked out the door. She'd beaten them again.

*　*　*

By the time they left Grapevine it was after seven. Rush hour traffic had all but disappeared and Dallas had settled into another uneasy weekend night. Rob drove and Frank brooded as they took the exit to Lamar Street.

"Always one step ahead," Frank muttered. He turned to Rob. "Now that the word's out, no use keeping anything secret. May as well warn Levern."

Rob flipped on his right blinker. "You don't think he already heard?"

"Who knows." Frank sighed. "Guy probably only watches Netflix and plays video games." Frank pulled out his phone and dialed the number. It rang several times before going to voice mail.

"My guess is once Jesse hears she's been outed, she's on the way out of town," Rob said.

Frank didn't answer. He dialed Levern's number again.

Levern said, "Hello?" His voice had a rushed sound, like he was late for something.

"Hey," Frank said, "you doing all right?"

Again the rushed tone. "Frank, love to talk but have a friend on the way up. Check in with you later—hot date with a blonde." And the line went dead.

It took about two seconds for Frank to make the connection. Cold crept through his blood. It was impossible for Jessie to snipe Levern or even get close enough for a pistol shot. But Jessie had shown herself to be versatile. Always did the unexpected. Had she managed to trick Levern into inviting her to his place?

Rob began his turn onto the ramp leading up to the parking garage.

"Stop!" Frank said. "Jesse's at Levern's."

Rob slammed on the brakes and shifted into reverse, doing a *bat-turn* in the almost empty parking lot. Frank redialed Levern's number. It went to voice mail. He tried once more—voice mail. He called Sims. Frank's nerves were raw. He spoke so fast Sims told him to slow down and repeat.

"I said, Jesse's at Levern's. Get some uniforms over there. We'll meet you."

* * *

When they rolled up to Levern's building, everything looked normal to Rob. The Cajun Crawdad was rocking, with the parking lot full and a line at the door. They parked in a fire zone beside the building. Nothing seemed out of place. Frank's forehead crinkled as he studied the scene. The restaurant's large windows spilled light onto the sidewalk out front. Rob scanned the customers inside.

"You see her?" Rob asked. He stepped out of the car and unsnapped his holster under his jacket. His stomach twisted. The adrenalin rush kicked in. He got this way every time—just before the shit slid down hill and he either had to get out of the way or get buried underneath it.

Frank edged to the wall beside the door and glanced through the windows again. "Not in the restaurant."

Rob looked over his shoulder as Sims pulled up with a two-man patrol unit close behind. They joined Rob and Frank outside the door. White crumbs clung to the corners of Sims's mouth as he slung a triple-X bulletproof vest over his head.

The parking lot patrons eyed them but didn't get out of line.

"Where is she?" Sims asked.

"Probably on the third floor," Frank whispered.

"Why you whispering?" Sims asked.

Frank blushed and cleared his throat. "Where are the other uniforms?"

Sims shrugged. "Friday night, manpower shortage, high priority calls—take your pick."

Frank faced the two young officers. "The woman we're looking for is most probably the sniper suspect. Killed close to a dozen people in the last couple of weeks. Wouldn't think twice about shooting you. Understand?"

They both nodded. The tall one said, "We got a briefing before signing on tonight. She's the blonde, right?"

"Right," Frank said. "We can't wait for any more backup." He swung open the door and took a right toward the back hall and elevator landing.

One of Levern's thugs, a young guy, leaned against the wall opposite the elevator with his arms crossed. He'd cut the sleeves out of his sweat shirt and wore his baseball cap turned backward.

"Where's Levern?" Frank asked.

The bodyguard took one look at the uniforms and mumbled, "I ain't saying nothing."

Frank pushed him against the wall, pulled his pistol, and pressed it to the guy's forehead before thumbing the hammer back. In his most menacing voice Frank very slowly said, "Where is Levern?"

The gangster's eyes crossed, staring at the pistol. He pointed. "Upstairs."

"He alone?" Frank asked.

The guy's eyes remained crossed. "No, Tabor's with him."

Frank holstered the pistol and stepped back. "Just Tabor?"

The guy swallowed hard. "Yeah, Tabor, and the hottest redhead I've ever seen."

"Redhead?" Rob and Sims said at the same time.

Frank looked Rob's way, his stare frozen in disbelief.

It was at that second Rob understood. Jesse knew her photo had been released—changed her appearance!

In a shrill voice Frank said, "It's her." He pointed at the thug. "Any of them come down?"

The guy shook his head.

"Get out of here," Frank told the guy. Frank motioned to the tall officer. "Stay here—nobody comes down the elevator or stairs. Understand?" Without waiting for an answer, he pointed at the other officer. "You and Sims take the stairs on the left"—Frank motioned to the stairs on the right—"and we'll take these."

When everyone pulled their pistols, the gangster bolted from the elevator landing. The shorter officer ran after Sims, who was already on the stairs, and Frank led the way as he and Rob charged up the other set. When they reached the second floor landing, Frank slowed and peaked around the corner into the empty room. Only the sound of the big-screen TV echoed through the vast open space. Not a soul in sight.

Frank rushed the stairs leading to the third floor.

Rob grabbed his arm. "Steady. If she's up there, no use running into a bullet."

Frank nodded and he and Rob slowly made their way up, one on each side, in the tactical combat shooter position. When they got to the third floor, it was dark and quiet. Rob searched the wall for a light switch—nothing.

The glow from the stairwell cast a faint light across the floor to Levern's bedroom. Rob's gut tightened at what he saw. A body lay crumpled on the concrete outside the door. From the size of it, Rob didn't have to guess. He and Frank eased beside it and rolled it over—Tabor. A small, neat hole between his eyes, leaking blood and a toothpick in the corner of his mouth.

Rob swallowed. *Oh, Christ!*

Across the darkness Sim's voice called. "Are you guys up here yet?"

"Yeah," Rob hollered back. "One dead. Send the uniform over."

The sound of the uniform's footsteps pounded through the darkness, preceded by the beam of his flashlight.

"Need me too?" Sims called.

"No," Rob yelled. "Hold the stairs."

The uniform trotted up and Rob touched his back. "We're going in that door," he pointed to the bedroom—dynamic entry. "You break right." Rob turned to Frank. "You break left, and I'll go up the middle. Any questions?"

Rob didn't like the set up. The whole stairs and darkness thing was a little too close to what they'd experienced that night at Ricardo's. Rob tried the door knob and it turned. He nodded to the others and said, "Go!"

When they blew inside, all the lights were on. Levern lay on his back, spread eagle on the bed, with the same neat hole in his forehead as Tabor. His lifeless expression had a surprised look. Time stopped for a few seconds and no one spoke. Frank let his hand holding the pistol drop to his side. He took a couple of steps back. His eyes were vacant.

Rob and the uniform cleared the bathroom and marched back into the bedroom. Frank hadn't moved. "She's not in here and she hasn't left the building," Rob said.

Frank turned to the uniform and in a quiet voice said, "Call for more backup. She's still up here."

They stepped out of Levern's bedroom into the silence of the dark warehouse.

Rob shouted, "Sims! Tabor and Levern are dead. Watch yourself! She's still up here somewhere."

"Oh, shit!" Sims yelled back.

Frank searched for a light switch—nothing.

"More backup's on the way," the uniform said.

Rob flattened himself against the wall and motioned Frank and the uniform over. "Everyone just be cool. She can't get out. We'll just contain her until reinforcements arrive."

A minute passed with no one saying a word. Everyone stayed low and out of the stairwell's light. The echo of breaking glass pierced the dark silence.

Frank stared at Rob with a questioning expression.

"That was a window. She's trying to get away," the uniform said.

"Call the backup units," Frank told the uniform. "Tell them to surround the building. She may be trying to escape from an upper floor window."

Rob understood the waiting was over. If Jesse had figured a way to escape, that changed everything. Knowing Jesse's attention to detail, Rob's mind whirled with ideas on how she was probably getting away right now. "We have to check it out." He looked at Frank. "Me and the uniform will do it. You guard this stairwell."

"I'm going with you," Frank answered, then nodded to the officer. "Give me your flashlight."

The uniform handed it over and Frank passed it to Rob. "Let's go."

Rob crouched near the wall and advanced toward the dark area where they'd heard the breaking glass. From his memory, they were heading toward the stinky sofa they'd seen on their first visit. He didn't turn on the flashlight. That would make them a target.

Frank's steady breathing behind him was the only sound as they slowly moved into the abyss. Rob stopped after a few steps and Frank's hand rested on his shoulder. They listened for a sound . . . anything that might give them an idea where she was. Rob ran each palm down his pants legs and got a new grip on the pistol. After a few seconds of dead silence, he started again. His stomach sick with dread.

The blood in Rob's head pounded so hard it made it difficult to hear. This whole thing was screwed up. He stopped and Frank's hand came to rest on his shoulder once more. Rob took a couple of deep breaths and whispered, "You think she could have night-vision goggles?"

Frank didn't answer immediately, but when he did it was typical Frank. In a soft voice he said, "Thanks a lot for sharing that at this particular moment."

Rob gnawed his lower lip and eased forward. Getting killed was bad enough, but what would happen to Carmen? It would push her over the edge. He forced the thought from his mind. Negative thoughts got guys killed. He needed all his attention focused right here, right now to survive.

A moment later, Rob's foot fell on something that crunched. He stopped. Must be near the broken window, but no light showed through. There were lights outside. He should have been able to see something. Reaching down, he felt what he'd stepped on. The first thing his finger touched was a jagged piece of glass. The second, the wet stem of some plant. He ran his finger up the stem and found the leaves and blooms. He lifted it to his nose.

A gladiola. We've been tricked!

A shot rang out from Sims's stairwell.

"Sims, what happened?" Frank shouted.

No answer.

"Sims," Rob yelled.

Still no answer. A sinking feeling filled Rob's gut. He and Frank raced across the warehouse to Sims. The uniform they'd left at their stairwell arrived at the same time. When they made the turn, a sprawled body lay on the floor near the stairs, automatic still in his hand.

The smell of gun powder hung in the air. Frank plucked the pistol from Sims's grip and rolled him over. Blood poured from his forehead. Rob checked him. A small caliber bullet had parted his hair. The wound was only superficial, but there was lots of blood. Of more concern was the red stain around a hole in his bullet-proof vest and shirt—very close to the heart. Rob's spirits sank. *No . . . no . . . no.* He probed under the vest.

Sims opened his eyes and sucked in gulps of air. Between breaths he said, "Came running out of the darkness, silenced gun. Think I hit her."

Rob jerked his hand from under Sims's vest and frowned at his red dripping fingers. He sniffed the syrupy goop and touched his tongue to it. "Sims, you idiot. This isn't blood. It's candy."

Sims flashed a sheepish grin. "Must have ruptured my ICEE Squeeze in my shirt pocket."

Frank jumped up and nodded at Sims. "You got him?"

"Yeah, we're good," Rob replied, wiping blood away from Sims's forehead with a handkerchief.

Frank turned to the uniform. "Follow me." And led him down the stairs.

* * *

When Frank got to the first floor, the tall officer they'd left guarding the elevator landing lay sprawled on the floor. Blood pooled around his head. *Damn!*

"See about him," Frank shouted at the uniform following, "and get us more backup and a couple of ambulances!"

Screams and shouts came from the restaurant around the corner. Frank charged the door, passing a bloody handprint smudged on the wall. Jesse had come this way, and she was injured.

Bedlam had erupted in the dining room. People streamed out as others crouched under tables. Drops of blood led out the front door. Frank ran outside and scanned the parking lot as another marked unit rolled up, red and blue lights still on. He quickly displayed his badge to the arriving uniforms.

Out of the corner of his eye he saw her. She leaned against a dark blue sedan, bent double. The gun in her right hand dangled at her side, and her left hand covered her midsection. Blood oozed between her fingers. She glanced around at the patrol unit and pushed off the car, staggering for the shadows of the building. A fist-sized red stain marred the back of her white dress.

A trapped and fatally wounded animal, struggling to survive. For a second Frank hoped there might be another way. There wasn't. He pointed at her as the uniforms approached. He didn't want to say it, but it was the fastest way to get their attention.

"She just shot two officers," he yelled.

Jesse swung around as he shouted, and they met eyes for the first time. Hers had a feral, determined look. A crooked smile crossed her lips. Her head wobbled as she stepped backward. As if in slow motion, she lifted the silenced pistol toward them.

Frank and the two uniforms fired. She tumbled backward over a curb and didn't move.

Frank lowered his gun. He slowly walked to her and stared down at over a dozen red blooms sprouting on her chest and stomach. The red wig had shifted. Strands of golden hair outlined her young face. Her dead-eyed stare caused his breath to catch. His gut knotted and bile rose in his throat as a wave of nausea passed over him.

Don't let me be sick.

40

The next morning when Frank woke up, he didn't go through his usual Saturday morning routine. He didn't do his yoga exercises or lovingly prepare his cup of *café au lait*. He was still tired. He and Rob had stayed with the homicide detectives, explaining what happened until after three in the morning. Terry made the shooting scene while Edna briefed the sixth floor. For the first time in weeks, the city seemed to relax.

Frank yawned and stretched, then fixed a large cup of strong black coffee. He wrapped himself in a blanket against the chill of the late October morning and sat on his balcony. Most of the day passed that way—thinking. About two o'clock Edna called.

"Doing okay, Frank?"

Frank let out a slow breath. "Yeah."

"Sorry about the shooting. Know that's not how you would have wanted it."

"Me too."

There was silence on the line for a few seconds before Edna cleared her throat. "Listen, Frank, there's another thing . . ." Another long silence. He thought he'd lost the call before she spoke again.

"Thank you."

"Huh?"

"Thank you for saving my ass. Higgins is so unpredictable, I was afraid of being relieved and reassigned. If it had gone on another couple of days, I'd be gone."

Frank didn't know what to say. Even felt a little embarrassed. He'd never been able to accept compliments graciously. "I'd never let that happen, Edna."

"Anyway, just wanted to check on you," she said. "Take care."

The line went dead and Frank closed his eyes. He doze off sitting in the patio chair. When he woke, it was dark. He grabbed a couple of bottles of red, wrapped himself in the same blanket, and started thinking. What could he have done differently? By bedtime he still hadn't come up with an answer. Just before turning in, Rob called.

"You okay," Rob asked.

"I'm okay. You?"

"I'm good. Carmen and I had a nice evening together."

It went without saying that when Rob used that phrase, he'd done the true cowboy thing. Two grilled T-bones with baked potatoes, a few beers, and made love with Carmen. His casual voice had returned. Sounded like the old Rob again.

"The newest drug appears to be working," Rob said, "haven't seen Carmen feel this good in weeks. May have turned a corner. Hope so."

"That's great," Frank said. He slurred a little. He didn't care. He was heart sick over the way the whole thing went down, especially over the officer by the elevator getting killed. Levern's death wasn't easy either.

Rob didn't answer for a few seconds. When he did he seemed to have read Frank's mind. "You know that was the only way it could have ended. Levern was a doper, bound to happen sooner or later. Jesse was a warrior. They don't do well in captivity."

Frank choked with emotion. "Yeah, I know."

"You alone tonight? I could stop by if you want? We could drink and talk it out."

"Love to, but I have company," Frank lied. "Thanks anyway."

"Okay," Rob said. "Guess you'll be off for a while until they finish the shooting investigation."

"Yup."

"You lucked out. Everyone believes the mysterious redhead you saw that night at Ricardo's must have been Jesse with the wig. Pretty easy explanation to close the loop on the whole thing and leave Alma out of it."

Fatigue swept over Frank. He mumbled, "I suppose I've always been lucky."

"You have, Dark Cloud, you really have."

The line went dead. Frank finished off the wine and stumbled to his bedroom.

*   *   *

Sunday morning Frank resumed his usual weekend activities. Just before lunch, Sims called. They'd kept him in the hospital overnight for observation and cut him loose Saturday afternoon.

"Hey," Sims said, "thought you'd want to know. My sergeant just called. The blonde hair found at the old house where the gangsters were killed tested out positive. It belonged to Jesse."

"Yeah, thanks," Frank said. "You doing all right?"

Sims's replied was distorted by the sound of something crunching. "No problems," he answered. "See you later."

By evening Frank had had all he could stand. He needed to get out and do something.

The sun was setting as he drove to White Rock Lake. Eventually, as he figured he would, he pulled into the driveway of Alma's cottage. Her car wasn't there. He hadn't spoken to her in three days. For reasons he couldn't explain, he just wanted to see her, hold her one last time, tell her things he should have said but didn't. Frank hadn't been in love in a long time—so long he'd almost forgotten the feeling. His attraction to Alma was something he struggled to explain. Could it lead to love? How far was he willing to go to find out?

Frank recalled another verse from the old Billy Joel song:

"Well, we all fall in love, but we disregard the danger, though we share so many secrets, there are some we never tell."

Yeah, having Alma as a love interest would be dangerous. She had more secrets than any woman he'd known. And some she'd never tell. He wasn't even sure he wanted to know. But he didn't care if it was a forbidden love. He might have a shot for true happiness again, and he was taking it. He'd put aside the whole "real witch" suspicion. It was silly. Everything that happened could be logically explained with enough imagination.

He followed the stone path to the front porch and rang the doorbell. When there was no answer, he cupped his hands against the glass and gazed into the dark, empty house. Just enough light drifted through the windows to see every stick of furniture was gone.

Frank meandered to the back and strolled into Alma's garden, a profane sadness overwhelming him. Along the path certain plants had begun to wilt—the ones not native to Texas. A gust of cold north wind ruffled Frank's hair as he took a seat on the bench under the arbor. The average first freeze wasn't for another month, but to Frank it already felt like winter.

Like every cop, he measured success by what he did to improve things. Nothing had been improved in this case. Levern squandered his second chance by becoming a criminal. Jesse squandered her good reputation for reasons Frank still didn't understand. He'd never gotten to know her—never gotten into her head. If there was a winner it had to be Alma. She'd gotten her revenge, and in the process triggered the whole mess.

A depressive wave of exhaustion coursed through Frank. He walked back down the path to the rear of the cottage. Crazy thoughts went through his mind. He had plenty of time now that he was suspended with pay for the next week or two until the shooting was investigated. It would take less than five minutes to find her on the computer. Perhaps go for a week's visit. See how things went. See if she shared the same feelings for him.

He sat on a garden bench for a while, thinking. As the last light of day faded, a cloud slid over the garden and another cold blast of wind caused the plants to sway. Yellow rose petals showered down around him. He stared at the giant Yellow Rose of Texas against the house. It was stripped bare. And then the realization hit him.

"Good-bye to you too, Alma," he whispered.

Acknowledgments

I am indebted to a number of people who read various drafts of this manuscript and made valuable suggestions. Thank you: Allen Holtz (Ret. DPD-CIU), Kelli Grant, Walt Baty, Melissa Lenhardt, Russell Conner, Natalie Enmon Mobley, and George Goldthwaite.

To my editors, Leslie Lutz and Jenny Chen for their magic with words.

To the staff of Crooked Lane Books for being easy to work with.

And last, but not least, the DFW Writers' Workshop for their critiques and encouragement.

Author's Note

Thanks for reading the new Rob and Frank mystery.

I love hearing from fans and always reply personally to each email. Write me at larry@larry-enmon.com with your feedback. Check out my website at larry-enmon.com and join my mailing list.

You can find my fan page on Facebook at www.facebook.com /larryenmonbooks/. I'm on Twitter @LarryEnmon, and Instagram @Larry Enmon.

Please post a review at Amazon.com and Goodreads.com if you enjoyed the book and tell your friends. Thank you.